THE HEAVENS
Before

THE HEAVENS
Before

KACY
BARNETT-
GRAMCKOW

MOODY PUBLISHERS
CHICAGO

Cover photo: © 2003 Daryl Benson/Masterfile.

Library of Congress Cataloging-in-Publication Data

Barnett-Gramckow, Kacy, 1960-
    The heavens before/Kacy Barnett-Gramckow.
        p.cm.
    ISBN 0-8024-1363-3
    1. Bible. O.T.—History of Biblical events—Fiction. 2. Noah (Biblical
figure)—Fiction. 3. Daughters in law—Fiction. 4. Noah's ark—Fiction.
5. Deluge—Fiction. I. Title.

PS3602.A8343H43 2004
813'.6—dc22

                                                          2003016997

                    1 3 5 7 9 10 8 6 4 2

            Printed in the United States of America

To my dear, wonderful parents, Robert and Sharon,
who surrounded me with brothers, books, and love—
and who taught me to love and fear the Lord.

Acknowledgments

I WOULD LIKE TO particularly thank Mary Busha, my amazing agent, and Editor Michele Straubel, who enthusiastically presented this work to the Moody Team. Also appreciation to Amy Peterson, Dave DeWit, Pam Pugh, and the whole Moody Team (if I haven't named you, it's because I haven't discovered your names yet)! Sincere admiration to wordmaster/editor, LB Norton, to Barbara LeVan Fisher for her beautiful artwork on the cover, and to Janet Chaiet for her professional encouragement.

Special thanks to John Woodmorappe for his kindness, and for writing his fascinating *Noah's Ark: A Feasibility Study*, which enabled me to envision the day-to-day details of life inside the Ark. In addition to countless secular sources, I would like to recognize: Answers In Genesis, The Creation Research Society, Christian Answers.net, Revolution Against Evolution, Creation Science, Creation

Evidences, Christian Science Research Center, and Christian Apologetics and Research Ministries, among others, for their many works, theories, opinions and, their debates. I have enjoyed studying their web sites and materials.

Also: Heartfelt gratitude to Kathi Macias, my editor /sister-in-law for motivating me. A hug to Auntie Jo Coila for volunteering to read, and to the family of Josie Dover, whom I miss. A medal to my brother Joe, who cheerfully endured my paranoia as I drove my car into a ditch during a blinding 1980 spring mudstorm—courtesy of a Mt. St. Helen's eruption that inspired some of the descriptions in this book. Loving thanks to my sons, Larson and Robert, for putting up with my addiction to words, and to my dear husband, Jerry, "Mr. Editor" who patiently answers my grammar quizzes and does housework. Thanks, Hon, for understanding, even when I confuse you (and me) completely.

Above all, to the Lord who granted me life and graciously provides every resource—which I can do nothing to deserve—my endless thanks and joy.

Prologue

THE ANCIENT tree of Havah stood in solitary splendor in a vast field, its pale green-leafed branches drooping softly, curtainlike, inviting passersby to come rest in the shade. It was said that Havah, Mother of All, had planted the tree after the untimely death of her favorite son, Hebel. The tree was not meant as a memorial to Hebel, but as a tranquil place where Havah might sit with her surviving children and nurture them through the remaining ages of her life.

If Havah had planted the tree herself or if she had not, it no longer mattered. For Havah and her children had passed into legend. Most people now doubted that Havah had ever lived. But the doubters were the ones who did not sit beneath the tree or climb its massive branches and listen to its leaves sighing in the quiet breeze beneath the rose-colored sky.

The doubters were also the ones who failed to recognize the countless signs about them, the marks of a young planet still resounding with the echoes of its creation. But the echoes themselves were becoming more discordant with each passing day. For the doubters were consuming the world with their own restlessness and destroying it with the violence of their desires.

One

ANNAH SIGHED and settled herself into a crook of the feathery branches of the ancient Tree of Havah. A morning mist shrouded the fields about her, and the cool rose-pink air made her shiver, but these minor discomforts were worth the temporary sensations of freedom and peace. Her family and the other inhabitants of the settlement still slept, exhausted after their usual night of feasting, visiting, dancing, and quarreling. Annah did not join in these festivities; she had nothing to celebrate.

I do not belong with the others, she thought.

To soothe herself, she pulled a carved wooden shuttle from her woven-grass bag, slung on a branch nearby, and began to work on the torn edges of her veil. Patiently she handled the light threads, knotting pale strands she had beaten from the stalks of soaked, crushed wildflowers. Over countless mornings, the knotted threads had become an intricate gossamer scarf, then a shawl, a head covering, and finally, an all-encompassing veil.

Aware of the shifting daylight and of her cramped, aching limbs, Annah gazed upward through the branches. The sun would be directly overhead soon. The sky was no longer the deep crimson of dawn, but a clear and bright pink, with a warm and welcoming sun.

Yerakh, her oldest brother, would wake soon. Annah shuddered, picturing his darkly bearded face, thinking, *Let Yerakh be happy today.*

She tied off one last knot, then tucked the small wooden shuttle into her bag. Shouldering her bag and veil, and smoothing her straight black hair, Annah clambered down from the tree. On the ground, she adjusted her soft leather tunic and stared upward into the tree once more.

Had Havah, the Mother of All, truly planted this tree with her own hands? Yerakh scoffed at this story, as he scoffed at all stories of old.

"If you believe that, you'll believe in the Most High next!" he would snap whenever his younger brothers or sisters dared to recite legends in his presence. Yerakh's dark arrogance and contempt usually silenced them all. But if contempt didn't work, he used his fists.

Let Yerakh be happy today, Annah repeated in her mind.

She scurried through the fields toward the grass-thatched settlement, aware of tiny creatures all about her, sensing their presence as they sensed hers. There was no fear between Annah and these creatures, only identification. Tiny mice, voles, and ground hens scrabbled near her feet, unintimidated by her presence. Insects hummed and darted before her while she admired their iridescent wings. Birds of many colors flew above the flowering grasses, twittering and singing songs as varied as their feathers. Annah envied them their wings. What did the birds think of her? She imagined them singing, *A human! . . . a woman! . . . a nothing!*

I'll show you, Annah told them silently. Pulling her veil away from her shoulders, she swung it expertly above her head as if to entrap some of the bright little songsters. They fluttered away excitedly, then returned quickly when the veil settled harmlessly over Annah's sleek, dark hair.

I am the creature who is trapped, Annah thought, eyeing her tiny companions through the soft mesh of her veil. She could almost hear their songs of sympathy. *Poor human! . . . poor woman! . . . poor nothing!*

~❦ ❦~

Kneeling on the earthen floor of Yerakh's lattice-enclosed workroom, Annah used a small wooden club to beat down the gold he had layered between sheets of membrane and leather. Her slender brown arm rose and fell in a pleasing rhythm of muffled thuds.

"Annah! Enough!"

Startled by Yerakh's booming voice, Annah flinched. For her own safety, she never looked directly at Yerakh. She dared not let him see the hatred and condemnation in her eyes, or he would kill her.

"Stupid," Yerakh hissed, snatching Annah's narrow club and threatening her by the action. "Move. Let me see what you've done. Move!"

With surprising delicacy, Yerakh checked the layers of leather, membrane, and gold leaf. He slapped the club hard into Annah's hand again. "Beat it until I tell you to stop. Understand? Work!"

I know how long to beat the gold. You don't need to tell me. The palm of her hand throbbed. As Yerakh strode from the workroom to his refiner's pit outside, Annah bit back her tears and raised the club.

Rhythmically, she beat her fury into the pile of leather, gold, and membranes, thinking with the tempo, *I-am-beat-ing-Yer-akh! I-am-beat-ing-Yer-akh!*

Eventually her rage thinned out with the gold. And like the gold, she felt fragile; the slightest breath could destroy her. The club felt heavy now, and her hands ached, but Yerakh would be angry if she stopped without his permission. Where was he? She beat the leather-clad gold more slowly. All at once she heard Yerakh's voice. He was returning to the workroom, and someone was with him.

"Stop, Annah!" Yerakh snapped. "You'll beat it to nothing."

As I've longed to beat you, Annah responded silently.

She glanced at her brother's big, bare feet, then at the feet of his companion, Naham the Iron-breaker. Naham's feet were the largest and filthiest in the settlement. Filth and soot were Naham's means of advertising his trade, but his size was enough to convince anyone that he deserved his name. Naham's footprint was more than twice the size of Yerakh's. And though Yerakh was as tall as any average man, he barely reached Naham's biceps. Scared, Annah bowed her head further, but didn't acknowledge their presence.

"In all the years I've known you, Yerakh, I've never heard her say anything," Naham rumbled, his voice mocking and deep. "Does she ever speak?"

"She can't speak. She has no mind." Yerakh answered, openly contemptuous.

14

Yerakh nudged Annah roughly with his foot, obviously displaying his power over her to impress his companion. She scooted away, hoping to evade further attention, but Yerakh snatched the club from her hand and struck her across the shoulders. She gave a sharp cry, then bit her lip to silence herself. The effort sent a chill of sweat from her scalp to her toes.

"There," Yerakh told Naham, satisfied. "A sound. But she's less than an animal."

Before Yerakh could strike her again, Annah scrambled to her feet and ran behind the leather curtain of the door leading to the main room of their lodge. Yerakh's scornful laughter echoed after her. *Let him die!* Annah thought, furious. *Any living thing in the fields has more kindness.*

"Stop!" A woman's sharp voice rose angrily. "Mindless creature. You'll spill everything."

Iltani, Yerakh's wife, was seated before Annah on an intricately woven grass mat. Curvaceous, with a long, gold-talismaned rope of black hair, Iltani flung out one tawny arm. Annah halted abruptly. She had almost stepped into a wooden dish of dried red beans and unpounded spices.

Annah averted her gaze as Iltani complained, her voice becoming louder with every word. "No manners at all . . . the way the creature behaves, she should be penned with the sheep. Where's her mother to take charge of her?" Hearing no response from any of the adjoining rooms, Iltani raised her voice. "Before she tramples our food!"

Staring at Iltani's plump brown hands, now extended clawlike over the bright red beans, Annah thought, *Don't worry, Iltani, I'm leaving. But if you possessed any kindness, you'd wonder why I'm running. You know Yerakh beats me.*

Annah snatched her grass bag and veil, then turned to leave the lodge. She was almost to the open doorway when a firm voice beckoned. "Annah."

Lowering her eyes, Annah turned toward her mother, Parah.

As lovely and severe as her gold-clasped, raven hair-braid, Parah spoke tonelessly. "Annah, I don't need the wife of my son screaming at me like this. I am busy."

Annah watched her mother's small, brown, bare feet, thinking in silent defense, *Iltani screams at everyone.*

Used to Annah's silence by now, Parah continued. "If you are finished with the gold, you can go to the orchards and gather some fruit. Take the baskets with you."

Hurt, Annah glanced at her mother's face. Parah was frowning, a delicate crease etched into her otherwise smooth and pretty brown forehead. Her large, long-lashed brown eyes—so like Annah's—reflected only exasperation.

My own I'ma, Annah thought, looking down in despair. *You of all people should understand me. Don't you see my pain? Why do you let Yerakh abuse us without speaking in our defense? It's the way you behaved when he killed my father. Not one word of grief or comfort. Why? I think you've never cared about any of us.* Tears filled Annah's eyes—tears she could not allow her mother to glimpse. Turning swiftly, Annah ran from the lodge.

"You forgot the baskets," Parah called after her.

I'll use my bag! Annah said in silent response. *But if I stay with you, I'ma, you'll beat me when you hear all the words I want to say.*

In her haste, Annah did not pull the veil over her head, but wore it in a great loop from her shoulders to her arms. Let others see her face today; she didn't care. Her tears and soaring rage affected the creatures of the fields as she ran. They fled before her, shrilling and squeaking beneath the ruddy sky.

Annah ran until her lungs burned like fire. Her mouth felt dry as dust, and her feet stung almost unbearably. Slowing her pace, she looked down and saw that the thorns of the fields had torn her feet. Even her ankles were bleeding. She would go to the river and rest, drink some water, bathe her cuts, and wash away her tears. *If only the river could rinse away my sorrow as easily as it will remove my blood.*

Her head drooping, her hair falling like a black curtain about her face, Annah walked through a thick grove of trees down to the sparkling, swift-flowing river. Sitting down heavily, she dangled her legs over the embankment and let the water rush over her feet, cool and soothing. The water directly before her was clear and lovely, but the middle of the river looked deep, fast, and disturbingly enticing. How easy it would be to slide into the water and simply drift out of this life.

Slowly she bent, dipped her aching hands into the clear water, and cupped the cool liquid to her mouth. Wiping her lips, she stared at the river, contemplating.

I'm not even forty years old—not even halfway to my first kentum. I'ma has lived two kentums, Yerakh one. Our father lived three kentums before Yerakh killed him. Father, you could have lived at least five kentums more if Yerakh had not been so greedy.

You were the only person who ever really loved me; I know that now. I wish I had not seen you die. After all these years my pain should be less. Why am I still crying for you?

Her grief flowed out now in streams of tears punctuated

by wracking sobs. *I must be going mad,* she told herself at last. *Yerakh will beat me for running from him. But I don't want to go back. I'm so tired of this life! I'm even tired of crying.*

Finally spent, Annah bent to rinse her face. She wiped her eyes with her veil and stared into the river once more. Perhaps she should let the river carry her away. Her pain would be over. No more of Yerakh's beatings or Iltani's scorn or Parah's indifference.

The rushing river seemed to beckon her, and she stared at the gleaming current, mesmerized, swaying faintly.

A sudden splash made Annah pull back. Before she understood what had happened, another fist-sized rock plummeted into the water before her. This time droplets of water sprinkled her face.

Astonished, she looked across the small river. A leather-clad young man stared at her from the opposite bank, his dark eyes quiet, intense. When she met his gaze, he gently shook his head at her, his long, dark curls shining in the sunlight. She could almost hear him thinking, *No, don't let the river take you.*

Annah sat back, stunned. Why should this stranger care if she died? No one in her own family would care. He watched her steadily, alert to her slightest move. *If I go into the water,* Annah realized, *he will die trying to drag me out again. He won't leave until he sees me returning to the settlement.*

As she thought this, another young man, obviously his brother, emerged from the trees lining the opposite side of the river. He was carrying netted bundles of long bark fibers. He had a quick, easy gait, and his eyes were alight with joy and mischief until his brother spoke to him and gestured toward Annah. The joy faded from the second man's face, and he stared at Annah. Like his brother, he shook his dark-curled head at her, and his lips actually framed the word, "No."

Discomfited, Annah pulled her veil over her face and stood. The brothers looked alarmed until she reached for her woven-grass bag and turned away from the river. She entered the shadows of the trees and circled back through the lush leafy undergrowth to study the two men.

The first one was still watching for her, but the second was kneeling and opening the bundles of bark fibers. Apparently, they would stay there for the afternoon, soaking the fibers and working them into ropes. As she watched, the second brother spoke to the first. Finally— perhaps because he could no longer see Annah or sense her presence—the first man knelt to help separate the long fibers.

They are at peace with each other, Annah thought, amazed. *They love each other. And they feared for my life, though I'm a stranger to them. Others would have watched me go into the river, and my death would be nothing but a story to tell their family or friends at the evening fire.*

To distract herself, Annah left the river and walked slowly through the fields toward Yerakh's orchards. If she was going to live, then she should pick fruit as Parah had commanded. *Although my I'ma certainly doesn't expect her mindless, nothing-creature daughter to understand a simple task like picking fruit,* Annah thought, grimacing.

Approaching the orchards beyond the settlement, Annah saw five massive, grayish, rough-skinned fruit-eaters. Taller than any of the lattice-and-grass houses in the settlement, the older fruit-eaters were grazing among the upper branches, their long, slender necks swaying here and there among the very tops of the fruit trees, choosing the most pungent and overripe fruits available.

The smaller, younger fruit-eaters, however, contented themselves with the lower branches, or fruits that fell to the ground.

Welcome, Annah thought, eyeing them. The fruit-eaters would clean the orchards. If the fruit were left to rot, it would attract wasps, which Annah detested almost as much as she did snakes. Strangely enough, as large as the fruit-eaters were, she was not afraid of them; like most animals of the field, they tolerated humans. As Annah approached, she spoke to them wordlessly. *Forgive my intrusion and ignore me if you like; I am a nothing, here to gather a few morsels for my family.*

The great beasts continued to nuzzle the ground and pick through the trees, clearly agreeing with her: *A human . . . a female . . . a nothing.*

Shouldering her veil and bag, Annah cautiously climbed into the tree's branches. Her fingers still ached, bruised where Yerakh had slapped them with the narrow club. Wearily, Annah picked her mother's favorite green-golden sun fruit, which had a warm, inviting fragrance. Suddenly hungry, Annah chose one, removed the pungent rind, consumed the glowing sweet-sour segments, and continued her picking.

By now one of the youngest fruit-eaters was exhibiting a mild curiosity toward Annah. Three times she turned to another branch, only to have the young fruit-eater suddenly whooshing its humid, heavy-sweet breath directly into her face. There was a softness in those golden-brown eyes that made her touch the wrinkled gray skin of the creature's neck. The feel of its skin was like the thick, toughened soles of her own feet.

One day you'll be very old, she thought to the young one. *You'll be large and stately, and you will have no desire to commune*

with a human-female-nothing. But I thank you. Three living crea-
tures have thought kindly of me today. Perhaps I will continue to live.

As if troubled by the dark turn of her thoughts, the
young fruit-eater pulled away and rejoined its small herd.
Seeming to be of one mind, they departed together, without haste. Annah sighed. Gloomily, she dropped the tart
green-gold sun fruit into her bag, added a few tiny, bright
yellow bitter-fruits, and heaped them with a cluster of
purple-black vine fruits. *I'll pick some of the sweet afals—the*
thin-skinned fruits—from the trees by the lodge, she decided. *That,*
plus what I've already picked, ought to be enough for tonight.

Glancing up at the sky, she saw the first violet hues of
night, then the first hints of the glittering reds, pale blues,
and gleaming whites of the stars. And the moon was
shimmering already, soft and lovely as a sea-stone she had
once seen about the neck of a food trader. The trader had
given Yerakh some pure white salt, brought from the far
edges of the land. Yerakh was so pleased with the salt that
he took the man feasting with him that night. *Perhaps,* Annah thought hopefully, *Yerakh will be gone tonight, feasting with*
Naham. Then I'ma and the others won't condemn me for running
away.

She turned toward the settlement, hurrying now. She
didn't want to be caught alone outside after dark. She was
just approaching the sweetly scented afal trees near Yerakh's lodge when she saw a man and a woman embracing
beneath the shadows of the low branches. At first the face
of the man was a mystery to Annah; she was too shocked
at the sight of the woman to pay him heed. His beloved
was her mother.

Annah's first coherent thought was, *Yerakh will kill them*
both, I'ma and her lover. Trembling, scared that they might
sense her presence, Annah sank into the tall grasses to

hide. As she crouched in the sweet grass, a new idea, half-hope, half-fear, crossed her mind. If Parah used this new love to break free of Yerakh's control, then their lives might change. But for good or bad?

Annah wanted to run away, but Parah would see her and be furious at being caught. It was best, Annah decided, to wait until her mother had parted from her beloved. She could hear them laughing softly in the shadows, murmuring intimacies to one another as they kissed. Mortified, Annah covered her ears. As soon as they left, she would go inside. *I can't pick afals tonight. I'ma will know I've been in the trees, and I've been beaten enough for one day. I wish they would hurry. I'ma,* she scolded her mother in her mind, *your children will be waiting for you. Go inside!*

Almost as if she could hear her daughter's thoughts, Parah's voice changed from inaudible intimacies to clear, tender urgency. "My family will return soon, and Yerakh will be angry if he finds us. Go now, please!"

"Yerakh will be feasting with Naham all night long," her mother's companion replied carelessly, laughing again.

By his laughter, Annah recognized him. He was Tseb-iy, a young, muscular, handsome—and much shorter—cousin to Naham. *But Tseb-iy's not much older than Yerakh,* Annah thought indignantly. *Why is he kissing my I'ma?*

She fumed as Tseb-iy kissed Parah again, whispering his farewells. *You're fools, both of you,* Annah thought, watching them leave. When they were finally gone, Annah stood, walked around the opposite side of the lodge, and crept inside.

Two

"PUT THEM in a basket. Do you understand? In a basket," Parah commanded, barely glancing up as Annah entered the lodge. Parah was busy as usual, arranging intricately carved wooden bowls and a basket of crisp grain cakes on mats set a prudent distance from the fire. Inhaling, Parah said, "You picked sun fruits; I can smell them."

You sound pleased, I'ma, Annah thought. *But I'm sure it's not because I've brought you sun fruit.* Silently she placed the fruits in a wide, shallow basket in the far corner of the dusky lodge. There, protected by the darkness, she studied her mother.

Parah was beautiful in the flickering glow of the central fire. Her figure was full, yet graceful. And when she bent to add more wood to the flames, the ensuing burst of light revealed the radiance of her skin, a smile about her lips, and a sparkle in her long-lashed dark eyes.

That wicked Tseb-iy has made you happy. You must love him. Did you love my father? I think not. But I mustn't consider these things or I'll go mad.

A piercing whistle sounded outside the lodge, and a young man's voice cried, "Have some food waiting, I'ma! The herds are penned for the night, and your children are dying of hunger!" Chathath, Annah's second oldest brother, bounded into the lodge.

Annah shrank back into the darkness. Chathath was not as muscular or as hot-tempered as Yerakh, but he had sharp eyes and a cruel, cutting way with words.

Smiling impudently, Chathath shook his long dark hair as if he were an animal, then confronted Parah, mocking her. "Feed me, woman."

"You and your belly," Parah sighed, her radiance fading as her irritation grew. "I spend all my time preparing your meals. One day you'll have to cook for yourself."

"If you're so tired of playing the mother, then speak to Yerakh for me," Chathath urged, his smile fading to a grim line in his handsome, angular face. "Tell him it's time for me to wed, then arrange a match for me."

Parah averted her eyes. "You know I can't do that. Yerakh would—"

"I know," Chathath interrupted. "Yerakh would refuse. He'd never allow one of his brother-slaves to marry and attain freedom. Where else would he find such cheap labor?" Chathath flung himself down on a mat near the fire. Snatching a grain cake from a basket, he bit into it savagely, talking as he chewed. "I'll have to run away without my inheritance, or fight him."

"And we know who'd win, dear brother," Iltani said, her round face smug as she entered the main room bearing a wooden bowl filled with steaming spiced red beans.

"Oh, Yerakh would win," Chathath agreed sardonically. "Unless I were to learn deceit from you, elder sister." Chathath pushed the entire grain cake into his mouth and glared up at Iltani.

Chathath's hatred of Yerakh spilled over into his dealings with Iltani, who encouraged Yerakh's unscrupulous treatment of his family. Chathath ridiculed Iltani's looks and her age, calling her elder even though they were both almost sixty years old.

Iltani scowled at him. "Be careful, dear brother. Another word and I'll pour these hot beans into your lap and put an end to your children before they're conceived."

Before their quarrel could endanger the food, Parah took the beans from Iltani and set them on the woven-grass mat beside the grain cakes.

Obviously feeling safer, Chathath taunted his sister-in-law. "Is that why you've had no children, Iltani? Did someone pour beans over you? I've thought it was because Yerakh despised you."

Enraged, Iltani swung an open hand at Chathath. He swiftly deflected the blow, then grabbed Iltani's arm and twisted it viciously, bringing her to her knees. "You won't win, elder sister."

"Ahahh!" Iltani shrieked, pain and rage contorting her features. "Let go!"

Watching from the darkness, Annah held her breath, fearing Chathath would push Iltani into the fire.

"Enough!" Parah cried, slapping her palms together. "Chathath, if you wish to eat here tonight, you'll let her go. Now."

"Certainly, I'ma."

Annah frowned suspiciously as Chathath's submissive

tone—and even as she did, Chathath gave Iltani a shove that sent her sprawling awkwardly over the grass mats.

"*Tan-neem!* A monster!" Iltani cried. "That's what you are!"

"Curse me, then," Chathath challenged her. "Go to the Nachash. Ask her and all the other Serpent-Lovers to call up spells from the deep to curse me."

Iltani looked aghast. Moving away from Chathath, she lowered her eyes.

Shocked, Annah huddled into herself. Had Iltani gone to the Nachash, who whispered ancient secrets and pronounced curses of darkness? By Iltani's yielding attitude and Chathath's triumphant smirk, Annah realized it was true.

Yerakh would beat Iltani if he learned of her actions. Yerakh had no use for legends or omens but, oddly, he feared the Nachash, and wanted nothing to do with her or her followers.

"Did you really go to the whisperers?" Parah asked, eyeing Iltani with distaste.

Iltani lifted her chin, her natural defiance returning. "Only once. I was curious. Your son must have followed me. Perhaps he was going to see them for himself."

"Liar," Chathath snorted. "I followed you to find out what you've been doing; and you've gone more than once."

Iltani's voice rose to a piercing shriek. "Monster! When do you work, if you spend all your time following me?"

"Hush!" Parah commanded sharply. "I'd like one evening of peace. Just one." Sighing her disgust, she knelt between the two quarrelers and spoke sharply to Chathath. "Where are your sisters and Gammad?"

Snatching another grain cake from the basket, Chathath shrugged. "They should be here soon, I'ma, don't worry. When I left, they were fastening the pens."

"You should have stayed with them until they'd finished," Parah scolded.

Chathath grinned. "They don't need me to protect them. I pity anyone who meets them in the dark."

As Parah fumed, a young woman's voice lifted in complaint from the entry of the lodge. "He's talking about us again, I'ma. Someone should cut out his tongue."

Haburah entered the lodge, proudly tossing back her flowing dark hair. Haburah was one full moon short of fifty, graceful, finely muscled, and peevish.

Behind her trudged their brother Gammad, forty-one years old, sullen, dark, and hostile toward everyone. He was followed by Ayalah, a lovely, sly-faced, bright-eyed woman of thirty-two—the only member of Yerakh's household younger than Annah. In Annah's opinion, Ayalah was also Parah's favorite—if Parah was capable of true fondness for any of her children.

Ayalah immediately settled between Parah and Iltani, nudging Iltani to the outermost edge of the woven-grass mat. Iltani's mouth went down in resentment.

Sitting next to my I'ma means nothing to you, Iltani, Annah thought indignantly. *You simply hate Ayalah more.*

As Parah began to serve the spiced red beans, using a deep, broad wooden spoon, Ayalah raised her voice. "I'ma, have you asked Yerakh's permission for my marriage to K'nan?"

Before Parah could answer, Haburah cried, "Why should I'ma say anything to Yerakh of *you* being married? She hasn't spoken to him for the rest of us! She's refused at least seven men who've asked for me. And she's never once spoken for Chathath or Gammad. Why should you be different?"

Parah continued to scoop the hot beans from the large wooden bowl into the wooden dishes, answering Ayalah without looking up. "As I told Chathath, Ayalah, I've said nothing to Yerakh. I know before asking him; he will refuse."

"Then make him change his mind!" Ayalah burst out, her eyes flashing, wrathful. "You're our mother; you should make matches for us and bargain for our futures. But you always give way to Yerakh. I want K'nan, and if I have to leave the settlement to marry him, I will."

"But does he want you enough that he's willing to leave the settlement?" Chathath asked, pleasantly sarcastic. "I think not."

"Shut your mouth!" Ayalah snapped, clenching her hands into fists. "K'nan wants me enough to leave the settlement, I'm sure."

"Chathath is right," Haburah said, obviously glad to destroy Ayalah's hopes. "If K'nan hears that he must give up trading here, trust me, he won't look your way again."

Ayalah nearly choked with fury. "You're all wrong. And if I have to live in this lodge with all of you for the rest of my life, I'll become like Annah . . . a mindless fool."

Wounded, Annah steadied herself. *I cannot react. But why am I so miserable today? I've endured all this before.*

Through her pain, she heard Chathath laughing softly. "Have none of you ever wondered why Yerakh refuses our help with the gold? Once we learned all his secrets, we'd be a threat to him. But poor Annah, with no mind to think and no tongue to speak, can never be a threat. And if she were to become one . . . he could break her neck. Snap!" Chathath snapped his fingers for emphasis, laughing again.

Ayalah began to cry, accusing the impassive Parah of neglect, while Haburah gloated over Ayalah's misery. Gammad and Iltani simply brooded, staring into the fire.

"We should kill Yerakh," Gammad muttered.

The others, as usual, paid him no attention, but Annah shivered. Perhaps Gammad was more dangerous than Yerakh. She continued to stare vacantly into the fire. *If I wish to survive, it is better to be considered mad. But do I wish to survive?*

She remembered the young man at the river this afternoon, shaking his head at her, his dark eyes telling her not to let the river take her. *Why were you there?* she wondered to him. *Did I imagine you? Am I mad after all?*

Before the mists of dawn had cleared to reveal the rosy sky, Annah was already at work, gathering wildflowers to make more of the fragile threads for her veil. *These need to be rinsed,* she thought, making an excuse to go down to the river. *I don't want to find dirt on them after they've dried.*

Reaching the river, she glanced at the other side. No one was there. *He was a vision. You have work to do before returning to Yerakh and the gold.* She settled into a patch of grass along the bank and sorted the flowers from the grass, rinsing the stems. Soothed by the simplicity of the work, Annah planned her day. She would sort the flowers, bind them, and hang them in the Tree of Havah. She would have to protect them somehow against the inquisitive birds and the morning mists. Suddenly she sensed a presence. *Someone is watching me.*

A rock plopped into the water beside her, and Annah looked up, her fingers still. *He* was watching her—the young man who had stopped her from taking her life.

Seeing him now, Annah caught her breath. In her misery the day before, she had not recognized the grace of his long, muscular body, the smooth tawny elegance of his features—unbearded because he was not yet married—and the wonder of his dark-curled hair flowing against his shoulders. He was real. She had not imagined him.

As she stared at him, he smiled—a pure, joyous smile reflecting his relief to see that she was still alive. Annah exhaled, grateful to be sitting; his smile made her weak. Feeling hot blood rush to her face, she reached for her veil to hide her embarrassment.

The young man raised his hands swiftly. *Wait*, his motion begged. *Not yet.*

He knelt, removing a leather-corded amulet from his neck. Curious, Annah watched. He untied a small leather pouch from his corded leather belt, emptied it, bound the amulet inside, and stood. Smiling, he lifted the pouch in a gesture of giving. *For you*, his eyes said, *if you'll accept it.*

Annah bit her lip, stupefied. Why should he give her a treasured possession—something he had cherished enough to wear resting against his own heart? As she watched, the young man retreated a step, calculated the amount of force he would need, then threw his precious offering across the small river. His aim was sure; the tiny leather-clad object fell within an arm's length in the grass to Annah's right. She hesitated, unable to believe that a stranger would give her something freely, without hope of anything in return. Looking at him, she begged silently: *Are you certain?*

Again, his hands moved lightly, urging her to take his gift. She could feel his eagerness. And his eyes entreated hers: *Open it.*

Opening the leather pouch, she pulled out a pale, highly polished oval of luminous shell, reflecting the tenderest rose hues of the midday sky mingled with the softest, most fragile blues of her favorite wildflowers. The edges were carved with intricate swirls, all flowing and curling like the waves of the river, and the center of each curl was pierced through, emphasizing the theme of water. It was a third the size of her palm, and slung from a leather cord, which meant it would be easy to hide from her mother and sisters. Most wonderful of all, it was real, cool and solid in her hand. Proof of her sanity. She looked at him, and her eyes filled with tears.

He lifted his dark eyebrows hopefully, eloquently: *Will you keep it?*

In response, Annah kissed the cool oval of shell lightly before pulling its cord over her dark head. He grinned, watching as she pulled her long hair out of the loop of the cord, then settled the luminous carving in place. On him, it had hung near his heart. On Annah, it rested near her stomach. She closed her hands about it protectively. Then, for the first time in years, she smiled at another person—at him.

Instantly, she was frightened by her happiness and reached for her veil to hide herself. But before she covered her face, Annah looked at him one last time, expressing her silent gratitude. His eyes were shining tenderly. Flustered, Annah scooped up the leather pouch and fled. An instant later, she returned to collect her half-rinsed pile of flowers. Through the mists of the veil, she saw that he was still watching her, and grinning. Mortified, she fled for the shelter of the trees.

In the lodge of Noakh, the young man seated himself before the evening fire, only to find that his father, his mother, and two brothers were staring at him; his father thoughtfully, his mother anxiously, his brothers frankly amused. His mother, Naomi, spoke first. Her voice was as gentle as her sweetly curved face and faintly graying hair.

"Shem, your brother tells me you've given some token to a young woman from the settlement beyond the river. Is this true?"

Khawm, his younger brother—the informant—was laughing, his leather-clad shoulders shaking, his dark brown eyes sparkling mischievously. Shem cast him a warning look, then cleared his throat. "It's true, I'ma. I gave her my sea carving."

"For a reason?" his father, Noakh, questioned softly, smoothing his graying beard.

Biding for time, Shem asked both his parents, "Did Khawm tell you what happened yesterday?"

Noakh merely smiled.

Naomi plaited her fingers together in her lap, speaking carefully. "Your brother told me that the young woman seemed ready to throw herself into the river, and that the two of you managed to dissuade her. This I understand. It was good that she didn't take her life. But was it wise of you to offer her the sea carving? She might believe something you did not intend."

"This woman and I . . ." Shem hesitated, then began again. "We understood one another perfectly, I'ma. And I wanted her to have the carving. She needs some token of kindness—she is in such pain. If you could only see her."

"Then, my son," his father agreed placidly, "if your gift was given in kindness, I am sure something good must come of it."

"But, my dear one," Naomi objected, her voice strictly controlled, "if the young woman is deluded enough to try to take her own life . . . Forgive me, I must ask: What good can come from insanity?"

"Beloved," Noakh said, his warm brown eyes sparkling, his mouth twitching with a suppressed smile, "remember that your husband is considered a madman. And his family must be mad to stay with him—deluded as he is. Surely this young woman will fit perfectly into our family."

Naomi actually allowed her mouth to fall open. Shem watched, fascinated, as she squeaked, "Who said anything about this young woman joining our family?"

Noakh turned to Shem, serious now. "Tell your mother everything, my son. For if you are my son—and I know you are—there is more to tell."

Shem was silent, trying to gather his fragmented thoughts. His mother was staring at him, her eyebrows raised in such a commanding way that he knew there was no escape. He blurted out the truth. "I knew, I'ma, that if she went into the river, I would lose the one the Most High had intended for me. She would not be replaced."

"But a woman about to kill herself!" Naomi protested, still shocked. "Does the Most High truly say such a one should marry my son? You knew this when you saw her?"

Shem lifted his hands helplessly, unable to fully explain. "She was like someone in mourning. Then, it was as if a voice behind me was whispering, 'Stop her.' Just after that, she began to move toward the water, so—"

"So he threw rocks at her," Khawm said, his expression mock-serious.

"Shhh!" Naomi frowned at her youngest son. Turning to Shem once more, she said, "So the Most High has said you should marry this woman. Did He say when?"

Unable to control himself any longer, Khawm cackled with glee, his eyes and teeth shining in the firelight, his long, narrow hands slapping the matting of the floor where he sat.

Seated quietly beside him, Yepheth, the oldest, nudged Khawm fiercely in the ribs. When that failed to hush him, Yepheth slapped his hand over Khawm's mouth.

Khawm wriggled free, still laughing. "Shem!" he cried, "did the Most High tell you where to find a wife for Yepheth? The Most High will have to promise her a thousand blessings to compensate for his ugly face."

Irritated at last, Noakh said, "Khawm, enough! Listen to me. Shem has done the will of the Most High. It's time for him to marry. It's time for all three of my sons to marry."

This announcement sobered Khawm immediately. He stared at his father. Noakh spoke sternly. "Even you, my undisciplined one. Unless you'd prefer an older wife to scold you when you behave as a child—I warn you—you must obey me and control your unruly tongue. Otherwise, your mother will choose a second mother to care for you."

"If I must, I will," Naomi agreed.

As his parents focused their attention on Khawm, Shem relaxed. For once, Khawm's irrepressible nature had solved a problem for him instead of creating one. He would not spend a second sleepless night wondering how he could explain to his parents that he must marry a young woman unapproved by his own mother. A young woman who had been contemplating death.

She's not mad, he thought defensively, staring into the fire. *She is grieving. What sorrow has she endured that would force her toward thoughts of death?*

He remembered her as he had seen her yesterday at the river, crying, then rinsing her face and gazing into the river. She had been so deep in thought that she had never noticed his presence. *What has hurt her so much that she wanted to die?*

Shem bit his lip, asking himself the same question. *What would hurt me enough to make me want to die? I think it would be to live until I was as old as the father of my grandfather; I could not bear to see my own children returned to the dust as he has done.*

Thinking of his great-grandfather, Shem excused himself quietly from the company of his parents and brothers. Taking a small, flickering clay oil lamp from the top of a wooden chest, he crept behind the woven reed partition at the back of the lodge. There, sleeping on a soft pallet, lay the feeble, diminished form of his great-grandfather, Methuwshelakh.

Most ancient of men, Shem thought fondly, watching the frail old man's eyelids flickering in his sleep. *I'm glad you have lived long enough for me to hear the stories of old from your own lips, as you heard them from the lips of Adam, the Father of All.*

Gently, Shem knelt and slid his fingers around the old man's thin, dry hand. Methuwshelakh stirred faintly. He spoke, his voice insubstantial as a breath sighed into a reed pipe. "What . . . what is it?"

"Father of my Fathers," Shem said respectfully. "Forgive me for waking you. I wanted to ask if you needed anything."

"Stay," Methuwshelakh rasped. He curled his ancient fingers around Shem's warm, young hand. "Nothing is needed . . . but you stay with me. There's no fear. . . ."

As he spoke, the old man slipped back into the twilight of sleep. Shem relaxed beside him, still holding his hand. Often in his sleep, the old man whispered names of loved ones long departed, sometimes grieving, sometimes joyful, occasionally in fear. And often, he would awake confused or in tears. At these times, he needed the presence of others to comfort him.

I'll sleep here tonight, Shem decided. As he held his great-grandfather's hand, his thoughts drifted back to the young woman at the river. He had not exaggerated to his parents; he had recognized her as his beloved. It was as if the Most High had led him down to the river to meet her. She was perfect. Her delicacy, the dignity she revealed in the midst of her pain—even her peculiar custom of wearing a veil—all drew him toward her. And when he saw her eyes, so beautiful and so expressive, he was captivated.

Be safe, he thought, willing her to sense his concern. *And come to the river tomorrow, so I can see you again.*

Three

ANNAH STIRRED in her sleep, then sank into the darkness of dreams. Her father's face, thin, kind, with a still-youthful beard of black, emerged from the mists. And Yerakh was there. They were in the workroom again, the three of them. Her father's voice was raised, yet reasoning. "There's enough for all, Yerakh. The flocks, the lands, and the gold will provide respectable marriage portions for your sisters and sustenance for you and your brothers. I've planned—"

"What you've planned is not my concern!" Yerakh cried, so enraged that Annah trembled to see him. Yerakh's dark face glistened with the sweat of work and hot fury. The muscles in his throat corded as he screamed. "Why should I even hear this? My brothers don't work the gold, and they will never work the gold. It's my work—my work!—that purchased this land!"

"Not only your work," their father reminded him, "but mine as well. And your brothers may not work the gold, but they do other work of equal value."

"My work has the most value!" Yerakh screamed. "Anyone can plant seeds and herd flocks, but not everyone can master the gold! And it is my hands that work the gold! These hands!" Yerakh lifted his hands, striking his father's face and knocking him to the earthen floor. "You'll not take what is mine! You'll not rob me with your foolishness!"

Stunned, their father sucked in a rasping breath, protesting, though Yerakh had him pinned to the floor. "It's not foolishness for a man to provide for his sons and daughters when they leave his household! And it's not foolishness for you, Yerakh, to share with your brothers. Now get up. You forget your duty to your father."

"Here's my duty!" Yerakh snarled, closing his hands about their father's throat and crushing the very breath from him.

Annah watched her father struggle to live. His face darkened. His tongue was forced out of his mouth. His eyes bulged and rolled back in his head. She ran to help him. At twelve she was too young and weak to be a threat, but she beat Yerakh's back and tore at his hair. When Yerakh finally noticed her, he threw her away like a stick of wood. By the time she recovered from the fall and scrambled to her feet, it was too late to save her father. He lay still on the earthen floor, his neck cruelly snapped, his eyes and mouth gaping, bloodied and ghastly.

As young as she was, Annah knew the look of death. A wail rose in her throat, high and piercing. Yerakh slapped his hands over her face and throat, squeezing

38

hard, threatening, "Not another sound. Not a word from you, or I'll kill you, too! Do you hear me? Not another word!"

Suffocating, Annah struggled against Yerakh's grasp until the light in the workroom faded to merciful blackness. When she awoke, she was alone with her father's body. In silence, she cried and clung to him. She kissed his cold hands and begged him—without words—to live. Finally, admitting to herself that there was no hope, she reached into his work pouch and retrieved something he had promised her for her marriage day; his small amulet of gold. If Yerakh should find the amulet, he would take it for himself. This precious bit of gold would never belong to Yerakh, who had murdered his own father. Who might also murder her.

Awakened by her terror, Annah lay sweating on her small grass-stuffed pallet in the quiet, dim lodge. Her heart was pounding so hard she thought she would die. Perfectly still and silent, Annah cried for her father in the darkness. *I wish you were alive. I wish I had not seen you die. Most of all, I wish Yerakh were dead for killing you!*

At last, taking a deep breath, Annah tried to relax. She remembered different things to comfort herself. The pink of the sky, the coolness of water, the fresh green of new leaves, her hands working on the veil, the smile of the young man at the river.

Saddened, she thought to the young man, *If only my brothers and sisters and I could work together and live together—as you and your brother do—in peace. I wish I knew your family. Do you think of me when you are not at the river?*

Her hands moved beneath her veil, down the front of her tunic to feel the wonderful shell carving hidden beneath the soft leather. Half-dreaming, she remembered the polished feel of the shell, its perfectly curled and pierced edges, and the luminous pinks and blues it reflected. In one short day, this bit of carving had become more precious to her than her veil. Somehow, she had to repay the young man for his kindness.

Stealthily, Annah reached for her woven-grass bag and explored its interior, seeking a closed grass pouch fastened near the bottom of the bag. This had been the best place to hide her father's cherished gold amulet. After his death, she had woven the tiny pouch to camouflage the amulet, then bound it neatly inside her bag with long, supple, sturdy blades of grass. She inspected the pouch often, but she never removed the amulet for fear that Yerakh would discover it and take it from her. He had never spoken of it after the murder; Annah hoped he didn't know it existed.

Does it still look the same? She fingered the contours of the amulet, recalling its pattern of a branch of tapering leaves in a disc of gold, half the size of her palm. *Father, would you approve if I gave the amulet to the young man at the river?*

Annah tried to remember her father's voice. She could see him in the workroom, busy with gold. He gathered the gold himself, with Yerakh's help, from the river encircling the land of Khawvilah. When he was working with the gleaming metal and stones, her father was always happy, humming as he worked. But as busy as he was, he always sensed her presence and turned.

She could almost hear him saying to her kindly, "My Annah-of-the-thousand-questions, why aren't you with your mother and sisters? Have you come to watch me work?"

As her father answered her childish questions, his nimble hands would deftly wind a long, thin strand of gold around a solid, narrow, grooved cylinder of iron, until the cylinder looked like an object of pure gold. Then he would take a long, sharp, wedged blade of iron, fit it along the groove in the cylinder, and rap the wedged blade firmly with a mallet. When he lifted the mallet and blade away from the cylinder, he would reveal a row of gold links.

Each time her father did this, he would challenge Annah to find a short link or odd end. She had always laughed and looked, knowing that each link would be shining and faultless. Her joy would last until Yerakh entered the workroom with rapidly cooling gold that had been fired to molten perfection in the small clay oven outside.

"I saw my face in this gold, I've made it so pure," Yerakh would say smugly. Then, with a sidelong look at Annah, he would say, "Why is *she* here?"

Now, in the darkness of the night, Annah thought to Yerakh, *You have always robbed me of my speech. Even before you murdered our father, you did all you could to silence me. Perhaps, one day, you will even kill me. But I'll be sure Father's amulet belongs to a man who is worthy of such a treasure.*

Touching the contours of the amulet once more, Annah hugged her grass bag tightly in the darkness. Parah, asleep on a nearby pallet, shifted and muttered incoherently. Haburah and Ayalah slept just beyond Parah, exhausted because they had quarreled late into the night. Annah could hear them breathing.

I wonder if your dreams are better than mine, my sisters. Do you ever fear to sleep because death itself might gaze upon you when you close your eyes? I think not. You have no fear of death, because you have forgotten the face of your father. But if I live for one thousand kentums, I will never forget.

Annah lay awake until dawn.

~♦ ♦~

At the river the next morning, Annah picked the amulet out of its dark hiding place. It was smaller than she remembered, but beautiful; a shining, flattened circle of gold embossed with a delicate golden branch of tapering leaves. Carefully she tied the amulet into the leather pouch the young man had used to protect the shell carving. When she was finished, the small leather bundle fit comfortably in her fist. *This is right,* she told herself. *This amulet belongs to him for saving my life. But I have to be sure I can throw it all the way across the river.*

She practiced throwing stones over the water at the opposite bank. To her immense frustration, every stone she threw fell short. If she lost the amulet to the river, she would mourn for it until she died. *Keep practicing,* she admonished herself. *If you don't throw accurately, and soon, you might as well give the amulet to Yerakh.* She moved upstream, looking for stones—until she sensed a presence and stopped.

He was on the opposite bank, his eyes shining dark and splendid, one black brow raised, questioning her: *What are you doing?*

Lifting her hands in a gesture of despair, Annah shook her head. Attempting to explain, she retrieved the small leather pouch with the amulet and extended it to him, then set it down, reached for another stone, and threw it—her best throw yet. Once again it fell short, perhaps two-thirds of the way across the river.

Perplexed, he raised his hands in the familiar gesture: *Wait.*

As Annah stared, he pointed to the small pouch containing the amulet, then lifted his eyebrows questioningly: *What's in there?*

He thinks I'm returning the shell carving, Annah realized. Anxious, she shook her head again, pulling the leather cord up from beneath her tunic to show him that she still wore the shell carving. His relief was visible. Annah sighed, grateful for his reaction. He did indeed want her to have the beautiful ornament. All the more reason for him to have the amulet. To inform him of the importance of her offering, Annah picked up the leather-clad amulet, cradling it protectively, willing him to understand: *This cannot be lost to the river.*

He smiled, his wonderful, breathtaking smile, and waded as far as he dared into the flowing water, almost to his chest. There, he flung his arms open wide, gesturing: *Throw it; I'll catch it!*

She eyed the river doubtfully. Had she been able to cast a stone that far? To be certain, she set the amulet down, picked up a stone half the size of her fist, and backed up to throw it. His eyes widened as Annah hurled the stone toward him. Alarmed, he swiftly lunged aside, almost toppling over before recovering his balance. They both watched the stone fall into the water, raising a froth of sparkling droplets. *Yes*, Annah decided, it was within his reach.

In obvious agreement, he nodded, lifting his hands meaningfully: *Throw it.*

Slowly, she picked up the amulet again and clutched it, working up her courage. *Please*, she thought—closing her eyes, the thought was so intense—*let this reach him.* Aiming as best she could, she threw the leather-padded amulet across the water. She threw it too far to his right.

He surged through the water for it, and fell. Annah sucked in her breath, horrified. He was gone. The amulet was gone. She had lost them both to the current. She sank to her knees on the riverbank and waited, trembling with apprehension. It seemed an eternity until she saw him again.

His left hand emerged from the water first, clutching the leather pouch. It was empty. As she watched in despair, he reappeared, gasping for breath. Wiping his eyes, he smiled at her mischievously, lifting his right hand. The leather-corded amulet dangled from his fingertips.

Melting with relief, Annah lowered her face into her hands. She felt as if she had been saved from some unknown danger. When she recovered, she looked over at him again. He was studying the amulet carefully, obviously fascinated by its leaf-patterned surface. Sensing her scrutiny, he gestured to the amulet, questioning: *Yours?*

Annah nodded and put a hand to her face, stroking downward on an imaginary beard: *From my father.*

The young man repeated her gesture, asking: *Your father's?*

She nodded again, then slowly drew her hand along a dry patch of the riverbank, gathering the tawny sand in her fist. Raising her arm so he could see, she let the sand drift down from her fingers to rejoin the sand on the bank—the customary gesture indicating death: *My father is dead.*

It was the first time that she had ever communicated the news of her father's death to anyone. In twenty-five years, no one in her family or in the settlement had ever spoken to Annah of her father. Not a breath of condolence, regret, or even a vague interest in justice. Nothing. Their lack of emotion had formed the most agonizing portion of her grief.

Now, the simple act of releasing the sand back to the earth was more than she could bear. The pain caught hard in her throat, and she tried to choke it down. Stinging, blurring tears filled her eyes and slid down her cheeks. Gathering another handful of sand, she flung it away. *Dead!* she thought, anguished. *And I'll go mad if I don't calm myself. He's watching.*

He had retreated to the opposite bank and crouched down, dripping wet, watching her, waiting. She could feel his gaze upon her. His mood was heavy now; she could sense that too. *He must think I'm mad.* Mournfully, she scooped some water from the river and dashed it over her face. As she dried her eyes, she heard the quiet plop of a stone in the water before her. He was beckoning her. Annah looked over at him reluctantly.

His eyes expressed no ridicule, only gentle sympathy and compassion. He repeated her gestures, imitating the beard of her father, and scattering the dust of death, but then he added his own thoughts. Pointing to her, he traced the path of a tear from his right eye down his cheek: *You mourn the death of your father.* Then, he tapped his chest, indicating himself, then drew the path of another tear down his cheek, and lowered his head: *I'm sorry.*

He did not lift his head immediately, and Annah realized he felt defeated by his inability to help her. Quickly, she snatched a small stone and threw it into the water before him. As he looked up, she managed a half smile and a shrug, then clasped both of her hands to herself briefly and extended them toward him: *Thank you,* she thought. *You are the first person to express any sympathy for my father's death. And you're not even from my own settlement.*

Now the young man lifted the amulet toward her,

worried: *Are you sure you want to give this to me?*

She nodded emphatically: *Yes!*

Reverently, with his eyes fixed on hers, he kissed the amulet gently and pulled it over his shining, dark curls. After shaking his hair loose from the cord, he threw a questioning look at Annah.

Confused, she tipped her head and gave him a questioning look of her own: *What do you want to know?*

He pursed his lips, obviously pondering how to ask his question. Apparently coming to a decision, he took a deep breath, extended his left hand toward her, pointed his right hand toward himself, and held the gesture. Watching her steadily, he clasped his hands together formally, in the manner of a man and woman pledging themselves to each other in a marriage ceremony.

Annah blinked. Surely he wasn't asking her to be his wife? But even as this wave of disbelief arose within her, she knew: He was asking her to accept him. He repeated the motions, his gaze compelling her to answer: *Can you pledge yourself to me?*

She managed to respond with a faint, questioning flick of her hand: *You and me?*

He nodded, echoing her gesture firmly: *You and me.* How? Annah wondered. *Yerakh would refuse anyway. And I would have to speak to him, using words.* The thought was frightening. Yerakh would kill her for deceiving him for so many years. But she couldn't refuse this young man. Instead, she raised her hands and shrugged to indicate her uncertainty. She did not have to express her fear, she knew; it was obvious.

He nodded and smiled comfortingly: *I understand.* Glancing up at the warm, pink sky, he indicated the midmorning sun.

He has to go, Annah realized. *He's probably stayed longer than he intended.*

As she perceived this, he gestured to her, then to the riverbank on which she sat. *He wants to know if I'll be here tomorrow.* She nodded.

His answering smile was radiant. To bid her farewell, he lifted the amulet to his lips and kissed it.

Dazed, Annah mimicked his gesture, kissing her treasured shell carving. Still unable to move, she watched him leave. He looked back at her once, smiled his enchanting smile, then vanished into the trees lining his side of the river. Annah had to remind herself to tuck the precious shell carving beneath her tunic once more. *How can I ever marry him? It'll never happen,* she thought despondently. *Not even if we live a thousand years.*

Annah sat on the riverbank, still too dazed to move. Lifting her eyes to the tranquil sky, she sighed, cherishing the sensation: He desired her. He wanted her to be his wife. Then she grimaced. *If he truly understood me, he'd never return to the riverbank. Why should he want me? I am a nothing.*

Despite her attempt to prepare herself for disappointment, the morning took on a new sweetness. The sparkling water seemed to reflect her elation, flowing before her, teeming with long, plump, many-colored fish. The fish slipped toward her, then away and back again, as if they were playing, coaxing her to join them.

How different the river looks today, Annah thought, gazing at the clear, swift-flowing water, enraptured. *How different everything is now, compared to the day when I first saw him. Has it really been only two days?*

She felt that nothing could touch her now. She felt only her joy; even if she never married, she could tell herself that he had desired her. To share her happiness, she gathered some seeds, berries, and snippets from nearby plants, and cast them into the river. The fish, obedient to her whims, sped after her offerings to nibble them; their unending curiosity and appetites served to cleanse the river of debris. Pleased that the fish had accepted her offerings, Annah retrieved her bag, swept her veil over her head, and turned toward the settlement. Her stomach was growling uncomfortably. She couldn't remember the last time she had felt such hunger.

You can eat as soon as you get to the lodge, she promised herself. But the thought of fruit, particularly the sweet, thin-skinned afals planted behind Yerakh's lodge, broke her resistance. Almost skipping, she cut through the field to the afal trees.

Choosing a honey-sweet golden-fleshed variety her father had always loved, she tossed her veil back against her shoulders, plucked one of the fat, soft-skinned fruits, and ate it quickly. Discarding the large, ruddy brown pit, she wiped the juice off her fingers, then picked more. She filled her woven-grass bag with the fruit, covered her head with her veil again, and started back to the lodge.

To her horror, Annah saw Yerakh and the formidable Naham at the entrance. Had they feasted all night without sleeping? They sensed her presence and turned immediately, staring at her.

I'll go to the back entry, Annah thought, ducking her head to appear as meek as possible. Her heart thumped uncomfortably. Edging away, she cast a wary, sidelong glance toward them through her veil.

Naham gave her a jeering, nasty look and approached

her, swaggering arrogantly. If she ran from him, Annah knew both men would take offense. She stood still, her head bowed.

"Little veiled one," Naham crooned, maliciously sociable. "Out so early? Have you been visiting your lover?"

As he laughed at his own wit, Annah began to sweat beneath her veil. His tone, his nearness, and his questions were unnerving her. Yerakh ambled up, his footsteps reluctant, like a man who wanted nothing more than sleep.

Sneering, Naham spoke to Yerakh. "Could she possibly have lovers, as the other women of your lodge do?"

"She's like a piece of wood," Yerakh muttered, obviously choosing to ignore Naham's gibe. "How can she have lovers?"

Naham grunted. "True. You know, this veil she wears outdoors has always disturbed me. Will she go mad if I remove it?"

"See for yourself," Yerakh answered.

Hearing his careless reply, Annah trembled inwardly. He would not speak for her or defend her in any way. Naham pulled at her veil, laughing softly. Annah kept her eyes lowered. Trying to control her fear, she concentrated on slowing her breathing. Naham dropped the veil; Annah felt it swish past her legs to the ground.

"She hasn't gone mad yet," Naham said. He was staring hard at her, Annah could tell. All her senses were screaming in alarm.

I'm going to run, she told herself. *I don't care if Yerakh beats me later.* But even as she thought this, she felt the pull of Naham's huge hand gliding down her hair, then edging in until his powerful fingers stroked the back of her neck.

"You know, Yerakh," Naham said, thoughtful now, "I've always wondered how you endure the women of your household. Troublemakers, all of them. But this one's different. Give her to me."

Yerakh snorted in disbelief. "To marry? She has no marriage portion. And you wouldn't want her after the first night anyway. I doubt your wives would want her around either."

Naham had taken three wives during his two kentums of life. His first wife was dead by his own hands. His two remaining wives were barren, embittered women.

"Oh, I'm not asking you to give her a marriage portion," Naham replied, still stroking Annah's hair, making her shudder in uncontrolled loathing. "It's well known how wretched your women are, Yerakh; you've kept them all without marriage portions or property of their own. I'm just asking you, as your friend—your only true friend—to give me this creature for a night. Just one night."

Annah stomach churned. She would vomit if she couldn't escape soon. Naham's touch repulsed her; his huge, brutish fingers, now clasping the back of her neck and her head, terrified her. She was barely half Naham's height. He could kill her with a swat of his hand. She would die if he took her for one night—or for any time at all.

Please, Yerakh, she thought desperately, *tell him no!*

When he finally spoke, Yerakh sounded exasperated. "Why do you want her? You know she has no spirit; as I said, she's like a piece of wood. Even so . . . I agree . . . for one night. But if she dies, or returns to my household unable to do her work—or if she's bearing a child—then you'll pay me half a flock, or one whole field."

Naham sputtered, clearly offended. "What? Half a flock? Or one of my good fields! For this no-wit creature?

She's not worth that!"

"She works with the gold—" Yerakh began, but Naham interrupted him, his voice booming as he flung Annah toward her brother.

"This is insulting! I'm your friend, and you demand things of me that you don't require of others. You should be fair, Yerakh. You should speak to K'nan before he gives Ayalah a full belly. Then you should beat Tseb-iy for everything he's done with your mother. As for Haburah— I asked your mother ten years ago to give Haburah to me as my second wife. Parah refused because she knew you would refuse.

"You don't want to part with any of your father's lands—not even for your sisters. And you're the richest man in the settlement! I didn't challenge you then because we've been friends, but if you reject any more men who ask for the women of your household, Yerakh, they'll all turn against you! Remember, I've warned you!"

Yerakh did not respond. If goaded beyond endurance, Naham could easily crush even Yerakh to death.

Thrusting one broad finger at Annah to emphasize his words, Naham added, "The only reason I asked for this creature is because I thought you wouldn't care. She has no value. No other man in the settlement will have her." Naham was leaving now, but he bellowed so loudly that the entire settlement could hear. "She's afflicted! You should have strangled her too, Yerakh!"

Keeping her face blank, her eyes lowered, Annah reached down carefully, trying not to spill the afals from her grass bag as she rescued her veil. She could hear Yerakh's breathing, harsh, deep, and fast. The sound frightened her. All over her body, inside and out, her skin seemed to be crawling, tingling with fear. Just as the urge to run seized her, Yerakh snatched a large handful of her hair and hauled her inside the lodge.

He had barely pulled her past the carved doorpost when Annah felt his first blow to her stomach. It knocked all the breath from her body and doubled her over, causing her to fall to the earthen floor, defenseless. The afals in her grass bag spilled and rolled everywhere.

Yerakh continued to hammer her with his big fists, uttering incoherent, throaty cries of rage until Annah was aware of nothing but pain. . . .

Four

UNABLE TO catch her breath long enough to scream, Annah curled up into a tight, quivering ball.

When Yerakh stopped using his fists, he kicked her back and legs, striking the most vicious blows with his heel. Then abruptly he left her and stomped through the lodge, roaring, "Ayalah! Bring your mother to me, Ayalah! Iltani, where are you? If you're hiding from me, I'll kill you! Haburah, come here!"

Terrified, Annah lay curled up on the earthen floor. It hurt to breathe. She could taste blood in her mouth, and she could feel her lips swelling. Her left jaw and cheekbone felt hot. And her precious shell carving had slipped out of its hiding place within her tunic. Furtively moving one hand, she tugged at it. The cord held.

She almost sighed with relief, but her ribs hurt too badly to take a full breath. Slowly, painfully, she tucked the shell carving into the neckline of her leather tunic. Then, tears of hurt seeping out from beneath her eyelids, she waited, listening for Yerakh.

He went out the back of the lodge, and she could hear him screaming, "Iltani! Haburah! Ayalah! Don't make me come after you! If I find you, I'll kill you!"

They've all run away, Annah realized. *And if he doesn't find them, he will come back here to wait until they return. But if he beats me any more, I'll probably die. I must get away.*

Moving weakly, she pushed herself to her feet, clutching her grass bag and veil as if they could save her from additional harm. Stumbling outside, she turned away from the settlement and headed for the river. She would hide in the lush leaf-shrouded trees and rest there. At nightfall, however, she would have to return to the lodge. Her fear of being caught outside in the dark was greater than her fear of another beating.

Her fear was not due to the darkness or to the creatures of the night, but because of feast-goers such as Naham and Yerakh—and because of the Serpent-Lovers, in particular, the Nachash. If any of them found her alone in the darkness, they would probably abuse her, then kill her.

By the time she reached the trees near the river, Annah was shaking from pain and fright. Suppose Yerakh were to come after her? Or worse, what if Naham decided to ignore Yerakh's demands and take her anyway? Fearfully, she watched the settlement. Perhaps Yerakh was still searching for her mother and sisters. *I hope they've managed to escape.*

Intent on escape herself, Annah crept into the deep green vines, fronds, and cloak-sized leaves of the undergrowth. Feeling safer, she leaned against a tree trunk and slowly eased her way down into the sanctuary of the leaves. The very act of sitting brought tears to her eyes. *I can't stay here*, she realized. *Sitting on the ground hurts too much. But I have to rest. And I'm thirsty.*

Groping inside her woven bag, Annah found one of the afals. There were only two left out of the heap she had gathered, and they were sadly bruised and crushed. *Like me*, she told herself ruefully.

Her jaw was so swollen that she had to break the fruit into tiny bits and push them between her teeth to swallow them. Slowly she ate them both, then pulled herself to her feet. She needed poultices for her wounds, but she was too weak to gather any herbs and pound them out.

All I can do is to soak myself in the river. Was I really there this morning? Impossible. I must have dreamed that I was happy.

She limped upriver to a sheltered, sandy inlet where the women of the settlement gathered occasionally to soak their garments and fleeces, and to bathe themselves and their children. Today, however, the inlet was deserted. Annah relaxed, grateful. She had feared some of the children might be playing in the water. The children were vicious, pampered creatures, preying on anyone they perceived as different, which she was. They usually threw rocks at her, forcing her away. She would not have been able to run from them today; the pain was too overwhelming.

Moving stiffly, Annah settled onto the inclined bank, scooting far enough into the water to cover her body without submerging her head. The water did ease her pain. She crammed her veil into her grass bag to make a pillow for herself, then leaned back and shut her eyes. The sound and the feel of the lapping water soothed her. She also sensed the fish hovering gently nearby, not touching her, but lingering, as if they understood her misery. Comforted, Annah slipped out of consciousness.

~◈◉◈~

Voices woke her. Opening her eyes, she recognized Parah's feet and those of Iltani, Haburah, and Ayalah. They were standing behind Parah, the water barely edging their brown toes. Annah didn't have to see their faces to know they were angry with her. Their annoyance showed in their crossed arms, or their hands on their hips, and she felt them watching her.

Why are you angry with me? Naham's the one who provoked Yerakh! And obviously, you've all escaped beatings. You don't have bruises. You aren't struggling to breathe. But you're just waiting for me to prove I can stand and walk, so you won't feel guilty for abandoning me.

Annah sat up, catching her breath at the pain. She wondered if she could stand at all. She felt shaky. Her ribs, her legs, her arms, and her jaw all ached and pounded miserably.

"Well, she's alive," said Iltani, her voice scornful.

"Ugh, look at her jaw." Ayalah sounded squeamish. "It's puffed out like a frog's. Almost the same color too. If we hadn't run, Yerakh would've beaten us the same way."

"He will catch us eventually," Haburah said, shifting from foot to foot. She was restless, angry. Her voice lowered conspiratorially. "We should find Yerakh before he finds us, and we should kill him."

Annah listened, appalled. Would Haburah really kill him? Could any of them—including herself—actually lift weapons against Yerakh? To cover her fear, Annah practiced her vacant stare, gazing at the sparkling, swift-flowing water.

"How?" Ayalah asked. Her lilting voice dared Haburah to act on her brave, impulsive words. "How would you kill him?"

"I said *we!*" Haburah retorted. "We will kill Yerakh. If you're too frightened, child, we could get Chathath and Gammad to help us."

"You sound as if you would actually do it!" Iltani burst out shrilly. "This is my husband you want to kill! Why do you say these things in front of me?"

"You should hear them," Haburah answered coldly. "You've been married to him for five years now, and you've given not one hint of bearing him a child. I'd wager every hair on my head that he's going to discard you soon and marry someone else. No man will have you after that. I say you should strike him first."

"Why aren't you saying anything, O mother of my husband!" Iltani demanded of Parah. "Are you too frightened to stand with me? Or do you really want your son to die so you'll be free to marry that seducer, Tseb-iy?"

"Tseb-iy has nothing to do with this," Parah answered, unmoving. "Yerakh is a tyrant, and it's only a matter of time before his family rebels. I warned your husband, Iltani; he chose a dangerous path by enslaving his own brothers and sisters. And he threatened to kill me for telling him so."

"He nearly killed Annah today," Ayalah added.

Hearing this, Iltani squealed indignantly. "So he nearly killed the creature! What would it matter?"

Annah stared into the water, feeling darkness rise within her against Iltani. She longed to scream, *I've never hurt you, Iltani! But if your husband did kill me, you would shrug and never think of me again. Why do you hate me so?*

Suddenly her thoughts were interrupted by a violent shudder beneath her. The trees lurched, groaning above her, while the river dashed cold water onto her chest and face, like a living thing subduing her. Gasping, Annah struggled to pull herself higher onto the riverbank. Her mother and sisters were screaming and falling to their knees beside her. Iltani fell with them, wailing in terror, clawing at her, then at Parah.

Wave after wave of river water rushed upon them as the terrible shaking of the earth continued. Annah tried to brace herself, feeling the sand seeping away from beneath her, fearing the force of the water would pull them into the river. But then the shaking subsided. Annah felt herself trembling helplessly. This was more frightful than being beaten by Yerakh.

Ayalah was sobbing like a child, and Iltani's wails faded to wretched groans. Haburah was the first to speak, all her courage apparently gone, crushed into a whisper of horror. "I'ma, has the earth ever shaken before?"

"No," Parah said, hushed. "I've never seen such a thing. And none of the stories of old tell of the earth moving."

"Will it shake again?" Ayalah whimpered. "Don't let it shake again."

As if we could prevent it, Annah thought, still in shock. *But how did it shake? What is strong enough to shake the earth?*

"The earth is alive," Iltani moaned. "The earth is angry because we were planning to kill Yerakh."

Haburah grabbed Iltani's arm and shook her, screaming, "Shut up about Yerakh! Shut up! If you tell him what we've said, we'll kill you before we kill him."

Haburah, Annah thought in despair, *you sound like Yerakh. Kill, then kill again.*

"Let's go back to the lodge," Parah said distractedly. "If the earth shakes again, I want to be away from the river."

They left quickly, without looking back. Biting her lip against the pain, Annah pulled herself to her feet, grabbed her sodden grass bag, and wobbled after them, dripping wet and weak with hunger.

Forcing herself to be alert, Annah searched for food as they tramped through the lush green undergrowth and trees lining the river. Soon, a soft humming and the scent of sweetness fell upon her. Seeing a graceful, broad-leafed tree covered with delicate white flowers, Annah sighed, thankful. She had found a resin tree with a colony of honeybees nested inside its trunk. Reaching painfully into the undergrowth, Annah plucked a broad, heart-shaped leaf from its fuzzy stem. She rolled the leaf into a cone and pinched the base together to form a hand-sized cup.

Gently, she slipped her free hand into the hollow of the resin tree, reaching down until she found a bit of honeycomb. The bees hummed around her lightly, scenting her, identifying her.

I am a human nothing, she thought to them wearily. She dropped the glistening chunk of honeycomb into her leaf cup and broke it apart. The bees inspected her work, then dismissed her, returning to the delectable white flowers of their sheltering resin tree. Grateful for the nourishing honeycomb, Annah ate it slowly, working the tiny pieces between her teeth, forcing her swollen jaw to move. She could hear her mother and sisters in the trees ahead of her, squabbling.

They were gathering stomach-soothing rhizomes and edible flowers in glorious shades of red, violet, yellow, and cream, but they disagreed loudly over which foods would appease Yerakh. *As if mere food would soothe his rage,*

Annah thought. *But perhaps the shaking of the earth has quieted him more than a meal ever could.*

Seeing Annah, Parah snatched the limp grass bag from her daughter's shoulder. "We need this," she said, not to Annah, but to herself.

Too wounded to struggle, Annah let her mother take the bag. But it grieved her to watch Parah snatch the still-wet veil from the bag and drop it disdainfully to the ground. Wincing at the effort, Annah crouched and retrieved the veil one-handed, guarding her leaf cup with its one last nip of honeycomb.

Iltani noticed Annah's leaf cup and snatched it. Gleeful, she ate the piece of honeycomb, smacking her lips.

"The creature found honey," she told the others. "We should gather some later."

"You do it," Haburah answered rudely. "Last time we found honey, you ate it all."

"You made yourself sick, too," Ayalah added, turning away from Iltani contemptuously.

"If anything makes me sick, it's you!" Iltani screamed. "I hate you all! Food is my one comfort. And if I ate all the honey myself, it's because you're all so heartless!"

Annah pulled the damp veil over her head. She wished she could find something to plug her ears against Iltani's complaints. Even the birds stopped singing at the sound of her loud shrieking. Walking away quietly, Annah began to gather herbs and her mother's favorite spicy golden-red cooking bark.

Will I'ma even notice I've gathered this for her? Annah wondered. *I doubt it. I'm sure she's too busy worrying about Yerakh, or Tseb-iy. I wish I could run away. I don't want to return to the lodge. Yerakh won't go feasting with Naham tonight, and everyone will be angry with each other, and with me.*

Yerakh was indeed in the lodge when they returned. His earlier rage was gone, replaced by anxiety. "Where were you?" he asked Parah. "Did the earth move there too?"

Keeping her eyes lowered beneath her veil, Annah dropped her collection of herbs and bark into a storage basket. She was trembling again, weak and in pain. She needed to hide and calm herself. Even so, one persistent thought gnawed at the edge of her mind: *What is strong enough to shake the earth?*

When the tremors stopped shaking the walls of their lodge, Shem looked at his brothers. They sat beside him speechless and awed, their midday meal forgotten. Their parents, too, remained silent. Noakh's eyes were dark and reflective, staring at the latticed walls of the lodge without seeing them. Naomi touched her husband's arm.

"My dear one," she began hesitantly, "I thought we had a year yet."

Noakh released a pent-up breath, rubbing one broad, stained hand over his bearded face. "We do have a year," he assured her. "This shaking of the earth was to warn the others. I pray they understand; soon, the Most High will lift the protection of His hand from the earth. Then the earth will turn upon itself. No one will survive."

"Except us," Khawm added, as if to reassure himself.

"Except us, by the mercy of the Most High," Noakh agreed. Sighing, he stood, brushed the crumbs of grain cakes from his beard and tunic, and went to look behind the screen that sheltered Methuwshelakh. Shem followed, peeking around from the opposite end.

Methuwshelakh was still asleep, the faintest of snores bubbling in his throat. Shem blinked at his great-grandfather, then grinned at his father. "He never moved. How could he possibly sleep while the earth was shaking?"

"His thoughts are beyond the earth," Noakh answered gently. "Soon he will leave us to sleep with his fathers."

"He's still asleep?" Naomi's voice rose in disbelief as she approached.

"He won't believe us when we tell him that the earth moved," Shem said.

Naomi was silent. Her attention was obviously focused on the dark leather cord encircling Shem's neck. "If you gave the sea carving to that young woman from across the river, my son, then what is this?" Suspicious, she pulled at the cord, raising the gold amulet from beneath his leather tunic.

Noakh eyed the gold amulet with interest. "From the young woman, my son?"

"I was going to speak with you after our meal," Shem promised his parents, "but I was interrupted by the earth's shaking."

Noakh pursed his lips, barely hiding the twitch of a smile. "One day you will learn, my son: Not even the earth's shaking will prevent your mother from spying some token of affection from a young woman."

Pretending offense, Naomi huffed. "If I were as clever as that, dear one, I would have seen this cord the instant he sat down to eat. And, so," she challenged Shem, "this is from the young woman?"

"Yes. Though it's not a token of betrothal on her part. She knows my thoughts are with her, but I think she's afraid of her family's reaction."

Naomi sniffed. "She should be afraid. I've not spoken

to her mother, and her mother has not spoken to me. How can this be a proper match?"

By now, Noakh had come around the screen to study the gold amulet. Seeing the pattern of leaves, his graying eyebrows lifted in recognition. "I know this family."

"And . . ." Naomi prodded eagerly, her eyes bright as a bird's.

"The Lodge of Zahar of the Tsaraph. But now, it is the Lodge of Yerakh; Zahar, the goldsmith, was killed by that son-who-was-no-son, Yerakh."

"But that was more than twenty years ago," Shem said, amazed, remembering snatches of news from the settlement after the murder. His father had been angered, his mother shocked. "She still mourns for her father after all these years?"

"That is just how a good and dutiful daughter should behave," Naomi said, nodding her head approvingly. But even as she approved, a shadow crossed her face.

By now, Yepheth and Khawm had finished their meal and were standing near Shem, fingering the gold amulet. Yepheth was stoic, but Khawm nudged Shem, enthused. "When do you marry this woman?"

"There's no betrothal yet," Shem replied, easing the precious amulet away from Khawm's avid fingers.

"I am not welcomed at the Lodge of Yerakh," Noakh told his sons gravely. "And you won't be welcomed if this Yerakh realizes you are my sons. When I heard of the murder of Zahar, I went to the leaders of the settlement and reminded them that such a crime must be punished for fear of the Most High." Noakh paused, sighing regretfully.

"Zahar was a kind, but foolish man. He was also the wealthiest man in the settlement. Yerakh claimed that wealth for his own. And with it, he claimed the loyalty of the settlement, including one of those giants—a *Nephiyl*. The leaders of the settlement scorned the Most High. As one, they escorted me down to the river, took possession of my reed-craft, returned me to this side of the river, and threatened me with death if I returned. And," Noakh added, disgusted, "when they crossed again to go back to the settlement, they broke the reed-craft to pieces. Zahar's death was never recognized, I'm sure. Now, I am an enemy to the Lodge of Yerakh."

Shem felt a sick churning in his stomach. "How can I have been mistaken in seeing her? It doesn't seem possible."

"You were not mistaken," Noakh told him. "She has been chosen for you. But the Most High must cause this young woman to come out of the Lodge of Yerakh according to His own plan. We must wait until the proper time."

Naomi fingered the gold amulet again, then straightened briskly, speaking to Shem. "I will go to the river with you tomorrow. I should see this young woman. Now, however, we must tend our ancient one. See if he is ready to wake up and eat."

Heartsick, Shem knelt beside Methuwshelakh, taking his hand and rubbing it gently. Stirring slightly, the old man opened his eyes. He recognized Shem and smiled. Lifting his thin, reedy voice, he said, "Son of my sons . . . am I dead? Your face looks like one of those who lament." Squeezing Shem's fingers kindly, Methuwshelakh rasped, "Smile."

Unable to resist the appeal of the father of his fathers, Shem smiled and bent to kiss the old man's withered cheek.

Methuwshelakh patted his shoulder. "It is a good day,"
he murmured. "A good day."

Five

HER WORKBASKET slung over one arm, Naomi emerged from the lodge, breathed in the soft midmorning air, and frowned. *I pray I like this young woman, for Shem's sake.*

At that instant, Shem came around the corner of the lodge. Seeing his mother, he grinned. "I'ma, are you ready to go? Or have you changed your mind again?"

Pretending irritation, she said, "No, I haven't changed my mind! Come here. Take these. . . ." She grabbed a thick coil of vines and a bundle of long, dried bulb-leaves, and thrust them into her son's arms. Then, deliberately taking her time, she picked up her workbasket and inspected its contents: wooden weaving needles, narrow iron cutting blades, tidy bunches of fiber threads. Still moving slowly, she gathered two more coils of dried vines from the storeroom inside the lodge.

All these supplies would let this young woman know

that she was not the sole reason for Naomi's visit to the river. Otherwise, she might infer too much and become proud, and later, unmanageable.

I will not live with a difficult woman, Naomi told herself. *And my Shem should not have to live with a proud wife.* She watched Shem lift the bundles to his shoulders.

His burdens settled, Shem gave her a wry, teasing look. "I'ma, when will you have enough baskets and ropes?"

"When I die," she answered briskly.

Obviously amused, her son said, "Six kentums more."

Naomi, halfway to her fifth kentum, feigned exasperation. "Humph! Since when does a person live for more than a thousand years? That would be too much of a blessing!" Gripping her coils of vines and her basket, she marched away from the lodge to the narrow dirt path that led through the trees, down to the river.

If she looked at her son she would smile, and her dignity would fail. He was so much like his father—a good, kind man. Thinking of Noakh, Naomi sighed. She felt truly blessed—certainly far more than she deserved.

As she walked, Naomi felt one of the coils of dried vines being tugged from her left arm. Shem pulled it away, adding it to his own burden, then moved ahead of her. He was hurrying her along. He had been hurrying her since prayers at dawn.

"Slow down. I shouldn't have to run to keep up with you. Why are you so eager to see some woman you've never spoken to before?"

"We've spoken, I'ma." He turned, walking backwards. "We don't need speech."

"When you've married her, you'll hear everything then," Naomi warned.

He smiled at her in response, his tender, heart-clutching smile.

Naomi almost faltered, thinking, *If this young girl does not love him, then she is incapable of love! But how can I let him marry? He's still too young.* She glared at her son. "Turn around. Watch where you're going!"

Obedient as always, he turned, leading her down through the trees lining the riverbank.

Naomi made mental notes of various flowers, vines, fruits, and types of bark. She didn't have enough of the tightly woven baskets that were best for storing grain. Nor did she have enough split-wood baskets to hold the various hard-shelled nuts that her husband and sons loved. She needed more time. No, she needed more help.

When my sons marry, Naomi thought, *then I will have women to keep me company. And grandchildren . . .*

"She's there," Shem announced, breaking into Naomi's thoughts, making her look across the river.

She—the cause of his joy—sat on the opposite riverbank, her right profile toward them, slender and vulnerable against the darkness of her long hair. Naomi raised her full, dark eyebrows, shocked. *What is my son thinking? She's a mere child, and much too thin. But she is lovely. And at least her hands aren't idle.*

The young woman was working on what appeared to be a long, pale, intricate piece of netting. When she sensed their approach, she turned slightly, anxiously. The instant she saw Naomi, she struggled to her feet, facing them fully, revealing the ghastly violet-blue contours of her swollen left jaw and cheek. As Naomi stared in dismay, Shem threw his bundles of leaves and coiled vines onto the riverbank.

"What's happened to her?" he cried, turning to Naomi

as if she could answer his question. She had never seen her son so angry; his face darkened and his eyes glittered with fury. He strode down to the water, screaming his rage across the river, not at his beloved, but at her abuser. "Yerakh!"

Immediately the girl backed away, clutching her meshwork, covering the pale sea carving slung about her neck. Her eyes were huge, terrified.

Setting down her basket and coiled vines, Naomi hurried to Shem, touching his arm, trying to calm him. "No, Shem, hush. If you scream again she'll run away—if she can run. Oh, look at her, the poor child!"

Moving away from Naomi, Shem angrily yelled to the young woman above the rushing current. "Did Yerakh do this to you?"

She nodded, obviously still frightened.

Once again, Naomi reached out to her son. "You must calm yourself."

"But look what he's done to her! She didn't have those bruises yesterday."

With an effort, Naomi kept her voice low. "And you've made her feel worse, I'm sure. No doubt she's heard enough screaming from her family; she shouldn't hear it from you. Look at her, poor child. She has to sit down." To convey her sympathy and concern, Naomi motioned to the opposite riverbank, urging the young woman to be seated.

She knelt slowly, stiffly, holding her meshwork.

Shem knelt also, rubbing one hand over his face. He began to talk, obviously thinking aloud. "How can we get her over here, away from him? If we simply take her into our lodge, that Yerakh would probably come after her. And once he catches her, he might kill her."

Naomi sank down beside her son, adding her thoughts to his own. "If Yerakh still has one of those giants—that *Nephiyl*—among his supporters, then we can only wait. She must be released with his permission, or his death—as the Most High wills."

"Until then she suffers," Shem muttered. Lifting his head, he gazed across the river. The young woman was watching him and met his look by lifting her hands and shrugging, conveying her resignation. As if to change the subject, she held out one hand and turned it gracefully, indicating Naomi.

After a brief hesitation, Shem tapped himself, then took Naomi's hand and put it on his head, rolling his lip out, looking miserable as he used to when he was very young and in trouble. Apparently amused, his beloved rocked back slightly, one hand to her mouth to cover a painful half-smile, the other hand clutching her side.

Perplexed, Naomi pulled her hand away, frowning at her son. "What was that about?"

"I told her that you're my mother. I couldn't think of any way to express it properly except to show her that you used to punish me when I was young. I think she would have laughed if she weren't in such pain."

Naomi swatted him, pretending exasperation. Shem grinned. The young woman tilted her head and studied this exchange, clearly fascinated, her dark eyes wistful. Then, as Naomi watched in wonderment, Shem and the young woman conversed silently through a series of hand motions and facial expressions. Their communication ended with the young woman lowering her head, clearly exhausted and miserable.

Shem looked at Naomi. "Yerakh beat her from head to heel! It hurts her to move."

Naomi shook her head sympathetically. "Ask if she has eaten today."

Shem tossed a stone into the river to make the unhappy girl look up. In response to his silent question, she touched her hand to her swollen jaw, then pantomimed drinking water from the river.

"She's had nothing but water," Naomi realized aloud. Scolding, she wagged her finger at the young woman, who drooped her head briefly in submission. Tapping Shem's arm, Naomi said, "Go back to our lodge and get my basket with the ointments and herbs."

"But, I'ma, how can you treat her from here?"

"You can throw the ointments to her. Go. Go!"

Sighing, Shem signaled to his beloved, asking her to wait. Then he quickly left the riverbank, heading back to the lodge. She watched him leave, shadows of fresh pain crossing her bruised, swollen face.

Naomi felt a new rush of compassion for the young woman. To distract her, Naomi tossed a small stone into the river, then motioned to the meshwork in her lap. In response, the girl finished off the knot she had been working, tucked her tool into a nearby bag, and shyly lifted the meshwork.

Naomi was amazed. It appeared to be very fine and light and was much larger than she had supposed. The young woman swung it over her shoulders, not displaying it, but huddling beneath it, as if it could protect her from further pain.

If I were beaten like that, I'd want to hide too, Naomi told herself.

As she lifted her hand to try to communicate, Naomi saw a young matron come out of the trees on the opposite bank. Round-faced and sulky, her rope of black hair tightly bound and decorated with gold talismans, the newcomer glanced at Naomi suspiciously, then ignored her and stalked over to Shem's beloved.

Aware of the matron's approach, the beleaguered girl covered the sea carving with her hand and cautiously slipped it into the neckline of her leather tunic. To Naomi's distress—and her growing fury—the matron didn't bother to greet the poor child, but snatched a handful of her hair and pulled hard. Wincing, the girl struggled to her feet, her expression blank and unseeing as a mask. If Naomi had not already communicated with her, and seen the life in her eyes, she would have thought the young woman was mindless. Aggrieved, she watched as the matron led Shem's beloved off into the trees.

Donning her veil, Annah followed Iltani through the trees, hurting and fearful. How had Iltani known where to find her? And why should her sister-in-law *want* to find her this early in the morning? Usually Iltani slept until midday. Mystified, Annah plodded behind Iltani up one of the many tortuous, almost imperceptible paths that cut through the thick undergrowth.

Iltani wandered, turning down this path, then that path, becoming more and more frustrated. At last she turned to face Annah, who looked down at Iltani's feet as the woman snarled, "You found it yesterday, little fool! Somewhere in that dull mind of yours, you know where it is!"

Confused, Annah stared at Iltani's plump brown feet. *What did I find yesterday that Iltani wants? Nothing except . . . the honey. That's it—the honey.* Relieved that the explanation was so simple, Annah hid her grim amusement. *If I weren't so tired and weak from hunger, Iltani, I'd lead you on a walk from here to your next kentum and back again. But I can't take you directly to it; you'd realize that I'm not mindless.*

To delude Iltani, Annah wandered aimlessly through the undergrowth, pushing aside leaves and stepping over vines, gradually approaching the honey-laden sweet-resin tree.

Iltani followed her, complaining aloud. "The creature doesn't know where she's going. Stupid-faced thing!"

At last, too tired to continue, Annah sat down in the undergrowth, within sight—and scent—of the resin tree. She could hear the bees humming softly.

Too engrossed in her own resentment to hear or smell anything, Iltani muttered, "I knew it! Worthless creature." Aiming a peevish kick at Annah's left shin, Iltani turned and walked toward the resin tree. She had just passed the tree when she looked back, laughing triumphantly. "Ha! I found it without the creature's help."

Gloating, Iltani gathered several dark, glossy, mantle-sized leaves from a nearby clump of rhizomes and spread them beneath the resin tree. Eagerly she reached into the hollow of the ancient tree and scooped out the glistening, dripping honeycomb. More than once she flicked away the bees, uttering little cries of pain.

Annah thought, *I've never been stung. I think there are some advantages to being a nothing-creature. Perhaps the bees recognize Iltani's greed and bad temper.* Pondering this, Annah threw a sidelong look at Iltani. She was still muttering and scooping out chunks of honeycomb.

When she had filled the center of the first massive leaf, Iltani knelt and folded the leaf edges over the pile of honeycomb, slipped a second broad leaf over it, then wrapped them all again with the third leaf. Then she stood, frowning as she surveyed the trees and vines. Her gaze swept toward Annah, who looked down at once. Iltani's feet pattered on the narrow trail of moist earth. Stopping in front of Annah, she snatched Annah's woven-grass bag.

Startled, Annah clutched the bag, trying to keep it. They struggled briefly, then Iltani wrenched Annah's veil away and kicked her hard in the side. A breathtaking jolt of pain shot through Annah's ribs. She fell sideways, releasing the bag. Laughing, Iltani gave her a final kick to the rear. Defeated, humiliated, Annah bit back her tears of pain and struggled to sit up, clawing the earth with her hands.

"Next time, you won't fight, stupid thing." Iltani snatched the grass bag, then paused. "What's this? A creature wearing an ornament?"

To her horror, Annah realized that the precious shell carving had slipped out of her tunic. Before Annah could hide her cherished possession, Iltani grasped the carving and swept it over Annah's head, tearing away some of Annah's hair as she pulled the cord away.

"Where did she find this?" Iltani wondered aloud. Still on the ground, Annah watched as Iltani looped the shell carving's cord over her own head, then tucked the leaf-wrapped honeycomb into Annah's grass bag. Clearly pleased with her victory, Iltani sauntered toward the settlement, never looking back.

Annah lay on the moist earth and wept.

Eventually, recovered enough to move, Annah got to

her feet and put on the veil. All the way back to the settlement, she blamed herself for not properly concealing the precious shell carving. *How could I have believed it was safe? I should have known someone would see it eventually. How can I go to the river and face him without the carving? I have to get it back.*

She entered the lodge warily. There was no sign of Yerakh, but she heard voices at the far end of the lodge, behind the taut leather partition where Parah and Iltani stored the dried grains, spices, and roots for cooking. Annah paused and listened. Iltani was actually chattering pleasantly.

"I found this while I was looking for the honey, and I'm so glad! I wanted a sea stone like the one that trader wore last year, but it's no use asking Yerakh for such a thing. Anyway, this is pretty, isn't it?"

"As you say," Parah agreed, noncommittal. "I haven't seen anyone wearing it in the settlement. You found it in the open? On the path?"

"Didn't I say so?" Iltani huffed. "Anyway, I'm going to use some of the honey for cakes tonight."

"Who could have dropped such a thing?" Parah asked, obviously still pondering the shell carving.

"I don't care who dropped it," Iltani said defensively. "I found it, so it's mine."

Liar, Annah thought, shutting her eyes. She had no strength to fight Iltani for the shell carving. She would have to bide her time and steal it back.

The sound of water being poured made Annah lick her dry lips. She had eaten no solid food for more than two days; by now she was so hungry that plain water seemed like a feast.

"Come here," Parah called out. "Annah, come here." Realizing that her mother had sensed her presence,

Annah lifted the veil from her face. Eyes lowered, she crept past the taut leather partition and knelt on the mat near her mother, like a trained creature.

She felt her mother's impassive scrutiny, then heard her sigh and turn away, apparently giving her attention to an assortment of spices, flavoring pastes, and grains she had gathered on the tray before her. Iltani's opened leaf-packet of honeycomb lay beside the tray, and Annah's discarded grass bag was beside the mat.

I'll get it later, when Iltani's not looking, Annah decided. *Now, however, I need some water. I'm dying of thirst.*

As Annah was thinking this, she heard her mother pouring water into a wooden cup and carefully setting the small clay water jug down on the tray.

"What are you doing?" Iltani demanded. "That's mine! I gathered that honeycomb, you didn't."

"And I gathered the last store of honeycomb, which you ate," Parah responded, wearily. "You can part with one piece."

"To sweeten water for that creature?"

"She needs nourishment, Iltani. She's missed at least a full day's worth of meals. Have you ever missed a meal in your life?"

"Are you saying that I eat too much?" said Iltani, her voice rising dangerously. "Next you will say that I don't deserve your son!"

Setting the cup down before Annah, Parah said, "I meant no offense, Iltani. And I know Yerakh does not admire women who are too thin. Now, if you aren't going to clean those sweet-bean pods, give them to me."

"Well," Iltani said, still irate, "from what I hear, Tseb-iy likes his women to be thin. And young."

"We will not talk of Tseb-iy," Parah answered quietly.

She began to split the long, dark sweet-bean pods with her thumbnails.

Annah sipped her honeyed water unobtrusively, casting quick, sidelong glances at her mother's hands. Parah was too busy, too intent upon her work. She looked tired. Bloodless.

Iltani sighed—a sweetly false sigh of concern—and scooped some dried grain from a deep storage basket. "Oh, I've upset you, I'ma. Don't worry; I won't mention Tseb-iy again. I'm sure you realize that he was the worst sort of man for you."

Parah dropped the split sweet-bean into the small clay pitcher of water. Later, it would be boiled, cooled, mixed with Iltani's precious honey, and added to finely crushed wheat to make cakes for their evening meal. Choosing another bean, Parah split it carefully, as if the task were more important than Tseb-iy.

"He has not abandoned me, Iltani, but I won't discuss him with you or anyone else." Parah stood, holding her tray of food. "These two beans should be enough to flavor your honey cakes. Now, I'm taking this water into the other room to boil it over the fire. If you wish, you may bring out the wheat, and I'll help you grind it. But I warn you: Any more of your little sighs and words about Tseb-iy, and I'll tear all the hair from your head for being so disrespectful to the mother of your husband."

"I was not being disrespectful," Iltani protested. Carrying her bowl of grain, she followed Parah. Passing Annah, Iltani aimed a kick in her direction. "Move!"

Annah cringed. She wanted to follow Iltani to keep watch over her precious shell carving, but decided it would be wiser to remain in the storage area. She had to finish her water and rest. Alone now, she retrieved her grass bag. Satisfied with this small victory, she covered herself with her veil and cautiously stretched out on the mat.

Closing her eyes, she remembered him, her beloved. He had been so enraged by her bruises this morning that she was terrified. But it was good to know that he longed to protect her. She was also glad Yerakh had not witnessed her beloved's rage; Yerakh would have found some way to challenge the young man and kill him—and Annah.

How do you know of Yerakh? Annah wondered to the young man. *Have you met him before? Did you meet my father?* Pondering these things, Annah drifted into sleep. Her dreams shifted between visions of her beloved, the river, the shell carving, the Tree of Havah, and Iltani's gloating, honeyed smile.

Suddenly Yerakh's voice intruded, bellowing, "Answer me! Who gave this to you?"

"I found it!" Iltani screeched in response. "If you want the truth, I found it on the creature. She was wearing it."

Fully awake now, Annah huddled on the mat. Yerakh was in the main room of the lodge with Iltani. But if he came after her in the storage room, she could not escape. She trembled, listening for his footsteps. Instead, she heard the sound of a slap, flesh against flesh. Iltani screamed. Then something small and light struck the taut leather partition of the storage room.

Annah could hear Iltani scuffling with Yerakh, crying, "I've done nothing wrong! Ah . . . I swear to you, the creature had it!"

"Liar!" Yerakh cried. Annah winced, hearing him slap Iltani's face again. "No man in this settlement would give that creature such an ornament. They won't even touch her; they know she's mad. Who gave this to you?"

Iltani sucked in a breath, whining, "Let me go. Ask your mother. She'll tell you."

Feeling a bit safer now, Annah crept over to the partition and peeked around its carved wooden frame. Yerakh was gripping Iltani's long, gold-decked braid of hair with one hand, while his other hand was poised to slap her again. But at the mention of his mother, he glared at Parah.

"She said she found it," Parah said, neither defending nor condemning Iltani.

"I've done nothing wrong," Iltani protested again, tearful. "You shouldn't punish me; I'm not the one who's bearing Tseb-iy's child!"

Hearing this, Annah clutched at the partition frame in horror. Parah gasped and fled through the open front doorway of the lodge. In a renewed fury, Yerakh ran after her. Iltani followed them, fearful but eager.

She wants to see Yerakh beating I'ma, Annah thought, sickened. She started to go after her mother when a pale gleam caught her eye: The shell carving lay on the earthen floor beside the partition. Elated, Annah picked it up and kissed it. She would bind it inside her grass bag to hide it from the others. Now, however, she had to find her mother. Wrapping herself in her veil, she tucked the precious ornament into her grass bag, then slipped out the back of the lodge.

Six

"I'MA!" HABURAH called, entering the lodge. Silent, Annah retreated into the shadows, watching her sister prowl through the storage area, then the sleeping area, then Yerakh's forbidden workroom. Unable to find Parah, Haburah sat down to wait in front of the fire. As she waited, she reached for one of the honey cakes that Annah had baked on the hearthstones.

Seeing Annah, Haburah sniffed disdainfully. "It's useless to ask you anything. I doubt if you know where you are."

Annah lowered her veiled head and picked the last bits of dough from her fingernails. Parah had not returned after the confrontation with Yerakh, nor had Yerakh or Iltani. Annah had eaten some dough to sustain herself, then finished making the honey cakes. She had also hidden her precious shell carving inside her grass bag, binding it into the same pouch that had held the gold amulet for so many years.

Now she waited silently for her mother to return. Even the appearance of Yerakh and Iltani would be a relief. She wondered if they had killed each other. As Annah's fears grew, even Haburah's indifferent presence seemed comforting.

But why should I care if you are here? Annah wondered, furtively studying Haburah's elegant profile. *You have never loved me, Haburah. Even before Yerakh murdered our father, you barely acknowledged my existence. I was a nuisance to you then, and now you detest me completely.*

Haburah ate another cake, then began to pace restlessly about the lodge, flexing her slender fingers. When Gammad entered the lodge, she snatched him by the arm, her black eyes glittering in the firelight. "Where are the others? No one is here!"

"How should I know? I've just come in from the fields. They don't answer to me." Shrugging her off, Gammad sat by the hearth and helped himself to the cakes.

"Ayalah's not here—she went off to find K'nan after we penned the sheep," Haburah said. "As for Chathath, he does as he pleases. But I'ma should be here. None of the other food has been cooked, just the cakes. It's not like I'ma to leave her work tray out. Something has happened; I feel it."

"You worry too much," Gammad told her brusquely, snatching another cake and breaking it between his fingers. "You also talk too much. They are probably all out visiting. Now leave me alone."

"Ox!" Haburah turned away from him, infuriated, and Annah stifled an impulse to smile. Gammad—broad, thick-muscled, and onerous—did resemble an ox.

A sharp whistle outside made them all look to the front entry of the lodge. Only one person whistled in that pitch: Chathath. He leaned inside the lodge, his mouth twisting sardonically. "We've been summoned to the lodge of our dearest friend, Naham the Bone-breaker—or do I mean the Iron-breaker?"

"Is I'ma there?" Haburah demanded.

Chathath shrugged carelessly. "Come see for yourself. But our presence is commanded, along with everyone else in the settlement."

Gammad scowled and stood, snarling, "Who gave Naham the authority to order us to come to him?"

"Are you going to fight him, brother-slave?" Chathath retorted. "He can beat you to dust with one fist." Pausing significantly, he added, "Tseb-iy is there."

Gammad rose and followed Chathath, and Haburah accompanied them reluctantly. Still hiding in the shadows, Annah hesitated. She longed to be sure her mother was safe. She also wanted to hear the others at this gathering—particularly Tseb-iy. But the memory of Naham's fingers creeping into her hair and caressing her neck made her shudder. What if he saw her and renewed his demand? Yerakh had no reason to protect her, apart from his own greed; perhaps he would give her as a peace offering.

If Yerakh gives me to Naham, I'll run away, Annah decided. *But how will I know if he decides such a thing? I have to hear what is said at this meeting.* Clutching her veil, Annah took her bag and some of the honey cakes, then slipped out the back of the lodge. The air was calm. The roseate daytime sky was giving way to the rich violet hues of night. The stars and the moon appeared now, glowing enchantingly, all whites, pinks, yellows, and blues. Annah paused to rest and look up at the stars, almost forgetting her physical pain and her fear for her mother.

If I did believe in the Most High, Annah thought, *I would believe because of the stars and the moon. How can they be so beautiful without the hand of a master craftsman? They are like jewels.*

Annah walked slowly between the lodges of the settlement. All of them were similar: woven split-reed lattice and grass walls, with wooden uprights framing the doors and grass-covered roofs open at the top to release the smoke of the evening fires. However, the lodge of Naham was the largest, to accommodate his imposing height.

Annah crept around the side of Naham's lodge and knelt on the hard earth near a lattice window. She could see the inhabitants of the settlement crowded into the main room. Naham sat on a thick heap of grass mats and hides in front of the carefully banked evening fire, his fearfully large body slouching, relaxed and comfortable. His two wives, remarkably alike, sat to his right. Both were slender, silent, and unmoving, their dark hair braided down their backs, fastened with only a few miserly gold talismans each.

Glancing behind them, Annah caught her breath. Parah was there, looking tired but uninjured. She was staring into the crowd gathered before Naham. Annah followed her mother's gaze across the crackling fire to Tseb-iy. He was completely at ease, laughing in the firelight, his teeth gleaming, his thick black hair falling over his shoulders.

He was surrounded by the other smooth-shaven, unmarried men of the settlement. Seated among them was K'nan, Ayalah's beloved, a well-built young man with deep-set eyes and a petulant lower lip. He looked bored, rolling his eyes upward as his companions talked and joked with Tseb-iy.

Look at all of you, so proud and pleased with yourselves, Anna thought. *Not one of you is as honorable and handsome as the man who loves me. Not even you, Tseb-iy.* Her gaze narrowing, Annah watched Tseb-iy. He never once looked at Parah. *He doesn't love her,* Annah realized, feeling a sudden pang. *He loves no one but himself. And, I think he and all his friends are hoping to make Yerakh angry—they're mocking him.*

Yerakh was seated nearby, glaring at them when he was not grimacing at Naham. Iltani sat beside him, her eyes downcast, her face swollen and marked as if Yerakh had slapped her again. Annah almost felt sorry for her.

As Annah watched, Ayalah slipped through the crowd, her eyes shining, her pretty mouth curving with a secretive joy. She knelt beside Yerakh, then turned and motioned to Taphaph, Tseb-iy's younger sister.

As attractive as her brother, Taphaph shook her lustrous black hair off her shoulders and delicately picked her way through the crowd, swaying as she walked. Her large dark eyes sparkled, and her smile was dazzling as she knelt beside Ayalah. Most of the men were openly admiring her; Yerakh actually licked his lips. Iltani sat up straight, clearly outraged.

Watching this interplay, Annah felt a reluctant stab of compassion for Iltani, mingled with a growing disgust at Ayalah, who was now giggling and whispering with Taphaph. The two young women were perfectly aware of the interest and tension their actions had created. The conversations of the other members of the settlement increased in volume. Tseb-iy scowled at his sister. K'nan frowned at Ayalah. Yerakh watched Taphaph from the corner of his eye, obviously distracted by her nearness.

And none of this escaped Naham's attention. Watching Yerakh's covetous expression, Naham leaned back on his pile of mats and whispered something to Parah. In response, Parah allowed Naham a hint of a smile. Seeming pleased, Naham straightened and spoke to his wives. At his command they passed baskets of grain cakes through the crowd—a reminder to all present that this was a peaceful gathering. Anyone with something to say would be allowed to speak. Naham lifted his hands and raised his voice over the chatter of his neighbors.

"Listen! Listen to me." Smiling as everyone hushed, Naham continued, his voice rumbling. "You are all welcome here tonight. Some have concerns they wish to share openly, so that everyone understands their worries. We must listen and agree on these matters. Also, there will be no fighting in my lodge tonight. I know you don't want me to break up anything . . . or anyone." He raised his huge fists, and the other members of the settlement were respectfully quiet.

Obviously satisfied with their reaction, Naham slapped his now-opened hands on his thighs. "Good. Let's enjoy each other's company, then part in peace. I'll begin with a matter that concerns more than one lodge." Pausing, Naham grinned wickedly. "Tseb-iy, some of the men believe you're too much of a distraction to their wives and daughters."

Everyone laughed, and Tseb-iy smiled and shrugged, lifting his hands as if to plead his helplessness against the attentions of the women of the settlement. "Do any of these women have complaints against me?" he asked. "Did I seek them? No, they sought me." His defense provoked sniggers from some of the men and murmurs of disbelief from the women.

Liar, Annah thought, shocked, glaring at Tseb-iy from behind the protective lattice. *My I'ma would never give her attentions to a man who did not encourage her. Shifting her gaze to her mother,* Annah became even more distressed. Parah's eyes were closed, as if in pain.

Everyone whispered and hissed until Naham raised his hands again, addressing Tseb-iy. "You are not of my lodge, Tseb-iy, but you *are* my cousin, and I'm tired of hearing complaints against you. We have decided that you should choose a wife or two, and stop causing problems for the families of other lodges. If you don't confine your attentions to your own women, you'll have to leave the settlement."

Again Tseb-iy smiled and shrugged, noncommittal.

"Do you agree?" Naham demanded, leaning forward.

Tseb-iy's smile thinned. Straightening, he said heavily, "I agree. I'll choose a wife soon. But she must have a proper marriage portion."

He knows Yerakh won't part with any of his fields, Annah thought, infuriated. *Tell the truth, Tseb-iy; you just don't want Parah of the Lodge of Yerakh.*

Chathath and Gammad pushed through the crowd. They stepped in among the young men surrounding Tseb-iy, forcing them to move so they could sit beside Tseb-iy, threatening him without words.

By now, Parah had recovered her composure. In silent dignity, she shook her head at her sons, but they did not look at her.

Apparently trying to distract Chathath and Gammad, Tseb-iy called out, "Now, I want to ask the opinion of everyone in this settlement: What should be done to a man who won't part with the fields and wealth his mother brought to the lodge of the Tsaraph? These possessions were for the use of Zahar of the Tsaraph, not for his son. Is it right for the son to deny his mother her own properties now that she is a widow?"

Yerakh leaned forward, his dark eyes kindled with rage. "You have no understanding of these matters, Tseb-iy! They're not your concern!"

Tseb-iy smiled maliciously. "Then who is concerned with these matters? What about your sisters? You have withheld their marriage portions, saying they have none. Now K'nan is concerned! And Naham was concerned years ago when he asked for Haburah. And what about your brothers? Why don't you give them their share of the inheritance your father planned for them? Do you think we're fools, Yerakh?"

"Answer him, Yerakh," K'nan yelled. "Then answer my question: If you, Yerakh, should desire another woman as a wife—such as Tseb-iy's sister, there beside you—would you believe her parents if they say she has no marriage portion? You would say that they're trying to cheat you!"

Yerakh turned to Naham accusingly. "You've told them to say these things! This whole meeting is planned to force me to agree with you!"

"This meeting was called to discuss problems brought to me by members of your own lodge, Yerakh!" Naham lashed back. "But now that the matter has been brought up, remember: I warned you yesterday that the other men in the settlement were becoming impatient with your ex- cuses. Now you will have to answer them before every- one." Ominously he added, "Later, you will answer me again: I haven't given up my earlier requests."

Naham stared at Yerakh until Yerakh looked away—in the direction of Taphaph. When Yerakh finally spoke again, he was subdued. "I'm not required to answer every- one here tonight. But I agree to consider these matters later." Before anyone could react to this, he straightened and called out, "Now I have something to say."

Pointing to Iltani, he said, "Everyone, look at this woman beside me. She's supposed to be my wife. But we've been married for five years and she has given me no children. Not even daughters. She's barren! She's lazy! She's bad-tempered and a liar! Today I found her wearing an ornament from another man! She would not reveal the name of this man, but it doesn't matter. I say to this man—whoever you are—if she doesn't bear a child of mine within the next year, then you may have her. I won't stop you, because I'll no longer consider her to be my wife."

Iltani burst into tears, doubling over, burying her face in her hands. Sickened, Annah looked up at the stars, all glittering, pure, bright, far removed from her troubles.

I'll wait, she decided. *I'm too weak to run away tonight. Perhaps Naham still wants Haburah, not me. But if Yerakh gives me to Naham, I will leave this settlement and never return.*

Flanked by his brothers, Shem stared into the evening fire, listening as his mother talked to his father, waving her hands in agitation. "I wish you could have seen her. The poor child! That other woman treated her as if she were less than an animal. It's obvious the child is pretending to be mindless, but why? Noakh, my dear one, we must bring her out of that settlement!"

Stirring, Yepheth spoke, his long, solemn face revealing an unaccustomed impatience. "Do we sit here and wait, Father? Or can we do something to help her?"

"I was going to ask the same thing, Father," Shem said. "But I feared such a question might be considered a lack of faith in the Most High."

Noakh answered them with the faintest of smiles "It will interest you, then, my impatient ones, when I tell you that I have also questioned the Most High concerning this matter." He stared into the fire, seeming to ponder the matter again, his expression distant, full of wonderment.

"And?" Shem questioned softly, "Can you tell us, Father? What is His answer?"

Stroking his beard absently, Noakh said, "His answer is that we are to build a bridge across the river. We have all the ropes and necessary supplies; it won't take long."

Naomi sighed, pleased. "Good! I'll feel so much better when we get the poor child away from that woman and her family. But think of it: a bridge—that will be a task."

As Yepheth grunted in thoughtful agreement, Khawm nudged Shem in the ribs. Then, in mock seriousness, he asked, "Forgive me, Father, but why must we build a bridge to cross the river? Couldn't we just build a little boat?"

Startled, Noakh blinked at his youngest son, then laughed.

Shem laughed with them, but his thoughts raced ahead. *A bridge, for her—his wife.*

Iltani trembled as she trudged through the dark fields. She knew she was not being followed; Yerakh, Chathath, and the others were still at the lodge of Naham. But her heart continued to pound horribly. Rage and distress welled up like bile in her throat.

"I hate you!" she cried to the absent Yerakh. "And I

hate your family—all of you!" She choked down a sob. *I wish I'd never left my family. Dull and backward as they were, they would never have shamed me the way you shamed me tonight.*

Stopping in the dark field, Iltani screamed, "You won't discard me, Yerakh!" It was stupid and futile to scream at him while he could not hear her, but she didn't care. He was a beast. He wanted to discard her because he was bored with her. And because Taphaph—the little bold-faced flirt—happened to sit beside him tonight, tempting him.

You knew what you were doing, Ayalah, thought Iltani, seething. *You wanted to distract Yerakh and humiliate me! As for my lack of children, that's nothing more than Yerakh's excuse for getting rid of me. If he had children, he would have to share his precious gold and flocks and fields! But if I do have a child, then he must swallow his own words.*

Iltani paused in the darkness, wiping away tears of frustration. In her mind she could hear the low, hoarse, guttural song of the Nachash and the other, less exalted whisperers calling to her, drawing her to their evening fire. They never showed surprise when she appeared unexpectedly. But then, they rarely displayed any emotions, beyond their arrogance and contempt for her gifts in return for their words of promise for her future.

Can they help me now? She hesitated. *Sometimes I wonder if they've ever helped me at all. Chathath knows I've visited them, and it won't be long before he tells Yerakh.*

The silent swoosh of an owl startled Iltani from her reverie. Instinctively, she stepped away from its flight path, toward the lodge of the Nachash. With this action, she felt that her course had been decided. She walked on, excited now, anticipating the alluring power surrounding the old whisperer and her companions.

She approached the lodge of the Nachash and paused beside a large, flat disc of bronze suspended from a bar set between two reed posts. A slender club of polished wood dangled from a leather strap, also attached to the posts. Grasping the club, Iltani struck the bronze disc once to warn the Nachash of her visit. Then she entered the reed-and-grass lattice lodge.

The Nachash and her five companions sat in a semi-circle before their evening fire, their eyes closed. All six were thin to the point of emaciation, their heads bare, their silvered hair disheveled, their rough-edged hide tunics stained with sweat, oils, and dirt. The Nachash herself wore a distinctive circular leather cloak, tooled and painted in sinuous patterns resembling the flowing lines of the serpent—the source, they said, of their wisdom and counsel.

They did not look up as Iltani entered the lodge, but the oldest of the companions croaked out, "Enter in peace and be seated."

Iltani knelt and waited until they were done sensing her and pondering her presence. The Nachash sat slack-mouthed and limp. Her eyelids—thin as the brown skin of a dried bulb plucked from the earth—rolled, then fluttered, revealing the whites of her eyes. The firelight played over her skeletal features, making her seem the least human of all humans Iltani had ever seen.

At last the Nachash sighed thickly, her voice rasping from deep in her throat. "You . . . your hands empty . . . why do you come?"

Iltani felt a prickling of sweat on her brow and down her back. "I didn't know I was coming until I was on my way here; otherwise I would have brought you a gift."

"Your gift must suit your purpose when it is known.

Tell us what you want."

"A child. I want to bear a child within the year."

The Nachash uttered a harsh, glottal grunt. "A child. A life. She wants a life from nothing? A life . . . and she has not paid."

"I've paid you before," Iltani protested, not daring to raise her voice. "You know I'll pay you again."

"Gold . . . for a life?" the oldest companion growled. The others muttered unintelligibly.

"Cakes . . . for a life?" The Nachash echoed her companion, then sighed again.

Iltani shivered; it sounded like the sigh of a dying creature. She leaned forward, feeling the heat of the fire against her face. Hardening her resolve and her voice, she said, "Name your price; I will pay."

"Do not ask for what you do not truly desire," the Nachash warned.

"I desire a child more than anything!"

The Nachash sighed again, then groaned softly. "A life . . . requires a life."

Uncertain now, Iltani moistened her lips, then swallowed. "A life?"

"A life," the oldest companion answered, her eyes shut tight as if in concentration. "This is the price: a life for a life, one heartbeat for another."

"You want me to take the life of another person?" Iltani faltered.

The oldest companion threw something across the flames. It landed heavily, tumbling toward Iltani's feet.

"One heartbeat for another," the Nachash sighed. "This is the price you will bring to our fire."

Sweating, Iltani took hold of the object the companion had thrown. It was a knife of stone.

Seven

ANNAH KNELT in Yerakh's workroom, polishing a blocklike wooden form used for shaping a small gold ointment pot. To Annah's knowledge, no one in the settlement had requested an ointment pot, and there had been no travelers for a number of days. *This is a whim of Yerakh's,* she decided. *This gold pot is for Taphaph.*

Slipping her right hand into a protective leather mitt, Annah sprinkled some fine river sand into the form—a hollow gouged into the dense, fine-grained block of wood. Patiently she rubbed her mitt-protected fingers over the sand in the hollow, smoothing the rounded interior of the form. If this ointment pot were indeed for Taphaph, then Yerakh would demand perfection.

He's infatuated with her, Annah thought. *I'm sure he will take her as his wife, even if Iltani does bear him a child.*

Since the night of the meeting, now ten days past,

Iltani had been unusually quiet. She also had been staring. First she had stared at Ayalah whenever Ayalah walked by, then at Parah, Chathath, and the others. She also cried frequently, clearly envious of Parah, whose belly was noticeably larger this past week. Parah had complained of kicks from the unborn infant.

Fascinated by the thought of an infant brother or sister, Annah worked the sand into the wood reflexively. *I am almost glad I'ma is going to have a baby. If I ever marry my beloved—which I doubt—I'd long to have a baby of my own. But babies turn into children, and all the children I've seen are spoiled, vicious, screaming, spitting little monsters who think nothing of attacking anyone. I'd despair, having such a child.* Annah shivered suddenly. Someone was behind her, watching her.

Shifting, she recognized Iltani's plump brown feet. Her sister-in-law was standing just inside the leather-curtained doorway of the workroom, perhaps three arm-lengths from Annah. *Why is she staring at me?* Annah tensed. She hoped she would not have to run: Her bruises and swollen jaw were finally beginning to heal, but her ribs still hurt whenever she took a deep breath. *Go away,* she thought, staring at Iltani's feet. To her surprise, Iltani retreated behind the leather curtain without saying a word.

Disturbed by Iltani's odd behavior, Annah pulled her work mat to the center of the room and knelt again, taking care to keep both doorways in full view. *Iltani is still watching me. I can feel her staring. It's as if she's waiting for something. But it's not like her to be so patient; it's almost worse than when she screams at me or kicks me.*

Annah tapped the fine powder of sand and wood dust out of the form, sprinkled fresh sand inside, and rubbed it some more. Still she sensed Iltani hovering behind the curtain. *Go away!* Too agitated to work, she pushed the wooden form away and discarded her mitt. Her hands were shaking, her heart thudding wildly as her fears blossomed into panic.

She jumped to her feet, snatched her grass bag, and swept her veil over her head. As she edged toward the doorway leading out to Yerakh's refining pit, Annah glimpsed Iltani coming into the workroom, clenching something in her fist. It was a knife of stone.

Terrified, Annah backed out of the workroom, keeping her eyes on Iltani's approaching feet. In the sunlight now, she retreated until something struck her veil-swathed arm. A clod of dirt.

"Annah," Yerakh's voice threatened, "is your work finished so quickly? Go back inside. Do you understand? Back inside!"

Annah hesitated, trembling, trying to conquer her fear. Rivulets of sweat trickled down her face. *I can't*, she told Yerakh in silence. *Iltani has a knife.*

Yerakh left the refining pit, crossed the hard-packed dirt ground, and grabbed her arm.

Annah trembled, wondering, *Who is more dangerous? Yerakh or Iltani?* As her brother dragged her back inside, Annah glanced around the workroom. Iltani was gone. Obviously, the sound of Yerakh's voice had frightened her away. And the sense of danger had vanished with her. Annah breathed an inaudible sigh of relief. When Yerakh shoved the wooden form back into her hands and compelled her to sit again, she did not resist. Throwing off her veil, she picked up her leather mitt and resumed her task.

Yerakh seemed satisfied by her compliance. To Annah's amazement, he did not strike her for trying to leave the workroom. Instead, he lingered, looking about, muttering noises of disgust. Then he strode into the main room of the lodge, bellowing, "Iltani, you stay out of my workroom! Don't deny you were in there; I could smell you!"

Annah heard Iltani protesting from a distance. "I did nothing wrong. I went to check on that worthless creature, and she—"

"She ran because you disturbed her! You leave her alone, do you hear me? If you go in there again, I'll beat you the way I beat her."

As she listened to her brother's shouts, Annah thought she would cry. She actually felt grateful to Yerakh.

Seated in her usual place by the river, Annah glanced up at the sky. Her beloved was late this morning, but she was content to wait and enjoy the sound of the river. She felt healed today. Her bruises had been gone for many weeks, and her ribs no longer hurt when she took a deep breath. Soon she would try to run between the river and the settlement.

At least I haven't had to run from Iltani, she thought. *I wonder if she still has that knife of stone. Anyway, she's not sneaking around, staring at everyone the way she did after that meeting. I'm sure she meant to kill someone.*

Annah pushed away thoughts of Iltani and went to work, winding more of the pale flower-fibers on her small, carved shuttle. Today, before leaving the river, she would wash her veil, and tomorrow she would mend it with the new thread. She had been neglecting her veil because of him; he was far more interesting than the veil. Thinking of her beloved, Annah smiled. *He is finer than any other man in this settlement. I wish we could marry. But even if I had the courage to speak, Yerakh would never agree. He would kill me instead.*

As she wrapped the last of her thread onto the shuttle, she sensed *him* approaching on the opposite shore. The liquid plop of a stone in the water confirmed her senses. She glanced over at him eagerly. His leather tunic was wet, and he wore a thick band of soft leather tied across his brow. Annah indicated the band: *Why are you wearing that?*

Answering with his irresistible smile, he pointed upriver on his side, beckoning: *Follow me.*

Annah hesitated, questioning him with raised eyebrows and uplifted hands: *Why?*

Again he smiled, motioned to her, then pointed upriver: *This way.*

He didn't answer my question, Annah thought, mildly indignant. Wondering at his secrecy, she scooped up her veil and bag, determined to keep pace with him as he hurried along the opposite shore. Now and then, as she straggled through areas of sand, he grinned at her. She wondered if he knew how very persuasive he could be. Encouraged by his glances, she hurried onward. But when they passed the boundaries of the settlement, Annah paused, anxious. He stopped.

Gesturing upriver, Annah questioned silently: *Is it much farther?*

He raised one hand soothingly, then brought his thumb and forefinger almost together in a pinching motion: *Only a short distance.* His eyes pleading, he urged her to look ahead. There was a bend in the river. *Around that bend,* he told her, using a sweeping motion. He waited, watching her. Annah understood that he did not want her to continue walking if she was reluctant to pass the boundaries of the settlement.

She wavered and mimicked his pinching motion: *Only a little farther?*

His answering smile and nod reassured her. Rounding the bend of the river, she stopped and gaped, hugging her limp grass bag. Six long, thick ropes hung from one side of the river to the other. Two young men were working in the ropes. One man stood on a log platform anchored precariously in the rushing water, weaving smaller ropes and canes into the side ropes, while the second man straddled the two lowest ropes, weaving stout canes into an emerging footpath. While they worked, an older man, gray and full-bearded, directed them from the opposite bank. *His father and brothers*, Annah realized. She recognized the young man straddling the lowest ropes—he had been with her beloved the day she nearly threw herself into the river.

The splash of a stone in the water made Annah look at the opposite bank.

What do you think? her beloved asked silently, lifting his eyebrows at her, tilting his head toward the bridge.

Dazed, Annah shook her head weakly, turning to stare at the bridge again. Obviously, they were nearly finished building it. *But why a bridge?* Motioning at the log platform, she moved her hand back and forth, indicating both sides of the river, then shrugged at the bridge, asking: *If you can move back and forth on the river with the floating platform, then why build this bridge?*

Lifting his hands, her beloved shrugged, perfectly serious: *I don't know.* He indicated his father with a slight shift of his hand: *My father's idea.*

Annah nodded. Certainly he must obey his father.

Keeping her distance, Annah sat down to rest and to watch. Her beloved went to help his father and brothers weave the sides and bottom of the bridge together. The ends of the bridge were bound to four tall trees; two on each side of the river, all reasonably well matched in height and distance. Four long ropes formed the bottom and sides of the bridge, while two longer ropes—suspended halfway up each tree on both sides of the bridge—swept downward to support its center.

Annah's beloved picked up a large bundle of canes and a coil of rope. Bracing himself, he hauled them into the current, carefully making his way toward the platform. His other brother—still a stranger to Annah—stretched out one long arm and took the bundle of canes, setting them on the platform before reaching for the coil. As the brothers passed the rope between them, they jostled each other until their father whistled at them sharply from the opposite bank. Chastened, they ducked their heads. Safe on his perch, their younger brother shook a cane at them and cackled, enjoying their disgrace.

Watching all this, their father gave a visible sigh and shook his graying head in fond exasperation. *He loves them,* Annah thought enviously. *Yerakh would scream at us in a situation like this, then beat us bloody.*

Her wistful envy intensified when she saw the mother of her beloved emerging from the trees on the opposite bank, smiling at her husband and sons. *I want to belong to this family,* Annah thought suddenly, the longing so fierce it brought tears to her eyes.

Catching sight of Annah, the mother of her beloved gave her a warm, welcoming smile and walked downriver to stand across from her. She motioned to Annah and patted her own face to convey her thought: *Your face looks better.*

Annah nodded agreement, then pressed both hands to her heart and extended them, smiling gratefully: *Thank you.*

The mother of her beloved nodded and flicked her hand in a genial, self-depreciating manner. Suddenly—as if remembering something—she lifted her hand, requesting Annah to wait. Hurrying to her husband and sons, she spoke to Annah's beloved. He had just emerged from the water and was dripping, but when his mother spoke to him, he kissed her, obviously thanking her. She shooed him off, pretending irritation that he had gotten her wet.

Amused and mystified by this exchange, Annah crept closer to the bridge. Her beloved was rummaging through a small heap of tools and supplies. Triumphant, he found a small leather packet and waved it at Annah, his eyes telling her: *This is for you.*

Before Annah could respond, he waded into the water and tossed the packet to his brother on the log platform, who called to the youngest brother to gain his attention. The youngest brother took the packet and grinned mischievously, waving it just long enough to cause his entire family to scream at him to throw the packet to Annah. Turning, he winked at Annah, then shook the packet at her, shouting, "Catch it!"

Fearing that the contents might be fragile, Annah ran. In her haste, she dropped her veil and bag, and almost tripped as she caught the packet. Her beloved yelled at his brother, clearly annoyed and worried—until Annah straightened up and smiled at him. She felt accepted now . . . and a little embarrassed, as they were all watching her. Uncertain, she glanced over at her beloved.

He pointed to the packet: *Open it.*

Self-conscious, she sat on a low, grassy bank to pick at

the knotted leather cord holding the packet together. Inside she found a broad comb of fragrant wood—patterned in the same manner as her precious shell carving—and a second leather pouch. Opening it, she found an assortment of small tools for her handwork: flat wooden threading needles, tiny metal piercing awls, and a diminutive cutting blade cleverly fitted within a slip of wood to prevent mishaps.

The fragrant comb was from him; she could tell by the carving. But the tools? She hesitated, lifting them toward his mother, questioning: *From you?*

His mother nodded and smiled. Annah thanked her, delighted to have tools of her own. And the comb smelled wonderful, like spices and sweet oils. She tested it shyly in a strand of her hair, then beamed at her beloved, gesturing to her bag: *I'll hide it in here.*

By now he knew that she had been forced to conceal her precious shell carving. He nodded: *Yes, hide it.*

After inspecting her new treasures once more, Annah tucked them safely into her grass bag. Her beloved and his brothers returned to their work on the bridge, and their parents lingered, watching them. It was now late morning, but Annah did not want to return to the settlement—to her own joyless, chaotic family.

I'll wash my veil, then I'll go, she decided. *It definitely needs to be cleaned now that I've dropped it in the sand.*

Taking her veil, Annah started toward the water. Suddenly she felt tremors and heard the sickening groaning beneath the earth. She lunged toward the grass again and clutched at it, terrified. The river churned violently, and the bridge rocked back and forth beneath the motion of its supporting trees. The brothers of her beloved clung to the ropes of the bridge while he and his parents crouched on the opposite shore and waited for the tremors to end. Annah was surprised by their calm acceptance. *It's as if they expect this to happen,* she thought, staring at them, open-mouthed.

When the tremors ended, his mother smiled, waved a farewell to Annah, and calmly departed. Equally calm, her beloved grinned at Annah, then went back to work. His youngest brother let out a whoop of celebration, apparently pleased with himself for not falling off the bridge. Despite her fear, Annah smiled.

～❦ ❦～

After finishing her evening meal, Annah crept into the shadows of the lodge where she could watch her family unnoticed. They were all on edge. Haburah was visiting the wives of Naham, while Naham roamed through the settlement with Yerakh. Annah suspected that Naham's wives had invited Haburah to their evening meal to warn her that Naham planned to marry her.

"I'd wager they're discussing her marriage portion," Iltani announced, taking another serving of honey cakes and nuts.

Chathath sneered. "Dear elder sister, how little you know. The wives of Naham have nothing to say about anything. And the only reason Yerakh would ever give Haburah a marriage portion is because he's afraid Naham will crush his skull—as I hope."

"Monster!" Iltani cried.

"Serpent-Lover!" Chathath retorted, adding, "It's not helped you, either, kissing those snakes."

Glaring, Iltani flung a nutmeat at Chathath. "Shut up!"

"When you do, elder sister," Chathath answered,

tossing the nutmeat into the fire.

Parah lifted her hands wearily. "Stop fighting, both of you. I'm tired enough bearing this child; I don't need you two arguing all the time."

Iltani glared at her in pure hatred. "The child again!" she snapped. "You should just spit in my face because you're bearing one and I'm not!" Throwing down her food, she arose and stalked out the back of the lodge.

"Nothing has changed," Ayalah complained. "K'nan is becoming impatient. If I don't receive a marriage portion soon, he's going to give up on me. And *you*, I'ma," Ayalah confronted Parah. "You've heard nothing from Tseb-iy at all since that meeting. You should go after him."

"I have no wish to marry Tseb-iy," Parah answered evenly. "One man is like another, and I'll be too busy to care about anything in a few months."

Brooding before the fire, Gammad said, "We should have crushed Tseb-iy into submission. You'd have been married long before now, I'ma."

All you ever think of is violence, Annah thought, watching Gammad's dark, self-absorbed face. She could not remember the last time she had seen him smile.

Parah frowned, her lovely eyes severe. "Listen, all of you. I will not marry Tseb-iy, so just forget him."

"You say that because he won't have you," Chathath responded scornfully.

Annah caught her breath at Chathath's insolence.

Parah's lips tightened. "You are wrong, my son, and I won't discuss him with you."

Iltani reentered the lodge, stalked into the storage area, and came out again with a cup of powdered herbs and a piece of honeycomb. They watched as she poured water into a small copper cooking pot and thrust it into the coals of the fire. "This is what you have reduced me to," she told them, scowling as she waited for her water to simmer. "I'm taking remedies to settle my stomach."

Chathath snickered, and Ayalah rolled her eyes upward in disgust. Parah looked down at her hands, folded over her fully rounded belly. Gammad, glaring into the fire, ignored them all.

Ayalah began to whine. "I'ma, please, won't you at least try to speak to Yerakh? K'nan doesn't expect a large marriage portion; Yerakh could afford one small field. Anyway, you'd think that if Yerakh's planning to marry Taphaph sometime soon, he'd prefer to have us all out of his lodge before then, so he could have Taphaph all to himself. You should mention that to him and see what he says."

Annah blinked, unable to believe that Ayalah had said such a thing in front of Iltani. But Iltani scowled, repeatedly testing the water in the cooking pot. Finally she snatched a leather mitt, lifted the pot out of the fire, and dumped some water over the herbs and honeycomb.

As steam wafted from the cup, Parah inhaled.

Iltani saw her and slammed the pot back into the coals. "I suppose you want some too. Well, if you're going to be staring at me the whole time I'm drinking it, you'd better take this one. I'll just go get my own. After all, you are bearing a child, and I'm not!" She plunked the cup in front of Parah and stomped back into the storage room.

Parah protested, "I didn't say a word, Iltani."

"Oh, stop!" Iltani hissed, returning from the storage room with another cup of herbs and honeycomb. "It's too late now."

"You're beginning to sound like a serpent, elder sister," Chathath taunted. "Why don't you go live with the

Nachash and save us all these scenes?"

"Someone should cut out your tongue!" Iltani fumed, pouring hot water over her herbs and honeycomb.

Ayalah leaned forward. "That does smell good."

"*You* can get your own! I'm not waiting on someone who thinks Yerakh should replace me with that Taphaph. Oh, how I'll laugh at you when K'nan takes another woman—and don't say he won't." Iltani slurped her hot drink noisily. "As much as you whine, K'nan will need a dozen wives to drown you out."

"You're one to talk!" Ayalah cried, indignant.

"Hush, all of you!" Parah screamed suddenly. "I'm sick of this fighting!"

"But I'ma . . ." Ayalah began, and Parah slapped her. Ayalah started to cry. "I'm going to stay with Haburah."

"Do it!" her mother snapped. Ayalah fled, sobbing. Defiant, Parah took her steaming cup and marched off to her pallet to prepare for sleep. Astonished by their mother's vicious outburst, Annah and the others silently followed her lead, preparing their sleeping places for the night.

Annah was just dozing off when she heard her mother groan, then shriek.

"I'ma?" Chathath called from the far corner of the main room. "What's wrong?"

Parah sucked in a ragged breath, then screamed again in agony.

Iltani came rushing in from the partitioned sleeping area she shared with Yerakh. "She's having the baby!" she cried. "But it's too soon! I'm going to get the other women." Highly excited, she ran from the lodge.

Trembling, Annah crept toward her mother. Parah was writhing. She shuddered, then stiffened up as if all her muscles were seized and paralyzed. Chathath and Gammad hurried outside, unwilling to be anywhere near a female in childbirth. *But this is not right,* Annah thought, terrified, gazing at her mother's rigid, mottled face. Parah could not seem to catch her breath, and the pain did not ease. Annah had seen women in labor before. Her mother's seizures and paralysis were not natural.

What should I do? Hearing women's voices, Annah retreated to a shadowy corner.

Haburah dashed into the lodge, followed by Ayalah, Iltani, and the wives of Naham. The wives of Naham had each miscarried before, and they questioned Iltani about Parah's contractions. Parah could no longer speak, or scream, or breathe, or even move.

Haburah turned ashen, and Ayalah began to sob. In her corner, Annah pulled her veil over her face and wept silently, watching as her mother delivered a stillborn son in mute, mortal agony.

Realizing Parah would not survive, Haburah, Ayalah, and the wives of Naham lifted their voices in high calls of mourning. They did not see Iltani's triumphant smirk as she took the body of Parah's stillborn son. But Annah stared through her veil as Iltani pulled a knife of stone from inside her tunic and cut the umbilical cord. As the lodge of Yerakh filled with mourners, Iltani sadly showed them the dead infant.

Later, Annah saw her pick up the infant's tiny, leather-wrapped body and sneak outside. *What is she doing?* Enraged, Annah snatched her grass bag and followed Iltani into the darkness.

Eight

HARDLY DARING to breathe, Annah crept through the fields, seeking Iltani. With every step, her rage grew. She could not think of her mother's death. Not yet. Pulling her veil away from her face, Annah listened to the sounds of the darkness, the croaking and rasping of hundreds of frogs and bugs and the faraway yipping of canines. She stopped. *This is not happening,* she told herself, swallowing hard against tears. *No. This is true. And I'm afraid. Why did you do this, Iltani? Why did you take my infant brother? He doesn't belong to you!*

She started out again, determined to learn Iltani's motive. She had to stay far enough behind her quarry that Iltani wouldn't sense her presence. *I'll risk being caught,* Annah decided. *I can't let her escape. She gave that drink to my I'ma; she wanted I'ma to die.* Maddened, Annah quickened her pace.

Iltani was moving south, away from the settlement, cutting through Yerakh's fields. Annah knew the Nachash lived just beyond these fields. She also knew that Yerakh—the bully—inexplicably feared the Nachash and her followers. He refused to drive them away during harvests when they helped themselves to portions of his grain.

How hateful, Yerakh, Annah thought to her brother. *You let strangers—whisperers and Serpent-Lovers—help themselves to grain from your fields, and you never demand payment from them. But if your brothers and sisters ask you for anything, even fields that are rightfully theirs, you threaten to kill them.*

Will you kill your wife for what she's done? I believe you will. It will be disgusting to watch you stand before the entire settlement and demand justice, when you refuse to submit yourself to the same authority.

Grimly, Annah passed the edges of Yerakh's fields. Here trees grew freely, as did flowers, shrubs, vines, and thorns. Annah searched for some sign of Iltani. Then, farther south, she saw a flickering light—an evening fire glowing in an unkempt lodge. Annah shivered, hugging her veil and her bag. Never had she dreamed she would seek this place.

"The Nachash will burn you to death," Chathath had told her once, before their father's murder. He had voiced her worst dream: The Nachash and the whisperers would steal her during the night. They would take her to their lodge and pass her, still living, through the fire until there was nothing left of her but bones and ashes.

Chathath had leaned close to her, hissing, "Then they will lick up your dust and the powder of your bones! After all, they are human serpents; they love the ashes of a dead child like you!"

I am no longer a child, Annah reminded herself now, suppressing her fears. *I'll find out what Iltani has done. And if I have to confront her before the entire settlement, using my own voice, then so be it. If I find her in the lodge of the Nachash, with the body of the child, then I will tell everyone that Iltani has committed two murders.*

Annah circled the lodge of the Nachash, looking for an observation point. When she saw glimmers of firelight through the roughly woven grasses of the west wall, she summoned all her courage and crept up next to the lodge.

Kneeling softly, she peered through a gap in the woven wall. Iltani was there, seated before a crackling, snapping fire. She had set the stillborn's tiny body off to one side, as if it were a bundle of refuse. Annah shut her eyes briefly, steadying herself against this new indignity.

Seated in a half-circle before the fire, the Nachash and the whisperers resembled dried caricatures of humans, whose individual characteristics had been sucked away by some vile, wasting blight. Yet they radiated a presence both compelling and dark. The strongest source of this dark presence was the Nachash herself. Encased in her circular, painted leather cloak, she exuded an arrogance that demanded submission.

And Iltani humbly offered it. Like a child expecting praise, she explained, "I used the seeds and leaves of death plants; the woman died bearing a child. You told me 'like for like.' Is this not your price?"

The Nachash sighed, low and harsh in her throat. "We will see what you have brought to our fire." From the depths of her cloak, the Nachash extended two withered arms, her skeletal fingers reaching over the fire. Iltani winced, forced to stretch her own arms over the flames to pass the small bundle to the Nachash.

The Nachash opened the bundle. "One heartbeat for

109

another," she muttered, a chuckling noise rasping in her throat.

Nauseated, Annah pressed a hand to her mouth.

Iltani sat down, obviously relieved. "Then you're pleased? You'll give me the remedies I need?"

The Nachash remained silent, swaying, fixated on Annah's stillborn brother. To Annah, this aged woman, leering at the body of a stillborn child, represented every horror clad in human flesh. *O Nachash*, Annah thought fiercely, *I hate you! You've demanded the lives of my mother and my brother. If I live a thousand years, I'll never forget what you have done.*

As if feeling Annah's rage, the Nachash turned toward the wall through which Annah stared, and flicked her eyelids open. Where there should have been the color of brown for her eyes, the Nachash showed only whites. Yet she recognized Annah. Enraged now, the Nachash screamed, deep and hoarse. "You, watcher in the dark! You, hating us! You! Will you demand justice? Will you accuse us before the Most High?"

The Most High? The Most High is the enemy of the Nachash? Does He exist after all? Confounded, Annah stared back through the tiny break in the wall, unable to move.

Now Iltani looked in her direction, suspicion dawning in her smooth, full face. "We're being watched?" she cried, horrified. "No. No!" She snatched the knife of stone from the earthen floor, gripping it in her fist.

The sight of it jolted Annah to her senses. Iltani was going to kill her. And this time even Yerakh couldn't protect her. Clutching her veil and her bag, Annah scrambled to her feet and ran toward the settlement. As she fled through the fields, she could hear Iltani behind her, running fast and hard.

Terrified, her feet shredded by thorns as she ran, Annah cried out, the words breaking from her throat in the faintest of voices, "Most High, help me!"

Hearing Iltani's snarls of rage mingled with gasps for air, Annah sped on through the darkness. Then she tripped. The earth seemed to rush up to meet her, knocking the breath from her body. *I'm going to die now. Iltani's right behind me.* Feeling smothered, almost suffocating with fear, Annah waited, bracing for a blow. But Iltani ran past her toward the settlement.

Annah lay perfectly still, her face pressed into the earth, unable to believe she had escaped. Why hadn't Iltani sensed her presence? Why weren't the whisperers following her?

Gradually, the smothering sensation faded. Annah waited, listening for the Nachash and the whisperers. She heard nothing. Only the croaking of frogs and the rasping of bugs. And night birds . . . singing joyously. Trembling, she sat up in the darkness and stared at the heavens, trying to gather her thoughts. *I'm alive,* she told herself, amazed. *I should be dead, but I'm alive.* The moon and the stars had never looked so beautiful. And she was comforted by an all-encompassing presence, the very opposite of the presence of the Nachash. *You're here,* she thought to the Most High. *I can sense You; it's as if You're touching me. But why should You notice me, a human-female-nothing?*

As she was trying to understand this, a distant clamor arose from the settlement, screams of rage and terror. Annah jumped up, panic-stricken, clutching her bag and veil. *Most High, help me. Where can I go?* Annah ran through the fields into the night.

Shifting on a branch in the Tree of Havah, Annah scanned the heavens, waiting for the first signs of dawn. From time to time she sensed the presence of others—men and women—and heard them calling to each other in the darkness. *Are they looking for me?* she wondered, trying to peer through the rising mist of the night. Suddenly sensing someone at the base of the tree, Annah climbed upward, groping for branch after branch, her heart thudding. *O Most High, save me from being discovered by this person.*

The person lingered briefly at the base of the tree, then hurried toward the river. Voices rose from that same direction, first in alarm, then in triumph. A woman screamed.

Iltani, Annah thought. Her eyes widened as Iltani's screams continued, mingled now with the curses and laughter of others, both men and women. The voices were moving, changing directions in the darkness. Unable to see through the deepening mists, Annah turned her head, following the sounds of the voices. Iltani's captors were apparently dragging her back to the settlement.

Sickened, Annah eased herself into one of the lower branches of the ancient tree. *Should I go back to the settlement and speak to the others, and tell them what Iltani and the Nachash have done? No, they'd kill me—Yerakh would demand my death. O Most High, stay with me. I'm so afraid.*

Annah leaned into a massive branch, clinging to it while she prayed. The presence of the Most High surrounded her, enfolding her. Reassured, she dozed. She was awakened by the sensation of her woven-grass bag sliding from her fingertips. Snatching it into her arms, Annah straightened, staring at the sky. The first ruddy hints of dawn glowed in the east.

I should go back to the settlement, she told herself. But she waited until the sunlight permeated the early mist, ending her night of fear. The light calmed her, strengthened her. *O Most High . . . thank You for saving me, and for noticing me—a nothing-creature. Why should You care that I exist? Why should You stay with me when I have nothing to offer You but words that I cannot speak? But how glad I am for Your presence; I'll remember forever that You were with me, protecting me when I was so afraid.*

She descended from the tree, wobbling a little as she turned toward the settlement. Birdsong pierced the morning mist from every direction. It was as if the terrors of the night had all been a dream; she would go back to her brother's lodge and find her mother, still pregnant and sound asleep.

No, I'ma's death, the hatred of the Nachash, and Iltani's screams when she was caught last night . . . all those things happened. Now I must face them. Slowly Annah pulled her veil over her head and entered the mist-shrouded settlement.

Everyone's still asleep, she thought. As she approached Yerakh's lodge, she noticed a woman curled up on the hard, trampled path near the doorway. Wondering, Annah crept around the prone figure, then stiffened, almost crying aloud. It was Iltani, eyes half-opened in a death stare, lying in a pool of her own blood. Someone had slashed her throat with the knife of stone.

Pressing one trembling hand to her mouth, Annah backed away from Iltani's body. There was so much blood. As she retreated, she just missed stepping into another patch of bloodstained earth near the front entry of the lodge. She stared at it, bewildered. Had they killed Iltani at the door, then flung her body out, disgraced and unattended? Annah shuddered, revolted by the thought.

Inside the lodge, Annah caught her breath and looked around. The wives of Naham were sharing pallets with Haburah and Ayalah, to the right of the hearth—on the same side of the lodge as the snoring Gammad. It was as if her sisters could not endure being on the same side of the lodge as their dead mother.

Bracing herself to see her mother's body, Annah turned to the opposite wall. She was surprised to see Chathath stretched out on a pallet next to Parah. Wondering, Annah approached them, staring at the two of them lying side by side.

I would never have believed Chathath was so devoted to I'ma. As she gazed at them, Annah realized that Chathath's face was bluish and unnaturally still. Refusing to comprehend the truth, Annah cautiously touched her brother's hand. It was cold and bound in place by cords at his wrists—prepared for burial.

Annah sat down hard on the earthen floor, thoroughly dazed. *How can Chathath be dead?* She half-expected him to wake up, mocking her, laughing over Iltani's death. She could still hear him quarreling with Iltani last night as they sat before the evening fire, their voices resounding with hatred.

Monster!

Serpent-Lover!

Shut up!

When you do, elder sister.

Annah winced, pained by Chathath's prophecy of his own death. *Iltani thought it was you spying on her last night,* Annah thought, gazing at Chathath's cold, still face. *It's my fault; you would not be dead if I hadn't followed her. When I fell and she didn't sense me, she came here—with that knife of stone—and killed you while you stood in the doorway.*

Stricken, Annah pulled away from the bodies of her brother and her mother. She had to get out of the lodge, away from the frightful atmosphere of death. Unable to endure stepping over Chathath's blood in the front entry, unwilling to see Iltani's sightless staring corpse again, she went out the back door of the lodge.

I'll go to the river, she told herself. But as she made her way through the afal orchard, she remembered her mother standing beneath these fragrant trees, embracing the faithless Tseb-iy.

If you had truly loved my mother, Tseb-iy, she would be alive today. The thought choked Annah, causing bile to rise up into her throat. She dropped to her knees, retching violently. When she could move again, she staggered through the fields, desolate, numbed beyond all feeling. The creatures of the fields skittered away from her approaching feet, and the birds flew before her in silence.

He was waiting for her at the river; Annah dimly recognized his presence. Uncomprehending, she dropped to her knees, watching the current as it rushed away. A small stone plopped into the river before her. She stared dully at the sparkling spray of water and the resultant rings emanating across the surface. A second stone fell, forcefully this time. The spray of water touched her hands, which were limp on the woven-grass bag in her lap. A thought came to her then, cold and clear, as if from a distance: *Look at him; he is waiting.*

With an effort, Annah lifted her head and met his gaze. He was wide-eyed, alarmed, questioning her silently: *What's wrong?*

After an instant of blank stillness, Annah reached down and scooped up a handful of river sand, letting it sift through her fingers, telling him: *Death. Death is wrong.*

He copied her gesture of the sand through the fingers, then raised his hands, desperately pleading with her to answer: *Who is dead?*

The intensity of his emotions finally reached her, breaking through her numbness. Annah took a deep breath. Trying to answer him, she raised four fingers: *Four people.* She lifted her hands to pull her hair back, indicating a mature woman. *One.* Then she depicted a full, pregnant belly, sweeping her hands downward fiercely to indicate the loss of a child. *Two.* Trying to convey the death of Chathath, she implied a smooth-faced person taller than herself, then clenched her hands and slammed them toward her heart as if holding a knife. *Three.* Following this, she pulled her hair back once more and drew her finger across her throat, indicating a fatal slash. *Four.*

This last action brought back the memory of Iltani's death-stare, causing Annah to press her hands to her mouth. She could not let herself be sick in front of him— though nothing but dry heaves could come of the sickness; her stomach was empty. Overcome, she began to cry, bowing her head into the sand, grasping fistfuls, flinging it away blindly as she sobbed.

When her sobs faded, she heard the plop of a stone in the water. Pulling herself up listlessly, she watched him, exhausted. He looked heartsick. Running his hands over his face, he held them out to her, displaying his tears: *I am grieving with you.*

Weakened by his show of emotion, Annah began to cry again. He gestured emphatically, pleadingly, pointing upriver: *Go to the bridge!*

She stood, not knowing what else to do. Wiping her eyes on the edge of her veil, Annah shouldered her grass bag and began to trudge upriver. The numbness was descending upon her again, and it frightened her. It would be too easy to allow the numbness to consume her, to suck her into a thoughtless, mindless madness.

O Most High, she thought wearily, *help me.* She sensed the Most High as she walked to the bridge—His quiet presence urged her steps forward, willing her to concentrate on her surroundings.

During their walk to the bridge, her beloved matched his pace to her own. Now and then he would toss a pebble in her direction, begging her to look at him, to reassure him that she was able to continue. Each time, she nodded in mute agreement and plodded onward. When they reached the bridge, he motioned to her, imploring her to sit on the riverbank and wait for him. Twice he looked back, asking with his hands and his wide, dark, eloquent eyes: *Will you wait?*

Exhausted, she knelt and nodded, patting the sandy riverbank to assure him: *I'll stay here.*

She watched as he ran up the riverbank and vanished into the trees. *He's afraid I might kill myself,* she realized. *But I'm too tired.* Using her veil and her bag to cushion her head, she curled up on the sand and shut her eyes. Almost immediately, she fell into a shock-numbed sleep.

The touch of a hand jolted her awake. Annah jumped, terrified, flinging herself away from the hand, as gentle as it was. Her beloved's mother stepped back, startled. Recovering instantly, she knelt, facing Annah, her dark eyes concerned. "Child," she murmured, low and soothing, "tell me what has happened."

Tell her? Using words? Annah felt the blood drain from

her face. Faint with fear, she lowered her head into her hands. His mother touched her again, comfortingly. Annah forced herself not to run from the touch, but she trembled. Had anyone touched her in kindness since the death of her father? She couldn't remember.

"You're safe," his mother whispered. "No one will hurt you now. It is not proper that my son should approach you yet, so I am here. Please, tell me what happened."

Talk! Annah commanded herself. Scared, she struggled to force sounds from her throat, past her lips. "Last night . . . my mother . . ." The effort of making words almost gagged her. Swallowing hard, she began again. "My mother . . . was bearing a child. My brother's wife is . . . was . . . barren."

Keeping her head down, she told the story in fragments. To her own ears, her words sounded abrupt and hollow. She told of her mother's death. She told of Iltani taking the stillborn to the Nachash. She described her flight for her life and her nightlong vigil in the ancient Tree of Havah, ending with the deaths of Iltani and Chathath.

The only detail lacking in her story was the presence of the Most High. She dared not confess Him to the mother of her beloved. Not yet. Her belief in the Most High would most certainly be accepted as evidence of her madness. Her beloved and his family might feel compelled to reject her. And today of all days, she would not be able to endure their rejection. Finished speaking, Annah waited, utterly spent.

The mother of her beloved touched her arm. "Child, look at me."

As Annah met her gaze, she said, "I want you to wait here while I speak to my husband and my son. They are over there." She inclined her head toward the opposite bank. Annah saw her beloved there, standing with his father. She could not see their faces; his father's hands were on his son's shoulders, their heads lowered as they talked. "Tell me you will wait," the mother of her beloved commanded.

"I will wait," Annah agreed tonelessly.

The mother of her beloved crossed the swaying bridge with amazing speed, her gait youthful, confident. Her husband and her son had finished their conversation and welcomed her approach. They talked briefly, their words accentuated by nods of agreement, their discussion ending with the three of them turning to study the bridge. Her husband spoke once more, and all three of them seemed satisfied. Once again, the mother of her beloved crossed the bridge to Annah, bounding off the last step, looking contented.

Annah stood, quivering. The mother of her beloved clasped her hand, speaking gently. "Child, if we were to speak for you, to bring you into our family as the wife of my son, would you come with us freely?"

"Yes, but . . ." Annah faltered, then burst out, "Yerakh would never agree. He won't give me a marriage portion."

"He will agree," the mother of her beloved answered firmly, forbidding argument.

Distressed, Annah lowered her head. "I must tell you . . . if you wish to be free of me, I will understand. I'm considered to be mad. I'm the most despised person in the settlement." She took a quick breath, tears welling in her eyes as she continued, "I have no value. I've avoided the others, and I haven't spoken to anyone since my father's death."

The mother of her beloved blinked, astonished.

"How? We remember your father. He died—what—twenty-five years ago? How have you said nothing for all these years?"

Annah looked away as tears slid down her cheeks. "Often I have been tempted to talk. But I feel Yerakh choking me—snapping my neck, as he snapped my father's."

The mother of her beloved lifted a corner of the veil. Briskly, protectively, she mopped Annah's tears, as she would wipe a young child's face, saying, "There will be no more of this! I'm coming to speak to your brother this afternoon. Whether he likes it or not, he *will* agree with me. This will be your last night in that place. Now, look at me."

Obedient, Annah looked.

The mother of her beloved smiled, resolute and tender. "You must return to your brother's lodge. Be as you always are; say nothing and let them believe whatever they believe. Today, they will honor the death of your mother and your brother. This afternoon, I will come to speak for you. By tomorrow night, you will be freed from that place." Pausing, she shook out the corner of the veil, which was damp from Annah's tears. "This is a beautiful thing, this veil."

"My family . . . they hate it."

"Child," the mother of her beloved answered softly, "we are your family now."

"I'ma, what is her name?" Shem asked as they were leaving the river.

Naomi frowned, wishing the young woman had not

already started back to her settlement. "I forgot to ask."
She glared at her husband as he laughed.

Nine

JUST AFTER midday, the entire settlement gathered to witness the burial of Parah and Chathath. Earlier, Iltani's body had been unceremoniously dumped into the waste pit; a disgraceful burial fitting a murderess.

K'nan and some of the younger men—Tseb-iy included—jostled each other and snickered as they lowered Chathath's leather-encased body into the grave beside Parah. Annah ducked her veiled head, biting her lip hard. She wanted to scream without stopping. The entire settlement would hear her giving words to her sorrow and rage. It pained her that these young men—Tseb-iy in particular—could enjoy themselves now. Only her sisters showed any grief.

Ayalah stood at the foot of the grave, sobbing. Haburah protested bitterly, asking the young men, "Did you hate my mother and my brother so much that you laugh over their bodies?"

Tseb-iy immediately became silent, but K'nan answered quickly, "I swear, Haburah, we aren't laughing because of your brother or your mother."

At that instant, Annah felt someone snatching her veiled hair, the action so fierce and swift that she fell hard on her rump. Again the young men snickered.

Ayalah said indignantly, "My mother is dead and you're laughing, K'nan. Stop it!"

"Enough!" Yerakh snarled.

The snickering stopped. Resentful, the young men shuffled their feet, impatient to cover the grave and be done with the burial.

Annah despised them all. She was raging inside, humiliated. *I know what they're thinking*, she told herself. *Why not just bury Parah's mindless daughter with her this very day? This is why they are laughing.*

As she got to her feet, Annah felt the children of the settlement shoving her. Not content with wrenching her to the ground, they were pushing her toward the open grave. She sat down again.

Being in the center of a crowd unnerved Annah. She could not hide in the shadows and slip away if she felt threatened. Worse, she could not sense one person from another because together they formed one overwhelming presence. And having to endure abuse from the children of the settlement only added to her distress.

The children continued to attack Annah, poking her, striking her, kicking her. *If I ever have children, which I doubt, I'll never allow them to behave as these children behave. But it's useless for me to even think such things; I'll never have a child. Yerakh will refuse the mother of my beloved this afternoon. I wish she wouldn't speak for me. Yerakh will laugh at her.*

The thought made Annah heartsick. She prayed the Most High would prevent the mother of her beloved from being shamed. She also feared to think of her beloved's face, and the faces of his parents and brothers, when they realized that she believed in a legend of old, the Most High. Her beloved's family probably would throw her into the river for believing such foolishness. Yerakh surely would—never mind that he feared and sheltered the Nachash, the enemy of the Most High. He didn't regard *her* existence as foolishness.

Grieving, Annah watched her brothers and sisters cast dust into the grave, honoring death. Fearful of attracting attention, Annah kept still. The children, having grown bored with her, watched the burial process instead.

Women from each lodge lowered remembrances into the grave: special pieces of burial pottery, flowers, and spices. As the final gifts were placed with Parah and Chathath, the young men quickly shoveled dirt into the grave, eager to be done. The remaining members of the settlement departed to their own lodges and fields. Tonight they would bring gifts of food to the lodge of Yerakh for a mourning feast.

"Why are you still here?" Yerakh snarled at Gammad. "Go check the fields. And you two . . ." He rounded on Haburah and Ayalah fiercely. "You have work to do. Come back later when you've finished tending the herds."

Gammad looked as though he would like to strike his brother. Naham was watching, however, and Naham would defend Yerakh. Gammad turned abruptly and strode away, his long dark hair flying back from his shoulders.

Annah sighed noiselessly, relieved. If Yerakh and Gammad attacked each other, one of them would die, and

Annah could not endure the death of another member of her family. Not even the death of Yerakh. For once, she was glad that Naham was nearby.

Obviously less intimidated by Naham's presence, Haburah pleaded with Yerakh, angrily. "Today of all days, Yerakh—"

He cut her words off with a wave of his broad, powerful hand. "Today of all days, you and Ayalah need to work and distract yourselves from this useless grieving. Now go away before I give you to Naham! Ayalah, go with her."

"I hate you!" Ayalah cried.

"You hate everyone," Yerakh answered, unmoved. "Go away and leave me alone."

He turned on Annah now, grasping her shoulders through the veil, pushing her toward the settlement. *He will have me work the gold today*, Annah thought, dismayed. *If I make any mistakes, he will beat me.*

As she stumbled toward the settlement, Naham walked beside Yerakh, laughing deeply. "So, my friend, if your sisters make you angry enough, you'll give me all three as their punishment?"

"Haburah's the most troublesome," Yerakh muttered.

"I'll manage Haburah," Naham assured him.

"She doesn't have a marriage portion."

"We'll agree on something. But you're sure you won't give me all three?"

"They'll cut your throat while you sleep."

"I'll tie them up at night before I close my eyes." Naham sounded gratified by the thought of having so many wives at his mercy.

Listening, Annah felt faint. Frightened by the sight of Naham's huge feet walking so close by, she tripped on her own. Yerakh steadied her, then shook her hard, saying, "If this one didn't have the gift of mimicking my work with the gold, I'd have killed her long ago."

"You're sure she only mimics your work?" Naham asked. "I've wondered if she really knows everything we do and say."

O Most High, Annah begged silently, barely able to continue walking, *save me from the idle thoughts of this wicked Naham!*

Yerakh snorted, contemptuous. "I've watched her enough over the years. She's incapable of true thought or speech. But if she deceived me in such a way, I'd kill her for that too."

"If you decide to kill her, then tell me," Naham urged. "I'll do it for you."

They both laughed, and Yerakh gave Naham a companionable swipe on the arm. "I'll remember your kind offer."

❧ ☙

Sweating, Annah clubbed gold sheets layered between folds of membrane and leather. This gold had to be perfect; it was for Taphaph. Yerakh had not said so, but Annah knew he would send this gift of gold to Tsillah, Taphaph's mother, as soon as it was finished. If she accepted the gold, then negotiations would begin. Taphaph would wear this gold on her wedding day.

And my life will be all the worse, Annah thought. *Taphaph is cleverer than Iltani ever was.*

Annah paused, hearing voices from the path outside Yerakh's workroom. Women walked by, laughing, then calling inside the lodge. But Yerakh, Gammad, Haburah, and Ayalah were all gone. Only Annah remained in the lodge.

You're not welcome here, Annah thought to the women, pounding the gold emphatically. How could they laugh, approaching a lodge filled with death? These were the mothers, sisters, and aunts of those little monster-children who had tormented Annah at the graveside this morning. Fuming, she thought, *I'm mindless. I don't have to acknowledge their presence.* She heard the women giggling as they entered the lodge, discussing how they should arrange their gifts of food—which Annah would never eat.

"Well, someone is here, if you can call her a someone." Annah recognized this voice as Taphaph's—young, gleeful, self-confident. Annah continued to beat down the gold, her rhythm unbroken. She could feel Taphaph watching her from the leather-curtained doorway.

Another woman spoke, Taphaph's haughty mother, Tsillah. "I've not seen her without that veil for ages. Truly, if she had any thoughts to match her face, she would be more beautiful than Haburah or Parah."

"Ugh! Well, she *doesn't* have thoughts," Taphaph replied. "She's a plain, stupid creature, and I don't want to discuss her. Let's go find Ayalah and Haburah."

"But what will you do if you marry Yerakh?" Tsillah demanded. "That Annah-creature lives here too."

"She'll have to live somewhere else," Taphaph declared.

In her thoughts, Annah could almost see Taphaph tossing back her long, thick hair, certain of her power over Yerakh.

Tsillah spoke, impatient with her daughter. "If Yerakh has managed to train her to work the gold, then you could train her to pound spices and grains. She could be useful to you."

Annah grimaced, trying to imagine being useful to Taphaph. Pressing her lips together firmly, she shifted the club between her hands and continued the rhythm of beating the gold, her thoughts chanting, *bride-gold-for-Taph-aph, bride-gold-for-Taph-aph.*

As she worked, she could hear children screeching in the main room of the lodge. Men were arriving now also: Yerakh, Naham, K'nan. Annah could hear them arguing.

Marriage portions, she told herself. *What else could they be discussing? I don't want to hear it. But the mother of my beloved will arrive before too long. I should go into the main room; she will want to see that I'm safe.*

Wearied, dreading the evening, Annah set her club down next to the bride-gold, then pulled her veil over her head. She slipped into the main room of the lodge and settled against the wall, not far from the men.

Gammad joined their circle. Belligerent, he faced Yerakh. "You'll have to hire another man to tend your herds and plow your fields. I can't do it all myself. And if Haburah and Ayalah marry and leave, you'll need to hire two more men."

"I haven't agreed to anything," Yerakh answered harshly. "And I don't need you to tell me what I will and won't do!"

Gammad's eyes kindled dangerously. "One day, Yerakh, you'll have to listen to me. You'll have to listen to all of us!"

Yerakh grabbed him by the throat, but Naham asked. "Yerakh, do you want to kill your only workman?"

Furious, Yerakh released Gammad and sat back, glaring. Gammad gave him look for look, while Annah held her breath. At last, Gammad looked downward in reluctant submission. Yerakh still held power over him.

Now Taphaph approached Yerakh, smiling. Her skin, hair, and eyes shimmered in the filtered afternoon light. She fanned herself delicately with her hands, then pulled her glossy black hair away from her neck, her movements graceful, lingering.

The men all stared at her, but Taphaph's smiles were for Yerakh alone. "Tell me that you're finished arguing, Yerakh, please. I want to sit near you, but my mother won't let me if she thinks you're going to fight."

"We've finished arguing," Yerakh told her, suddenly smiling and genial.

Taphaph knelt beside Yerakh, sure of herself. Yerakh reached behind her back with sly, secretive fingers and began stroking and caressing her hair.

Annah was disgusted. They acted as if this were a marriage feast instead of a mourning feast. A soft murmur arose from the others. Annah presumed it was in response to Taphaph's flirtation—until she looked up and saw the mother of her beloved entering the lodge, carrying an intricate oblong basket heaped with grain cakes.

Her graying hair rich and heavy with gold talismans, she moved quietly through the crowd and set her basket on the mats with the other dishes brought by the women of the settlement. Everyone was watching her, but she seemed oblivious to them all. She straightened, completely dignified, her hands clasped respectfully, displaying a fine pair of matching gold cuffs on her wrists. Turning toward the seat of honor, held by Yerakh, she said in calm, carrying tones, "Yerakh of the Lodge of the Tsaraph. I am Naomi of Those-Who-Carve-Wood. We live north and west of the boundaries of your settlement."

Naomi, Annah thought, clinging to this bit of information.

Yerakh inclined his dark head. Naham, K'nan, and Gammad all moved away, allowing her to approach. Taphaph, however, stayed beside Yerakh. He frowned slightly, focused on the elaborate gold cuffs adorning Naomi's wrists. At last he said, "Welcome. How do you know me?"

"My family was acquainted with your father," she answered, lifting one dark eyebrow.

Annah caught her breath at this; it was precisely the way her beloved lifted his eyebrow when questioning her at the river.

Naomi continued, saying, "I have come to express my sorrow for the death of your mother."

"How do you know she's dead?" Yerakh demanded, astonished, almost rude.

"There are ways of knowing," she told him firmly, her tone allowing no questions or doubts. "I also wish to conduct business with you before all these witnesses, though I ask your forgiveness for speaking of it, today of all days. This will be my only chance to meet with you, and I must have your answer immediately."

Yerakh studied her, then indicated one of the mats set before him. Naomi knelt formally, her hands calmly folded in her lap. As if remembering his manners, Yerakh straightened, his tone cool, polite. "Will you have something to eat?"

"Two of my sons are waiting for me; we have only a short time to conclude our business," she answered, her words soothing. "I do not wish to offend you."

Yerakh turned, glaring at Haburah. Ducking her head obediently, Haburah selected a small dish of dry grain cakes and brought them forward. Annah held her breath, wondering if the mother of her beloved would refuse this offering of food; to accept food in the house of a stranger was to acknowledge peace between host and guest. Naomi smiled politely at Haburah and took a grain cake. They watched as she broke off an edge of the cake and ate it, accepting Yerakh's courtesy. Annah relaxed slightly.

Finished with her piece of grain cake, the mother of her beloved straightened, purposeful again. "I have come to ask you for one of your sisters; my second son has seen her and desires to have her as his wife."

Annah's heart pounded hard and fast. It was difficult to keep still; her hands were sweating. As she expected, Yerakh frowned. "You'll have to tell your son to look for a wife elsewhere. My sisters have no marriage portions."

Waving one dismissive hand, her gold wrist-cuff glittering, catching light, Naomi said, "It is not our custom to accept marriage portions. My son has seen your sister and he desires to have her as his wife. He asked me to offer you five hundred of his finest animals and half the grain from his fields for this year."

Yerakh sat back, visibly stunned. There was not a sound in the lodge; every member of the settlement was trying to absorb the shock of having one of their most basic customs overturned by a stranger. Yerakh shook his head as if he did not understand. Carefully, he asked, "Your son is willing to pay five hundred of his finest animals, and half his harvest, for one of my sisters?"

He looked at Haburah and Ayalah, who were staring at their guest, speechless. Annah gaped beneath her veil, unable to believe what she was hearing.

Naomi waited patiently, watching Yerakh. As if to encourage him, she said, "My son has harvested and threshed his grain; it is ready to be used."

Yerakh swallowed. Annah shut her eyes, feeling his

greed. To offer a man grain, already gathered and threshed, was to offer him ease. Grain was the basis of every meal, difficult to raise, more satisfying than the sweetest fruits or beans. She could only think of all the days her beloved had worked in his fields, sweating, fighting the thorns and his own weariness to gather his harvest, merely to offer half of it to Yerakh for her. Annah longed to protest against this sacrifice.

"He measured out the containers this morning," said the mother of her beloved. "His brothers had to help him; the grain fills two handcarts."

Yerakh stared. "Why should he offer this much?"

"Because our fields have prospered and he wants a wife."

Glancing at Taphaph, then at his sisters, Yerakh smiled. "I accept. But which of my sisters could be worth all this?"

"The veiled one."

Yerakh's smile faded. Like a man condemned, he said, "Your son won't want her; she cannot speak."

"Then she cannot argue. And my son will have peace in his lodge. As for myself, I say if she can bear him children, then nothing else matters."

Naham growled at Yerakh. "Fool! Accept her terms!"

Everyone laughed, and Yerakh smiled, obviously enjoying the conspiratorial looks of all his family and friends. "I accept."

Annah clenched her hands in her lap, overcome, struggling to maintain her composure.

Naomi stood, dignified. "My sons will bring the herds and grain throughout the day tomorrow. Have her ready tomorrow evening." As if remembering something trivial, she said, "Please, forgive us. This is a place of mourning.

We do not expect a wedding feast; it would be inappropriate. And your sister should bring only what she can carry in her arms. Nothing more."

Inclining her head respectfully to Yerakh, and to all present, she departed. Annah watched her go, as stunned as everyone else. *I don't believe this,* she thought, numbed. *This did not happen.* She felt everyone staring at her now, trying to see her in the shadows. Their sudden interest terrified her. *Be nothing,* Annah told herself. *A nothing-creature.*

His eyes narrow with suspicion, Yerakh stood and crossed the short distance between them. Reaching down, Yerakh dragged Annah to her feet, pulling her veil away. She gazed at the floor, keeping her face slack, her eyes vacant, seeing something that didn't exist. Yerakh grabbed her jaw, turning her face toward his, bellowing, "Look at me!"

Annah looked past him vaguely, now fixing her eyes to a point somewhere beyond the roof of the lodge. Disgusted, Yerakh let her go. Annah slouched down again beside the lattice-and-grass wall. Slowly, absently, she gathered her veil to herself and pulled it over her head, then leaned into the wall and shut her eyes, as if nothing was more important than a nap. Even with her eyes closed, she could feel the others staring at her. Some of the young men snickered.

"What did she do to make him desire her?" Tseb-iy asked, expressing everyone's disbelief. He laughed softly, the sound full of unspoken, lascivious imaginings.

How can you laugh, Tseb-iy? Annah almost shook with rage. *My mother died last night, bearing your child, and you stand in her lodge now, and you laugh and think of vile things.*

"Now, we'll talk!" Naham announced loudly, rumbling,

jubilant. "This worthless creature has brought more wealth to the lodge of the Tsaraph. So, Yerakh, no more excuses. You'll give K'nan one hundred animals for Ayalah's marriage portion."

"One hundred and fifty," K'nan argued. "Because he's kept me waiting for so long."

"And one hundred fifty animals for Haburah," Naham agreed, accepting K'nan's terms as his own.

"Then you owe me at least one hundred fifty animals," Gammad said menacingly. "That leaves you with all the grain, fifty new animals, and the promise of a marriage portion from Taphaph. You have no reason to disagree with us now, Yerakh."

Curious, Annah opened her eyes to peer through the veil. Yerakh looked murderous. Taphaph was pulling away from him in response to fervent signals from her mother.

Tsillah, thin and imperious, spoke as if alarmed. "Nothing has been decided for my daughter, and I'm not ready to part with her yet!"

"I'ma!" Taphaph protested. But Tsillah steered Taphaph out of the lodge, lifting her high-arched brows at Tseb-iy. Sullen, he stalked after them.

"Get out!" Yerakh ordered Gammad. "You've caused enough trouble for tonight. You can sleep in the pen with the sheep!"

Gammad hesitated, then snatched several handfuls of grain cakes and stomped outside. Yerakh scowled, watching him go. Still angry, he looked at Naham. "You won't give me any peace until you have Haburah, will you?"

"None," Naham agreed.

"Then you may have her, and the animals you requested from the five hundred. And K'nan will have the one hundred fifty animals he requested for Ayalah."

Hearing this, Ayalah screamed with delight, while Haburah closed her eyes. All the women whispered among themselves, amazed.

Yerakh ignored them. He beckoned Naham quietly. "I'll pay you an extra fifty animals, if you'll do as I say."

Annah shuddered at the coldness in his voice. Hushed, Yerakh muttered instructions to Naham, who smiled and narrowed his eyes, pleased. *What is Yerakh planning?* Annah wondered. She watched the two men for the remainder of the evening, but their words and actions revealed nothing.

At the end of the evening, Yerakh called to the wives of Naham. "I'll give you each a talisman of gold if you'll guard that creature tonight in your own lodge, and prepare her for her marriage. Be sure she doesn't run away in the morning. Haburah, Ayalah, go with them. Naham will stay here with me."

The other guests were leaving now, and the wives of Naham stopped to gather some remnants of the feast to take back to their lodge. Grimly, Haburah grabbed Annah by the elbow and pushed her toward the doorway of the lodge. *My bag,* Annah thought, suddenly anxious, halting in the doorway. *My comb, my shell carving.* She had left them in a corner of Yerakh's workroom.

"Go!" Haburah shoved her out into the dusk. Ayalah and wives of Naham followed them, gossiping. Stars sparkled in the violet-red evening sky. Annah focused on them, calming herself.

"Don't think that I'll spend the entire night with the four of you," Ayalah told the wives of Naham. "I'm going to find K'nan!" She paused, listening to sounds in the distance. They all turned, hearing the low, protesting calls of sheep and the sharp whistles of approaching herders. "It must be Annah's fool—he's too impatient to wait until tomorrow." Ayalah laughed at the thought.

The sounds of the sheep and the whistles of two herders roused the men of the settlement. They were coming from all directions now; among them Yerakh, Naham, Tseb-iy, K'nan, Gammad, and Tseb-iy's father—the portly, gray-haired Bachown, who was the settlement's expert in testing metals. Already the men were quarreling about how to divide the herd. Annah guessed there were at least a hundred animals. Yerakh was talking to the lead herder, whom Annah recognized as the older brother of her beloved.

I wish you were here, she thought to her beloved, knowing he had deliberately stayed away. *It would comfort me to see you again.*

As she stared at the gathering of men and at the sheep, Annah saw Gammad arguing with K'nan, then with Yerakh. Naham stepped between Yerakh and Gammad, then very pointedly turned his massive back on Gammad, cutting him off from the others. Annah felt chills of fear creeping downward from her scalp.

"You can forget about seeing K'nan now," Haburah taunted Ayalah. "The men will be arguing for the rest of the night. Come. Let's leave them to their stupid sheep." She gripped Annah's shoulders and turned her toward the lodge of Naham. Annah resisted, longing to scream out a warning to Gammad. But her sisters dragged her away, and fear kept her silent.

Ten

IN THE late-morning sunlight, the wives of Naham immersed Annah in the river, then scoured her with sand and rinses of cleansing herbs. Finished, they led her and her sisters back to their lodge. There they rubbed scented oils into Annah's hair and skin. Haburah and Ayalah were indifferent to Annah's appearance, but the wives of Naham were unhappy. The first wife, Shuwa, slim and meticulous, was especially displeased.

"This is like trying to bring a stone to life!" Shuwa complained, combing Annah's hair. "It can't be done. Does your brother expect me to make her appear to be a normal woman, with her eyes staring away like that?"

The second wife, Qetsiyah, laughed curtly. "From what you've said, sister-wife, you must have looked exactly like this creature the day you married Naham."

Shuwa stopped combing Annah's hair. "Well, from

what *I* saw, the day you married Naham, you *did* look like a stone."

Clearly impatient, Ayalah plucked the comb out of Shuwa's fingers. "I'll do this. We've been working on Annah since this morning; I'm sick of looking at her. K'nan's waiting for me."

"May he always be waiting for you," Shuwa muttered, but her words sounded more like a curse than a blessing.

Kneeling on the mat beside her, Haburah slapped an oblong basket of cakes in front of Annah and the wives of Naham. "I wouldn't concern myself with Annah's appearance. A man offering anything for a dumb creature like her can't have much of a mind himself." Lowering her voice, she added, "Perhaps I'll become as mindless as Annah the day I marry Naham."

"You'll survive," Qetsiyah answered, subdued.

Shuwa and Qetsiyah evidently lived from day to day, dealing with Naham. Oddly enough, both wives had the same build as Haburah: slender, hinting at elegance. Annah wondered if Haburah eventually would become like Shuwa or Qetsiyah; an almost-nothing woman, her elegance and spirit crushed by Naham's brutality.

"I don't want to just survive him," Haburah said, snatching a grain cake. "I want to kill him."

Silent, the wives of Naham perused the basket of cakes. Annah recognized the oblong basket and the cakes made by the mother of her beloved. Pretending nothingness, she took a cake and nibbled it. The taste was sweet, faintly spiced, and delicate, crumbling gently in her mouth.

"At least she can feed herself," Shuwa sighed.

"Her tunic is old," Qetsiyah said. "We should persuade Yerakh to let us find some other garment among the belongings of his wife or mother. We wouldn't want that fool-of-a-man to receive his wife in an old tunic."

"You can't use one of I'ma's beautiful garments on her," Ayalah protested.

"You'd give her one of your own?" Qetsiyah asked, skeptical.

"It's well past midday," Shuwa interrupted, addressing Haburah. "Will your brother allow us to return to his lodge and search for proper marriage attire?"

"I'm beyond caring what Yerakh thinks!" Haburah declared savagely. "Or Naham!"

"Naham's other wife—the one before me—used to speak in such a way," Shuwa told Haburah somberly. "Naham broke her bones, then buried her alive because she argued with him."

"He showed me her grave," Qetsiyah added. "He laughs about her death."

"Let him try to break my bones." Haburah stood, brushing the crumbs from her tunic. "He'll have to catch me first. Come, let's take Annah to our lodge."

As Haburah pulled her to her feet, Annah grasped Naomi's basket of cakes; she would not leave it in the lodge of Naham.

"Why should she take that?" Shuwa asked indignantly, her tone informing them that she wanted to keep the basket.

"She's probably hungry," Ayalah told Shuwa. "Anyway, the basket was presented by the mother of her husband. She ought to keep it."

You aren't defending my right to the basket, Ayalah, Annah thought to her sister. *You want to insult Shuwa and Qetsiyah because you don't like them. Even so, thank you.*

Clutching her basket awkwardly in one hand, Annah

pulled her veil over her head with her free hand. It fell across her face in uneven, bedraggled folds, partially obscuring her view. She stumbled as she followed her sisters out into the sunlight.

Shuwa sniffed disdainfully. "That fool-of-a-man will demand all his animals and grain back when he realizes that your sister has no true mind."

"He'll have to fight most of the settlement," Ayalah scoffed.

As they walked, Annah peered ahead. The men of the settlement were gathered before Yerakh's lodge, watching Yerakh, Naham, and K'nan divide yet another group of sheep—perhaps fifty this time. Gammad was not there. Yerakh beckoned Haburah, spoke with her briefly, then waved her toward the lodge.

Haburah motioned for Ayalah and the wives of Naham to follow her. Ayalah gripped Annah's elbow, pushing her into the lodge.

Inside, Haburah said, "Yerakh agreed that we should take whatever Annah needs from I'ma's storage chest. But we're not to go into his workroom or touch the bride-gold."

"Why would we use bride-gold on Annah?" Ayalah demanded. "Such a waste!"

"It might distract others from her stupid staring eyes," Shuwa argued. "Yerakh should definitely use the bride-gold. And she needs a tunic and some hair bindings." Shuwa opened Parah's short-legged storage chest, set against the wall of the lodge. The sight of the chest pierced Annah with fresh stabbing grief. She knelt on the earthen floor, staring numbly through the mist of her veil, feeling the mindlessness descend upon her.

Naham's wives sorted through the chest, removing

combs, beads, cords, carvings, tunics, pieces of gold, bracelets, hair bindings, and amulets—the remnants of Parah's life. Haburah watched these proceedings stonily, but Ayalah gathered the choicest articles in her lap—beads, carvings, and ornaments of gold.

Unable to bear the sight of the greedy Ayalah snatching at a bracelet, Annah looked away from her mother's belongings. Shuwa and Qetsiyah argued, finally choosing one of Parah's long, soft leather tunics. They removed Annah's veil and slid her old tunic down to her feet while pulling Parah's tunic over her head. Annah inhaled the remnants of her mother's distinctive scent of spices and sweet oils. Overcome, she twisted away from the wives of Naham, snatched up her veil, and ducked past the leather curtain to Yerakh's workroom.

Knowing that her sisters would check on her, Annah retrieved her grass bag from the corner and knelt with her back to the doorway. Struggling for self-control, she focused on the far corner of the workroom and caught her breath. There, against the wall of the workroom, was the grain offered to Yerakh by her beloved, stored in six impressively large, tightly coiled baskets. Someone had spilled some of the grain carelessly over the earthen floor, as if it meant nothing.

My beloved's work is wasted on people who despise his sacrifice, Annah thought. *I should be bringing wealth to his lodge. Instead, he's enriching Yerakh and the others for a nothing-creature like me.*

Annah shut her eyes. She would cry if she thought about her beloved, and she could not weaken, not with her sisters and the wives of Naham watching. *I have to calm myself,* she thought. *I'm in the workroom now; I can work.*

The bride-gold for Taphaph was untouched from yesterday. She could continue to beat it. Lifting her club,

Annah pounded a steady rhythm against the leather-draped heap of gold, as the wives of Naham peeked at her from the doorway.

"We don't need to guard her," Haburah announced, pulling the others away. "She's trained to stay here."

Alone, Annah contemplated all the time she had spent here over the years. This room had been terrifying in Yerakh's presence, yet comforting in his absence. And the gold was like a medicine to Annah, its brilliance and beauty distracting her from sorrow.

I can't give up the gold, she realized, pounding the heap of leather and membrane-clad gold. *Surely my beloved will allow me to teach our children to work the gold. But I need tools.*

She would be allowed to take nothing but what she could carry in her arms. *My father's tools haven't been touched since his death. Yerakh won't miss them. And I've earned them by all my work in the past twenty-five years. But how can I hide them?*

Keeping her face vacant, Annah set down her club and wandered into the main room, past her sisters and the wives of Naham. They were still picking through Parah's belongings, discussing them eagerly. Pretending indifference, Annah drifted over to the mat in front of her mother's now-empty storage chest and retrieved the oblong basket of cakes made by Naomi. Holding the basket, Annah wandered absently into the workroom again, eating one of the cakes along the way to make them believe she was still hungry.

For a time, she beat the bride-gold to lull her sisters. Then she tucked her club into the basket and swiftly, stealthily pulled her father's leather bag of tools from his storage chest in the far corner of the workroom. Quickly, Annah placed the heavy bundle inside the basket, covering it with her woven-grass bag, her veil, and the last of the cakes. Sensing her sisters approaching, she ate another grain cake, staring into nothingness.

"See," Ayalah said, "I told you she wouldn't run away. She's trained to be in the workroom at this time of day. And . . ." Ayalah faltered. "Usually I'ma is preparing the evening meal now. I forgot about the evening meal; we haven't prepared anything for Gammad, and he's never late for his food."

"Yerakh asked if I'd seen Gammad," Haburah said, sounding perplexed. "It's strange that we haven't seen him, today of all days. I thought Yerakh was going to give him a share of the animals from that fool-of-a-man."

"Gammad was quarreling with everyone last night," Shuwa sniffed.

Annah listened to them, swallowing, the spicy-sweet cake going down hard. *O Most High,* she thought, staring up at nothing beyond the grass-thatched roof of the workroom, *don't let Gammad be dead! There's been too much death in this family.* But she knew that he was dead. The numbness descended upon her again, and she welcomed it as a covering for her despair.

Breaking the sudden silence, Qetsiyah said, "I suppose we ought to cook something. What do you have?"

Their voices faded as they went into the storage area. Trying to shake off the mists of the numbness, Annah thought, *Yerakh, why couldn't you give Gammad fifty sheep, then banish him from the settlement? Why did you have to take his life? Will you ever be repaid for the harm you've done to others? But I can't consider these things now. If I do, I'll scream like a madwoman.*

Her thoughts clearing, she looked around the workroom. *This is the last time I will see this place. I won't miss it; except for the memory of my father.* Her gaze settled upon Naomi's beautiful, intricate oblong basket. *Thank you for making this basket, Naomi. I hope I'll be able to carry it away tonight without anyone inspecting it.*

Annah checked the five remaining grain cakes. They were too good to waste on anyone here. She would take them back to Naomi. *I'll learn to make these cakes,* she promised herself. *They must certainly be a favorite of my beloved's and his family.*

"Haburah!" Yerakh bellowed from the front entry of the lodge. "The animals are counted and separated. That fool will be coming soon. Is she ready?"

"She's in the workroom," Haburah answered indifferently.

Lie down, Annah told herself. She must not make Yerakh suspicious. What could be more innocent than a nap?

By the time she felt Yerakh's presence at the doorway of the workroom, she was curled up on her work mat, feigning sleep. Yerakh strode into the workroom and nudged her sharply in the rump with his foot. "Get up. Up!"

She sat up slowly, her gaze deliberately unfocused. It was not difficult to pretend that she was tired; her fears for Gammad had kept her awake half the night. *Murderer,* she thought to Yerakh as he crouched on the opposite side of the heap of leather-clad bride-gold. *Because of your greed, your father, your wife, your mother, and your brothers are dead. O Most High, repay him.*

As she thought these things, Annah practiced her vacant expression. Yerakh growled, disgusted. "Piece of wood! Let's cover your ugliness."

With the utmost delicacy, he rolled the top layer of leather away from the bride-gold. Then, holding his breath, he peeled the layer of pale, dried membrane away from the shimmering layer of beaten gold beneath.

It's perfect, Annah thought, aware of the gold from the edge of her vision. She had beaten it to a uniform thinness, so light and fragile that it would float on the merest breath. She remained slack and apparently mindless, breathing as shallowly as possible.

Still holding his own breath, Yerakh eased the exposed layer of gold—and its layer of supporting membrane—up off the remaining layers beneath. As he brought the gold up to the level of Annah's chin, he exhaled softly, steadily. The layer of gold lifted off the membrane, drifting upward into the air like glowing ash released from a fire. It flowed toward Annah, splitting and settling in curling, feather-light pieces on her oil-smoothed skin. Her hair, forehead, eyelids, nose, and cheeks were all gilded and shimmering. The remaining wisps of gold fell here and there, clinging to her oiled shoulders, her forearms, and her hands.

Gold purified by a murderer, she thought bitterly.

Yerakh grabbed Annah's wrists as if she were something noxious and set her hands on the edges of the basket containing her veil. "Carry that," he muttered. "And come. Do you understand? Come!"

Behaving as his trained creature, Annah lifted the basket, stood, and followed Yerakh into the main room of the lodge, where her sisters and the wives of Naham were arguing with each other loudly.

"Hush," Yerakh commanded. They hushed.

Then Ayalah giggled, as if struck by a thought. Swiftly, she approached Annah, snatched the five remaining cakes from the oblong basket in Annah's arms, and carried them back to Haburah and the wives of Naham. They were pleased. Even Haburah seemed amused. "Trust you to get out of work and trouble," she told Ayalah.

"I've saved us all!" Ayalah laughed, shoving the cakes into a dish.

"What are you four doing?" Yerakh demanded.

Before they could answer, a clamor arose from outside the lodge, in high, echoing cries of celebration. The men of the village were entering the lodge now, and Annah quivered. *He* was coming for her.

"Hold her!" Yerakh snapped. Obedient, Ayalah grabbed Annah's elbow and took her to stand beside Haburah. Annah stared at the floor.

You do not care, Annah reminded herself. *You are indifferent to everyone and everything. You will not look at him. Be a nothing-creature.*

Indirectly she observed the feet of the men, women, and children of the settlement coming into the lodge. A man, K'nan, stood behind Ayalah. She tittered, whispering to him.

"Ayalah!" Yerakh snarled. Ayalah stopped whispering. Now Shuwa, wife of Naham, darted away into the crowd. She returned quickly, dumping a heap of garments and gold-talismaned hair-bindings into the basket in Annah's arms.

I didn't want those, Annah thought, staring past the garments.

A wave of murmurs swept over the crowded lodge now; the feet of men, women, and children were moving, clearing a path. Three young men stood before Yerakh, and Annah listened with all her being as her beloved spoke, his voice calm and low.

"I am Shem of Those-Who-Carve-Wood. My brothers and I gave you payment as agreed. We have come for my wife."

"Welcome," Yerakh said, actually sounding cordial.

He lifted a hand and signaled to Haburah and Ayalah. They each took Annah by an elbow and propelled her forward.

Shem, Annah thought. *Appointed one. Or "to desolate." Which meaning is your true name, beloved?*

Haburah passed the clay dish of Naomi's cakes to Shem and his brothers. Slowly, they each took a cake, broke it, and ate a portion. Almost in unison, they hesitated, then quickly finished their cakes. Without a word, Shem offered his left hand to Annah. His fingers were long, capable, and callused. And he was taller than she had believed. She stared beyond him, unmoving. Ayalah tugged the basket from Annah, nudging her toward Shem. Yerakh reached down and lifted Annah's right hand, placing it in Shem's, palm to palm. Shem's fingers curled warm around her wrist. *Nothing,* Annah told herself. *You feel nothing.* To Ayalah, she thought, *Do not notice how heavy my basket feels. Think of K'nan instead.*

"I give you my sister," Yerakh said tersely. "May you have many children."

"Thank you for your kindness," Shem responded. Annah felt the quiet anger beneath his words. She prayed Yerakh would not notice, or care.

"Here," Ayalah whispered to Annah, pushing the basket at her, grabbing her left hand, forcing her to obey. "Take it."

Annah accepted the basket, grateful that Ayalah hadn't noticed its weight.

"We've been warned that you are in mourning," Shem told Yerakh politely. "Therefore, we'll leave you in peace."

"As you say," Yerakh agreed, amazingly courteous. Annah suppressed a dark smile. Yerakh wanted to be rid of Shem quickly, fearing he might renounce their bargain.

Gently, Shem took Annah's arm and guided her outside, followed by his brothers. As they stepped out beneath the rosy late-afternoon sky, Annah heard the other members of the settlement talking and laughing uproariously. Annah did not dare to look at her husband as they walked out of the settlement, toward the river.

Eleven

SHEM'S OLDER brother walked beside Shem and Annah as they made their way along the riverbank toward
the bridge. Quietly, without turning his head, he said,
"Shem, we're being followed by some men from the settlement."

Annah felt a wrenching, sinking movement in her
stomach. Seeming to comprehend her fear, Shem tightened his fingers around her arm, urging her onward.
Without missing a step or looking back, he asked, "How
many men?"

"Four."

"Is the giant with them?"

"No."

Annah sighed, relieved. If Naham was not with these
men, then Yerakh meant to let her go. *But why should any of
the men from the settlement care to follow us?* She didn't dare to

turn and look at them. Shem and his brothers had no weapons, unless they used her father's piercing awls and hammers, hidden in her basket.

"Should we challenge these men?" the younger brother whispered.

The older brother released a pent-up breath. "I say no. Others in the settlement might come after us. I say we cross the river and wait in the trees to see what they do."

"I agree," Shem replied. He lifted the basket from Annah's arms. She was grateful to him for this; the tools were heavy and her arms were aching. Despite her gratitude, she did not look at him. If these men from the settlement saw her looking at Shem or talking, they would certainly tell Yerakh.

Even now, Yerakh would come after us. And I would die rather than let my husband and his brothers suffer for my sake.

Shem and his brothers walked faster, hurrying Annah along. By the time they reached the bridge, she was panting. Mounting the wooden step to the bridge, she halted, eyeing the gently swaying ropes and cane pavings uneasily.

Shem bent, whispering, "Beloved, listen to me: between last night and this afternoon, we herded five hundred animals over this bridge. All crossed safely. Even my brothers survived crossing this bridge!"

Remember how Naomi almost ran across this bridge yesterday, she encouraged herself. *And as you hesitate, the men from the settlement are approaching.* Resolute, she trotted forward, her hands skimming the high, woven rope sides. Halfway across—without slackening her pace—she heard the roar of the current beneath the bridge. *I'm not as brave as Naomi,* Annah admitted. *I think I'll never care to do this again.* Her legs shook as she stepped off the bridge. Shem was just behind her, carrying the basket. Without words, he urged her up the bank and into the trees.

Breathless, Annah scurried into the lush undergrowth of a young cone-bearing tree and peered back at the bridge. Shem's brothers were just stepping onto the bank, their expressions wary. As her husband and his brothers hurried into the protective trees, Annah looked downriver at their pursuers, who had just reached the river bend.

K'nan! Why should you follow us? And Tseb-iy, she thought, enraged at the sight of his handsome, self-certain face. They were accompanied by Tseb-iy's father, Bachown, and by K'nan's brother, Dahar, a sulky, sly-eyed young man of perhaps forty. All four men stopped to stare at the bridge. *You had no idea this bridge existed, did you?* Annah thought to the four men, grimly pleased by their shock.

Tseb-iy turned to his father, flinging an arm toward the bridge, arguing. Bachown, proud, broad, and graying, pushed Tseb-iy aside and approached the bridge. By now, Dahar was disagreeing with K'nan, waving his hands wildly. K'nan ignored him, following Bachown instead.

"Why are they here?" Shem's younger brother demanded. "They have the sheep and the grain. They ought to be satisfied."

"Those men will never be satisfied," Shem answered softly.

Still watching the four men, Shem shifted the basket into his left arm and put his right arm around Annah's shoulders protectively. Acutely aware of his touch, Annah looked down at his fingers, curving warm around her gold-flecked right shoulder. It was strange to be embraced. She felt awkward and uncertain of the proper response.

Shouts arose from across the river. Tseb-iy was

screaming at his father, and Bachown—now at the bridge—screamed in response. At last Tseb-iy stomped away, heading toward the settlement. Dahar followed him. Bachown and K'nan talked briefly, then K'nan shook his head and turned away from the bridge. For an instant, Bachown stood at the entrance, obviously longing to pursue Shem and his brothers. Then he flung his hands up in frustration and followed Tseb-iy, K'nan, and Dahar back to the settlement.

Watching the four men retreating from the bridge, Shem's younger brother cackled gleefully. But Shem breathed out in a reverent whisper, "O Most High, thank You." He bent, kissing Annah's hair, speaking fiercely. "You are free of them!"

Annah pressed her hands to her mouth, trembling, amazed. *O Most High.* She had heard him say those words with her own ears. There would be no secrets to keep from her beloved. No fear of rejection. Helpless with relief, she began to cry. And once she started to cry, she could not stop. Her sorrow for her mother and her brothers—suppressed with such difficulty these past two days—welled up within her. Grief drove Annah to her knees as her sobs rose in agonized wails.

She was aware of Shem kneeling beside her, holding her, saying, "I know, beloved. This has all been too much, too quickly. But you're safe now."

Unable to respond, she simply leaned into his arms and cried. He held her, rocking her gently and stroking her hair until her sobbing eased. At last he said, "Come, beloved. I think you've frightened my brothers; they've gone ahead to warn my parents. They are expecting us."

Sighing shakily, Annah let him help her to her feet. She wiped her hands over her tear-streaked face, then stared blearily at her fingers. The gold glinted at her in a fine, lustrous powder. She grimaced. *I must look wretched. I hope I've cried all this gold off.*

"Don't worry," Shem told her, amused. "You still have plenty of gold all over your face and in your hair. For once, your brother was generous; he wanted to prevent me from seeing you." Serious now, Shem said, "If Yerakh had known the truth, he would have demanded all my grain and flocks for you. And I would have given him everything."

Annah looked up at him, astonished. Then she knew what to say, although she could barely speak above a whisper. "Thank you."

He smiled, compelling her to smile in return. He had glints of gold here and there on his mouth, his chin, and his cheeks; proof that he had been kissing her. Annah thought she should wipe all this evidence from his face, but she hesitated, embarrassed.

"Let it stay," he said, as if reading her thoughts. "My parents would be concerned if I didn't kiss you, today of all days."

He kissed her again, on the lips this time, then bent to pick up her basket. Taking her hand, he guided her up the path from the river. As they emerged from the shadows of the trees, Annah put up a hand to shield her eyes from the ruddy, lowering sun. "This way," Shem said.

Turning, Annah stopped, uncertain of what she saw. The lodge of his parents was of average size and situated in a smooth, level field. But it was utterly dominated by an enormous, darkened rectangular structure of wood behind it. *It's like a storage chest for a giant above all giants,* Annah thought, blinking, stunned. *Countless lodges would fit inside it!*

"That's the pen," Shem told her, perfectly calm, as if

153

all families had such overwhelming structures situated behind their lodges.

"The pen . . ." Annah faltered. "For keeping animals?"

"Eventually."

"But, why?"

"No one in your settlement has ever spoken of it?" Shem asked, surprised. "The men know it exists; it's one of the reasons my father isn't welcome in your settlement."

"No, I've never heard of it. But I spent most of my time avoiding the others. They do not talk to me."

"My father has been working on it since before he married my mother. And my brothers and I have helped him almost from the time we could walk. We'll show it to you later. Now, look over there." He motioned gently, toward the softly flowing fields west of his family's lodge. The distant fields were filled with sheep, tended by various herdsmen. "Those are our herds, and those men are my father's cousins. They come and go in our service depending on their moods and whether they are hungry or not. They aren't fond of us, so you won't see them too often. I know you'll be cautious, but if you see them coming, you should stay with my mother inside the lodge."

"Don't worry; I'll avoid them," Annah promised. The herdsmen of the settlement were fierce, independent men, avoided by all but their employers. She looked at the pen once more, trying to comprehend the reason for its existence.

Diverting her attention yet again, Shem balanced the basket in his hands, obviously curious. "What do you have in here? Something of metal?"

Annah pushed aside her shock at the sight of the pen and forced herself to think. *What do I have in that basket?* "Tools," she answered, remembering suddenly. "My father's gold-working tools."

Hearing this, Shem smiled, his face beautiful, captivating. "You work the gold?"

"Yes." In a whisper, she pleaded, "I can't give up working the gold. It's been one of my few comforts."

"I don't want you to give up working the gold." Shem kissed her hair and grinned. "If you give up working the gold, then who will teach our children? But come now. My parents are eager to welcome you, and I don't want them to worry."

Annah followed Shem into the peaceful main room of his family's lodge. Naomi embraced her, delighted. Then Shem's brothers introduced themselves, the older brother calling himself Yepheth, the younger brother giving his name as Khawm. Annah was too self-conscious to speak to them, but they didn't seem to care; they were relieved to be in their own lodge once more. And they were glad to frighten their mother, telling her of the four men who had pursued them from the settlement. While his brothers talked, Shem said, "Come meet my father."

By now Annah was anxious and overwhelmed, reverting to her habit of looking down at the floor—at the feet of others. The feet of Shem's father were work-hardened and stained here and there with what she presumed were wood resins. His hands also were stained and calloused.

He welcomed Annah kindly, bending to kiss her forehead. "Daughter," he said, his voice genial and completely sincere. "Welcome. Your husband has forgotten his manners: I am Noakh."

"Forgive my bad manners," Shem said to Annah. His

eyes sparkled; he seemed to be laughing at himself. "Dear wife, now that we are married, please, tell us your name."

She felt the blood rush to her face. Bracing herself, she explained, "When I was very young, I talked constantly and asked so many questions that my father called me Annah . . .'Oh now.' I've been called Annah ever since." Lowering her voice, she admitted, "I don't remember my true given name."

Noakh chuckled soothingly. "If it pleases you to be called Annah, my daughter, then we will call you Annah. If you would prefer another name, then that's for you to decide. But now, you must meet the father of my father. He wants to see the two of you."

The father of his father? Annah glanced up at Shem, incredulous. *Noakh was obviously vigorous, but he was not a young man. He has celebrated at least five kentums,* Annah thought. *He must surely be approaching his six hundredth year. How can the father of his father possibly be alive?*

"It's true," Shem whispered, as he led Annah to a finely woven reed partition. "His name is Methuwshelakh, but I call him 'Father of my Father.' He is 969 years old."

Annah did not quite believe Shem until he pulled her behind the partition. There, on a soft, thick pallet, beneath a light fleece cover, she saw the frailest wisp of an old man she could ever have imagined. Insubstantial, thin-skinned, with a fine down of silver hair, he didn't seem real. Yet he was breathing, slight, faint, rhythmic breaths. Annah watched Noakh kneel beside the old man, take his hand, and kiss him reverently on the cheek. As the old man stirred, on the verge of waking, Noakh motioned to Shem and Annah, silently urging them to kneel beside him.

"Father of my Father," Noakh said gently, "open your

eyes; Shem has brought his wife to meet you."

Methuwshelakh opened his eyes, blinking first at Noakh, then at Shem, and finally at Annah. After an instant of confusion, his soft, dark old eyes lit with understanding. "A wife . . ." he muttered almost dreamily. "A wife . . . for a son of my sons." He groped now, stretching out his dry, ancient fingers toward Shem. Smiling, Shem took his hand, kissing it, listening attentively as the old man lifted his feeble voice. "Now you will have joy . . . many children . . . blessings of years . . . and years."

"Eat with us tonight," Noakh urged Methuwshelakh.

The old man sighed and patted Shem's hands. After a brief pause, he said, "These children do not need . . . such an old man . . . at their wedding feast."

Annah loved his sweetness and his mild spirit. Hesitant, afraid she might be too bold, she covered his fragile hand with her own. "If you can, most ancient of men, please eat with us. I would be honored by your presence."

He looked at her mistily, sighing again. "Who can refuse . . . such an agreeable request?" To Noakh, he said, "Only for the meal . . . I will not be more of a burden."

Obviously delighted, Shem gathered Methuwshelakh into his arms as tenderly and easily as he would a young child. Noakh quickly lifted the old man's pallet and carried it to the center of the lodge.

By now Methuwshelakh was fully awake and bright-eyed, peering at Annah. "She wears bride-gold?" he asked Shem wonderingly. "Is she of wealth?"

"She's from the Lodge of the Tsaraph," Shem answered, carrying Methuwshelakh to his pallet, now arranged beside Noakh's mat at the hearth.

"The Tsaraph?" The old man's voice lifted in surprise. "What have you done . . . to deserve such a privilege . . .

from those who work the gold?"

"I consider myself blessed," Shem told him. As he spoke, he looked down at Annah, standing beside him. Deeply affected, she had to bite her lip to prevent more tears. To busy herself, she helped Naomi arrange extra pillows for Methuwshelakh's pallet so he could recline comfortably while eating.

Shem's father prayed and gave thanks to the Most High, then sat down with Methuwshelakh, spooning a broth of lentils to him, encouraging him to eat. Annah sat between Shem and Naomi during their meal, cherishing their company, listening more than eating.

Still elated by the day's events, Shem's brothers told their parents everything that had happened: coaxing the sheep across the bridge, listening to the men of the settlement quarrel, bathing in the river, then enduring the amazingly brief wedding ceremony. "That Yerakh couldn't wait to be rid of us," Khawm told his parents, as his brothers nodded and Annah smiled in agreement.

Shem looked at Annah now, raising one dark eyebrow. "I am curious . . . those cakes your sisters offered us in your lodge . . . they tasted just like I'ma's cakes."

"They did," Khawm agreed as Yepheth nodded. "But how could those cakes have been I'ma's?"

"My sisters forgot to prepare food to offer you," Annah confessed, mortified. "I was guarding the last of your mother's cakes and her beautiful basket. I couldn't bear to leave them in the settlement. But my sisters remembered the cakes and took them from me. They didn't care that you would eat cakes from your own lodge during your visit."

Now Yepheth actually smiled, his stern features becoming pleasant. And he spoke, his voice low and thoughtful. "Then, because we ate none of their food beneath their roof, we have no obligations to the Lodge of Yerakh."

As pleased as her sons, Naomi patted Annah's hands. "Thank you, child, for saving my basket. It is good to know that my sons are not obligated to your brother. And if they're not obligated, then neither am I." She jerked her chin emphatically, saying, "Do you agree, my dear one?"

"I agree, beloved. Truly, the Most High has saved us from evil." Noahk paused in feeding his grandfather to study Annah. His eyes were so kind.

Annah wanted to smile at him, but began to cry instead. Shem touched her arm, distressed. They all hushed, looking at her. Even the fragile Methuwshelakh noticed her tears.

"Why should she cry?" Methuwshelakh asked worriedly.

Annah managed a smile and wiped her face with her hands. The wretched bride-gold was all over her fingers. Recovering, she turned to Naomi. "When I spoke to you at the river yesterday, I was so afraid that you would reject me . . . I didn't tell you everything that happened at the lodge of the Nachash."

The word "Nachash" caught the attention of Shem's entire family. They stared at her, wide-eyed and unmoving. "Did you tell them everything?" Annah asked Naomi.

"Yes," Naomi answered softly, her eyes dark and anxious. "My husband and sons were so angry that they began to herd the sheep toward your settlement last night. They wanted you to be free as soon as possible. But tell us what you could not tell me yesterday."

Shem took Annah's hand, clearly wanting her to look at him, but she looked at Noakh instead; unlike Shem and

Naomi, Noakh was perfectly serene. "When I saw the Nachash holding my stillborn brother, I hated her for demanding his life. I hated her so fiercely that she sensed my presence and screamed at me, asking if I would accuse her before the Most High. Then I knew; the Most High is not a story. And I knew—as the enemy of the Nachash— He would welcome me. When my brother's wife, Iltani, came after me with the knife, I called to the Most High."

Overcome, Annah stopped. Taking a deep breath, she continued shakily, "I had not spoken aloud since the death of my father. And when I called to the Most High, I could barely hear my own voice. But He heard me. I fell into the grass, face down—all my breath gone. I was sure I would die! I waited for Iltani to stab me with the knife. But she ran by me. She should have sensed me, but she didn't."

"The Most High covered you with His presence!" Noakh exulted, almost spilling the dish of lentil broth on the bewildered Methuwshelakh.

Unable to speak, Annah nodded agreement. Beside her, Naomi was weeping. But Shem laughed, pulling her into his arms and kissing her hair. Annah felt tears spilling down her cheeks. She thought she would never finish crying. Shem consoled her, whispering, "Annah, beloved . . . shhh. I think you need some time to rest and to mourn. Listen: stay here with my mother and rest for a few days. That will give me time to prepare a place for the two of us; then I will come for you."

Annah stared at him, fearful. "Won't I see you?"

He grinned, as mischievous as his younger brother, Khawm. "Don't worry; I'll be here at every meal."

Her grass bag in her lap, Annah began to pick her precious shell carving out of its secret pouch. She felt better this morning. Rested. And lulled by the peace in the lodge of Noakh. *I've been here since yesterday evening and I haven't heard one quarrel in this place*, she realized, freshly amazed, looking around.

Sunlight warmed the main room of the lodge, while Methuwshelakh dozed in his sheltered pallet behind the woven reed screen. She could hear Naomi in the storage area, humming—music from the heart of a contented woman. *Will I be like her one day?* Annah wondered. She hoped she would be as happy as Naomi.

But the fears bred within her over the past twenty-five years continued to affect all her actions. During the morning meal, she had to remind herself that she could look at Shem and his family and speak to them without fear of punishment. And she felt almost naked without her veil. Her fingers twitched with the urge to snatch it from her basket, but she fought the impulse. She wanted to prove to herself that she could live without its protection.

Pressing her lips together, Annah forced herself to concentrate on her precious shell carving. She picked out a few more stitches and found the leather cord. Triumphant, she eased the shell carving out of her grass bag. *I'd forgotten how pretty it is*, she thought, admiring its luminous pink and blue glow and its pierced, curl-carved edges. Delighted, she kissed the carving, pulled the cord over her head, and swept her hair off her neck. *Now*, she thought, *I can use my comb!*

She found the carved, scented wooden comb still in its leather pouch and untied the knots holding it within the bag. Naomi's gift of tools for handwork also was in the bag. Annah spread these out, studying them while she combed her hair. The flat wooden needles and the cutting blade would be perfect for making garments for Shem and their children. Meanwhile, the old tunic she wore now, and the newer tunic from her mother's storage chest would be sufficient.

"You can also use those to make baskets," Naomi said, coming in from the storage area. She carried a large, flat basket stacked with dishes of beans, edible tubers, bulbs, dried fruits, nuts, grain cakes, and spices and herbs.

"Please, teach me to make baskets," Annah begged Naomi. "Once I stopped speaking no one taught me anything except ordinary work. And I want to learn from you; your baskets are more beautiful than any in the settlement."

"Baskets are like everything else," Naomi said. "A lot of time and a little skill. With practice, you will do very well." She set down her burden and handed Annah a dish of cakes, dried fruits, and nuts. "Here; these are yours. And don't tell me you're not hungry; you are too thin. Between last night and this morning, I saw how you don't eat. A bite of this and a pinch of that won't do!"

Not daring to argue, Annah tucked her comb into her bag and reached for the dish of food. Some of the fruit was sweet, some tart, and the cakes and nuts were crisp—a perfect match to the sweetness of the fruit. She decided she was hungry after all. As she ate, she watched Naomi prepare the midday meal.

"May I help you?" Annah asked, wanting to be useful. "Do you need more water from the well?" By now she had discovered that Noakh and his family had their own wells: a distant one for the herds, and one behind the lodge for Naomi's convenience. This was a luxury. All the lodges in the settlement shared two wells. And Annah, a mindless-nothing-female, had never been trusted to carry water. Now she longed to do that task, to be considered trusted and normal.

"Finish eating," Naomi scolded mildly. "You are supposed to be resting today, not working. You'll be tired of well water soon enough."

"Mother of my Husband," Annah began tentatively, "if you have wells for water, why do you use the river so often?"

Smiling, Naomi said, "We rarely go to the river. The first day my son saw you, he and his brother decided they would enjoy using the river to soak the fibers for ropes. Of course it was the will of the Most High that my son see you there; we know that now."

"Oh." Annah blinked, grateful, but wondering at the will of the Most High. Why should He notice her?

Using a thin, fine metal blade, Naomi peeled the bulbs and edible tubers, humming beneath her breath until a sharp whistle sounded from outside the lodge. Her dark eyebrows lifted. "That's Noakh. Something's wrong."

Annah scrambled to her feet, clutching her food. Noakh entered the lodge, raising his grizzled eyebrows at his wife. "We have visitors from the settlement." He turned to Annah. "Child, please go look through the lattice in the storage room and tell us who these people are. Why should they visit us twenty-two years after forbidding us to enter their lands?"

Sick with dread, Annah went into the storage room and peered through the lattice of the far wall. In the distance, she saw one man and two women. Bachown, Tsillah, and Taphaph. Slowly, Annah faced Noakh and Naomi, who had followed her. "They are Bachown and

Tsillah and their daughter, Taphaph. My brother, Yerakh, wants Taphaph as his wife. But I think her parents would rather have you offer grain and sheep for her, as you offered them for me. That's why those men pursued us yesterday, and why Bachown and Tsillah are coming to visit you now. I'm sure Tsillah will offer Taphaph to Yepheth or Khawm."

Fingering his beard thoughtfully, Noakh said, "Then Yerakh will make trouble for us if we take his beloved. We must be rid of this family without giving offense."

"I wish you could tell them that you've chosen wives for Yepheth and Khawm," Annah whispered, deeply distressed, hugging her bowl of food.

"That would be a lie," Naomi sighed.

But Noakh's eyes shone, suddenly mischievous. "Thank you, daughter, for your concern. Now listen; go out the back of our lodge to the pen. Don't be afraid, but run up inside that big door and hide there. We will come for you when this family is gone."

Annah offered the dish of cakes, fruits, and nuts to Naomi, but Naomi flapped her hands vigorously. "No, take it with you; I expect you to eat it all by the time our guests have departed. Hurry. And don't spill your food!"

Impossible! Annah thought. But she slapped one hand over the food and scurried out the back of the lodge. She heard Noakh chuckling as she ran.

Twelve

ANNAH PAUSED to summon her courage before approaching the formidably vast structure her husband and father-in-law called the pen. The door of the pen was actually a long ramp of dense, multilayered wood stretching from the ground up to the inner level of the structure. Each layer and surface of the ramp was permeated with hardened black resins. Annah stepped on the ramp, testing its feel with her bare foot; it was warm, smooth, rock-solid, and not at all sticky. Reassured, she trotted up the ramp, her toes gripping the narrow holds built into the surface of the wood.

Reaching the top of the ramp, she crept inside the pen, wondering if Bachown or Tsillah and Taphaph had seen her. *Not that it matters if they did,* she thought defiantly. She resented their intrusion into the lodge of Noakh. Why had she believed she could be rid of the members of the settlement just by crossing a river? *O Most High,* she begged, *please make them go away peaceably!*

As her eyes adjusted to the filtered light inside the pen, Annah forgot about Bachown, Tsillah, and Taphaph. To her left and her right were endless rows of wooden stalls of varying heights and widths, built in orderly formations throughout this level of the pen. Each row of stalls was separated by long rows of what appeared to be covered water troughs. The trough covers were cut open at carefully spaced intervals, to allow the would-be occupants to drink comfortably. Above, long resin-blackened reed pipes hung suspended by ropes from the rafters; the ends of these pipes were jointed and turned downward— seeming ready to spill water into the troughs at any time. There were also open bins beneath each trough—feed bins, Annah decided. At the rear of each row of stalls, shallow gutters were built into the floor, as if to catch and contain animal waste. Annah frowned at these.

Do they really plan to keep their animals here? she wondered, perplexed. *This pen is too elaborate for that, and these different-sized stalls don't make sense.* Her feet pattering over the bare floor, she inspected large baskets and tall bins, also placed at convenient intervals near the stalls. These held an overwhelming abundance of coarse grains, seeds, pellets, dried fruits and vegetables, oddly dark grain cakes, twigs, dense bundles of bark, and countless varieties of dried grasses, leaves, and pine needles—all weighted by stones to pack them down tight within their containers.

Seeing this abundance, Annah remembered her dish of food. Randomly pushing the fruits, nuts, and bits of grain cake into her mouth, she chewed avidly while exploring several large herding areas. Apparently, these would allow selected animals freedom from the stalls. *As if they won't go outside,* Annah thought. There were also numerous large cages—barred with metal and built against the walls—completely separated from the more open stalls. Annah touched one of the chilling metal bars, baffled. *Why metal?*

Turning from the barred cages, she studied the far walls of the pen. Here she found endless rows of stacked reed cages. Each cage had its own slanted board beneath, to propel animal wastes into long communal pits behind the cages. *These cages are for very small animals,* Annah decided. *And there are hundreds of them. Why should my father-in-law and my husband keep small animals of no practical use?*

Curious, Annah approached the ramp near the center of the pen. This ramp led upward into the next level. Near it was a rail, guarding an opening in the floor. *Another ramp leading downward,* Annah realized. *There are three levels. Why?*

Annah crept up the ramp to the higher level. Here she paused, sucking in her breath, awed. This level was much brighter, lit by a high, double row of raised, continuously roofed, open-shuttered windows, which extended the entire center-length of the pen's gradually peaked ceiling. The clear, restful pink of the sky and the distant calls of birds filtered through the windows; Annah admired them while she finished her snack. Full now, she explored the upper level.

There were more cages and bins here. Annah gaped at the enormous netted enclosures at each end, hung with countless dried tree branches and more water pipes. *These are beyond understanding,* she told herself, gazing at the massive netted enclosures. *I'm sure I don't want to know their purpose.* Near the enclosures, Annah noticed ladders built into the wall. The ladders, stout and sturdy, extended to

167

the high windows and also descended through the floor, accessing the lower levels.

Reluctant to try the ladders, Annah retreated, still exploring the upper level. She discovered several small cubicles built into the walls, equipped with open-holed seats—waste pits for humans. There were also four comfortably spaced rooms in this upper level, set far apart from each other like a vast lodge. *Does my husband's family intend to abandon their lodge and live here?* Annah wondered. *There is no other explanation for all these supplies. Even so, why should they keep so many types of animals and foods? Have they stored food for themselves too?*

Suspicious now, she eyed row after row of large, coiled storage baskets; the same sort of storage baskets her beloved had used to convey his payments of grain to Yerakh. *But there are so many more baskets here,* Annah thought, stupefied. *It will take years to eat all this food.* She peeked into basket after basket, bin after bin. All of them were filled with grains, beans, spices, dried fruit cakes, dried vegetables, gourds, dried olives, huge quantities of seeds, nuts, and—to her amazement—large clay jars of oil and wooden vats of honey. There were also large quantities of dried honeycombs. In addition, many bins contained scented resins and huge stacks of dried, fragrant wood, obviously intended for burning. Wondering, Annah looked for the hearth.

She found it just beyond the ramp—a small hearth, encircled by stones lined, paved, and mortared with clay. Oddly, the sight of the hearth shocked her. She sat beside it, staring, trying to make sense of this entire pen; it had no logical, normal explanation. Annah bit her lip, thinking, *Perhaps my husband's family is more than a little strange.*

As she sat beside the hearth, staring, she heard footsteps

coming up the ramp. Not Naomi's quick, brisk footsteps, but the calm, deliberate footsteps of Noakh. *Why?* She thought to him, sensing his quiet presence. *Why?*

He emerged from the ramp and turned, obviously sensing her near the hearth. His face was peaceful, but somber, as if he knew she would question him. Slowly, he approached the hearth and sat a proper distance away, facing her.

"It's safe for you to leave now, if you wish, child," he said, giving her the option of a swift retreat to the normality of the lodge. His eyes were gentle and dark, like Shem's, and he smiled—a patient, waiting smile. He seemed willing to answer any questions she wished to ask.

"Father of my Husband," she began hesitantly. "Why? This pen doesn't make sense. Why all these supplies and this hearth?"

He released his breath quietly, gazing up at the long row of windows, contemplating his answer. At last he looked at her. "Child, do you love your husband?"

Startled, she said, "Yes." *Why do you ask?*

"How much do love your husband?" Noakh persisted. "How would you measure your love?"

A measure of my love? Pondering this, Annah remembered her first glimpse of Shem at the river: the intensity of his eyes, the sunlight shining on the darkness of his hair. She could still feel the shock of realizing that he would not hesitate to follow her into the river; it was nothing to him then—or now—to risk his life for her sake. Drawing on this memory, she said, "I would give my life to save my husband's life."

Noakh smiled approvingly. "That is the true answer of love. But what if your husband turned against you? What if he ignored your words and despised your love and your beauty? What if he actually laughed in your face and spoke of you with scorn and contempt when from the beginning you have only wished to share with him the treasures of your innermost heart?"

Annah felt the blood draining from her face, unable to imagine such a possibility. Swallowing, she said, "I would try to reason with him and be patient and hope his feelings might change."

"What if you gave him years upon years of perfect love and patience, and he refused to change? What then? What if his feelings turned to violence against you and against the people and the things you love? What if his hatred began to destroy things that were precious to you? What if he began to destroy the lives of others? What then? Would you finally feel compelled to turn from him and seek another way?"

"Yes, but . . . Shem wouldn't . . . ."

"He wouldn't," Noakh agreed, smiling sympathetically. "But this is how men have turned against the perfect love of the Most High." Serious, Noakh pursed his lips, his long work-stained fingers smoothing his graying beard. "Now, daughter, think of when you go out to the fields and the trees, where the animals and birds live. You sense them and they sense you. They know if you're pleased and if you're angry. Am I right?"

Annah considered the reactions of the birds, the field mice, the fruit-eaters, and even the fish. "When I'm happy and at peace, they come to me. When I'm angry, they become agitated. They flee."

Noakh nodded. "This is how the Most High created them: to respond to man. This is how He also created man and the earth. When man is at peace with himself and with the Most High, then the earth itself is at peace.

When man is full of violence and shuns all good—including the Most High—then the earth, too, is corrupted and given to violence."

Annah shivered, the first hints of horror gripping her. "Then the earth shakes."

"The shaking of the earth is only the beginning," Noakh answered gently. "Tell me, daughter, have you met any man, woman, or child in the settlement—ever—who has called upon the Most High, and who has not been filled with rage, but with lovingkindness?"

"No." She could not help staring at her father-in-law.

"Nor have I. Through the years I've met countless people, in your settlement and far beyond. None will believe in the Most High. And none call on the Most High who loves them, though I've tried to reason with them, to warn them. I tried to warn the people of your settlement years before you were born."

Annah frowned. "Warn them? Of what?"

Taking a deep breath, Noakh said, "Because of the violence and evil of mankind, the earth will turn upon itself with violence, bursting open, creating a great flood—the most horrible destruction! No creature that draws breath through its nostrils will be left alive on the earth. Only those sheltered in this pen will be saved."

Unable to comprehend such devastation, Annah blinked.

Noakh smiled at her reaction. "This is why my sons and I built this pen. This oversized storage chest is constructed as the Most High commanded. This is how He has chosen to save those of us who love and obey Him."

"But," Annah protested, "if the Most High created the earth, then can't He restore it? Can't He prevent the earth from turning upon itself?"

"Child, listen." Shaking his head firmly, Noakh said, "Understand me. For almost one hundred and twenty years now, it is only the merciful hand of the Most High that has prevented the earth from turning upon itself. He has extended every sign of love to men, but men despise Him. He has granted them all these years of mercy to give them the chance to turn toward Him again—away from the violence of their desires—to prevent this destruction. But they laugh and deny His very existence. He grieves, child. Soon, He will be compelled to lift His hand from the earth. Yet, He will be merciful; some day, He will send us the Promised One to bring us into harmony with Him."

"The Promised One?"

"Child, what stories do you remember of Adam and his Havah, Mother of All?"

"I know that Adam and Havah were tempted by that Serpent, then forced from the Garden of Adan by the Most High because they neglected His commands," Annah offered, uncertain.

Noakh's mouth twitched in reluctant amusement. "There is more to the story, child—and one day you will be able to recite it in whole. But, simply told . . . after the rebellion in Adan, the Most High promised that one day a man born of woman will crush our Adversary, that Serpent adored by the Nachash and her whisperers."

Annah leaned forward, pleased that the Serpent—and possibly the Nachash—would be crushed. "May I ask one more question? Who will be this Promised One? How will we recognize him?"

"Two questions!" Noakh teased. "But listen, daughter. This Promised One will make himself known at the proper time as one of the sons of my son Shem. We will recognize him by his unfailing love and obedience toward the Most High—and because he will restore us to harmony with the Most High, as it was in Adan."

Taken aback, Annah struggled to form the words, "Then one of the sons of my husband . . . a child I will bear . . ."

"Will be—or be a father of—the Promised One," Noakh finished quietly.

"But I'm a nothing."

"Am I any better?" asked Noakh, smiling. "No one, daughter, including me, deserves anything but punishment from the Most High. But He loves us enough to send the Promised One. Who are we to argue?"

"We don't deserve such mercy," Annah murmured, overwhelmed. Wondering, she said, "You went to the settlement before I was born. You spoke to the men there. Did you see my father and tell him all this?"

Looking away, Noakh said, "When the Most High warned me of the coming destruction, I also knew that I should marry my beloved, Naomi. Our mothers had spoken to one another many, many years before." Smiling faintly now, gazing up at the high windows, Noakh said, "It is not a pleasing or flattering thing for a woman to be kept waiting by her pledged husband. And I confess, I did keep her waiting far too long: Her childbearing years were almost gone. To soothe her feelings, I sought out a renowned goldsmith: Zahar of the Tsaraph. I asked him to create a pair of bracelets for her; gold is soothing to the heart of the wearer."

Annah nodded in silent agreement. She didn't like it that her father-in-law was avoiding her gaze.

Noakh hesitated. "I spoke to your father, child. He was a kind man. He listened politely when I spoke of the

Most High. Then he spoke of the gold."

When her father-in-law fell silent, Annah realized that there was no more to tell. Her father had rejected the Most High. Her throat and eyes burning, her chin quivering, Annah said softly, "My father was merely polite to you. I'm sorry. Undoubtedly . . . he would have also scorned me."

Noakh sat looking down at his hands, his brow troubled, his mouth working this way and that. Annah could not bear his distress. She choked down her tears. "Thank you. At least I know you spoke to him."

Noakh looked up, and Annah was astonished to see telltale glints of moisture in his dark eyes. Smiling mournfully, he said, "I've had countless men, women, and children laugh at me, spit on me, turn their backs on me. . . . It was nothing compared to having to tell you this now. And, excepting my wife and sons, you are the first ever to listen to me or to question me without mockery. Thank you, daughter."

Annah wiped her face, sighing ruefully. "I should stop asking questions. I rarely like the answers, even when I agree with them." Hearing footsteps, quick and certain on the ramp, Annah turned. Shem appeared, his hair in damp, wild curls as if he had recently emerged from the river. The very sight of him revived her.

Seeing Annah, he lifted his eyebrows, obviously concerned: *Are you well?*

She nodded faintly, motioning with her hands: *Thank you.*

His answering smile was radiant. As he approached, she gazed at him, enraptured. *How I've missed you! No man alive can compare to you.*

Glancing at Noakh, Shem said, "I'ma sent me. She

said you are both so late for the midday meal that if you delay any longer it will be evening and she won't bother to cook again today."

"Then we must hurry," Noakh answered agreeably. "I like my evening meal at the proper time."

Shem helped Annah to her feet and kissed her. She sighed, welcoming the warmth of his touch.

Noakh watched them, his eyes gleaming, amused. "Yes, help your pretty young wife to her feet, my son, and forget that your father is an old man."

Laughing, Shem pulled his father to his feet and kissed him. Noakh pretended to scoff. "Bah!"

Outside the pen, with the sunlight touching her face, Annah remembered Bachown, Tsillah, and Taphaph. *I prayed that the Most High would make them go away*, she thought, fearful of her own selfishness. *Now, it seems that He will. But when?*

⚓ ⚓

Naomi was indignant. "That Tsillah is a proud, rude woman! And her daughter is no better. I wouldn't have Taphaph in my lodge for anything in the world. She *sulked*, child. And she made such a face at her mother that I was amazed her mother lived. Here now, eat; Yepheth and Khawm left a little."

Naomi uncovered the clay dishes containing the remnants of the midday meal: flat cakes of parched grain, olives, a thick paste of spiced beans, and boiled, mashed tubers, delicately seasoned with precious salt.

"I'm sorry they were rude to you, Mother of my Husband," Annah said, eyeing the tubers uncertainly—Parah had always left tubers whole.

"Don't apologize for them. It's not your fault they were rude."

"What did you tell them, I'ma?" Shem asked, spreading bean paste on his flat grain cake.

Naomi knelt beside Noakh, patting his hand fondly. "At the suggestion of your father, I told them that the wives of Yepheth and Khawm have been chosen and we are waiting for them." Shem's eyebrows lifted teasingly. Naomi became stubborn. "It's true! The Most High knows who the wives of your brothers are, and we *are* waiting for Him to bring them to us. But even if it had been a lie— may the Most High forgive me—I would have said anything to keep that Taphaph out of my lodge and away from my sons."

Turning to Annah, Naomi said, "I can guess how she would treat you, daughter! We'll have no women from that settlement in this lodge. Here, child, eat some more." Naomi scooped some of the mashed, seasoned tubers onto a flat, parched grain cake and presented it to Annah. "Don't worry about being too tidy; after years upon years of watching these men eat, you can't possibly disgust me."

Annah ate self-consciously, certain that Shem was just waiting for her to drop her food so he could tease her. But she finished the cake and the mashed tubers neatly. And she liked them enough that she wanted more, which pleased Naomi. "It's the olive oil and salt, and some of the savory bulbs," she explained. "Not pretty, but good."

Later, when Noakh went to work in the pen, Shem took Annah's hand. "Come, walk with me to the edge of the trees."

When Annah hesitated, Naomi shooed her off kindly. "Go with your husband." But she scolded Shem. "Remember, she is supposed to rest today."

"I haven't forgotten, I'ma," Shem promised. Lowering his voice, he added, "Though I'd like to." His tone of intimacy brought a rush of warmth to Annah's face. Shem led her out into the daylight, beneath the low, soft-pink sky. They walked together in silence, then Shem asked, "Did my father tell you why we built the pen?"

Reluctantly, she said, "He told me that the earth will be destroyed. I think I believe him."

"It's all I've ever known," Shem explained. "I've always accepted it as the truth. But I suppose, to anyone else, the thought of such a flood—such destruction—would be more than they'd want to believe."

"I don't *want* to believe that the earth could turn upon itself, but your father is right; the earth is filled with violence. Ever since those first tremors, I've been wondering what could be strong enough to shake the earth."

Shem exhaled, sounding relieved. "At least you've been wondering. None of the other people we've met seem to care. They all mock us."

They turned onto the path leading down to the river. Birds sang from every direction, while ground hens, lizards, and rodents skittered around them. A snake, tawny and black, undulated over the path. Edging closer to her husband, Annah said, "Your father told me that he went to the settlement and spoke to the men there."

Shem nodded. "Yes, when my father heard that Yerakh had murdered your father."

Annah halted, staring at him. "He didn't mention my father's murder. When did he go to the settlement to speak of my father's murder?"

"Twenty-two years ago. Didn't you know? That's when they banished him."

"I didn't know." *Twenty-two years ago,* Annah thought.

Three years after the murder. That year, I began to make the veil. Aloud, she asked, "What did your father say to the men in the settlement about my father's murder?"

"He reminded them that murder was an offense to the Most High. He asked for justice on behalf of your father. Yerakh and that *Nephiyl*—that giant—shouted him down, and all the men took him out of the village. They brought him to this side of the river, destroyed his river craft, and threatened him with death if he ever returned."

"I'm amazed they didn't kill him. But how did he hear of my father's death?"

"A food trader borrowed my father's river craft to cross over to the settlement. When he came back, he told my father of the murder. At that time, I believe it was just hearsay. I think my father's visit somehow confirmed the rumors; that's why Yerakh was so angry and afraid."

"Then someone did demand justice. I never heard a word of it. But at that time, Yerakh had me imprisoned in the workroom during his waking hours. He wanted to be sure I wasn't a speaking, thinking creature—a threat."

"You're free of him now." Shem pulled her close, hugging her as they walked again. "Let's not talk about Yerakh or the settlement anymore. Listen, next week I have to return to the fields and help my brothers. But I think, in two days or so, I'll have your dwelling place ready. Will you come with me then?"

Annah was amazed that he would even ask. She was his wife; he could command her as he pleased. But her husband and his family were not like other people. "When you have everything ready," she agreed.

By now they had reached the edge of the trees. Shem led her into the shade, out of sight of his family. There, without a word, he enfolded her in his arms and kissed her, tenderly, passionately, thoroughly. Annah clung to him, shaken, yet elated by the dizzying rush of feelings his kiss evoked.

Before she could recover from this, he lifted her up and swung her around like a child at play, kissing her again, making her gasp before he set her down. "I can't believe you're here," he said, his eyes sparkling. "I look at you, and all I can think of is that I love you! I've loved you from that first instant I saw you at the river, and as long as I live, Annah, that will never change."

Suddenly shy, Annah was unable to speak; she couldn't even look at him.

Touching her face with his work-roughened hands, Shem said, "Never be afraid of me, Annah. You're my dearest friend on earth. No one else will know me the way you know me. Above all"—Shem bent, making her look at him—"I need you to talk to me."

"It's still too strange," she confessed. "I've forgotten what it's like to talk freely, to touch and be touched . . . to allow myself to look at others." She dared to caress his face, warm and rough with unshaven whiskers. "I do love you. But you'll have to remind me not to behave as if I'm still wearing the veil."

"Gladly." Smiling, he kissed her again, lightly this time. "I'd better finish my work. And I'ma will be looking for you."

Annah took his hand, reminding herself to look up at him. "Shem, this destruction of the earth . . . does your father know when it will happen?"

His smile faded. "We don't know the exact day. When I first met you, it was about one year. Now we have perhaps eight or nine months. But the true indication will be the life span of the father of my fathers.

Have you considered his name?"

Annah hesitated. Like so many others, Methuwshelakh's name held a twofold meaning. Spoken one way, he was called Man-of-the-Darts. This had been Annah's interpretation, until now. Methuwshelakh's other, less obvious name, was He-Who-Departs-before-the-Waters. Annah caught her breath.

"You understand now," Shem said quietly. "When he is gone, the waters will come."

Thirteen

PROPPED UP on his pallet behind the woven reed screen, Methuwshelakh watched, bright-eyed, as Annah opened her father's leather tool bag. She pulled out the tools one by one, staring at them, wondering if they had been touched since her father's murder.

As she showed the tools to the ancient man, Annah kept a mental inventory, noting piercing awls, a tapering iron cylinder—used to make rings—scrapers, flat and curved working blades, hammers, pincers, wedges, and grooved rods for fashioning chains. There were also chisels.

Delighted, she held them up to Methuwshelakh. "These are carving tools! I can make my own molds and forms for casting and shaping the gold. My father had so many tools. No wonder they were so heavy." Her elation faded as she stared at them.

It will be years before I learn to use all these tools properly, she thought, dismayed. *But I know I can do this. I just have to be patient and practice.*

Puckering his thin, lined lips, Methuwshelakh studied the tools. Tremulous, he said, "You need more than . . . these tools . . . to work the gold."

Annah nodded. "I need a refiner's pit, wooden forms, stone forms, salts to separate the impurities, and hides to protect the gold while beating it." She frowned in disgust. "I forgot to bring my leather mitts."

Methuwshelakh released a snorting laugh. "Ha! The bride can't . . . mar her hands! You have . . . nothing else?"

To prove to the ancient man that nothing remained in the bag, Annah turned it over. There *was* something inside. Four plump, glistening pebbles of gold and a small leather bag fell out. Annah touched the gold and the bag in disbelief.

"Open it!" Methuwshelakh flapped one fragile hand toward the small bag, curious as a child.

Annah emptied it into the palm of her hand. It held another hoard of gold. Some had been clipped from the edges of previously worked items, but most of it was in natural pebbles. In addition, Annah found a bent talisman, cut from a hair binding.

"Humph," Methuwshelakh grunted. "Now . . . you have gold . . . to pound!"

Studying Methuwshelakh, Annah realized that he was indeed proud to have a son of his sons marry a woman from a Lodge of the Tsaraph. She didn't deserve such regard. Gold work was no more important than any other labor. But if it pleased this most ancient man to know that she worked gold, then she was glad.

As she inspected her small hoard of gold, Methuwshelakh watched her, his eyes becoming distant. He was falling asleep. Quietly, Annah slipped the loose gold into the pouch, then put her tools away, sensing Naomi's approach.

"Child," Naomi whispered, "you need to prepare yourself and gather whatever you need for tonight."

Motioning her thanks, Annah smiled at Naomi, then tipped her head toward the dozing Methuwshelakh.

Naomi nodded her understanding and returned to the hearth, while Annah gathered her tools and crept out from behind Methuwshelakh's sheltering screen. Softly, she knelt beside Naomi, who was patting out the spiced, scented dough Annah remembered from her wedding day. "Mother of my Husband, please, let me help you make these cakes."

Still forming the cakes with her oiled hands, Naomi smiled. "Next time, child, you can make them all yourself! I'll be glad to let someone else do this. But not today: This is a wedding feast, and you are the bride. Now, please, go do whatever you need to do to prepare for this evening."

Annah hesitated. "I've been thinking . . ."

"And?" Naomi paused, raising one dark eyebrow.

Lowering her head, Annah said, "A blessing from Yerakh is more like a curse; my marriage ceremony didn't feel like a marriage ceremony. Would it be improper to ask the father of my husband to bless us tonight?"

Chuckling, her fingers coated with sweet oil and dough, Naomi gave Annah a brief, awkward hug. "I will speak to my husband, child, but I'm sure he will be delighted to give you his blessing tonight—he would have anyway. Now, go wash your hair and rest, or do as you please. Go. No, wait! Take these." Snatching up a small dish, Naomi shook some roasted nuts into Annah's hands. "Eat."

Obedient, Annah scooped up her grass bag and hurried out into the late-morning sunshine, eating the nuts quickly. She had already decided that she would go down to the river and wash her hair, following the custom of the women from the settlement. On her way to the river, she unearthed some pink-flowered stalks from a clump of cleansing plants. When rinsed and thoroughly beaten, the stalks, leaves, and roots of the cleansing plant produced a froth used by all the women of the settlement for scrubbing their hair and skin. At the river's edge, Annah found a flat stone and rinsed and pounded the plants.

As she worked, she glanced at the opposite riverbank. *Was I on that bank only a few days ago? It seems like a bad dream. This is like a good dream, and I don't want to wake up. I wonder if Yerakh has given Haburah to Naham.* Annah shivered. *You killed Gammad, I know you did,* she thought to Naham. *Where did you hide his body? If I know you, Naham, you hid it where you didn't have to work at breaking the earth.*

Annah slowed her beating of the cleansing plant, appalled. *O Naham, you buried Gammad's body in the waste pit with Iltani. Then you hurried off to laugh with Yerakh. You are less than animals, both of you!* Furious, she beat the cleansing plant into green-flecked foam. *I hope your killing price of fifty sheep pleases you, Naham. I hope those fifty sheep are barren! And I have to stop thinking of you before I go mad.*

Deliberately, Annah turned her thoughts from Naham, Yerakh, and everyone in the settlement. Careless of her old tunic, she waded into the river and scrubbed her hair, then enjoyed the water. Naomi was right; the work would come soon enough. *This once, I'll waste time and play with the fish.* She let her hands rest weightless and motionless in the water, tempting the fish to approach. A massive gray berry-eater—almost as long as a man—slipped through the water, scented her fingertips, then glided away. But the minnows were more persistent, darting back and forth, touching her fingers over and over, until Annah pulled her hands back, sensing that she was being watched.

Where are you? Who are you? She scanned the nearby fringes of the trees. A small rock plunked into the water before Annah, splashing her, causing the minnows to flee. Shem. Smiling, Annah felt along the river bottom until she found a stone of the proper size. She threw the stone up at the riverbank and made an impudent face, telling her husband: *Go away!*

Emerging briefly, Shem staggered as if wounded, then he grinned teasingly and sauntered back up into the trees. *You looked like a little boy,* Annah thought as his presence faded away. *Perhaps the Most High will bless us with a son just like you. And perhaps our son will be the father of the Promised One. That is a blessing I don't deserve.* She waded out of the river, smiling.

After the evening meal, Noakh beckoned Annah. "Daughter, please bring me your veil."

My veil? Wondering, Annah went into the storage room and removed her veil from her basket of tools. She had intended to leave the veil here tonight; she saw no reason to take it to her new dwelling place. She had already folded her stiff-dried work tunic into her grass bag, with her comb, her gold hair bindings, her wooden needles, and Naomi's gift of handwork tools. *Why should I need the veil?*

When she returned to the main room of the lodge, Shem was standing respectfully before his father.

Methuwshelakh watched approvingly from his pallet while Naomi, Yepheth, and Khawm knelt around him, pleased witnesses to Shem and Annah's marriage blessing.

Annah offered her veil to Noakh, still curious. He took the veil, smiled at her fondly, then shut his eyes, praying silently. Finished, he beamed at Shem and Annah. "As old as I am, children, this will be the first time I've performed such a ceremony, so you must be patient with me."

Annah could not help smiling at him. Feeling Shem's fingers curling warmly around her own, she turned her hand beneath his, palm to palm, twining her fingers with his. Shem winked at her, then they looked at Noakh.

Shaking out the veil, Noakh admired it aloud. "See what a beautiful thing the wife of my son made during her years of sorrow!" To Annah, he said, "You created this veil as a shield against the eyes of others. It protected you. It sheltered you. It was your comfort. Yours alone. But now . . ." He swept the veil over Annah and Shem, covering their heads but not their eyes. "Now, you must allow your husband to share this place with you. There will be no veil between the two of you, because the Most High has chosen to bring you together as one. There will be no hiding from each other. No turning away in times of anger or grief."

His brown eyes glistening, Noakh said, "And may all your many children see that you are united by your love for each other. Then they will be filled with joy! May the Most High give you long lives together, and may you always turn to Him as your protection, your shelter, your comfort, to the last days of your lives."

Her eyes filling with tears, Annah said, "Thank you, Father."

Nodding as if deeply moved, Noakh kissed Annah's

cheek, then Shem's, saying almost gruffly, "Kiss I'ma before you leave."

Following Shem, Annah kissed Naomi, then Methuwshelakh. Yepheth and Khawm each kissed her shyly, before taunting Shem. "Now you'll leave us with even more work," Yepheth grumbled.

But Khawm pretended indignation, his dark eyes dancing in evening firelight. "I'm not doing his work! Do you hear, Shem? We're saving all your work for you. You'll be so tired next week you won't be able to move—not even to kiss your wife!"

"I'll remember that when you marry," Shem threatened, swiping Khawm lightly.

"No wrestling!" Naomi scolded. She filled a basket with cakes, nuts, olives, and fruit from their evening meal, and presented it to Shem. "Carry this for her; be sure she eats enough."

Before they left, Noakh said, "Wait." He went into the storage room and reappeared with a resin-soaked torch. "You need this."

As Shem thanked his father and lit the torch at the hearth, Annah kissed Naomi again, whispering, "I'ma, thank you for being concerned about me. And when I come back next week, you *will* let me help you with your work."

Naomi nodded and patted her, teary-eyed. Fearing she would cry too, Annah snatched her grass bag and followed Shem outside. Then, realizing she was still holding her veil, she hesitated. Shem chuckled. "You have to keep it now; it was part of our marriage blessing."

"You're right," Annah sighed. She wadded the veil into her bag, then walked with him, taking the path toward the river. The flaring torch was comforting. And the stars and the moon were glowing now, luminous in the deep violet sky. Annah stared up at the heavens, remembering the last time she was out at night: The Nachash screaming at her, staring at her with those white, sightless, knowing eyes . . .

Shem scattered her unwelcome thoughts, saying, "I'ma put half her storage room in this basket."

"I'll carry it for you," Annah offered worriedly; the torch was wavering as he shifted the basket onto his shoulder.

"No, I have it. I'ma wouldn't want you carrying this heavy thing."

"She's been feeding me constantly," Annah told him.

"That's I'ma." Turning his head slightly beneath the burden of the basket, Shem studied her face. "You look as if you feel better; perhaps you do need to eat more."

"Perhaps. I was never able to enjoy meals with my family, but I do now."

"In spite of our bad manners?" Shem asked, grinning. "I'm glad. Also, it was good to see you playing in the water today. You looked happy, almost like a child."

Annah smiled. "I thought you looked like a child."

"Oh?" His eyes gleamed in the torchlight. "Well, if I hadn't been so eager to finish our shelter, I would have come into the water to play with you. But never mind that. Look there." Lowering his chin, he indicated the dark outlines of a small hut, set a short distance from the shadowy trees lining the river. Apologetic, he added, "It's small; we won't need a lodge of our own for a few years."

"It's enough," Annah said, following him into the clearing surrounding the dark reed hut. A small, stone-enclosed hearth was outside in front, its wood and resins neatly arranged and ready to be lit. Shem carefully lowered the basket from his shoulder, then lit the hearth with the resin torch. As he tended the fire, he said, "I brought some water from our well; it's in that container near the doorway. And the waste pit is just behind those trees. I covered it so you wouldn't fall in."

"As if I *would* fall in!" she said, feigning outrage. But she went to visit the pit. When she had returned and washed her hands, Shem gave her a flickering clay oil lamp.

"Go inside, beloved; see if I've forgotten anything."

Entering the low reed and grass hut, Annah looked around. As Shem had said, it was small, sheltering only a wooden storage chest and a sleeping area of pallets covered with fleeces and two pillows. Annah set the lamp on the chest and inhaled softly. Shem had placed evening flowers in each corner of the hut. Cut from a bush, the evening flowers had glossy tapering oval leaves edged in yellow, framing delicate clusters of rosy, four-petaled flowers, which were the deep violet-pink of the evening sky. Their fresh, sweet fragrance permeated the air. Smelling them, Annah relaxed and sat on the edge of the fleece, hugging her grass bag. Everything was soothing and peaceful. She sighed. *Thank you.*

Shem came in, carrying the basket, his face solemn and handsome in the light of the lamp. Quietly he said, "I'll check the hearth once more tonight. If you were wondering, I put some dishes and cooking pots in the storage chest. Did I remember everything?"

"Yes, thank you. Everything's perfect."

Silent, he placed the basket next to the storage chest, then approached Annah and sat just behind her on the fleece. Very softly, gently, he caressed her hair, smoothing it away from her neck. Annah flinched inwardly, closing her eyes, struck by the unwelcome memory of

Naham's massive hand in her hair, his huge fingers curling possessively against the back of her neck. But Naham had wanted her without loving her. And Naham would have never kissed her neck the way Shem was kissing her now, his lips warm, ardent, stirring an equal response from her innermost being.

Folding his arms around her, Shem kissed Annah's cheek, whispering, "What are you thinking?"

Trying to think clearly, Annah said, "I never expected this . . . to be here with you. I always thought Yerakh would kill me as he killed my father."

Shem tipped her back slightly, gazing down into her eyes. He smiled, his wonderful, radiant smile. "No, beloved, forget Yerakh! Listen to me: We are going to live to be very, very old. And we will have many . . . many . . . children." He started to kiss her again, but then he paused, his lips just above her own as he whispered, "You know, I could be jealous."

Jealous? Of the children? Annah stared at him, confused. But he smiled again, murmuring, "I wish you would hold me the way you're holding that bag."

Captivated by the thought, Annah dropped her grass bag and let her husband lower her down onto the softness of the fleece.

Her gold talismans dangling against the back of her neck, and her grass bag looped over her shoulder, Annah left the lodge of Noakh. In her arms she carried a light, netted bundle of long, dried, husklike sheaths that Naomi had stripped from the giant grass canes growing near the river, north of the lodge.

I should use water from the well, Annah thought, making excuses. *But I'd rather go to the river.* Shem was working in the fields between the lodge and the river, and Annah hoped to catch a glimpse of him. *I won't interrupt him. I just want to see him, and then I'll go to work on these sheaths.*

She walked along the edge of a recently turned field. Khawm was in the far fields with the sheep today, but Yepheth was here with Shem. Their backs were toward her as they slowly worked through the greening field, hacking a profusion of weeds and creeping thorns out of the stubborn earth. Both brothers were stripped to their waists, and both wore bands of soft leather around their heads to prevent the sweat from trickling down into their eyes. Also, both had tied back their long, curling dark hair to keep it out of the way. The strong resemblance between the two brothers might have been confusing, except that Shem now had the neatly trimmed beginnings of a black beard, marking him as a married man.

As Annah walked past them along the edge of the field, both Shem and Yepheth turned, sensing her presence. Without breaking her stride, Annah smiled at her husband, lifted her bundle of sheaths slightly, then tilted her head toward the river to convey her intent.

She could feel him watching her as she walked all the way down to the trees. Annah smiled. It was wonderful to see her husband, but it was even more wonderful to know that he was watching her so intently—equally infatuated. Blissful, daydreaming, Annah made her way through the trees down to the riverbank. There, just north of the bridge, she chose a calm, moist, sandy area marked with large, deep, webbed footprints.

A giant lizard, Annah thought, measuring her feet against one of the webbed imprints. Her feet were nothing beside these prints, which were fairly fresh. She must have just missed seeing the creature.

Regretful, Annah went to work. She pushed the netted sheaths down into the cool, gently lapping water, using several stones to prevent them from drifting away. Now, sitting cross-legged on the sandy bank, she rummaged through her grass bag. Touching a coil of finely plaited cordage, created from the sheaths, Annah pulled it from her bag and slipped the coil over her left foot to hold the plaiting taut. The four strands composing the plait trailed lightly over and between her wrists as she folded them tightly back and forth. Later, as she needed more plaiting materials, she would cut them from the damp, husk-like sheaths, using the blade Naomi had given her. Just as she fell into a steady rhythm with her plaiting, Annah paused. Someone was behind her.

Looking back, wide-eyed, Annah saw Shem coming out of the trees. His expression was peculiar; smiling, but disgusted as well. Alarmed, Annah asked, "What's wrong?"

"You," he said, kneeling to kiss her neck. "You are the most terrible distraction!"

"I didn't mean to distract you, but I had to see you, just for an instant." Slipping the coil of plaiting off her foot, she turned to face him.

Shem pulled away. "You shouldn't touch me; I'm covered with dirt and sweat."

"One kiss won't matter," Annah said, edging closer. "But even if I were to touch you, I could wash off in the river."

"Give me a kiss then, and we'll both go back to our work. I just wanted to see you." He leaned forward. Annah kissed him, wrapping her arms around him tight. His skin was warm, and he smelled of earth. Annah snuggled closer, and Shem objected, "I should go back to work. Yepheth is waiting."

"I wish you didn't have to go."

"Annah . . ." Sighing, he surrendered and put his arms around her. Then he laughed quietly, picking apart her talisman-decked hair bindings. As her hair fell around her shoulders, he said, "I hope my brothers find wives for themselves soon; they'll begin to hate me."

"They'll forgive you eventually." Annah reached up to unfasten his hair. When he raised his hands to stop her, she said, "You've pulled off my hair bindings."

"That's different," he answered, grinning.

"How?" she challenged him, smiling in return. They sat unmoving, daring one another silently, her hands on his hair, his hands on her wrists. With a sudden growling laugh, Shem overbalanced them both, taking Annah with him down into the sand. Annah squealed and released his hair. Before she could gather her wits, he kissed her. Elated, she responded, kissing him in turn, winding her arms around his neck.

"Annah," he murmured, "we should return to our work."

"I know. It's unfair to Yepheth that you've abandoned him." She was suddenly uneasy, sensing that they were being watched. At first she thought it was Yepheth, but Shem sat up, pulling her with him, holding her protectively. His face tense and quiet, he stared over her head toward the bridge. Turning, Annah saw two women just coming off the bridge, both gaping, astonished.

Dazed herself, Annah thought, *Haburah. And Ayalah. They are wearing talismans in their hair. And they've seen me kissing my husband and talking.* She felt sick with fear. They had seen her talking. They would tell Yerakh, and he would come to find her. *I'm dead,* she thought, half-faint. *Yerakh is going to kill me.*

"Don't be afraid," Shem whispered. "I won't leave you alone with them. But they've seen us now, and it's too late to make them think anything but the truth."

Slowly, willing herself to move, Annah reached for her bindings and tied back her hair. As Shem helped Annah to her feet, he said, "You have to speak to your sisters. Don't worry about the sheaths, I'll pull them out of the water for you."

Still silent, Annah picked up her grass bag and the coil of plaiting. She hesitated, then walked to the bridge, keeping her eyes fixed on their faces, not their feet. *The nothing-creature-Annah no longer exists,* she thought to them and to herself. Haburah and Ayalah continued to stand and stare as if they were carved of wood. Annah wondered if they were thinking at all, they looked so utterly stunned.

Finally, Ayalah said, "Annah? You can't be Annah."

Annah took a breath. "Ayalah. I see Yerakh finally allowed you to marry K'nan. Haburah, welcome." Unwillingly, she remembered her manners and said, "Please, come up to the lodge of my husband's parents. They will be glad to welcome you."

By now, Shem had pulled Annah's bundle of sheaths from the water, and he approached. Haburah and Ayalah gaped at him, astonished. He gave them a long, level look and nodded briefly. *He detests them,* Annah realized, startled. *He can't even speak to them.* Silent, carrying the dripping sheaths, Shem took Annah's hand to escort her—ahead of her sisters—up to the lodge of Noakh.

Fourteen

ANNAH WAS aware of her sisters watching her—and
Shem—all the way up the riverbank and through the
trees. When they emerged from the shadows of the trees,
she turned to watch their faces when they caught sight of
the pen.

Haburah stared at the vast wooden structure without
comment, her graceful profile unmoving, but Ayalah
laughed. Haburah shoved her, snarling, "Shut up!"

"Don't push me!" Ayalah snapped, aggrieved.

Annah bit her lip, her anxieties mounting. Her sisters
weren't even trying to be polite.

Turning to Shem, Annah saw his loathing. She tightened her fingers around his, urging him to look at her.
When he glanced at her, Annah lifted her eyebrows,
pleading silently: *Don't be angry.* She needed him to be
calm, to steady her own unsettled emotions. He smiled

somberly, then lifted her hand, kissing her fingertips. Annah felt her sisters staring, fixated on his gesture of love. She doubted that K'nan was often tender with Ayalah, and knew that the best Haburah could expect was an occasional snort of condescending approval from Naham.

You're furious with me now, Haburah, Annah thought. *I can feel your rage. I think you want to tear my hair out.*

By the time they reached the lodge, Noakh and Naomi were waiting in the doorway, their expressions formal and courteous. Noakh took the bundle of damp sheaths from Shem, saying, "I'll put these in the storage room, my son, while you go wash." As he spoke, Noakh gave Shem's bare torso an oblique look, silently implying that Shem also should cover himself with a fresh tunic.

Shem nodded, but Annah knew he was reluctant to leave. She pressed his hand gently to reassure him. He responded by kissing her cheek and running a light hand over her bound hair before he left the main room. Again, he did not look at her sisters, but they watched him leave—Ayalah's glance frankly appraising and admiring.

When her sisters turned toward her, Annah saw their unspoken accusations. She did not smile. *This isn't what you expected, is it, my sisters? You thought it would be amusing to come visit your nothing-creature sister, so you could laugh at her later. Instead you realize that I am happy here, and you are furious.*

Reluctantly clearing her throat, Annah turned to Noakh and Naomi. "These are my sisters, Haburah, wife of Naham the Iron-breaker, and Ayalah, wife of K'nan, the tradesman."

Noakh smiled at Haburah and Ayalah. "Welcome. Forgive me, but I'll put these sheaths away before I sit down to visit with you." He dropped the bundle of sheaths inside the storage room, then returned, pausing briefly to peer behind Methuwshelakh's screen.

By Noakh's quiet expression, Annah knew the ancient man was asleep. *Please, let him stay asleep,* Annah prayed. If Methuwshelakh met Haburah and Ayalah, he would probably mention the gold and tools Annah had brought from the lodge of the Tsaraph. Then her sisters would tell Yerakh. *I would be dead by the end of the day,* Annah thought, her stomach tightening.

"Daughter, please, come sit down," Naomi said to Annah. "And you, Haburah and Ayalah, please." Naomi indicated an array of finely woven floor mats, already spread and set with an assortment of fruits, cakes, and drinks. "Sit and rest."

Seeming unimpressed, Haburah knelt, her hands folded stiffly in her lap. Ayalah was not so formal. She eyed the fruits and cakes hungrily—leaning forward until Haburah elbowed her in an unspoken rebuke. Furious, Ayalah glared at Haburah. "Stop!"

Annah bit her lip, embarrassed by their rudeness. Mindful that she was expected to offer food to her guests, Annah knelt near Haburah and warily offered her a dish of fine grain cakes. Haburah took one, broke off a piece, and nibbled it disdainfully. Ayalah followed her lead. Annah felt Haburah's bad temper and Ayalah's peevishness. If they behaved at all, it would only be out of deference to Noakh and Naomi—now seated to Annah's right, facing her sisters.

"This has been a long walk for the two of you at the height of the day," Naomi said, pouring fruit juice from a plump, glazed clay pitcher into rounded, matching clay cups. She handed the filled cups to Annah, who passed them to her unhappy sisters.

Feeling obligated to speak, Annah asked the question

foremost on her mind. "How is Yerakh? If you both are married now, then he must have the lodge to himself."

Haburah remained obstinately silent, but Ayalah smiled, her delicate face alight with a secret, malicious pleasure. Looking at Noakh and Naomi, then at Annah, Ayalah said, "I doubt you know, so I'll tell you; Yerakh is going to marry Taphaph tomorrow. Bachown offered Yerakh fifty sheep and the use of one field as her bride price, and Yerakh accepted. Now Bachown is complaining to everyone that he shouldn't have to pay a bride price because Yerakh has so much already. But Taphaph is overjoyed; she told me she would have despised any other man."

"I hope Yerakh and Taphaph will be happy," Annah replied, hearing Naomi take a quiet breath of indignation at Ayalah's blithe, indirect insult to the Lodge of Noakh. Annah was equally offended, thinking, *What a wretch you are, Ayalah. You know that Bachown offered Taphaph as a wife to one of my husband's brothers, and you just couldn't resist cutting my in-laws with a spiteful little comment. If Noakh were as cruel as Yerakh, he would beat you and throw you out of his lodge.*

Now Haburah stared at Annah, embittered. "You haven't wished me well for my marriage, Annah. Naham took me to his lodge the day after your wedding."

At a loss, Annah looked down at her hands, folded in her lap. Finally she said, "I know you're grieving, Haburah; I'm sorry."

Haburah responded with a swift, vicious, open-handed slap to Annah's left cheek. Annah cringed, putting up her hands to ward off a second blow. She heard Naomi utter a cry of fury and saw Noakh start up off the mats, then sit down again.

Hands—warm, callused, and protective—settled on

Annah's shoulders. Shem glared at Haburah, his eyes glittering dangerously. "Don't touch my wife again, woman! She's suffered enough at your hands. You're a family of vipers, all of you—it's a wonder she's survived."

To Annah's amazement, Haburah burst into tears, covering her face with her hands as she cried. Annah had never seen Haburah cry before, not even when Parah and Chathath were murdered.

Ayalah put her arms around Haburah defensively, saying, "She couldn't help it. She's so unhappy. The wives of Naham begged me to take her out today to try to cheer her up. But now, instead of being consoled by this visit . . . well . . ." Ayalah faltered. "If Naham had known that Annah was not mad—and that she could speak—he would have taken her as his wife instead of Haburah. Haburah can't help being angry."

Shem gave an abrupt, disbelieving laugh. "Am I supposed to accept that as an excuse? Am I supposed to be glad that Naham-the-Iron-breaker-monster would have preferred to abuse my wife instead? As for unhappiness, where were you when Naham caused Yerakh to beat Annah five months ago? In fact, where were the two of you when Yerakh killed your father before Annah's very eyes, then turned on Annah and choked her half to death—and she was no more than a child! Who consoled her then?"

Staring at Shem, then at Annah, Ayalah lowered her eyes. "I didn't know."

Annah summoned her courage. "No one ever told you, did they, Ayalah? But then again, it wasn't terribly important to anyone else. Yes, I saw Yerakh beat our father bloody, then strangle him and snap his neck like a dry branch. Then Yerakh grabbed my throat and told me not to say another word. He choked me until I lost consciousness. I was surprised to wake up, Ayalah! Then I was afraid to utter one sound because Yerakh had threatened me. I was a child, and I obeyed."

Ayalah swallowed, her expression squeamish. Annah looked at Haburah—who was now wiping her face, recovering from her fit of tears. Very quietly, Annah asked her older sister, "Didn't you wonder why I never dared to speak? Why I always looked away? Why I hid beneath the veil? It was to save my life, Haburah!"

Infuriated by Haburah's dark silence, Annah continued, "You've decided to be angry with me because you were forced to marry Naham. But years ago, you knew that he had asked for you. You could have prevented this. When Naham asked for me, I decided to run away before he could take me into his lodge. I'm sorry, Haburah, but you chose to stay in the settlement." She paused, compelling the defiant Haburah to look her in the eye. "As for living in sorrow . . . for the past twenty-five years I was waiting to die, and you never once comforted me. Didn't you care?"

Her eyes fierce, shadowed with tears and rage, Haburah said softly, "Ma'adannah, O cherished daughter of my father! O delightful one. Or so our father said. Ma'adannah!" Her voice rising, Haburah sneered, "I was *glad* when you stopped speaking, stopped asking so many questions, dear Ma'adannah! But now you've found your voice again, and all the questions are coming out. Well, I'm not going to stay and listen!"

Haburah stood and nudged Ayalah with one bare, slender brown foot. "Come. We're leaving this lodge of the insane!"

Startled, Ayalah argued, "But we're still visiting—we haven't eaten yet, and I'm not ready to leave."

"Oh, yes, you are!" Haburah reached down to snatch her sister's arm.

Ayalah ducked away. "Don't! I'll come. Go on ahead of me."

"Stay then." Haburah turned and marched out of the lodge. Annah was relieved to see her go, but equally frightened. *Haburah will tell Yerakh everything she saw and heard here today, which means I am dead.*

Obviously ready to end the visit, Shem stood, helping Annah to her feet, then helping his parents to stand. Naomi was thoroughly distressed and silent, but Noakh was thoughtful. Curious, Annah followed Noakh's gaze. He was watching Ayalah.

Annah saw that Ayalah longed to stay and visit. *I don't want you to stay*, Annah thought to Ayalah. *But then again, my feelings have never mattered to you, my sister. You are nothing more than a rude child.* Unwillingly, Annah offered her sister a courteous but less-than-loving hand.

Encouraged by Annah's polite gesture, Ayalah took Annah's hand and hurried outside, forgetting to thank Noakh and Naomi for their courtesy. Even so, the older couple followed their guests out of the lodge.

Ayalah began to chatter, lightly, sweetly. "Ma'adannah, I never knew how much Haburah despised you! But where is Haburah?" She peered at the fields. "Never mind, there she is."

Annah saw her stalking down the path toward the trees that shielded the bridge.

In her loudest voice, Ayalah called out, "Haburah, are you so eager to return to the lodge of Naham?"

Haburah stopped almost midstep and lowered her head, acknowledging the truth; she was not eager to return to the lodge of Naham. But she wasn't willing to return to the lodge of Noakh, either. Instead, she sat in the grass beside the path to wait for Ayalah.

Smiling gleefully, Ayalah said, "I always have to do as she pleases; this once she can just wait for me." Pulling Annah along, she commanded, "Show me this giant's box behind your lodge."

In despair, Annah looked back at Shem. He shrugged and followed them. Before she turned the corner of the lodge, Annah saw Naomi run her hands over her face in a gesture of furious, tearful disbelief. Noakh took Naomi in his arms, soothing her. Annah could not bear to see her mother-in-law so distressed. Exasperated, she pulled her hand from Ayalah's grasp.

Unaffected, Ayalah headed for the ramp leading up to the massive darkness of the pen. She talked all the way up the ramp, her tones honeyed yet disparaging. "This is unthinkable; why should that Noakh bother to build such a useless structure? K'nan said that the father of your husband has been a madman for as long as K'nan could remember. Does that Noakh really believe in the Most High?"

Annah stopped inside the doorway of the pen. Shem halted just behind her, grim and quiet. Unwilling to allow her sister to deride Noakh, Annah said, "I'd rather ask you a question, Ayalah. What do you believe in?"

"What should I believe in? Things are as they are. And Yerakh is right; the Most High is nothing but an ancient story."

"But Yerakh believes in the Nachash," Annah persisted.

"But the Nachash is real," Ayalah countered indignantly, her wide dark eyes flashing in her pretty, childlike face. "She exists."

"She's an old woman," Annah said softly. "She's an old

woman who takes grain from Yerakh without payment. Have you ever heard of Yerakh allowing anyone to take anything from him? Particularly an old reed of a woman?"

"No—o," Ayalah agreed, uncertain now. "And you're right, I've never understood why he allows the Nachash and those whisperers to do as they please on his lands."

Annah stared at her sister hard, willing her to understand. "It's because he believes they have all the powers of their beloved Serpent. And if Yerakh believes in the powers of the Serpent, then why should he scorn the existence of the Most High?"

Rolling her eyes impatiently, Ayalah said, "Ha! Don't make me laugh, Annah. Next, you'll say you believe in the Most High too."

"I do believe in Him. And knowing that He exists causes everything else to make sense. Think, Ayalah; what about when the earth moves? Don't you wonder why it shakes?"

"No, I don't. The earth shakes, then it stops, and everything is as it was before. Really, Annah, you're every bit as empty-headed as you've seemed all these years. I won't discuss your Most High. Now, show me this place. Are all these stalls for animals? And look at all this food!" She opened baskets and bins, peering inside.

Watching her sister, Annah thought, *She is not moved by this place as I was. She's only eager to satisfy her curiosity and to have something to tell K'nan at their evening fire.* Shem stood with Annah now, wrapping an arm around her shoulder, then caressing her cheek where Haburah had slapped her. Annah leaned into him, watching her sister.

Ayalah opened a basket of dark, rock-hard grain cakes. Without asking permission, she took one, nibbled it, frowned, then nibbled it again. Annah heard Shem suck in a quick breath; he actually shuddered. Wondering, she glanced at him. He was staring at Ayalah, seeming oddly fascinated, yet thoroughly repulsed and queasy. Perplexed, Annah looked back at her sister.

Still holding the dark grain cake, Ayalah grimaced. "This tastes odd. What did you use to flavor it? Whatever it was, you shouldn't use it again."

"If you say so," Shem answered, his eyes now sparkling roguishly.

They followed Ayalah through the pen, leading her up and down the ramps, letting her look at everything until her curiosity was satisfied. "It's all madness," Ayalah declared as they were leaving the pen. "That Noakh put more than a hundred years of work into this foolishness—more than a kentum of his life! Not to mention wasting all this valuable timber on something so useless. No wonder everyone laughed the other day when Bachown talked about him."

Stopping at the base of the door ramp, she said, "I should go find Haburah. I wish you well, Annah, even if you did make fools of us for all these years. What *will* Yerakh do when he realizes you can talk?" Dropping the cake, she walked away, smiling, self-satisfied.

Watching Ayalah saunter off, Annah thought, *You and Haburah are eager to tell Yerakh about me, I know. You hope he kills me. And my death won't affect you in the least.*

Hugging Annah, Shem chuckled. "Well, we've had our first animal in the pen, and she was a carrion-eater."

Annah blinked. "What?" Carrion-eaters were all the sharp-toothed creatures of the earth that ate the bodies of fallen animals—a nasty but necessary function. "Why do you call Ayalah a carrion-eater?"

"That cake she ate—my brothers and I call those

blood cakes. They're made with raw meat. And your sister took two bites. Wait until I tell my father and brothers!"

"Ayalah ate the flesh of another creature?" Horrified, Annah thought, *I'm glad she didn't kiss me before she left.* She shuddered and accused her husband, "You watched my sister eat flesh and you didn't warn her."

"She ate it before I could say a word," Shem protested. "You know, beloved, she's too quick to use her mouth, but not her mind." He chuckled again, coaxing her to enjoy the joke. "It's laughable. Admit it."

"I think it's sickening."

"Never mind; my father and brothers will enjoy hearing it." Shem bent to kiss her hair. "But one day I'll hear you laugh."

I can't find much to laugh about, Annah thought, burying her face in her husband's warm, leather-clad shoulder. *Yerakh's going to come after me soon, though his marriage to Taphaph will keep him busy for a while. Perhaps he will wait another week. O Most High, give me some time.*

"You are worth more than both of your sisters," Naomi told Annah fiercely as they rinsed the clay cups and pitchers after their evening meal. "I cannot believe you're still sane after living with them for all those years."

"*They* believe I'm mad," Annah said, stacking the last of the cups into a basket. "And it's just as well; if they believe I'm mad, they might leave me alone."

"That sort never leaves you alone," Naomi sniffed, setting a pitcher into the basket with a muffled clatter. "Look at those herdsman-cousins of my husband, always coming and going from the flocks, always leaving us and sneering at my Noakh. But as soon as their bellies shrink a bit with hunger, they're back again, pretending nothing happened." Sighing, she passed a weary hand over her face. "Sometimes I wonder how many times must I forgive those fools for calling my dear one a madman."

"As many times as he is willing to forgive them himself?" Annah guessed.

Naomi smiled, shaking her head. "I'm not as patient as my husband." She settled the last of the wooden serving spoons into the basket. "There. Finished."

Before Naomi could take the basket, Annah grabbed it and stood. As she carried the basket to the storage room, Annah called back over her shoulder, "Don't touch the rinse-tub, I'ma! I'll take it out to your garden and empty it."

Annah enjoyed stacking the cups inside their fragrant wooden storage chest. It felt good to behave as a normal-speaking person should behave. She would be completely happy, if only she weren't so afraid of Yerakh. *But I am afraid,* she thought, her emotions suddenly raw, eating at the pit of her stomach. *If only I could put all thoughts of Yerakh away until I see him coming to kill me. O Most High, please calm my fears.*

Naomi was sitting near the hearth when Annah returned to the main room. She smiled and patted the mat beside her. "Don't empty the rinse water yet, daughter. I want to talk to you."

Curious, Annah knelt beside her mother-in-law and waited. Naomi had her hands carefully folded in her lap, hiding something from Annah's view.

Moistening her lips, Naomi said, "Your father must have loved you completely to have given you such a name, Ma'adannah. I've been thinking that if he had been alive, he would have worked gold for you, anticipating your wedding day. He would have given you something special, like this." Lifting her hands, Naomi held out one of her beautiful gold cuff-bracelets to Annah. "Take it, child."

"But this was from your husband," Annah objected, shaking her head in disbelief. "How can I take this?"

"My husband has given me many gifts, including another bracelet like this one," Naomi said, almost stern. "But your father is gone. He never had the chance to give you a wedding gift. You must have this—the work of his hands."

Tears welled up in Annah's eyes. The gold danced and glittered before her. "My father wouldn't listen to your husband. He rejected your husband's words, as he would have rejected me."

"Does that make the bracelet less beautiful?" Naomi argued. "Does that make your father less than your father? No. Forgive him and go on, child. Remember him kindly; he did love you." As she spoke, Naomi took Annah's right hand and pushed the bracelet over her wrist. On Naomi, the bracelet fit her wrist. On Annah, it stopped securely at her forearm. "There." Naomi sounded satisfied. "Now, give me a kiss and go empty the water. Your husband will come looking for you soon."

Wiping the tears from her face, Annah kissed her mother-in-law and hugged her. "Thank you, I'ma!"

"Empty the water, then go find your husband," Naomi repeated, affecting impatience. "Go."

Carefully, Annah lifted the carved, resin-coated water tub and went out the back of the lodge. The evening air was scented with moisture, and the sky glowed a deep ruddy pink as the sun lowered in the western horizon.

Calmed now, Annah lugged the tub to Naomi's garden, off to the right of the door. Stepping cautiously into the dark, loose soil of the garden, she tipped the tub gently, allowing the water to trickle over Naomi's cherished root vegetables and herbs.

As she worked, Annah sensed the presence of others near the pen. Shem and Yepheth emerged from the great door, trotting down the ramp. Shem grinned at her. Annah smiled in return, unable to resist him. She spilled water on her feet. *Don't become distracted,* Annah scolded herself, returning to her task. By the time the tub was empty, Shem was beside her, pulling it from her hands.

"Put this thing down and come with me," he urged. "Have you climbed up to the roof of the pen?"

"No. Should I?"

"Come see for yourself," he said, taking her hand.

As they moved away from the lodge, Yepheth called out, "Remember, brother, it's your turn tomorrow night to keep watch over the herds!"

"You'll be gone tomorrow night?" Annah asked Shem, dismayed.

"I take the watch from Khawm tomorrow," Shem answered regretfully. "But forget that now; we'll miss the sunset."

He hurried her northeast along the base of the pen until they reached the far corner. There, he pulled Annah up a series of steps leading to a broad platform, then up more steps to a second platform above.

By the time they reached the second platform, Annah was swallowing hard, trying not to look down. *Why should this be any different than climbing a tree?* But the steps were not as solid as the pen itself, and this unnerved her. A final series of steps above the second platform led to the roof of the pen. Encouraged by Shem, Annah gritted her teeth and climbed onto the roof. Though the roof of the pen was broad, solid, and gently sloped, Annah felt insecure enough to snatch at Shem as he stood beside her.

He laughed. "I didn't think you'd be afraid, but I won't argue if you want to hold me."

"Don't tease me about this!" she warned him. "I've never been this high off the ground before, though obviously you think it's nothing."

"Then let's sit here. Although, I thought we would walk to the other end. . . ."

"No, please, don't ask me to walk along this entire roof!"

They sat, facing westward. "Look," Shem persuaded Annah, wrapping his arms around her. "See how beautiful everything is from up here?"

Slowly Annah relaxed and looked out over the landscape. It was beautiful. She had never thought of being so high up off the ground and able to see the sweep of the land, the low, dark curves of the distant mountains, the rose-gold gleaming of sunlight slanting over the fields. The light also illuminated the leaves of the treetops, gilding them. And the rose-violet sky seemed nearer than ever before. Annah felt that she could almost touch the first stars of the evening.

"There are the herds," Shem said, nodding toward the western fields.

"And you'll be out there tomorrow night," Annah whispered.

"Every third night from now on," Shem agreed. "And when Yepheth and Khawm get married, I'll take their turns out there for a few weeks—as they've done for me."

"I suppose I'll stay with your parents," Annah sighed.

She wouldn't be able to sleep alone in their hut near the woods. Except for that one night in the ancient Tree of Havah, she had never spent the night away from other people. *And Yerakh might find me alone and kill me,* she thought. *But it would be worse if he found me at the lodge of my husband's parents . . . I'd endanger their lives as well.*

Shem kissed Annah's cheek, then smoothed her hair, interrupting her thoughts. "Perhaps you should avoid the river for a while. I'm sure your sisters will tell Yerakh that you've been able to talk all these years. If he decides to come after you, then you should be here with us."

"Perhaps." Annah deliberately made the word sound like an agreement. But as her husband was talking, she thought, *If you were to meet Yerakh and fight him, then you might die. I can't allow that to happen. Therefore, I won't avoid Yerakh.*

"I was also thinking," Shem said, kissing the palm of her hand, "that Ma'adannah is a good name for you; your father chose well. I know it means 'delicate' and 'delightful' as he intended, but it also means 'influence'. And later, when we're old, you will be an influence on others."

"I like my name," Annah agreed. *If I live long enough to become used to it.*

And if I ever can forget the hatred in Haburah's eyes.

Haburah, it hurts that you and Ayalah hate me. What have I ever done to either of you, but to exist? Now, you'll tell Yerakh. And my husband is in danger because of me.

"What are you thinking?" Shem asked, fingering the gold bracelet on her forearm. Annah leaned against him, watching the sunset.

"I am thinking that I love you."

How much do you love your husband? Noakh had asked her. *How would you measure your love?*

I would give my life to save my husband's life.

That is the true answer of love.

Remembering this, Annah shut her eyes against the beauty of the heavens. *O Most High, help me not to be afraid.*

Fifteen

ANNAH PICKED the weeds out of Naomi's garden, casting them by handfuls into growing heaps around the edges of the garden. All the while, she was eagerly anticipating Shem's return from his night of keeping watch over the herds. Tonight, Yepheth would go out to the herds, tomorrow night it would be Khawm's turn, then Shem would go out again the following night. *I cannot complain,* Annah lectured herself. *Every third night is reasonable, and I enjoyed visiting with my husband's family last night.*

Her husband's parents and brothers had amused her with their banter around the evening fire. Later, Methuwshelakh had joined them, smiling as a dreamer smiles, enjoying the laughter of his great-grandsons. Even more wonderful, at Naomi's request, Yepheth had retrieved a polished wooden harp from the storage room and played it.

Annah was astonished. She never would have suspected that the somber, taciturn Yepheth could play so beautifully. Not to be outdone, Khawm had produced a set of reed pipes and joined his brother, his music by turns lilting, soothing, and spirited. Annah could have listened to them all night.

"Does my husband play music like this?" she had asked Naomi, amazed.

Khawm laughed. "Why would you care to listen to him? He's only your husband!"

Naomi silenced her youngest son with a sharp look, saying to Annah, "All three of my sons have learned music; the sounds are soothing to the herds."

There was no music in the lodge of Yerakh, Annah thought now, wrenching another thorny weed from Naomi's patch of beans. *No music, no joy. Only quarrels and hatred.*

"Daughter!" Naomi scurried out of the lodge, carrying a tapering clay water vessel. "Yepheth says there are traders approaching. We need water. Don't worry about the weeds; wash your hands and feet, then come help me."

Her heartbeat quickening, Annah took the clay vessel from Naomi. She bounded onto the dark wooden platform built over the well and plunked the vessel down next to the carved wooden dipping bucket, which was attached to the platform with a rope. Kneeling, she lifted the small, square well cover built into the surface of the platform, then lowered the dipping bucket into the water.

When the dipping bucket was full, she had to stand to haul it up. Feeling like a child, she splashed the deliciously cool water over her dirty hands and feet. *No playing,* she scolded herself. Briskly, she checked her hands and feet for any last traces of dirt, then she filled the clay vessel. It took two buckets of water to fill it almost to the top. Satisfied, Annah replaced the well cover, then braced herself to shoulder the tapering curves of the clay vessel. The surface was rough against her cheek, but she didn't care; the work was a joy.

"Do you still love going to the well?" Naomi asked as Annah entered the lodge.

Her hands and feet tingling from the water, Annah lowered the vessel to the earthen floor. "Yes, it's good to be able to go draw water from a well like a normal person."

"I'll ask again in a few days," Naomi chuckled, busily arranging grain cakes and nutmeats in polished wooden bowls. She began to think aloud. "These and the juice of the vine-fruits, and some olive paste, flatbreads, and pressed afal cakes should satisfy our visitors until the evening meal. Now, child, carry these mats outside, and I'll bring the food; the traders won't want to leave their goods, so we'll ask them to sit in the shade on the eastern side of the lodge. Yepheth is leading them here."

Annah carried the rolled woven-grass mats out to the eastern side of the lodge, where the shade was beginning to creep over the grass. Unrolling the mats, she created a large sitting area that would eventually be covered by the shade. Then she helped Naomi set out the food. Just as she was placing the last dishes on the mat, Annah heard the squeaking clatter of a cart and Yepheth's low voice calling out, "I'ma, they are here."

Hovering at the corner of the lodge, Annah watched the trader approach with his ox-drawn cart, which was heaped with goods and protected with a covering of leather hides and cords. Behind the cart were the trader's wife, one grown son, one round-faced boy-child, and a young woman—the trader's daughter, Annah decided.

They all stared up at the overwhelming darkness of the pen until Yepheth spoke again, abruptly. "This way." As Naomi approached, Yepheth simply said, "I'ma, this is Qeb-al of the Kinah, seller of wares."

Qeb-al beamed at Naomi, his brown face ruddy with the warmth of the day, his black hair rough and barely contained by a headband of leather. With a brief, respectful nod, he said, "Mother of Yepheth, I am pleased to happen this way; my family is favored by your son's kindness."

As Naomi inclined her head politely, Qeb-al waved his family forward, saying, "This is my firstborn, Pa-sak; my younger son, Saiyr; and my wife, Etsah. That is the daughter of my brother—he is gone from us now. Her name is Ghinnah."

Qeb-al's sons were like their father, rough haired and flushed, but their expressions were surly. Etsah, the trader's wife, was slim and glum, her hair held back with—Annah guessed—cheap bronze talismans lightly coated with gold. Qeb-al's niece lingered behind the others, leaning against the wagon, apparently tired and bored. Annah could not see her face.

"Welcome," Naomi said. "Please, bring your cart this way. You can guard it while you rest. Daughter . . ." Her tone gently urged Annah to help tend their guests.

Quickly, Annah led the trader and his family to sit on the mats. She was aware of the trader, his wife, and sons staring at her as she passed the grain cakes to them. Only the young woman, Ghinnah, did not look up.

As Annah passed the cakes, Naomi said, "Yepheth, please find your father. He went out to the herds to speak to his cousins."

Yepheth nodded silently and strode away. Now An-nah saw Ghinnah look up, furtively glancing at Yepheth's retreating back. Swiftly, she lowered her eyes again, her mouth curled faintly at one corner, her expression unfath-omable.

What are you thinking? Annah wondered to Ghinnah. *Kindness or mischief?* Intrigued, she knelt near the girl, study-ing her overtly from the corners of her eyes. Ghinnah was small, with clear brown eyes and a rounded, pretty face. Her hair was soft, with flowing dark waves, and her brown skin was pink-tinged—a tender variation of the trader's heated flush.

When Ghinnah merely nibbled at a grain cake, Annah scooted the dish of pressed fruitcakes toward her, then poured some juice into one of the rounded clay cups. As she placed the cup to Ghinnah's right, Ghinnah blinked at her, startled. Summoning her courage, Annah smiled.

Ghinnah bit her lip, then smiled, the bloom in her face deepening. Qeb-al frowned, subduing her with a glance. Then he stared at Annah, his expression politely discouraging her from talking to his niece.

Clearing her throat, Naomi said, "Qeb-al, Etsah, this is Ma'adannah, the wife of my second son."

Qeb-al's dark eyebrows lifted in obvious disapproving surprise. "But if Yepheth is the first son, then . . ." Recov-ering, he straightened. "Forgive me."

Completely dignified, Naomi said, "By the will of the Most High, my second son has married before my first—to our own surprise."

"The Most High? Ah . . ." Qeb-al's brow smoothed immediately, as if dismissing Naomi's foolishness in the interest of conducting business. He inclined his head po-litely toward Annah. "We wish you many sons."

But no daughters? Annah wondered to Qeb-al, disquiet-ed. *I think you despise women; your wife and the daughter of your brother are very unhappy with you.*

Etsah was pressing her lips together in tight displea-sure, while Ghinnah looked down at her hands. But Qeb-al and his sons were eating heartily, obviously hungry and glad to rest. Ghinnah sipped at her cup of juice and took a pressed fruitcake. But before she could eat it, her boy-child cousin, Saiyr, snatched it from her hand.

Annah was disgusted by his rudeness. As she watched the boy, Naomi asked Qeb-al, "How long have you been traveling?"

"Months of days, Mother of Yepheth," Qeb-al an-swered, his mouth full of grain cakes. "And I will say that no others have received us as kindly; we thank you again."

"It is only right to receive strangers with courtesy," Naomi answered. A piercing whistle startled them. Nao-mi and Annah stood as Yepheth came around the corner of the lodge, followed by Noakh and Shem. Smiling, Naomi said, "Here is my husband, Noakh, and my second son, Shem."

Annah watched as Shem placed his leather carrying pouch and tall, carved herder's crook against the lattice wall of the lodge. *How I've missed you,* Annah thought to him. *And you are so tired.* She was incapable of looking at anyone else now; all her attention was focused on her husband.

Wearily, Shem kissed Naomi, greeted their guests, then smiled at Annah, asking her with a look: *Are you well?*

She answered him with a small nod, then knelt to pour two cups of juice: one for Noakh and one for Shem, as Naomi served Yepheth. They accepted the juice grate-fully.

Noakh's eyes sparkled. "This time, I am served first? Thank you, daughter."

They sat down, and Annah knelt beside Shem, content just to be near him.

Noakh questioned Qeb-al. "Tell me what you've seen during your travels."

"Many wonderful things and many kind people. But none so kind as the family of Noakh," Qeb-al said. "The most peculiar and fearful thing we've seen—"

"The carrion-eaters!" his elder son, Pa-sak, interrupted, his color rising. "Tell about the carrion-eaters!"

"As I was saying," Qeb-al continued brusquely, ignoring his son, "the most peculiar and fearful thing is that in many places now the carrion-eaters are no longer waiting for creatures to become carrion before they eat flesh from their bodies."

Shem frowned. "The carrion-eaters are consuming living creatures?"

"Exactly." Planting his hands on his knees, Qeb-al leaned forward. "And it's not just one sort of carrion-eater. Multitudes—the great lizards, the saw-toothed fish, the clawed beasts and birds—all are doing this, as if they enjoy the act of the kill. Between that and the shaking of the earth . . ." he sighed, rolling his eyes dramatically. "This is a time of many wonders. And I have acquired many marvelous things to show you! But later, later. For now, it's good to visit as friends, eh?"

Allowing her thoughts to drift away from Qeb-al's patter, Annah looked at Shem. His eyes were tired, but shining, admiring her. Leaning toward Annah, he whispered, "I'm going to check on the father of my fathers, and then rest a while. But don't let me sleep too long; I want to visit everyone and be near you."

He looked as if he wanted to kiss her, but such an open display of affection might be considered offensive by their guests. Annah smiled, silently encouraging him to go rest. Nodding politely to their guests, Shem stood, gathering his tall herder's crook and leather pouch as he excused himself. Annah watched her husband until he disappeared around the corner of the lodge. When she turned back, she saw Ghinnah studying her enviously. Embarrassed, Annah looked away.

Settling herself on a short grass mat behind the lodge, Annah poured a measure of fine wheat into a broad, low, stone mortar. She smoothed the pale, bran-coated grains around the central peg of the mortar, picking out stray bits of straw and sharp-ended husks. As she reached for the wooden-handled grinding stone, she sensed someone approaching.

"Please, let me help you with that," said Ghinnah. "Even doing heavy work is better than the company of my aunt."

They lined up the hole in the middle of the grinding stone with the wooden peg in the center of the mortar and lowered it gently onto the heap of wheat, laying it flat like a dish.

Ghinnah sighed, remorseful. "I shouldn't have said that."

"I'm sorry you must avoid her." Annah pulled the wooden-pegged handle that turned the stone within the mortar. "Are you very unhappy living with them?"

"I haven't been with them long," Ghinnah replied. "My father has been dead for less than a year. I was a disappointment to him, but my mother loved me. She said I was as wonderful to her as all the flowers of her garden, which is why I am called Ghinnah."

"Do you have brothers and sisters?" Annah asked, careful to keep her eyes on the grinding stone.

Ghinnah shrugged. "My father sent my two sisters away as soon as he could find husbands for them. My only brother stole a large portion of goods from my father several years ago and left like a thief during the night. My father never spoke his name again. My mother died the following year—of a fall, my father said. I think he pushed her from the roof of our home while they were fighting. We lived in a city, so the roof was high, and the paving below was solid."

Ghinnah nudged Annah's fingers away from the handle, taking the work from her. She continued, "My father was killed last year while fighting with another man. The husbands of my sisters didn't want me, not even as a concubine, because my uncle claimed all my father's possessions—even my bride price. My uncle didn't take me as his second wife because Etsah threatened to maim him in his sleep. Qeb-al is a coward. Etsah has hated me ever since. Now I am a burden to them—an unwanted woman."

"How awful." Annah swallowed, grieved by the other young woman's pain.

"Don't worry about me," Ghinnah said, her voice hardening. "I'm fine."

No, you're not, Annah argued with her silently. *You've only pushed the pain away for now. It will strike you again when you're not ready for it—as sharp and hard as ever. You'll go mad.*

Glancing around cautiously, Ghinnah said, "You've been kind to me, so I'll warn you: Qeb-al uses hollow weights and shortened rods to measure out his goods. The father of your husband should insist on an additional fourth. And my cousins and my aunt have stolen things from time to time; small things that won't be missed immediately. And before you condemn them, please understand; I've done the same. One day, we'll be caught and killed."

Annah gaped at her, confounded. "Why should you trust me? I could go to the father of my husband and have him chase you all away."

"I hope you won't," Ghinnah answered, averting her eyes. "But that's your choice. As it was my choice to warn you." Then, smiling a little, she said, "I'll tell you, too, that I envy you for loving your husband and his family as you do. When you are with your husband, you caress each other with your looks, and I can feel the passion you have for each other." Ghinnah sighed, finally looking up at Annah. "Do you think we should check this grain?"

As Annah sifted the wheat-flour through a woven-fiber sieve into a broad wooden bowl, Ghinnah poured more grain from a nearby basket into the large mortar. Looking up at the pen, she said, "Tell me about this big dark box that the father of your husband built. We heard rumors of this thing, but we didn't believe them."

Without excuses or mincing words, Annah told Ghinnah of the Most High's warning to Noakh: about the earth turning upon itself because of the violence of men, and about the preparations Noakh and his family had made for all the animals they expected to shelter.

Smiling, Ghinnah said, "I've heard of more peculiar things in my life. And I would say that if your husband and his family treat you well enough, then you could accept living with such an oddity."

"What if I were to tell you that I believe as they do?" Annah asked, challenging her mildly. "What if I said that the Most High is not a legend, but that He exists?"

Ghinnah bit down a smile. "I'd have to think about that."

They carried the bran-flecked flour into the lodge, where Naomi was visiting with Etsah, measuring out olive oil as she talked. "Thank you, daughter," Naomi said, eyeing the amount of flour in the large wooden bowl. "This will make enough dough for tonight and tomorrow. Now, please go ask our ancient one and Qeb-al if they will accept something to drink."

Obediently Annah went to the sunlit area near the front door, where Methuwshelakh was propped up, visiting with Qeb-al. Seeing Annah, the ancient man's eyes brightened. In his fragile, faded voice, Methuwshelakh said to Qeb-al, "Did the son of my son tell you . . . this child is of the Tsaraph? She has tools . . . to work the gold."

Qeb-al looked at Annah with new interest. Discomfited, Annah looked away. Qeb-al asked Methuwshelakh, "Is there a lodge of the Tsaraph nearby?"

"Yes . . . her family is across the river," Methuwshelakh answered proudly.

Licking his lips in evident anticipation, Qeb-al said, "Perhaps I should cross the river tomorrow."

Methuwshelakh lifted one frail old hand. "There is a bridge . . . though your cart is too . . . big. Only handcarts fit."

Annah flinched inwardly, turning away from Methuwshelakh and Qeb-al, forgetting to ask them if they wanted something to drink. *I'm going to be sick,* she thought, hastily stepping outside the lodge. *Qeb-al is going to visit Yerakh, and then I'm going to be killed.*

Seated near the evening fire in his lodge, Yerakh stared at the trader. Then he looked at his sisters. Haburah and Ayalah knelt nearby, eyeing him, hateful and smug. Yerakh glared at them, longing to slap them both.

Unintimidated, Ayalah tossed her head. "Listen to the trader, brother, since you wouldn't listen to us. Annah has made you a fool."

Leaning forward, Yerakh frowned at the trader. "You spoke to my sister? And she spoke to you?"

Clearly unnerved, Qeb-al stammered, "Ah, um, well, she n–never spoke directly to me, but we were there for all of last evening and half of today. I saw her talking to the daughter of my brother. And I was told that she— your lovely sister—has tools to work the gold."

"You saw these tools?" Yerakh snapped, no longer caring to be polite.

A haze of sweat broke out over the trader's red-brown face. "No, I didn't see the tools, but their ancient one described them to me. I'm sure he spoke the truth."

Yerakh sat back, seething. *I'll kill you,* he thought to Annah. *I should have killed you years ago. Where did you get tools?* As far as he could remember, he had used all of his tools since Annah's marriage. None were missing. Unless she had taken those old, deservedly forgotten tools belonging to his father.

Controlling himself, he asked, "Where is the daughter of your brother? I want to hear what she has to say about my sister."

The trader gaped at him, clearly offended. "Forgive me, Yerakh of the Tsaraph, but I doubt my worthless niece could say more than what I've told you."

Kneeling beside her husband on the grass mat before Yerakh, the trader's thin little wife spoke. "I'll tell you where she is."

Yerakh frowned at the woman, contemptuous of the ridiculous would-be-gold talismans in her hair.

She shifted uncomfortably. "We left her at the lodge of Noakh to guard our cart and to visit with your sister; they seemed to enjoy each other's company. Our cart would not fit over the bridge, so my husband and I carried our wares over on our backs. See . . ." The trader's wife opened a leather bundle, spreading out various carvings, combs, and scent-pots.

Ayalah and Taphaph edged over to inspect these offerings, but Yerakh ignored them.

If you've stolen my father's tools, then you are dead, he thought to Annah. *Tomorrow morning I will cross that bridge, find you, and strangle you!*

Without another word, he left his seat and strode into his workroom. Tensing, he opened his father's storage chest and rummaged inside, reluctantly breathing his father's scent among the herbs and spices. He patted his hands through his father's garments, his favorite stone molds, his windings of stiffened leather cords. He searched the entire storage chest without finding the tools. *They were here,* Yerakh thought. *I know I put them in here the next morning.*

The next morning, after his father's death. After a terrifying night of digging, sweating, and cursing as he struggled to bury his father's body beyond the far edges of his fields. He could still hear the hoarse laughter of the Nachash when she discovered him working that night. Her rasping, avid voice still echoed in his mind.

Bloody, bloody man! Can you hide blood? No. Blood is alive! It

follows us! Can you bury blood? No! One drop grows like a seed!
Like a stream, blood flows until you drown! You!

Even now, after all these years, he was sweating, re-membering the Nachash—her wild hair, her death-odor, those sightless, staring eyes. She was the essence of all his youthful nightmares. Shaking his head, Yerakh forced himself to clear his mind. The tools were gone. Annah had taken them. She *was* working the gold; she had de-ceived him for twenty-five years.

You'll beg my forgiveness! he raged silently, remembering her pretense of a vacant face. *You stole my knowledge and made a fool of me. For that, I will kill you.*

Kneeling on the softness of their bed, Annah kissed her husband's cheek, then combed out his thick, dark curls, cherishing the feel of his hair winding about her fingers.

"You can comb my hair tonight," Shem teased her. "Yepheth and my father are waiting for me."

"No, I can't comb your hair tonight," Annah said, smoothing his curls into the confines of a black leather cord. "You have to go out to the herds again, remember?"

"I'd rather not remember," he sighed, turning to kiss her. "Will you stay with I'ma and Ghinnah again today?"

"Later," Annah murmured. *If I live. That Qeb-al was in the settlement last night, and I have no doubt he's told everything to Yerakh.*

His eyebrows lifting almost sternly, Shem pulled An-nah into his lap. "You will remember what I said? You'll stay away from the river?"

Annah focused on his beard, brushing it lightly. "If

225

Yerakh is determined to kill me, beloved, he will kill me. And if he brings his favorite weapon, that Naham-the-Iron-breaker, then you and your brothers won't be able to fight them. I would die anyway."

"The Most High did not bring you across the river to let you die," Shem reminded her gently. "He has other plans for your life, and He won't change them. Even so, it would be wise to take precautions and watch for Yerakh."

"I will." She stood, allowing him to rise.

After tying a soft leather band across his forehead, he bent to kiss her again, nuzzling her. "Remember what I said: Stay away from the river."

She hugged him tight, then smiled and handed him his herding stick. "Don't worry. I love you, but you have to go. Your father and Yepheth are waiting. If you see I'ma and Ghinnah, tell them I'll come a little later, when I've finished tidying up here."

She watched him leave the clearing surrounding their hut, waving at him once when he turned to look at her. As soon as he was gone, she smoothed their bed, filled the oil lamp, then carried a dish of nutshells and fruit peels out to the waste pit. Returning to the hut again, Annah rinsed the dish and threw the rinse water into the grass beyond the doorway. Then she deliberately pulled the precious ornament from her neck and tucked it beneath her pillow. She would not give Yerakh the option of strangling her with the cord of her beautiful shell carving. Shouldering her grass bag, she willed her feet to move toward the river.

She already knew where she would wait—on the south side of the bridge. Her husband and his brothers wouldn't see her there. But Yerakh would see her immediately.

Perhaps I should throw myself into the river now and be done with the waiting, she thought, as she approached the bridge. *It would be easier and certainly less painful.*

No. The thought came to her, firm and undeniable. *If I die today, then let it be because Yerakh has taken my life.*

She knelt on the sand and waited, sweating. Once in a while, she dipped her hands into the water to cool them and to calm herself. Then she thought of her shuttle; she hadn't touched it since before her wedding. By now, she never used her veil, but she could still use her shuttle.

She groped inside her woven-grass bag. Pulling out the shuttle, she stared at it as if she had never seen it before. *Everything is different now,* she thought. *I no longer need this.* But she unwound a length of the delicate thread and began to knot it loosely. The thread was neglected, brittle and difficult. By the time she had worked a cord the length of her palm, she sensed a presence. Glancing across the river, she saw Yerakh, his darkly bearded face staring, gloating. Her heart began to thud.

I am afraid, she admitted to herself, her hands shaking, clenching the shuttle. *O Most High, help me. I'm afraid. Shield me as you did the night of my mother's death. Yerakh is eager to kill me; I can feel it.* She swallowed hard, praying. *If I am to speak to him, Most High, please give me the words. And if I am to die, then let me die quickly. Also, if I must die . . . please, I want to take Yerakh with me.*

Sixteen

YERAKH CROSSED the bridge eagerly, staring at Annah. She was kneeling in the sand near the bridge, simply waiting for him.

Haburah and the others claim you do have a mind, he thought, sneering. *Though it can't be too clever a mind if you're so easily caught, Ma'adannah.*

He had not thought of her given name in years, but he remembered it now, hating it as much as ever. Hating her. He had always despised her; she had been an irritant, a troublesome child. Always full of questions, always thinking of new things. *Little fool. I'll be glad to know you are dead.*

He stepped off the bridge, still staring at her. She hadn't moved. She was kneeling in the sand, her head lowered, her eyes almost closed. She looked better— cared for. Actually beautiful. Not the Annah who had cringed before him for so many years.

Yerakh slowed, then stopped, trying to comprehend the difference. A new presence surrounded her, swirling about her and washing over him like strong, unstoppable waves. He felt confused, alarmed. His mind told him this was Annah, but his senses told him this woman was someone else. Uncertain, he hesitated. "Annah?"

She did not look at him, but she spoke, her voice low and firm. "The Annah you remember is dead."

Frowning, fighting down his uncertainty, Yerakh narrowed his eyes. "Really? If Annah is dead, then who are you?"

With grace and dignity, she stood and looked him full in the face. Her eyes were his mother's eyes. But unlike his indifferent mother, this woman's eyes were passionately alive and full of power. A wave of fear passed through him. Catching his breath, he asked again, "Who are you?"

"I am an enemy of the Nachash, whom you have sheltered, O Yerakh of the Tsaraph!"

The Nachash has an enemy? Stunned, Yerakh stepped back. Annah, or the woman he had thought was Annah, moved toward him in a torrent of words.

"And because you have sheltered the Nachash, Yerakh of the Tsaraph, you are cursed. You have condemned yourself by your love of violence: choking the life from your father, then causing the deaths of your mother, your wife, and your brothers. Listen, Yerakh!"

She advanced on him, her eyes kindling. "Because you have done these things, Yerakh of the Tsaraph, your new wife will never bear a child. And you will die a violent death, but not by the hands of a man; you will see your death coming. Your fear will be so great that the death of your brother Gammad will seem like a mercy. You will long for the quiet of his grave—in the waste pit beside your first wife, Iltani!"

Hearing this, Yerakh began to shake. *She knows Gammad's burial place! But how? Naham swore he would tell no one.*

Yerakh retreated to the bridge, but she followed him, calling out, "Your body will be torn to pieces, and your bones will be crushed and scattered like bits of straw!"

Yerakh scuttled across the bridge, barely able to see where he was going. But her words followed him, lifting across the water. "There will not be one person left who will mourn for you, Yerakh. You are cursed! The heavens themselves will turn upon you!"

On the opposite side of the river, Yerakh charged up into the trees lining the riverbank, desperate to get back to the settlement, terrified that she would follow him. He could still feel the presence about her, sweeping out against him like a mighty lash. The combined powers of the Nachash and her whisperers were nothing compared to this boundless tide.

Annah was shaking, unable to believe Yerakh was gone. *But it's true.* Amazed, she retrieved her grass bag to put away the shuttle. She had been clenching it so hard that its outlines were bright red against her palm. Still unable to believe what had happened, she looked at Yerakh's footprints, fresh, damp, and leading to the bridge.

I did not imagine this, she thought. *Yerakh is gone, and he won't return. I am free. O Most High, thank You!* She hugged her grass bag and—like a child—spun in a joyous circle, lifting her face toward the warm, ruddy sky. "Thank You!"

Elated, she slung her grass bag over her shoulder and

ran up to the trees. Someone was there. Ghinnah emerged from the undergrowth, obviously shocked, the soft bloom fading from her cheeks. "Annah!" she cried. "I came looking for you. Was that your wicked brother? You said such horrible things—I thought he would soil himself."

"He's gone, and he won't return!" Annah hugged the astonished Ghinnah, dancing around her, pulling her in a circle. "I'm free! Where's my husband?" She hurried through the shadowy flowering trees.

Ghinnah trotted after her, panting. "But . . . those things you said about his death, and his bones being crushed, and no one mourning him . . ."

Annah halted, her elation dampened by Ghinnah's fear. "Ghinnah, I know those things must have sounded horrible to you. But they were the truth. I knew it, and Yerakh knew it, which is why he was so frightened. And he ran because he felt the condemnation of the Most High, though he won't perceive it that way. He will make up an explanation of his own."

"Your Most High frightens me."

Somberly, Annah touched Ghinnah's arm. "If you're not His enemy, then you have no reason to fear Him. He simply desires that you call to Him—and listen to Him in love. As for me, He is better than my own father. He has saved my life twice. He also brought me out of that horrible settlement and gave me a true family. I owe Him everything. Whatever happens in my life, I'll never say a word against Him."

Ghinnah didn't respond. Annah smiled again, her joy returning. "O Ghinnah, in one day you've been more kind to me than my own sisters have been for all my life. Please be happy for me now. My brother is gone! I'm going to live, when I was so sure I would die!"

"You thought he would kill you?"

"I knew he would. But the Most High surrounded me and gave me words. Now I will live! Please, be happy for me."

Reluctantly Ghinnah smiled, but she changed the subject from the Most High. "The mother of your husband will wonder where we are. I promised I would find you and bring you immediately."

"Then we should return to the lodge."

They found Naomi seated just outside the lodge, weaving cordage through the ribwork of a new basket, obviously waiting for them. Seeing Annah and Ghinnah, she said, "I knew you would be playing and taking your time."

Kneeling, Annah put her hands over her mother-in-law's hands, unable to conceal her happiness. "We weren't playing, I'ma. I have to tell you—"

"Wait, please," Naomi interrupted, seeming anxious. "While you are both here, and before Qeb-al and his family return from the settlement, I must tell you something." She looked at Ghinnah, now kneeling beside Annah. "This morning before you awoke, Ghinnah, my first son asked me to speak to your aunt for you."

Color rushed to Ghinnah's face. "To speak to my aunt . . . of marriage?"

Hastily Naomi reassured her, "I will only speak to her if you wish to accept marriage with my son. If not, then we won't be angry. My son will not coerce you."

"But . . ." Ghinnah faltered, "he hasn't said a word to me."

Annah patted Ghinnah's shoulder comfortingly. "My husband's older brother doesn't speak often. He must admire you tremendously if he has spoken to his mother."

Distracted, running her hands through her hair, Ghinnah said, "This is too much. I have to think." She wandered into the lodge.

Annah turned to Naomi, worried. "Ghinnah had a fright, I'ma, and it's my fault. Yerakh found me this morning."

"Child! Why didn't you tell me!"

"I'm telling you now." Eagerly, she told Naomi about her confrontation with Yerakh. When she finished, Naomi dropped her basketwork, agitated.

"Forgive me, child. I must find my husband and my sons."

Shem strode into the lodge and stopped in front of Annah, staring at her. For an instant he seemed incapable of speech, then he pulled Annah into his arms. "I should be angry with you for not listening to me! If Yerakh had touched you . . ."

"You would have tried to kill him," Annah said, giving his thought words. "Or he would have killed you and your family. I couldn't risk your lives for mine."

Giving up, clearly relieved, Shem sighed, holding her close.

Noakh entered the lodge and said calmly, "Now, daughter, I hear you had a pleasant morning."

"Yes, I did, Father of my Husband," Annah agreed, beaming at him. "But I frightened Ghinnah."

"Where is Ghinnah?" Wondering, Noakh looked around, but their guest had gone out the back door to be alone. Noakh exhaled thoughtfully. "Well, I am sure that she must have time to think, as we must have time."

He believes Yepheth has decided hastily, Annah thought, startled. *He has doubts. And Ghinnah has doubts. Was I too eager to be friends with her? Was I mistaken?*

Equally solemn, Naomi entered the lodge. "Yepheth and Khawm are coming, so we will have our midday meal soon. Is Ghinnah outside? I wonder if Qeb-al and Etsah might return this evening. I told Ghinnah she should make her own decision concerning Yepheth's request; I won't mention anything to her family unless she is willing to stay."

"What do you think of her?" Shem asked Annah beneath his breath, his arm now encircling her waist.

Annah answered, "I've enjoyed visiting with her. But I have to remind myself that she's still basically a stranger."

"I agree—although *we* should still be strangers; we've known each other for only five months. I'm afraid we didn't provide the best example for my brothers."

"That was beyond our control."

"True. The Most High allowed us no choice. But Yepheth has decided for himself that he wants Ghinnah, and he won't change his mind. That's why my parents are so worried."

Naomi interrupted their furtive conversation. "Daughter, if you will bring in some water, I would welcome it. Perhaps you should also find Ghinnah."

Hearing Khawm's laughter in front of the lodge, and knowing that Yepheth was probably with him, Annah nodded. Lifting the clay water vessel in her arms, she slipped out the back door. There was no sign of Ghinnah. Quickly, Annah filled the vessel at the well. By the time she returned to the lodge, Noakh, Naomi, Yepheth, Shem, and Khawm were all engrossed in a serious conversation.

Annah set the water vessel just inside the door, then crept outside again. *Ghinnah,* she thought, *where are you?*

She found the young woman on the eastern side of the lodge, sitting near Qeb-al's wooden, solid-wheeled trader's cart, watching Qeb-al's ponderous grazing ox. As Ghinnah looked up, Annah said, "I'll stay with you for a while."

"The one they call Khawm . . . I heard him laughing. Was Yepheth with him?"

"Yes." Smoothing her tunic over her knees, Annah knelt beside Ghinnah. "They're all inside; I thought I should leave them alone."

Ghinnah looked alarmed. "They won't fight, will they?"

"No," Annah soothed her. "They don't fight. They talk."

"You've never seen them arguing?" Ghinnah asked, incredulous.

"No. As I said, they talk. They truly love each other."

"And they love you."

"Yes, they do love me," Annah agreed quietly. "I am blessed."

Ghinnah sighed, stretching her legs straight out before herself. "Two days ago, I said that I envied you for having your husband and his family. Now I'm afraid. Does this Yepheth believe in the Most High?"

"Yes. Everyone in this lodge acknowledges Him."

"And what if I can't?" Ghinnah demanded. "Years from now, will this Yepheth cast me off and take another wife who does believe in the Most High?"

Annah shook her head. "Yepheth would never do such a thing."

"And do you believe in the coming destruction—this

dreadful story of the Most High allowing the earth to turn upon itself?" Fierce now, Ghinnah stared into Annah's eyes, demanding perfect honesty.

Annah spoke carefully. "Yes. I'd prefer not to think of it, but when—or if—this great destruction happens, then I will accept it."

"So you're not entirely convinced of it either!" Ghinnah sounded satisfied.

"Don't misunderstand me," Annah warned her gently. "I only said that I prefer not to think of it . . . but I will accept it if it should happen."

"Then, I won't have to accept it unless it happens." Bitter now, Ghinnah said, "So, I can choose to marry a non-speaking man who believes in an ancient, unbelievable story, or I can continue to lie, cheat, and steal with my uncle's family, hoping I'm never caught."

"You hate both choices," Annah whispered, distressed. "I'm sorry."

"Don't! I won't be an object of pity."

"It's better than being an object of contempt, as I was for twenty-five years."

Subdued, Ghinnah hung her head. "I admit I've been fortunate by comparison. My uncle was robbed and beaten twice last year before I came to live with his family. And Etsah never feels safe when we're traveling. But nothing terrible has happened to me, beyond the death of my mother. Look . . ." Ghinnah sat up straight. "There are Qeb-al and the others. I didn't expect them to return so soon."

"I'll go tell my husband and his family," Annah said, getting to her feet. "I'ma will want to feed them again, I'm sure."

Ghinnah stood, staring at her approaching relatives. The color ebbed from her cheeks. "Qeb-al is angry. And Pa-sak is injured."

There's been trouble in the settlement, Annah realized. *Someone beat that rude Pa-sak.* Fearful, she hurried into the lodge, her gold talismans fluttering against her neck.

Still fuming, Yerakh entered the lodge of Naham. The giant ironworker was eating his midday meal, his massive, dark-haired hands clutching the huge, flat grain cakes he favored. His wives, Shuwa, Qetsiyah, and Haburah, were hovering nearby; Naham expected them to wait on him until he had eaten his fill.

Seeing Yerakh, Naham folded some grain cakes into one substantial bite, shoved it into his mouth, and spoke. "Come in, my brother." Pointing to his wives, he said, "You, you, and you, go away."

Quietly they filed out of the lodge. Only Haburah dared to look at Yerakh. She was thinner and doleful.

Yerakh thought, *I should have given her to Naham years ago.* When they were gone, Yerakh sat beside Naham.

Slapping one of the large soft grain cakes at him, Naham said, "Eat! You look sick. Isn't your wife tending you?"

Ignoring his question, Yerakh asked quietly, "Did you tell anyone where you buried Gammad?"

His mouth flecked with food, Naham reached for a pitcher of juice. "No. I haven't even thought of it since that night. Why do you ask?"

"Someone else knows."

Naham gulped from the pitcher and wiped his mouth on the back of one enormous hand. "Impossible! Who? Someone else you want me to kill?"

Do I want him to kill that Annah-who-is-not-Annah? Yerakh wondered. He recalled the force of the presence about her. Trying to decide, he scowled at his knuckles, which were raw from beating that impudent young trader, Pa-sak. At last, sighing heavily, he said, "No. Not yet."

That Annah-who-was-not-Annah was more fearsome than the Nachash. If he tried to kill her, or have her killed, she might curse him to die immediately. *I'm already cursed*, he reminded himself. *I must persuade her to withdraw her words. But how?*

Seventeen

ANNAH HURRIED outside the lodge to stand with Ghinnah near the trader's cart. Qeb-al dropped his pack and screamed at Ghinnah as he approached.

"You've been nothing but trouble since the day I took you into my care! You're a curse to me!" Pushing her against the broad wheel of the cart, he cried, "Because you've befriended this stupid woman and her insane family, look what her brother did to my son!"

Pa-sak's eyes were swollen shut. His lips were split and his teeth were bloodied. The tearful Etsah was holding his hand, guiding him. The boy-child, Saiyr, was glaring at Ghinnah.

Provoked, Annah thrust an arm between Qeb-al and Ghinnah. "If you must be angry, then be angry with me. Ghinnah has nothing to do with my brother's bad temper."

"You," Qeb-al muttered, flushing. "I ate bread with the family of your husband. You should have warned me about your brother and the people in that settlement!"

"Would you have listened to me?" Annah wanted to know, struggling to keep her voice soft. "I'm sure you would have sneered at my warnings."

By now Noakh, Shem, Yepheth, and Khawm were standing alongside the angry Qeb-al, curbing him with their presence. Speaking mildly, Noakh said, "We will give you compensation for your son's injuries. Tell us what you consider to be fair."

Shaking with rage, Qeb-al pointed at the silent Ghinnah. "Take this useless burden off my hands. Give her to one of your sons or chase her off your lands, whatever you please. That's what I want!"

"We will do whatever Ghinnah decides," Naomi said quietly, standing beside Noakh. "If she wishes, Ghinnah can marry my firstborn son."

"She'll have no marriage portion from me," Qeb-al warned. "Not after what's happened to my son!"

"We won't demand a marriage portion," Naomi agreed.

"And if she decides not to marry my son," Noakh added, "I will pay restitution for your son's injuries."

While they were speaking, Annah was aware of Ghinnah looking first at her, then at Noakh, then at Yepheth. *She feels she has no choice,* Annah realized.

Downcast, Ghinnah walked behind Noakh and Naomi, passing Shem to stand beside Yepheth.

Clearly uncomfortable, Yepheth cleared his throat. "If you are unwilling to marry me, Ghinnah, then my parents and I will do whatever we can to help you."

Lifting her chin at him, Ghinnah asked, "If I become

your wife, will you ever reject me and put me aside?"

"No." Yepheth seemed genuinely shocked. "If you marry me, then how could I put you aside? Whatever happens, I'd never reject you."

Ghinnah stared at him for a long instant, then put out her hand. Yepheth smiled. He was, Annah thought, almost as handsome as Shem. Clasping Ghinnah's hand, Yepheth addressed the smoldering Qeb-al. "I'll offer you the same terms my brother offered for his wife: five hundred sheep and half my grain from this past season. Everything's counted and waiting, if you agree."

"And," Naomi added, "as it was with Ma'adannah, you must agree that Ghinnah may bring with her only as much as she can carry in her arms. Nothing more."

Qeb-al stared at Yepheth as if he were mad. "You'd give me five hundred sheep?"

"And half my grain," Yepheth reminded him. "As my mother said, she is to bring only what she can carry in her arms."

Etsah frowned. "What do you mean, 'only what she can carry in her arms'?"

"Hush!" Qeb-al snapped. To Yepheth, he replied, "I agree. You're holding hands now, so she's yours. Have many sons and long lives. Now, I'll take the sheep and the grain."

"Annah." Ghinnah released Yepheth's hand and motioned furtively to Annah. Stepping apart from the others, she whispered, "What did you carry away from your family?"

"One of my mother's best tunics, her hair bindings, and my father's tools."

Ghinnah laughed softly, snatching Annah's hand. "I need your help."

"I can't carry anything for you."

"No, but you can load my arms."

Marching over to Qeb-al's wooden cart, Ghinnah loosened its protective leather cover.

Qeb-al protested. "What are you doing?"

"Fulfilling my portion of the agreement," Ghinnah answered defiantly. "I'm taking what I can carry in my arms. Annah, hold these until I'm ready for them." Rummaging through the goods in the cart, Ghinnah dislodged a small red storage box.

Etsah screeched, "You can't take that!"

"But you took it from my father's house," Ghinnah argued. "I'm only taking what should have been mine when he died."

Ghinnah next removed a smaller, more elaborately painted storage box. Qeb-al started to object, but Yepheth, Shem, and Khawm moved closer, and he shut his mouth. Annah bit her lip, hiding a smile.

Ghinnah nudged Annah impatiently. "Ma'adannah, take this one too." Turning yet again, she tugged out a third, larger box. The effort made her sweat.

"You can't possibly carry all those," Qeb-al told the girl smugly. "If you drop anything, it will be mine again."

"You will see what I can carry," Ghinnah answered with equal confidence, her clear eyes wide. "Even if I break both my arms, I will have what belonged to my parents." She jumped from the cart, facing the corner of the lodge. Grabbing the largest box, she said, "Ma'adannah, give me that box first, then the small one on top."

She's going to drop them. They're too heavy. But Annah complied.

Balancing the boxes, Ghinnah gasped, "I have them. But I can't see."

"Forward," Annah urged her. "I will tell you when to turn."

Ghinnah struggled forward, sweating, followed by Yepheth.

"You can't help her!" Qeb-al cried. "And if she drops them, they're mine!"

"If she drops them, she can try two boxes instead," Khawm answered, taunting Qeb-al with his peculiar cackle.

"Turn!" Annah called to Ghinnah as they reached the corner of the lodge. Blindly Ghinnah obeyed, sweat streaming down her face.

"Don't you dare," Shem said sharply. Annah saw him step in front of the boy-child, Saiyr, who had apparently tried to trip Ghinnah to make her fall.

By now, Ghinnah was staggering.

"Three steps, then turn," Yepheth told her. She grunted, managed three steps, turned, then dropped all three boxes inside the lodge, falling on top of them. Yepheth rushed to help her, with Annah just behind him. They hauled her to her feet.

"Did you hurt yourself?" Annah asked.

Very softly, Ghinnah said, "I hurt . . . everywhere."

"You probably crippled yourself," Qeb-al told her, as if he hoped it was true.

Yepheth gave the flushed trader a long, even stare. Calmly he said, "Bring your ox and your cart to the back of the lodge. My brothers and I will bring your grain and sheep so you can leave at once."

As Yepheth led Qeb-al and his family away from the lodge, Annah heard a persistent tapping from behind Methuwshelakh's screen. *He's awake*, Annah realized, *and he must be worried*. She started toward the old man's pallet to

243

reassure him, but Noakh overtook her. "Don't worry, daughter. I'll speak to the father of my fathers. Stay with your sister."

Ghinnah is now my sister, Annah thought, delighted.

"Annah." Naomi gave her a tapering clay vial. "Here; this oil should ease Ghinnah's pain. And I'll brew some herbs." Clucking her tongue regretfully, Naomi added, "She won't be able to move tomorrow."

Ghinnah groaned. "I don't think I can move now." But she smiled at Annah and whispered, "My husband does speak after all."

"When it's important," Annah agreed.

"Well, I'm glad it was important to him that Qeb-al should leave. And Etsah should be happy; she's always wanted to settle down and raise grain and sheep. But they'll have to force Pa-sak and Saiyr to help them." She winced. "Ow, my neck."

"And your arms, and your legs, and your mind, I'm sure," Annah scolded gently, rubbing the aromatic oil on Ghinnah's neck and arms. "You shouldn't have carried those boxes. They were too heavy."

"But worth the pain," Ghinnah said, taking some of the fragrant oil in her palms to rub on her shoulders. "My mother's clothes, her ornaments, her weaving weights, and my father's sunstones are in those boxes."

"Weaving weights?"

"My mother used to weave garments for wealthy people in our city who were too far above the rest of us to wear plain leather. The weaving weights hold the threads taut at the bottom of the frame. They've been unused since her death. Etsah wanted to learn to weave, but she couldn't bear learning from me."

"And what are sunstones?"

Biting her lip, Ghinnah rubbed some of the oil into her legs. "Sunstones are like cold fire—a great mystery. My father never let me touch them."

"Cold fire?" Naomi asked, dubious, offering Ghinnah a cup of pungent, steaming, brewed herbs.

"I'll show them to you," Ghinnah offered, painfully reaching for the smallest, most elaborately painted box.

"No, you can show us later," Naomi told her firmly. "I want you to drink this brew. And I'll finish preparing our midday meal."

By now, Noakh was carrying Methuwshelakh out from behind the screen. The ancient man was alert, watching Ghinnah. "I knew she would stay," he announced in whispery, cheery self-congratulation.

Swiftly Annah gathered fleeces and pillows for the ancient man's comfort.

Noakh smiled at her. "Thank you, daughter."

Unable to turn her head, Ghinnah crept over to a mat and knelt down. She reeked of the aromatic oil, and she could barely move, but her eyes sparkled. Ghinnah loved Methuwshelakh's company. Whenever he spoke, she listened to his every word. It seemed to Annah that Ghinnah was accepting her marriage and her new family.

Resting in a place of honor, Methuwshelakh lifted a frail hand toward Ghinnah, rasping happily. "Child . . . now I will tell you. When I was . . . about your age . . . my father took me on a journey . . . to visit the Father of All. At that time . . . the Father of All was . . . in his seventh kentum. Seven generations before me!"

Ghinnah stared at Methuwshelakh, confused. "The Father of All, Ancient One?"

Sighing, Methuwshelakh said, "You don't believe . . . the stories of old. The Father of all my Fathers . . . was created from clay, near a river. His first breath . . . was the breath of the Word—the Most High. And his color was . . . your color . . . red in the brown of his face . . . even in his old age. He was Adam . . . for the red in his face."

As she helped Naomi set out dishes of lentils, flat bread, and olives, Annah listened, fascinated. Eager to hear more, she asked. "Did you meet Havah, the wife of Adam?"

"The same Havah." Methuwshelakh sighed again, his eyes faraway. "She was . . . even in her old age . . . everything lovely and . . . pleasing in a woman. The Father of All called her . . . his Mischief . . . and Life-giver. Later, when she departed this life . . . he no longer cared . . . to live. One day . . . he said he was tired. He went to sleep . . . because he missed her."

When Ghinnah continued to stare at him, clearly bewildered, the ancient man said, "You do not believe. But one day . . . you will remember what I have said. And . . . I tell you now . . . it is good to see . . . Adam's color . . . in your face."

Annah knelt beside Ghinnah and smiled, leaning over to whisper in her ear, "Now you are thinking, *My husband's family is more than a little strange.*"

Unable to turn her head to look at Annah, Ghinnah widened her eyes, whispering, "How did you know?"

"Because," Annah replied, "that's what I thought on my first morning here, when I saw everything in the pen behind the lodge."

Ghinnah bit her lip, surprised and uncertain. Pleased, Annah thought, *Perhaps you are wondering whether or not you should believe the stories of old. But you wouldn't dare to call our Methuwshelakh a liar, even in your own mind. I think you'll eventu-*

ally believe in the Most High. Smiling, she helped Naomi serve their food.

"You look sad this morning," Ghinnah told Annah. "Are you thinking of your cruel brother and your family again?"

"No." Annah knelt behind Ghinnah to comb her hair—Ghinnah's arms still hurt too much to reach behind her head. "I'm disappointed. My time of seclusion has begun, and I wish it hadn't. I long for a child."

"You've been married only a short time," Ghinnah reminded her.

Annah sighed. "I suppose I'm too eager. I'm sure that in a few years, we'll be tearing out our hair because our children will be running everywhere and questioning us about everything."

"*Your* children will do that," Ghinnah answered, pretending hauteur. "My children will sit quietly like their father. They'll be perfect."

"With you as their mother?" Annah teased. "I doubt it."

"Then I'll send my children to play with your children, and you can tear your hair out over all of them and leave me alone."

"You can send them all to me," Naomi announced from her place beside the hearth. She was kneading dough in a polished wooden bowl, her hands glistening with oil. "I'll teach your children to behave, then I'll send them back to you."

Annah smiled at her mother-in-law. "You say that now, but I think you'll spoil them and send them back to us. As far as our children are concerned, we'll be nothing in their eyes when compared to you, I'ma-Naomi."

"We will see," Naomi said, smiling in return. "It will be good to hold a child again. Perhaps by this time next year, you will both have children."

"Perhaps," Annah agreed. She eyed the dough in Naomi's hands. "I'ma, after I've helped Ghinnah, I'll be glad to make those cakes."

"I'd forgotten, I promised—" Naomi stopped and turned.

Annah looked up, sensing Noakh's presence even as he approached the back of the lodge.

His arms and face were covered with dust and sweat from working the earth. He glanced at his wife, raising his grizzled eyebrows significantly, then he turned to Annah. "Daughter, I must warn you that your sister—the talkative Ayalah—is coming to visit, with Tsillah and her daughter, Taphaph."

Stifling a groan, Annah finished smoothing Ghinnah's hair with the carved wooden comb. *Ayalah, Tsillah, and Taphaph! Why should they come here except to cause trouble?* She looked from Noakh to Naomi, dismayed. "Am I allowed to refuse them entry into the lodge?"

"Let's carry the mats and food outside," Naomi suggested. "That way they won't disturb our Ancient One. Also, we will offer them only cakes and water this time. I've had enough of those women. They won't change."

"Can I meet them?" Ghinnah's curiosity apparently overwhelmed her misery.

Annah stood to pick up the mats. "Can you move that far?"

"For the chance to meet one of your sisters, I will," Ghinnah assured her.

"They'll be here soon," Noakh warned.

Hurriedly Annah carried several mats outside, placing them near the eastern wall of the lodge. Ghinnah followed her slowly, holding a clay pitcher of water. When Annah had arranged the mats properly and helped Ghinnah to sit down, Naomi joined them with a basket containing only plain grain cakes and six cups for water. Satisfied, Annah went out to the path to meet their guests.

Ayalah was leading them, her sly, pretty face alight: She was enjoying herself. "We won't stay, Annah!" she called out. "I mean, Ma'adannah."

Annah put her hands out to greet her sister properly, though not affectionately. Then she looked at Tsillah and Taphaph, who had stopped more than an arm's length away. Tsillah looked proud as ever, but Taphaph seemed older, tired and hard-eyed, her lustrous hair swept back severely into a sparkling, gold-talismaned hair binding. In her arms, Taphaph held a small parcel of leather.

"There," Tsillah sniffed, nudging her daughter. "Didn't I tell you? That Annah-creature is more beautiful than Parah and Haburah, now that she has a mind."

Thank you, Tsillah, Annah thought without rancor. She nodded to them politely. "Will you sit with us and have something to eat and drink?"

"No," Taphaph said abruptly. "We won't stay. My husband is waiting for us to return to the settlement." She hesitated.

Life with Yerakh has not pleased you as much as you'd hoped, Annah thought to Taphaph, seeing the strain in her eyes.

Moving stiffly, Taphaph held out the leather parcel. Acting as their go-between, Ayalah took the parcel and gave it to Annah.

Feeling its weight, Annah realized at once that the parcel contained a solid bar of gold.

Taphaph cleared her throat. "Yerakh wants peace in his family. He knows you have your father's tools, and he says that you should keep them. He won't come after you again. But he wants you to lift this curse you've placed upon him."

Annah looked at the parcel in her hands. Yerakh must be terrified to offer her so much gold and the ownership of their father's tools. Very gently she said, "Tell your husband that I feel compassion for you both. But the curse was already upon him as soon as he killed our father. The earth was never meant to receive such an act of violence."

Taphaph looked desperate, her eyes filling with tears. "Please! My husband has not been the same since you spoke to him! He is distant . . . full of despair. And . . ."

When Taphaph could not continue, Annah said, "He has beaten you."

The other woman nodded mutely.

Annah sighed. "There is nothing I can do. Yerakh is the one who—"

"You mean you won't do anything." Taphaph burst out. "You're the one who spoke the curse!"

"Yerakh brought his own curse upon himself. All I did was give it words."

"Then what can he do to escape this curse?" Taphaph begged. "I want my husband to be as he was before!"

"Yerakh must be willing to submit to justice for the death of his father, and for causing the deaths of Gammad and the others."

"You mean he should seek his own death?" Taphaph said, not believing what she heard.

"He should acknowledge his wrongs and give himself

over to justice."

"You know he can't do that."

"I know he *won't*," Annah agreed. She held the gold out to Taphaph. "This has not served Yerakh as he wished. Take it back to him."

Alarmed, Taphaph retreated. "No, I can't return it to him. He will be angry enough when I tell him what you have said."

"Tell him before many witnesses," Annah urged. "Then stay away from him until he's calm."

"No! I don't want any more of your advice—you've caused enough trouble!" Covering her ears, Taphaph ran toward the river.

Glaring, Tsillah spat at Annah's feet. "You cursed my daughter as barren!"

As Tsillah strode off, Annah remained silent. She could not tell them what they wanted to hear; it would be a lie.

Ayalah loitered, smirking. "Your advice about telling Yerakh in front of witnesses was good, Ma'adannah, but I doubt Taphaph will listen."

"Make her listen," Annah urged her sister. "Or you will share the blame if she's killed."

Ayalah widened her eyes at this, indignant. "Why should I be blamed? I can't control Yerakh when he's angry. Enjoy the gold, Ma'adannah. Yerakh must have felt like he was tearing out his guts to give it to you. Perhaps you'll see me again, dear sister, and perhaps you won't. Until then!" Waving a careless farewell, Ayalah followed Tsillah and Taphaph down the narrow path through the trees to the river.

Annah felt a sinking pain in her stomach. *Why did I think I could be rid of Yerakh and the others so easily? What a fool I am! O Most High, what will happen now?* She watched her sister and Tsillah and Taphaph until they vanished into the trees. Then she returned to the lodge of Noakh.

Eighteen

SEATED ON a grass mat in the sunlight behind the lodge, Annah listened to Ghinnah's humming as they sorted a small hill of tiny, smooth-skinned, violet-blue berries. Ghinnah looked better today; she moved more freely, and she hadn't complained of her neck or back hurting even once this morning. But it was her obvious happiness that pleased Annah the most. Pretending to complain, Annah said, "Why are you making so much noise? You're supposed to be miserable, marrying a non-speaking man."

Startled, Ghinnah looked up from stemming the berries. Then she smiled. "You're teasing me! But Annah, please, don't ever tell Yepheth I called him a nonspeaking man; he'd feel hurt. Besides, he doesn't need words, the way he watches me."

"Then you are happy you stayed?"

"I think I am," Ghinnah agreed, the lovely color deepening in her cheeks.

She's thinking of Yepheth, Annah decided. Clearing her throat, she said, "When we've finished here, we should go bathe. Then I'll help I'ma with the food for tonight while you do nothing, because you're the bride this time. I thought Yepheth would never finish building your dwelling place."

"He was being very careful; it had to be perfect," Ghinnah said, mildly defensive.

"I'm sure it will be." Annah stopped, sensing the approach of another. *Shem*, she thought, standing eagerly. He waited at the corner of the lodge, exhausted and wild haired because he had just returned from his watch over the herds.

Shem grinned at Annah, admiring her even as his eyes appealed to her silently: *I need to talk to you.*

"Wait for me, I'll return," Annah said to Ghinnah.

"If my husband ever gives me such a look, *I* won't return," Ghinnah replied airily. "Just to let you know."

"I'll remember that." Annah hurried to her husband, who quickly led her around to the west wall, out of Ghinnah's sight.

"I'm tired, I'm dirty, and I'm hungry, but I have to ask you two things," Shem whispered, staring at her as if she were lovely and infinitely desirable. "My first question is, will you be staying here again tonight?"

Pleased by her husband's tenderness, Annah wrapped her arms around his neck. "No, I'll leave with you as soon as we've sent your brother and Ghinnah away after the celebration. My time of seclusion is ended—for this month, at least."

Shem's expression softened. "Don't worry, beloved;

254

the children will come soon enough. Until then, we can keep each other company." He bent, kissing her cheek, then her throat.

Annah sighed. "Tell me, before we both forget, what was your second question?"

Reluctantly Shem paused, trying to remember. "Yepheth wanted to ask if Ghinnah needed him to carry anything in particular out to their shelter. Utensils, lamps, storage boxes? He's worried he might forget something."

Annah planted a quick kiss on her husband's lips. "Wait here; I'll go ask her."

Still sorting berries, Ghinnah laughed at the question. "Tell your husband to tell my husband not to worry. I'll gather a few things later. We aren't traveling far."

Annah relayed the message, then asked, "Are you going to sleep for a while?"

"And bathe and eat," he agreed. "Give me another kiss, then I'll go. Yepheth is expecting my help. We won't be here for the midday meal, but I'll see you tonight."

When he was gone, Annah returned to sort berries with Ghinnah. After a brief silence, Ghinnah said, "I've been thinking . . . Qeb-al and Etsah took my mother's gold hair bindings to pay off a debt. Could you make some new ones for me? I'd be willing to pay you for your time. . . ." Her words trailed off, nervous and unsure.

"You said your mother knew how to weave," Annah mused aloud. "I'll be glad to make your hair bindings as a gift. But later, will you teach me how to weave? None of the women in the settlement had such a skill. It was more practical for us to wear plain leather."

Ghinnah beamed. "Gladly! I'll teach you everything about weaving."

"I know how to make threads from the stalks of certain

plants—" Annah stopped, tensing as the earth quivered beneath them.

"Oh no!" Ghinnah gasped, terrified. A rumbling, echoing groan seemed to lift from the earth to the sky; they both looked up, following the reverberation of the sound.

It sounds like the cry before a death tremor, Annah thought, horrified. Oddly, the memory of her mother's fatal convulsions welled up in her mind. As the shaking of the earth intensified, Ghinnah screamed, huddling against Annah. Clasping her protectively, as if Ghinnah were a child, Annah watched as everything around them shuddered and trembled sickeningly. Then, as suddenly as it began, the shaking stopped.

Gulping, Ghinnah cried, "I'll never be used to the earth shaking! I hate it!"

"But it's over now," Annah soothed. "We're safe."

"How can you be so calm?" Ghinnah demanded, straightening, almost furious with her. "How can you sit there and pretend it's nothing?"

"I don't pretend it's nothing; the shaking of the earth is to warn the others of the destruction to come. This is only the beginning, Ghinnah. I used to be as frightened as you are. But now I know why the earth shakes, and it no longer scares me."

"Your Most High again," Ghinnah choked out, wiping her eyes with her hands. "I know! Don't tell me—I don't want to hear it."

Annah shrugged, trying to remain unaffected by Ghinnah's anger. "You asked me, and I answered you. Next time, Yepheth will be glad to comfort you."

"I'm sorry, I didn't mean to offend you."

"You didn't. At least not much." Annah frowned, picking up the berries that had bounced out of the bowl and rolled everywhere. As Ghinnah helped her, Naomi came out of the lodge, looking satisfied.

"Our Ancient One was awake this time, Ma'adannah. He didn't believe us the last two times when we told him that the earth shook, but he believes us now. Ghinnah-child, leave the berries; I'll take them. You two go bathe. Then," she added, smiling at Annah, "I'll let you make the cakes. The hearthstones are heating, so don't be too long."

"Let's go to the river," Ghinnah urged Annah, her mood brightening.

Annah hesitated, reluctant. "If that's what you want. But I meet too many unwelcome people at the river."

Naomi laughed. "Your husband should hear you! Listen: Go north, past the place where we gather sheaths from the reeds. No one from the settlement ever wanders up there. Hurry, or I'll make the cakes without you."

Yerakh moved through the darkness, watching shadows and studying the flickering lights of the fireflies that swarmed beyond his reach. Some members of the settlement netted the glowing flies, trapping them in containers of oiled membrane, then using the resultant lights to see in the darkness.

I don't need help from mere flies, Yerakh told himself smugly. *I can see well enough.* But he slowed his pace as he approached the lodge of the Nachash. Doubtless she was inside, aware of his presence and gloating, feasting on his fear. *I wish I could break her neck,* Yerakh thought. *Disgusting creature. And her whispering companions are no better. But I need to find some way to defend myself against that Annah-who-is-not-Annah.*

Yerakh seethed, thinking of that heavy, gleaming gold in Annah's traitorous hands. *I should have killed you the day I killed our father. I underestimated you—a mistake I won't repeat.* Reluctantly, Yerakh trudged into the clearing surrounding the lodge of the Nachash. He saw the disc of bronze suspended between the posts, and the slender, polished club hanging beside it, and he scowled. *If that old woman and her stinking companions have the powers they claim, they'll know I'm here even if I don't warn them.* Ignoring all formalities, he strode into the lodge and sat down before the glowing, crackling hearth.

The whisperers scratched at their filthy leather tunics, glaring at Yerakh as they took their places near the hearth. The Nachash was silent, swaying faintly within the confines of her painted leather cloak. She was thinner than he remembered, and her scent was strong and harsh, evoking thoughts of death-rot.

It's enough to persuade a carrion-eater to come looking for her, Yerakh thought, grimacing.

The Nachash stirred and sighed. Without opening her eyes, she spoke hoarsely. "You . . . bloody, bloody man. We remember you. Why have you come to our fire?"

With an effort Yerakh spoke politely. "Tell me, Nachash, who is your enemy?"

The whisperers shivered and bared their ancient yellow teeth. "He asks . . ." the oldest whisperer croaked, swaying in her place to the left of the Nachash. "Without paying a price . . . he asks us to name the Enemy."

"Bloody man," the Nachash growled. "Rude! Can we say the name of the One who is against us? Can you resist

Him? No!" She exhaled loudly, contemptuously, over the fire. "We feel your fear. The Presence of the Enemy is against you. But you were warned. Blood calls him from the earth, bloody, bloody man! You!"

The eldest whisperer groaned as if in pain, her eyes shut tight. "The Presence was here the night of the child. It is against us, as it is against you, cutting you off from life."

"How did you know?" Yerakh demanded, aghast, wondering if Taphaph or any of the other women of his family had spoken with the Nachash. "Who told you this?"

"Your fear tells us," the oldest whisperer muttered. "That, and the Enemy's anger."

"And how do you resist this Enemy?" Yerakh asked. "Tell me."

The Nachash opened her thin brown eyelids, revealing the whites of her eyes. Her face twisted with rage. She screamed at him, her voice rasping. "Resist? Fool! Leave us! You, with your hands empty. Even with a price, to resist the Enemy . . ." A tremor seized her body, making it shake as the earth had shaken that very morning. Suddenly desolate, she said, "We do not resist. Only hate. Out. Leave us with our fire."

Outside, Yerakh passed a hand over his face. He was drenched in sweat. *We do not resist. Only hate.* He shivered at the words of the Nachash, fearing the weakness they implied. *If the Nachash and her whisperers can't even say the name of their enemy, then how can I free myself from this curse? I feel it hovering, waiting to take my life.*

Not knowing what else to do, Yerakh turned again toward the settlement. Toward Taphaph, who now hated him as much as Iltani had once hated him. Nothing in Yerakh's life pleased him now, and this was baffling, because everything he had longed for was in his hands. He had expected pleasure from his marriage to Taphaph, joy from his wealth, and peace from being completely rid of Iltani and his family. Instead, he felt cheated, as if he had mistakenly exchanged a box of gold for a box of ashes.

Wielding a slender iron pick, Annah gently pressed the gold talisman back into shape on her broad, flat work-stone. Finished, she stretched briefly, glancing around at the peaceful clearing surrounding her hut. Flowers of white, blue, and golden-yellow edged the clearing. Hundreds of birds sang from the trees beyond. A beautiful morning. *I must resist daydreaming. It'll be midday soon. Shem will return from his night of watching, and I'ma-Naomi will be waiting for me at the lodge. I also promised Ghinnah I would work on the talismans.*

She studied the gleaming talisman's flower-petal design and the pierced tab where the leather hair bindings were inserted. *I'm not as skilled as my father or Yerakh, but I think I can make something that will please Ghinnah.*

Using a shard of clay, Annah gently traced the edges of the gold talisman against the work-stone, then moved the talisman and traced it again. She repeated the motions until she had a row of seven talisman tracings across the stone. Cautiously wielding a thin iron chisel and a bare hammer, she outlined the edge of one of the tracings, enjoying the feel of the tools in her hands.

A faraway whistle interrupted Annah's concentration. Brushing chips of stone from her lap, she looked toward the noise, sensing the approach of Yepheth, Ghinnah, and Khawm.

"We've come to visit you," Ghinnah called out. "But since you're finally using those tools, we should leave. Perhaps I'll have decent hair bindings soon; it's only been two weeks since we discussed them."

"Well, I won't ask where you've been for most of those two weeks, dear sister," Annah retorted mildly, pleased to see all three of them. She moved her tools to stand up, but they waved aside this courtesy and sat down, Khawm to her right, Yepheth and Ghinnah to her left.

"We thought you might be lonely, waiting for your husband to return from the herds," Ghinnah explained. "Not that I'm eager for him to return, because then my husband will leave me." She leaned against Yepheth, sighing dejectedly.

"You'll be too busy talking and playing to miss me," Yepheth said, kissing her hair. Marriage with Ghinnah had lightened Yepheth's spirit; he talked more, smiled more, and actually seemed to enjoy being teased by his wife and his family.

"You know I'll miss you—even while I'm talking and playing." Ghinnah fingered Yepheth's new black beard, then tweaked his curls lightly, making him grin, though he pulled her hands away from his hair.

"Look at them." Khawm nodded in mock disgust at Yepheth and Ghinnah. "They're sickening; always holding hands, kissing, staring at each other, ignoring the rest of us." With a sly look at Annah, he said, "They're almost as lovesick as my brother Shem and his wife."

"May your wife rule you," Yepheth muttered placidly, glancing at Khawm.

"I agree," Ghinnah said, lifting her chin. "Say you agree, Annah."

"I'm busy." Annah picked up her tools, hoping to excuse herself from the conversation, and from offending Khawm. She believed he felt isolated, being the only unmarried member of his family. As if recognizing her silent defense of him, Khawm sighed dramatically.

"At least someone refuses to speak against me! Not that it matters anyway." Khawm sounded impatient, his mouth turning downward. "The way I'ma's fussing and picking, I doubt I'll ever marry."

"She's had enough young women to choose from," Ghinnah said derisively. "I think my uncle told every person from here to the end of the earth that this family will pay a bride price instead of demanding one."

"It's just as well that he's sending them," Yepheth pointed out. "Otherwise, we wouldn't have so many families offering their daughters for Khawm."

"But that's the problem," Khawm grumbled. "I'ma has seen so many that she's being too fussy. The family that left yesterday—the young woman was beautiful."

"She was scowling," Ghinnah reminded Khawm. "She looked as if she would rather bite you than kiss you. I think I'ma-Naomi was entirely correct."

"Perhaps it's also because our marriages weren't settled according to the usual customs," Annah said.

"Mine won't be either, if I'm paying the brideprice," Khawm argued, picking at some chips of stone. Annah had never seen him look so unhappy.

"You don't resent having to pay the brideprice, do you?" Ghinnah asked Khawm, her soft color fading, her expression anxious.

Sighing, Khawm shook his head. "No, not at all. I simply want the matter to be settled. But the way I'ma is behaving, it won't be decided for months."

Yepheth changed the subject now, staring at Annah's

tools. "When you were in the settlement, did you learn how various metals were handled and prepared?"

"I saw some of the iron being tested and shaped, and the copper," Annah said tentatively, "but I usually avoided others in our settlement. Most of my work was with the gold, or mixtures of copper and gold."

"Even so, you know more than the rest of us," Yepheth said quietly. "Much knowledge will be lost. . . ." He paused, obviously remembering Ghinnah's aversion to talk of the predicted flood.

Already, she was taking Yepheth's hand to distract him. "I'ma-Naomi will be waiting for us, and we don't want her to think we're being forgetful. Annah, will you come back with us?"

Annah began to pack her tools into the leather bag. "Yes. But I'll bring these with me; the bar of gold is at the lodge. Perhaps I'll cut some gold off the bar and test it tonight."

She checked inside the hut to be sure there was fresh water and food waiting for Shem. He would sleep here after the midday meal. As an afterthought, Annah opened the storage chest and removed the fine gold cuff bracelet that Naomi had given her. Annah's father had beaten the gold of this bracelet flat, then embossed it and tooled it delicately in a pattern of stylized vines and fruit. Studying the bracelet might give her ideas for Ghinnah's hair talismans.

Annah pressed the bracelet over her forearm and hurried outside, ready to leave. Yepheth held the leather bag of tools, prepared to carry them for her. She smiled, touched by his consideration.

Ghinnah admired Annah's gold cuff bracelet. "It's so beautiful! Did your father really make this before you were born?" Without giving Annah the chance to reply, she said, "I'll do your chores this evening, if you'll work the gold."

With Yepheth and Khawm leading, and Annah and Ghinnah lingering behind to visit, they followed the path edging the trees. As they approached the lodge, Khawm sighed, disgusted. "Look, here's another family for my mother to send away."

A wooden, two-wheeled handcart was outside the lodge, guarded by a brooding, fully bearded man of about two kentums. The man eyed Khawm speculatively.

Clearly discomfited, Khawm nudged Yepheth. "You greet him. I'm going inside."

Silent, Annah and Ghinnah followed Khawm into the lodge. Annah felt the stranger staring at them and disliked him at once. Inside the lodge, she breathed in the scent of fresh grain cakes and simmering fruit. Naomi was seated near the hearth, formal, but smiling at three women who sat on a mat opposite her.

The oldest woman was slender, lovely and haughty, with tightly braided and bound hair that curled luxuriantly at the ends. She was undoubtedly the mother of the two younger women who sat to her left, for both of the younger women were also slender with long, richly curled black hair. The younger, smaller daughter was pretty, but restless. She was pinching and nudging her elder sister, who repeatedly swiped her hands away. At last their mother admonished them, "Behave. You shame me, both of you!"

The younger daughter wrinkled her nose and stared at Annah boldly, as if to say, *Who cares what my mother thinks— I do as I please.* But the older daughter clasped her hands tightly in her lap and looked up at the reed-and-grass roof of the lodge. Despite her unapproachable air, her eyes were lustrous, her black eyebrows exquisitely arched, her nose delicate, her mouth full and wonderfully curved.

She's more beautiful than Taphaph was before her marriage to Yerakh, Annah thought, amazed. Kneeling beside Naomi, she glanced up at Khawm. He was staring at the older sister, obviously staggered by the sight of her.

Naomi reached up, patting Khawm's hand to get his attention. "Be seated, my son. Ghinnah, please sit down. Ma'adannah, this is Ce'appah, and her daughters, Tirtsah and Hadarah. They will be staying the night."

Annah watched Khawm obliquely. He gazed at the older daughter, Tirtsah, and his expression hardened. Raising his eyebrows at his mother, he pressed his lips together, clearly threatening to rebel if she sent this young woman away. Naomi returned his look, equally hardened, silently demanding his respect. At last Khawm lowered his eyes. But his rebellion remained.

Nineteen

WARMED BY the afternoon sun, Annah strode through the grass toward the slender, aromatic spice-fruit tree, followed by the chattering Ghinnah and the silent Tirtsah. Each woman wore a sturdy tapering basket slung across her back to hold the spice-fruits that flavored Naomi's special grain cakes. At Naomi's request, they were also searching for any other ripe fruits. They could pick whatever pleased them; nothing was wasted in the lodge of Noakh. To Annah, however, picking the fruit was less important than being outside; she hoped the work would clear her thoughts.

Oblivious to Ghinnah's chatter, Annah chose a heavily laden branch and began to pick the fleshy, yellow, palm-sized spice-fruit. Ghinnah started to pick at a branch to the left of Annah, Tirtsah to the right. As they worked, Annah watched Tirtsah from the corner of her eye. *O Most High, if only I could perceive this woman's thoughts. She worries me. I think she wants nothing to do with us.*

Since the departure of her parents and sister two days before, Tirtsah had been quiet, impassive, and remote. She acted with proper courtesy toward everyone, kept her hands busy with work, and ate and slept normally, but with no tears, no frowns, no laughter, and no attempts at conversation. *Yes. No. Thank you.*

"Ma'adannah!" Ghinnah called out irritably, pelting Annah with one of the yellow spice-fruits. The fruit split in half, revealing its plump red-and-violet-brown seed as it fell away from Annah's shoulder.

"What?" Annah stared at Ghinnah, bewildered.

Ghinnah stared back at Annah, enunciating her words, sweetly, carefully, as if addressing a child. "I just asked if you would speak to my husband's parents for us."

"Speak to them . . . ?"

"About combing the sheep to get fibers for weaving. You haven't been listening to me at all! Are you becoming like her?" Ghinnah jerked her head toward Tirtsah. "Will you become once again a woman of no words, Annah?"

Annah bit her lip, distressed. "Ghinnah, I'm sorry. I was thinking about something else. But why do you need me to speak for you? The parents of our husbands will listen to you."

"But they'd be more likely to agree with both of us," Ghinnah argued. "Or with all three of us—though one of us seems likely to refuse." She turned to Tirtsah, none too fondly. "Tell me, O Tirtsah—now that we're away from the lodge and you may talk freely—do you hate us so much that you intend to say nothing for a lifetime?"

Her hands poised in the act of picking, Tirtsah stared at Ghinnah and Annah. Toneless, she asked, "What

267

should I say?"

"Anything but yes and no, which is all you have said for the past two days!" Ghinnah cried. "Are we so horrible, so beneath you that we don't deserve your companionship?"

Tirtsah frowned and continued to pick in silence. Ghinnah flung a yellow spice-fruit at Tirtsah, striking her forearm.

"There!" she snapped. "Now you can hate me with reason. Whether you like it or not, you're bound to us, sister!"

"Ghinnah." Annah spoke softly, quenching Ghinnah's tirade with a word. Looking at Tirtsah, she said, "Before I married my husband, my life was nothing but silence and hating others. If you don't speak, Tirtsah, you'll eventually die of the hatred."

Tirtsah's dark eyes burned and her delicate nostrils flared as she scowled at Annah, then at Ghinnah. Her voice husky with rage, she asked, "Again, what should I say? Should I say I'm happy to be here in the wilderness, away from the city and my friends? Should I be pleased that my parents exchanged me for sheep and grain, then left me with no marriage portion for my old age?"

While Annah listened, appalled, Tirtsah continued. "Do you want me to pretend that I'm glad my husband purchased me for his own use? No, I won't!" She clenched one small fist, striking herself at the base of her throat. "How can I be glad? I should be able to lift my head high and say that I've brought something of value to this family—something other than my own body and an armful of clothes. Instead, I have nothing, and I'm shamed by it!"

Annah shook her head. "No—it's no shame."

Tirtsah didn't seem to hear. "And as for you—all of

you—are you insane? What about that monstrous box behind the lodge? That 'pen'? I can hear my parents laughing even now! It's just as well that I'll never see my friends again; they'd point to me and say, 'There's poor Tirtsah, who was sold to that madman's family—the ones with the giant's box behind their lodge.'"

She was crying now, the tears sliding down her cheeks. Pained, Annah shut her eyes briefly, then faced Tirtsah, determined to make her listen.

"It's my fault, Tirtsah. If you blame anyone for your misery, blame me. My husband is the one who first offered to pay for a wife—for me. It was the only way he could free me from my family."

As Tirtsah glared in sullen disbelief, Annah explained, "When my husband offered a brideprice for me, I was as shocked as you are. But I was also grateful to him; he loved me enough to part with half of all he owned for my sake. And, out of loyalty to my husband, his brothers have made the same offer to the families of their wives."

Tirtsah looked unconvinced. Annah sighed. "Tirtsah, I assure you, your husband does not consider you a thing purchased for his own use. Ghinnah and I are cherished and respected by our husbands and their parents, as you will be cherished and respected. Please, I'm telling you again, if you blame anyone for your unhappiness, then you should blame me, not your husband and his family."

"I suppose you're going to say you're responsible for that pen, too!" Tirtsah snorted, challenging her. Before she could reply, Tirtsah said, "No, don't try to explain *that!* It won't make any difference—you're all insane!"

"Well." Ghinnah glared at Tirtsah. "You're very sure of yourself! So, tell us, what will you do now? Run away?"

"Where could I go?" Angrily, Tirtsah wiped her eyes,

then snatched at the plump yellow spice-fruits, flinging them over her shoulder into the basket as she talked. "I can't go back to my parents. They were glad to sell me. You should have seen the looks on their greedy faces when that Qeb-al told them I could be sold for five hundred animals and a cartload of grain. I hope they lose everything on the journey home."

She gave a bleak little half-laugh. "It didn't occur to my parents that they would need help on their return journey with all that grain and all those animals. *I* certainly wasn't going to tell them. Anyway, my father never listens to anyone but himself." Tirtsah sneered at Ghinnah. "Your uncle may have had five hundred animals when he left the lodge of Noakh, but he didn't have that many when he arrived at my home. He claims he traded them, but I think he was lying to cover his own stupidity in losing them."

"As I believed he would," Ghinnah said airily. She turned away from Tirtsah and continued to pick spice-fruit.

But Annah studied Tirtsah quietly. Obviously, Tirtsah was still seething. Fearing that Tirtsah would eventually subject Noakh and Naomi to a similar display of rage and scorn, Annah said, "Tirtsah, please, won't you even give us the chance to befriend you? Everything would be easier for you—for all of us—if you would let us understand you and help you."

Tirtsah snapped a tiny branch from the tree, the lovely curves of her mouth rebellious. "Why should you care? You're strangers, and I don't need you to care for me—obviously no one else has ever cared for me." She shook her dark-curled head decisively. "No, I have nowhere to go. So I'll stay and be a wife to that Khawm. It doesn't matter." Her voice dropped dangerously. "Now, leave me alone."

"Gladly," Ghinnah muttered. To Annah, she said, "Did I sound like this the day I agreed to marry my husband?"

"Only for an instant," Annah whispered. "But I'm afraid Tirtsah will be angry for much longer than that."

O Most High, she pleaded silently, *help us gain this Tirtsah's love before she destroys us with hatred.*

Crouching in the predawn darkness, Annah lit a slender, resin-soaked taper from the banked coals in the hearth before the hut. Cupping the flame protectively, she carried it into the hut and lit the solitary oil lamp. Shem stirred, rubbing a hand over his face. Annah smiled, loving the sight of her husband. She blew out the taper and sat beside him, taking his hand.

Still half-asleep, Shem pulled her into his arms, his voice slow and drowsy. "You're awake before me?"

"I didn't sleep well," Annah confessed, nestling into his warm shoulder.

"Hmm," Shem responded in soft agreement. He stroked her unbound hair and yawned. "I knew you were too quiet last night. Talk to me now."

Propping herself up on her elbow, Annah said, "Tirtsah hates us. I've been trying to understand her these past four days—trying to appease her. But she simply hates us."

Shem opened his eyes wide in the lamplight, as if forcing himself to concentrate. "How do you know this when she refuses to speak beyond yes and no?"

"She said much more than yes and no the day before

yesterday. She said that she despises our entire family. And yesterday, while we were combing the sheep to gather fibers, she wouldn't even look at us. I dread facing her today."

Shem tightened his arms around Annah, caressing her. "What will you do today?"

"I'm going to work on Ghinnah's hair bindings this morning, then we'll go down to the river to wash the fibers we've combed from the sheep." Feeling Shem tense, Annah straightened defensively, sitting up again. "Ghinnah insists that it'll be easier to work at the river. She knows you don't want us going down there, so she wouldn't insist if we could do this work some other way. We'll try to finish quickly and return to the lodge as soon as possible. I promise we'll be careful. Actually, I'm more afraid of Tirtsah now than anyone. Even Yerakh or Naham."

Groaning in apparent disgust, Shem sat up, pushing one hand through his loose, heavy curls. "What has Khawm's impulsiveness brought into our family? I heard my parents talking the first night Tirtsah came to our lodge. They were displeased with Khawm's rebellion, but my father said that Khawm should have his way and accept the consequences for himself."

"But those consequences might affect us as well."

"Yes," Shem conceded reluctantly. "And I'm afraid that some day Khawm's impulsiveness will anger my parents so much that they'll send him away."

Annah's stomach tightened in agitation. "Khawm is impulsive, but there's so much joy in him too. I can't bear the thought of having to part ways with him."

"I pray that day will never come." Leaning forward, Shem kissed Annah's lips, then wrapped his arms around her. "Speaking of prayers, if we sit here much longer, we will miss the dawn."

From the first morning of their marriage, it had been their custom to walk out into the fields surrounding their hut to watch the stars, see the sky brighten, and listen to the songs of the birds. To Annah, it seemed the most perfect time to pray. Everything was peaceful and lovely at dawn. And she needed that peace now.

As they walked outside together, Annah asked, "What about Tirtsah? I don't want to tell your parents. That might make things worse."

"Let's be patient, and trust the Most High," Shem murmured, taking her hand as they walked together. "And you are right; don't tell my parents, not yet, anyway. Though I suspect they understand her nature already. I almost wonder if Tirtsah was placed before Khawm by the Adversary—our enemy, the Serpent."

Annah blinked, startled. *The presence of that Serpent—beloved of the Nachash—is trying to use Tirtsah to divide us.* Shivering, she said, "Then let the Most High deal with the Adversary, and with Tirtsah—and let Him save us from her hatred."

"According to His will," Shem agreed. "But we shouldn't shun Tirtsah, unless she forces us to do so. For Khawm's sake, I hope she doesn't."

"I agree." Sighing, Annah leaned comfortably into her husband's embrace as they stopped to look up at the sky at the first hints of dawn.

Later, when the sun was shining warm and full in the early morning sky, Annah watched Shem leave to go help his father work in the pen; then she went to work on Ghinnah's hair bindings. Ghinnah had requested a starburst pattern instead of flowers, and Annah was secretly relieved. A starburst required less skill, but reflected light more brilliantly, dazzling the eyes of onlookers. To create it, she had cut six intersecting lines into one of the tracings on her work-stone. Each line was delicately etched in the center, then deepened and broadened toward the outer edge of the talisman.

To form the talismans, Annah placed a beaten, tabbed disk of gold—cut from the bar sent to her by Yerakh—into the carved stone etching. Now, pressing her father's smallest leather-padded hammer over the gold, Annah pounded it with another hammer until the gold assumed the design cut in the stone. Then she pierced the tab and worked it into a suitable shape so it would dangle lightly from Ghinnah's hair bindings.

Lifting the talisman from the stone, Annah studied it, dissatisfied, thinking, *This would look so much better if I had a refiner's pit, with foot bellows for the fire, and the proper tools to manage the heated gold. Then I could just pour the gold into the stone carvings, and each edge would be sharp and perfect. But this is what I can do now; Ghinnah will have to understand. Perhaps I'll etch the back of the talismans for her. Then the talismans would look more finished and presentable.*

Deeply engrossed, she continued to work until mid-morning, when she sensed the approach of another person. Two people: Ghinnah and Tirtsah. Ghinnah was swinging two empty buckets in rhythm with her stride, while Tirtsah followed her reluctantly, carrying four puffy, netted bundles of unwashed wool.

"Have you finished my hair bindings?" Ghinnah called.

Smiling, Annah waited until her sisters-in-law were near enough that she didn't have to raise her voice. "You have seven talismans, Ghinnah, but whether I've finished them or not depends upon you."

"I don't care what they look like," Ghinnah responded. "I'm wearing them *now*."

"I'd like to finish the edges and the backs for you." Annah tipped the seven loose, sparkling discs of gold into Ghinnah's outstretched hands.

"No," Ghinnah said, lifting her chin, pleased and willful. "I have them now, and you won't get them back. If I know you, you won't be satisfied with them for another year. Even then, you'd change your mind. You can play with Tirtsah's bindings. If she wants any."

Annah looked at Tirtsah wonderingly. But Tirtsah turned away, seeming unsettled. Khawm had sent word to the lodge last night that he expected to have Tirtsah's dwelling place ready this afternoon. He would take Tirtsah away with him tonight after the evening meal. Feeling a reluctant pang of compassion for the unhappy girl, Annah said, "If you decide that you want hair bindings, then tell me. I'll do what I can for you."

While Annah was talking, Ghinnah was busy knotting the seven talismans to the thin black leather cords of her hair bindings. Finished, she tied them in her hair and stood, triumphant. "My aunt—that Etsah—would choke with envy if she could see me now. Qeb-al used her gold as payment for a wager. Annah, thank you!"

Ghinnah kissed Annah's cheek enthusiastically, then hugged her, saying, "Let's go wash these fibers, and then we can play for a while. I'ma-Naomi isn't expecting us back before the midday meal, so we have plenty of time. Do you have one more bucket? And perhaps an extra roll of leather or a hide?"

Tirtsah trailed after them as they left the clearing around Annah's hut. Under Ghinnah's direction, Annah picked various scrubbing plants as the three of them walked through the cool green of the trees and undergrowth down to the river. There, she noticed Tirtsah staring at her. *What are you thinking?* Annah wondered, watching her beautiful, unmoving face. *I wish I knew.*

Ghinnah was in full command as they pounded out the cleansing plants, soaked the fibers clean and rinsed them, then allowed them to dry on the clean rolls of leather Annah had provided. To Annah's surprise, Tirtsah seemed willing to work near them today—although she refused to speak as they worked.

They were just rinsing the last of the fibers when Annah sensed the presence of another person watching them from the trees across the river. Ghinnah and Tirtsah also looked up, frowning.

"Is someone hiding over there?" Ghinnah demanded, irritated.

Annah studied the opposite shore. They were not far from where the women and children of the settlement bathed and worked. But who would care to linger and hide while watching them? In answer to her unspoken question, Tseb-iy emerged from the undergrowth on the opposite shore. He was staring at them like a man enchanted, as if they were the most fascinating women in the world.

"Who is he?" Ghinnah asked. "Annah, you must recognize him."

"He is Tseb-iy," Annah said softly, keeping her voice neutral. She wondered what her sisters-in-law would think of the charming, presumably irresistible young man.

Still staring at him, Ghinnah said, "He's handsome. Not as handsome as our husbands, of course, but it's as if . . ."

"As if he's the most perfect man?" Annah suggested. "As if he could adore you forever?"

"Yes," Ghinnah agreed, obviously discomfited by her own reaction. Tirtsah was also gazing at Tseb-iy, seeming entranced. Annah smiled at their expressions. But she was glad to have the river between Tseb-iy and her sisters-in-law, just as Tseb-iy was probably regretting this same river—though he might choose to walk to the bridge.

"I will tell you about this beautiful man," Annah said, her voice conveying a calm she did not feel. "There's not a woman in that settlement who doesn't desire him. They all want to marry him, but he hates the thought of marriage and avoids choosing a wife."

"Did you love him, Annah?" Ghinnah demanded, still gazing across the river. By now, Tseb-iy was sitting on the opposite shore, watching them, smiling at them, then leaning on one elbow as he stretched out and made himself comfortable in the sand beside the river.

"At one time, years ago, I was as captivated as any of the young women," Annah told Ghinnah. "You see how he is—how his smile and his eyes implore you to look at him. But he didn't notice me. I was the least desirable and least valued of all the women in the settlement. I was nothing to him."

Tirtsah stared at her, openmouthed. "You? The least desired? How could he not look at you?"

"As I said, I was nothing." Annah secretly marveled at Tirtsah's stunned expression, wondering if the young woman was not as hardened as she seemed. Sighing, Annah continued, "Also, he has taken lovers from every lodge, all of them willing. My mother was the one he chose from our lodge. She was very beautiful. And she loved him more than anyone else in her life."

"Your mother?" Tirtsah asked, surprised.

Annah spoke smoothly, as if she had not been interrupted. "Tseb-iy made my mother very happy. For a short time. But he gave her a child, then abandoned her for the attentions of others, because that is his way."

As Ghinnah and Tirtsah stared at her in disbelief, Annah said softly, "My mother died bearing his child. And he laughed as he helped to bury her. He was able to enjoy himself on the day of my sorrow—this man you think is so wonderful. He is like death to the women who love him. He helped to kill my mother."

Despite her resolutions, Annah felt the tears burning her eyes. Unable to speak, she removed the last of the fibers from the rinsing bucket and placed them on the protective layer of leather.

Ghinnah stood and spat vehemently into the river toward Tseb-iy. He jumped and looked startled, which made Annah feel somewhat better.

"We're leaving," Ghinnah announced firmly. They gathered the buckets, the leather, and the dripping fibers, then departed into the trees without looking back at Tseb-iy on the other side. Annah hoped she would never see him again.

As they walked along the path through the trees, Tirtsah said, "When you make my hair bindings, I want them to be shaped like leaves, long and slender."

"Gladly," Annah agreed, staring at Tirtsah's masklike beauty, wondering for the hundredth time what she was thinking.

⁓❡ ❦⁓

"It was as if she cast a spell on them," Tseb-iy complained to Taphaph, as he sat beside her in the lodge of Yerakh.

Busy slicing tubers for Yerakh's midday meal, Taphaph smiled at her brother's chagrin. "Obviously it was that Annah. Poor, dear Tseb-iy. Perhaps you are simply not as attractive as you once were. You should marry before you lose your charms altogether."

"How could this woman be Annah?" Tseb-iy asked, still fuming. "She looked nothing like that creature."

"She hid herself well, didn't she," Taphaph agreed, curling her soft, full lips contemptuously. "Your loss, dear brother. If you'd paid any attention to her at all, she might still be here now. Just think; you might have married her."

"Let's not talk about marriage," Tseb-iy muttered. "The way she turned those other women against me with just a few words . . . she's dangerous. We should have killed her and buried her with her mother and her brother. Is Yerakh still afraid of her?"

Taphaph stared down at the tuber in her hand. "Yes," she said at last. "He's still afraid of her. She changed him completely; he's not the man I married."

"Someone should kill that Annah," Tseb-iy told his sister. "We'd all be better off for her death."

"Would you kill her for us?" Taphaph asked softly, not looking at her brother.

"No." He grimaced and took a piece of the raw tuber from her hand to eat it. "I won't kill others with my hands, unlike your husband."

Her eyes glittering furiously, Taphaph thrust the thin iron blade toward her brother. "Get out, before I cut you!"

"She's gotten to you as well," Tseb-iy sneered, leaning away from the blade. "Perhaps you should kill her yourself." Still eating the raw tuber, he stood and sauntered outside.

Taphaph threw down the blade and burst into tears.

The stalks of grain were heavy, coarse, and tawny. Annah loved the look of them as she worked with Ghinnah and Tirtsah to bind the stalks into sheaves. This crop was beautiful, surpassing all their expectations—as if the Most High had released all His blessings upon this particular harvest.

Time has gone so quickly. Standing, holding some sheaves, she glanced at Ghinnah and Tirtsah. They were sweating beneath the late afternoon sun, but they didn't complain. The grain was as precious to them as it was to Annah.

Even Tirtsah seemed pleased today. The past few months of marriage to Khawm had made her a little less sullen. But any improvement was welcomed to Annah. And Khawm loved Tirtsah. He followed her with his eyes whenever she was near. Annah suspected he could deny her nothing.

As Annah was stretching, she saw Naomi running toward them from the lodge. Naomi was panting for air, her expression fearful, stricken. "I'ma!" Annah dropped the sheaves she held and ran to her mother-in-law. Holding out her hands, she cried, "I'ma, what's wrong?"

Naomi clutched her, in tears. "Daughter, go tell your husband and his father and brothers . . . I can't wake our Methuwshelakh. He's dying."

Twenty

GENTLY, FOLLOWING Naomi, Annah cast a handful of sand into the grave, scattering it over Methuwshelakh's leather-shrouded body. It pained Annah that she had been unable to tell the ancient man anything in his last hours; he had never once opened his eyes. But she had comforted herself by giving Methuwshelakh one last token of her affection; she had struck a small disc of gold, patterned after Ghinnah's starburst, then tied it about his neck as they were preparing him for the burial. Now she watched as Noakh slipped the first shovelful of dirt into the grave.

Standing beside Annah, Ghinnah cried softly. Tirtsah, however, remained unmoved. Methuwshelakh's presence had never touched her as it had touched the other two. Annah studied Tirtsah, resenting her lack of emotion. *I think that the grief of your husband's family hasn't affected you at all.*

Now Yepheth, Shem, and Khawm were helping Noakh cover the ancient Methuwshelakh's grave, their expressions wearied and sorrowful. Shem shoveled dirt steadily, but he paused once and looked at Annah. His expression was despairing, telling Annah silently: *This is the end. And the beginning of our sorrows.*

Moved by her husband's pain, Annah lowered her head. Tears stung her eyes. *I will miss you,* she thought. *Methuwshelakh. Man-of-the-darts. He-who-departs-before-the-waters. Now that you're gone—if my husband and his father believe the truth—the waters will come to sweep everything away.* Thinking of this, Annah begged silently, *O Most High, if there is a way to avert this destruction . . .*

She stopped suddenly, feeling the prayer fall back upon her like a stone; it would change nothing. Noakh had been praying and speaking to others for more than a hundred years, hoping this calamity might be averted. And yet, because of the unchanging evil and violence of men, ruin was approaching. Annah sensed heaviness in the air about her. Unnerved, she looked at Noakh, trying to discern his thoughts.

Her father-in-law was carefully shoveling the loosened earth over his grandfather's grave, but his eyes were distant and deeply troubled. When the grave was covered, he turned away silently, walking off into the trees lining the river. Annah gazed after him, understanding his need for solitude.

Later, when Noakh returned to the lodge to share their midday meal, Annah and the others looked at him, waiting for him to speak. Slowly, as if forcing out the words, he said, "From this day on, we harvest everything. Everything."

Annah watched Ghinnah and Tirtsah's reaction. Both

young women looked confused, obviously thinking, *But we've been harvesting everything already. How can we possibly need so much?*

Seeing their rebellion, Annah shut her eyes. *We are to harvest everything,* she thought. *The father of my husband means more than just grains and fruits. And if he is so reluctant to face this harvest of "everything," then I'm sure I don't want to know what "everything" means.*

~✥ ❦~

"We need your help today," Shem said quietly, looking away from Annah, toward the dawn. The sunlight barely showed above the mist-filled clearing before their reed-and-grass hut. "We will be working with the herds."

Hearing an unspoken meaning in his voice, Annah stepped in front of her husband, facing him, willing him to look at her. "Please, tell me what you mean. You and your father and your brothers have been coming and going from the herds for three days already. And when you come to me at night, you say almost nothing. You obviously don't like what you have to tell me, so I want to hear it now."

"We're going to harvest the herds," Shem answered bluntly. "I've been helping my father and brothers set up enclosures to hold the animals while we butcher them. Their flesh will serve as food for the carrion-eaters while we are together in the pen. I'ma will help us. But we also need your help to cut the flesh and set it out to dry."

Annah felt the blood draining from her face. "*All* the animals of your herds?"

"Virtually all, yes."

"That will take longer than just one day," Annah said,

reluctantly forcing another unwilling admission from her husband's lips.

"Yes, it will take more than a few days."

Sickened, Annah swallowed hard. *To cut into flesh, over and over for days. No, I can't do this.* She wavered and turned away.

But Shem caught her and pulled her into his arms, holding her tight. "Listen to me," he whispered. "You know I would never ask such a thing if it weren't necessary. We can't depend upon my father's cousins to help us, and we know that Ghinnah and Tirtsah will consider this as further proof that we're mad. Most likely, it will be just the six of us doing all the work. We need your help, beloved, please."

Annah sucked in a quick breath. It was ridiculous of her to be squeamish. Her garments were of leather, and whenever she worked the gold, she worked with leather and membranes. And she had seen death already: useless, senseless, bloody death. This would be different; the deaths of these animals would have a saving purpose. Their flesh would give life to other animals. Bracing herself, she nodded. But as her husband bent to kiss her, she clutched at him again, begging, "Please don't ask me to kill any of the animals."

"You'll stay with my mother and help her," Shem promised. "You won't be near the animals when we take them."

They ate a quick morning meal. Then Annah helped Shem gather what they needed: cutting tools—blades of stone, bronze, and iron—a sharpening stone, a bucket, cleansing herbs and pale, coarse, dried gourd fibers for scrubbing their hands. Annah also packed some food in a basket, though she was certain that she would be unable to eat anything. Silent, they walked through the misty fields, toward the herds, away from the rising sun. Noakh, Naomi, Yepheth, and Khawm were already at work, separating the herds, urging them into small, woven-wood enclosures, despite the protests of three angry, leather-clad men, Noakh's cousins.

As they approached his family, Shem spoke to Annah beneath his breath. "I don't need to tell you to stay away from my father's cousins. They are wild men. The two with the graying hair are brothers, Pathal and Akar. The younger one is another cousin, Othniy. Don't speak to them, even if they speak to you. Stay with I'ma."

Naomi greeted Shem and Annah first. She was quiet and tense, her eyes flicking back to the herds, where Noakh was trying to placate his cousins. The two brother-cousins, Pathal and Akar, were almost as old as Noakh, wiry and sharp-eyed, their hair grizzled and thick with curls, their beards flowing and rumpled. Noakh's third cousin, Othniy, was much younger and, to a startling degree, resembled Shem. His eyes were large, dark and intense, and his features were strikingly handsome, but he was completely lacking in manners. He was now screaming at Noakh, gesturing wildly with his hands, his voice hoarse, raging.

"You're a fool! You've always been a fool! And now you'll ruin us all—that's what you want to do, isn't it? Why should you cut down perfectly healthy animals?"

"Othniy, listen to me," Noakh answered mildly, reasonably. "I will pay you as we agreed when you returned from your last journey. If you prefer, you may take one hundred animals now and leave. But if you stay to help us, you may save one hundred twenty animals for yourself."

"Why should I help you destroy my livelihood? "

Othniy sputtered. "No, I'll take my hundred and leave! The death of that old man gave your weak mind another turn!"

"That old man was the father of your father," Noakh reminded Othniy firmly.

But Othniy refused to be concerned with any familial respect. "Father of my father or not, that Methuwshelakh was an old storytelling idiot. And his idiocy has been passed from you to your sons. No wonder your sons had to pay bribes to get wives. You're all insane."

Hearing this, Annah put a quick hand on her husband's arm. Shem was angry, his eyes glittering, his lips pressed together hard. Annah met his look swiftly, shaking her head, silently reminding him: *Be calm. Your cousin is speaking in rage. We know the truth.*

But Khawm was obviously stung, and snarled at Othniy, "Your hatred of us hasn't kept you from demanding our food and work all these years, when you've lost everything and we've had plenty. Who is truly the fool, cousin?"

Infuriated, Othniy charged at Khawm, but the two older cousins held him back while Yepheth grabbed Khawm, restraining him. Othniy bellowed, "I'll kill you now! Let me go! I'll dash his brains all over this field!"

"You'll take your animals and go," Noakh told him, so harshly that Annah barely recognized his voice.

Shem already was moving toward the herd to help his father count out one hundred animals for Othniy's wages. Freed now, Othniy glared menacingly from Noakh, to Shem and his brothers, then to Naomi and Annah. Othniy paused and stared at Annah, his expression voracious.

Annah looked down at her feet, scared. *My husband could have been just like this Othniy. They are of the same family, and their features are the same. The only difference between them is that my husband loves the Most High, while this Othniy shuns Him.* Annah longed for the secrecy of her veil. More than anything, she wanted to hide from Othniy's cruel, staring eyes.

"Daughter," Naomi whispered, putting an arm around Annah, "come with me to the well. We can prepare our work area while my husband and sons deal with these men."

Annah followed Naomi obediently, but she was still frightened, watching the men anxiously from beneath her lashes. Noakh's cousins were quarreling with each other as Noakh, Shem, Yepheth, and Khawm goaded one hundred animals away from the herd. At last, Othniy picked up his staff and his pouch, then strode away, driving the animals before him. They were reluctant to go, but Othniy hissed and whistled sharply, chasing the animals onward, Annah thought, by the sheer force of his rage.

In contrast to Othniy, the two older cousins, Pathal and Akar, seemed willing to stay and help, apparently lured by Noakh's promise of extra animals in return for their work.

I wish they would go too, Annah thought, feeling sick, watching the brother-cousins prepare their blades by sharpening them against stones. *I wish they didn't have knives.*

To keep herself busy, Annah brought water from the nearby well, then helped Naomi to unpack their own cutting blades. Almost before she knew it, Shem and Yepheth came toward her, carrying a gutted, skinned, decapitated carcass.

As they set the once-living form in front of Annah, she shut her eyes, willing herself not to retch. *This is necessary,* she told herself firmly. *It has to be done.* Slowly, she picked up a knife and moved with Naomi to kneel beside the still-warm carcass. Annah let Naomi make the first cut, then she followed her motions numbly. *Don't think about this,* Annah told herself. *Just work.*

Moving quickly, Annah cut slice after slice of the flesh, her fingers becoming sticky and stained with blood. Like a mindless creature, she worked until she heard Naomi release a low, sobbing breath. Startled, Annah looked at her mother-in-law. Naomi continued to slice at the flesh of the carcass, but tears were coursing down her cheeks. Her own misery forgotten, Annah whispered, "I'ma?"

Naomi sniffed and swallowed hard. "It's nothing, child." She sighed and continued. "I can't help but think of all the nights my husband and my sons have spent out here, tending these animals. Now, to do this is horrible. I have to tell myself that this is necessary."

"That's what I've been telling myself."

Taking a deep breath, Naomi said, "We should keep telling this to each other."

They worked as quickly as possible, stopping only to rinse their hands and sharpen or exchange their cutting blades. Several times, Shem and Noakh came to help them.

"Look," Shem told Annah once, his voice soft and concerned as he took her knife in his bloodstained fingers. "You're trying too hard. The flesh doesn't have to be cut perfectly, or evenly; just thin enough to be sure it dries well." Almost inaudibly, he said, "Thank you, beloved."

Annah nodded, biting back the tears. *It's necessary,* she reminded herself again. *It has to be done.*

"I made Yepheth tell me where you were," Ghinnah said to Annah the next morning. Her eyes were fierce as she knelt beside Annah. "At first I didn't want to believe Yepheth when he said they were harvesting the herds, but there was blood all over his tunic. Even so, I'd rather be out here with you and I'ma-Naomi than closed in the lodge one more day with that sulking, bad-mouthed Tirtsah."

As Ghinnah spoke, Yepheth and Shem dropped two more carcasses in front of them. Sitting back, Ghinnah looked at Annah, her eyes huge, horrified. "You did this all day yesterday?"

"All day," Annah agreed, her muscles aching, her fingers swollen. She pressed a knife into Ghinnah's hands. "Tell yourself that it's necessary. Don't think too hard. And sometimes, you have to put down the knife and just tear the flesh with your bare hands. When we're finished with this one, we'll hang the flesh on the cordage between those poles." Annah motioned to numerous rows of cordage slung between narrow reed poles, set a short distance away.

"But you've ruined your tunic," Ghinnah said, as if this was more important than anything else.

For the first time in two days, Annah smiled. Her tunic was stained and stiffened with blood. It looked the way she felt: as if she would never be clean again. "Dear Ghinnah," she said, keeping her words gentle and agreeable, "I am far beyond caring about my tunic."

"We will make new tunics for ourselves when this is done," Naomi said, kneeling beside them. Too tired to smile, she greeted Ghinnah wearily. "It's good to see you, daughter, and good to have another pair of hands working with ours."

Ghinnah said nothing, but her fading color and troubled expression betrayed her doubts. Watching her, Annah thought, *Now you are sure that the father of your husband is mad. And, most likely, you are even wondering about your husband's sanity. And mine. Perhaps I should wonder as well.*

Annah demonstrated her carving skills for Ghinnah. Though nauseated and wincing at first, Ghinnah learned quickly. Soon she was slashing into the carcasses, her movements almost ruthless, as if she were taking her rage and fears out on the lifeless flesh before her. Annah could almost feel her inner turmoil.

But what can I say to comfort her, when I can't even comfort myself? Praying now, she thought, *O Most High, comfort me! Remind me that Your plans—Your infinite, loving plans—will someday include the death of Death—as it was in the Garden of Aden. Assure me that some day the Promised One will destroy Death. How I long for that day! Now, however, I must live in this day.* Thoroughly miserable, she continued to work in silence.

Near midday, Annah sat back and stretched briefly. She was about to offer to prepare the midday meal when one of Noakh's cousins, Pathal, let out a piercing yell. He was working near the woven enclosures, but Annah heard him raging at Noakh.

"See, I've cut my hand! I've had enough! I want my animals now. I'm done with you and your accursed family!"

Noakh tried to reason with his cousin, but Pathal waved him off. "I'm going now! Give me my animals, and I'll leave you to your Most High! You'll get whatever you deserve, fool!"

Even as Pathal was screaming, Shem, Yepheth, and Khawm went to count out the animals—obviously, they were glad to be rid of him.

One cousin left, Annah thought, casting a sidelong glance at the grizzled Akar. *I wish he would go too.*

Sighing, disgusted, Naomi lifted her eyebrows at Annah and Ghinnah. "We'll let that Pathal-child leave before setting out the midday meal. Why should we feed him? That rude thing . . . screaming at my dear one."

As soon as the angry Pathal had departed, Naomi urged everyone to scrub, then eat. But Noakh's remaining cousin, Akar, took handfuls of grain cakes and fruit and flung himself down in the scanty shade on the northern side of one of the woven enclosures, clearly shunning Noakh and his family.

Apparently disturbed by Pathal's departure, Noakh ate standing, watching Pathal goad his flock through the distant northwestern edges of his fields.

Touching Annah's arm, Shem gave her a grim little smile. "I'm amazed Pathal stayed as long as he did. We gave him two extra animals for his cut hand."

"I suppose that's fair," Annah said, her voice low. "This hasn't been easy work."

Shem nodded somberly, caressing her cheek. "I wouldn't blame you if you wanted to run away. This isn't the sort of work I'd ever wish for you to do."

Suddenly Noakh cried out, alarmed. "What am I seeing?"

They all stood and followed his gaze northwest toward the departing Pathal. A trio of great lizards loped toward Pathal and his retreating flock.

"Those are monstrous carrion-eaters!" Ghinnah clutched at Yepheth.

Taller than men—their leathery long-necked heads and bodies counterbalanced by long tails—the carrion-eaters charged the distant flock and scattered it. *Like children playing,* Annah thought, stunned, unable to believe her eyes. Normally, carrion-eaters avoided humans, ignoring them—as if humans were mere gnats, or flies, or little nothing-creatures meant to be disregarded.

"That's what my uncle was saying," Ghinnah cried, distraught. "It's as if the carrion-eaters are too impatient to wait for the carrion to become carrion!"

Even from this distance, Annah could see the sheep of Pathal's herd being flung about like sticks. The carrion-eaters were amazingly agile, snapping at their victims with their teeth and razing them with great hooklike claws. Annah stepped back, as if she could retreat from the scene. Catching her by the arm, Shem said, "Hurry! We need to move the herds closer to our lodge."

Akar, Noakh's last remaining cousin, screamed a death wail. "Pathal, my brother! How can he survive against those terrible monster-lizards? He's dead! He's dead!"

"The carrion-eaters must smell the blood of the herds on him," Yepheth said, as he helped the terrified Ghinnah gather their supplies.

"The carrion-eaters have departed from their purpose," Noakh said, grieving. "The violence of the earth has affected them—as man is affected."

Appalled and silent, they hastily decamped to the lodge of Noakh.

"Am I supposed to accept this?" Tirtsah's beautiful face was ferocious as she confronted Annah and Ghinnah amid the flocks, which now surrounded the lodge. "Am I supposed to be silent while my husband and his family destroy their wealth?"

"Yes, please be silent!" Ghinnah retorted. "I'm sick of your complaints. I had enough of you yesterday. Even cutting flesh today was preferable to listening to you again. And the only reason we're here now is to save ourselves from those terrible lizards—though I'm sure you wouldn't mind if they killed all of us!"

Undeterred by Ghinnah's hostility, Tirtsah challenged Annah. "Do you accept this madness? This cutting down of the herds?"

Exhausted and frustrated, Annah said, "Yes. I accept it. And whether you like it or not, you must accept it as well. Now, you can help us, or you can go tend the lodge. But please, sister, don't say another word against your husband and his family."

Annah marched back to her task of cutting and drying flesh. She could feel Tirtsah staring after her in disbelief. *You'll have to make your decision soon,* Annah thought to Tirtsah. *Will you go or stay?*

Entering the lodge the next afternoon, Shem knelt beside Annah and pulled her into his arms. Softly, he said, "We found Pathal's body and buried him. He was crushed and torn almost beyond recognition. At least those carrion-eaters have not acquired a taste for the flesh of humans."

Absorbing the full impact of his words, Annah shuddered and pressed a hand to her mouth. *Don't think about it,* she commanded herself. *Carrion-eaters chewing the flesh of a man, then spitting him out.* Overwhelmed by nausea, she ran out of the lodge.

"Today we rest," Noakh said quietly, his dark eyes sweeping over them all as they sat together for their morning meal. "There's nothing more to be done. Tomorrow we will move into the pen and prepare ourselves. In seven days, the waters will come."

Naomi lifted her eyebrows. "The Most High has told you it is time?"

"It is time," Noakh agreed, without enthusiasm.

Annah felt Shem's warm, callused fingers curling around her hand. Clearing his throat, he said, "Then we should all go to our shelters and pack everything."

"No. You must rest today," Noakh commanded them sternly. "Enjoy the sun, the earth, and the skies. This will be our last day of calm and freedom. Do nothing except rest and pray. By tomorrow evening, we should have all our belongings inside the pen. Everything else will be destroyed—as the Most High has said."

Annah and Shem left the lodge, accompanied by Yepheth, Ghinnah, Khawm, and the sullen Tirtsah. Unsettled by Tirtsah's smoldering expression, and by Ghinnah's obvious unhappiness, Annah slowed her steps. Shem, Yepheth, and Khawm went onward, engrossed in their own subdued conversation. Ghinnah and Tirtsah lingered to talk with Annah.

Ghinnah spoke first, her vivid color rising with exasperation. "Do you still agree with them, Annah? Should we leave everything and move into that pen tomorrow?"

"Ma'adannah, you *have* to agree that this is madness,"

Tirtsah spat, siding with Ghinnah. "They've cut down all but a handful of the sheep, the oxen, and the goats. And now, we're to abandon our own dwelling places? No, I won't do it!"

"What could possibly happen if you do?" Annah asked, staring at them, unyielding. "You don't agree with your husbands. But they are your husbands, and unless you intend to leave them, wouldn't it be better to go into the pen for at least seven days? At the end of that time, you'll know who is right—the two of you or your husbands. And if you are right, you can laugh about it for the remainder of your lives. Now, I'm going to rest and enjoy my day of peace."

Annah sat beside Shem near the open hearth, enjoying the early evening fire and the first violet-red hints of dusk. Smiling, Shem kissed her hair, her forehead, her lips. "You're more beautiful than that sky. I'd rather look at you."

"Greedy man." Annah nuzzled his bearded face. "You've had me to yourself all day long. Aren't you tired of me yet?"

Shem laughed. "Never."

A sharp whistle cut into their conversation. They turned and saw Khawm, Yepheth, and Ghinnah hurrying toward them in the ruddy evening light. Khawm looked desperate; his eyes were enormous.

He snatched at Shem, saying, "Tirtsah has been angry all day. We quarreled, then she ran off into the trees, and now I've lost her. Please, help me find her."

Annah felt a chill of sweat prickle over her face, her

neck, her arms, her back. If Tirtsah had abandoned Khawm, where else would she go but to the settlement? Without explanation, Annah ran into the woods and toward the bridge.

Twenty-One

BREATHING HEAVILY, Annah scurried off the bridge, followed by Shem and Khawm. Yepheth and Gh-innah stayed on their side of the river, hoping that Tirtsah had not abandoned them altogether. *Are you worth all this?* Annah wondered to Tirtsah in a growing, gnawing attack of fear. *Are you worth my very life? If anyone from the settlement finds me on this side of the river, I will be killed.*

Annah pushed her fears aside as she hurried up the riverbank and into the trees. Surely if the Most High had chosen to save her from the settlement, He would not change His mind now.

"Annah!" Shem called out, just loudly enough to catch her attention. "Slow down. We can't go running into the settlement. Let's search the trees; if we don't find Tirtsah here, then we'll make some sort of plan."

"If she has gone into the settlement, then we've lost

her," Annah whispered. She paused in the shadowed undergrowth, clutching her hands to her stomach. "If we follow her there, we'll be killed."

"If Tirtsah has gone into the settlement, then I'll go after her myself," Khawm told them. "And if I don't come back, then tell our father and I'ma not to come looking for me." Eyeing Shem and Annah, Khawm said, "That includes you as well. Whatever happens, don't come after me. Why should we all be in danger?"

"We'll talk about that later," Shem replied, peering ahead, carefully stepping between the bare tangled roots of a honey-flower tree. "It's getting dark; let's pray we find Tirtsah soon."

I don't sense her, Annah thought, anxiety making her heart race and flutter. She tried to console herself. Perhaps Tirtsah hadn't crossed the bridge to go to the settlement after all. Even now, she might be pacing around the hearth before her dwelling place, waiting for Khawm. *I pray that's where she is,* Annah thought, *because she's not here in the trees.*

They searched all along the river between the bridge and the settlement. By the time they reached the fields, the sun had set and the light was fading rapidly. Now, crouching beside Shem and Khawm in the shadows of the trees, Annah looked over at the clusters of lodges, all of them marked by the rising smoke of their evening fires. *I don't miss any of you,* she thought.

"She must be there," Khawm said, speaking slowly.

Equally reluctant, Annah looked away from the settlement, studying the huge field before them. The only thing breaking the outlines of the darkening field was the magnificent, flowing shape of the ancient Tree of Havah—the one place, she suddenly realized, that Tirtsah might be hiding if she were afraid.

Excited, Annah patted Shem's arm to get his attention. "Tirtsah could be in the Tree of Havah! I used to sit there in the mornings. Let me go look; if she's still angry, she'd be more likely to talk to me than to either of you."

"It's almost dark enough that you won't be seen," Khawm agreed eagerly.

Shem touched Annah's face, his voice filled with concern. "If she's not in the tree, please, come back here at once. Don't go into the settlement."

"I won't ever go into that place again," Annah assured him, meaning every word. "If she's not in the tree, I'll come right back. But if she is there, you must give me time to talk to her."

Lowering her head, Annah scurried through the field. *I wish this tree were on my side of the river,* she thought, admiring the flowing, restful contours of the shadowed branches. *There's no other tree half so wonderful in all the world.* She was glad to reach the Tree of Havah, delighted to touch it again. And she was even more pleased to sense the presence of another person sheltered within its branches.

Annah reached for the lowest branch and pulled herself up easily. She knew every bend of each branch; she didn't have to concentrate on climbing. She focused on Tirtsah instead. Tirtsah was seated high in the crook of a branch, turned toward the settlement. She didn't look at Annah, though she undoubtedly knew Annah was near. Stepping onto an adjacent branch, Annah sat down, sighing with relief.

For a brief time, they were silent, then Tirtsah spoke, almost rudely. "Why did you come to find me?"

Annah ignored the question. Instead she looked over at the settlement and said, "The last time I sat in this tree was the night of the deaths. I listened as everyone in the settlement hunted for my brother's wife, Iltani. They were so ready to kill someone that it wouldn't have mattered whose blood was spilled. I stayed here all night in the branch above you."

Silent, Tirtsah looked up at the branch.

More somberly, Annah said, "That was the night my mother died. Iltani, too. When the searchers from the settlement caught her, they slit her throat because she had killed my second brother, Chathath."

Swallowing, Annah continued. "I was the one who should have died, not Chathath. When I saw his body the next morning, I was on the very edge of true madness. I had no thoughts, no words. I wandered down to the river like a mindless nothing-creature. Shem was so sure I would kill myself that he begged I'ma-Naomi to offer a brideprice to my brother."

When Tirtsah remained silent, Annah went on. "Yerakh was always so greedy. He gave me to Shem without question the next day. But if he had perceived my thoughts, he would have killed me instantly. If anyone from the settlement finds me here, they'll kill me and claim a reward from him."

Tirtsah looked at Annah, shocked. "Then why are you here? Why should you risk your life for me?"

Annah sighed, speaking carefully. "Your husband loves you, Tirtsah. He has made you my sister by marriage. And I am here now, sister, because this is how a family behaves to survive. Each member considers the others, and each member truly cares about the others—to the point of sacrifice, if need be. I'll tell you now, Khawm is ready to go into the settlement after you, knowing he's not welcomed there."

"They'd kill him for trying to find me?"

"Yes. Then they'd throw his body away and laugh. Khawm would be forgotten almost immediately. It would be worse for you—they would allow you to live." Annah prayed Tirtsah would listen. "If you go into the settlement, the men of the settlement will follow you and use you according to their desires because you have no one to protect you. The women will hate you because of your beauty. Later, the men will grow tired of you, and you'll have to find some way to survive. No one will help you, because you have nothing of value but your beauty. If you should disappear or die, they'd never look for you. And," she added, "your death would most likely be the result of violence from someone in the settlement."

"That's what I've been thinking," Tirtsah admitted. Straightening, she sucked in a sharp, angry breath. "I'm trapped then! I have no choice but to go back to the family of that madman, Noakh!"

"You *will* have a choice," Annah retorted, offended for Noakh's sake. "And you'll have that choice because the father of your husband is not a madman. He's kind and loving. He will have compassion on you now, even though you hate him. Just as the Most High has compassion on you now, Tirtsah, though you hate Him." Seeing Tirtsah stiffen defiantly, Annah gritted her teeth, struggling with her own impatience.

When she could trust herself to speak, Annah said, "Tirtsah, listen to me. Stay with your husband for the next seven days. On the eighth day, if nothing has happened, then you can laugh in our faces and demand to go back to your family, wherever they are. Your husband and his father and his brothers will honor your request. I know this because Yepheth offered a similar choice to Ghinnah the day he married her. Also, if nothing happens and you choose to leave us, I'll give you the last of my gold."

"But you don't think there will be an eighth day," Tirtsah said, not quite arguing.

Annah shrugged in the twilight. "As I told you this morning, someone will be right. Now, be honest; if there is no eighth day, wouldn't you rather be with us? Please, Tirtsah, come down from this tree before Khawm goes looking for you in the settlement."

Suspicious, Tirtsah leaned toward Annah. "You will insist that my husband and his family help me if I don't want to stay?"

"I'll insist," Annah agreed. "If you don't believe me, then you can take your chances in the settlement."

"No, I'll go with you," Tirtsah said sullenly.

They climbed down out of the tree, then scurried across the field. The last traces of sunlight were gone, but if anyone from the settlement should come out into the western fields, they would sense Annah and Tirtsah at once. Annah was trembling with relief when they reached the safety of the trees.

Shem grabbed her immediately, hugging her. "We were getting ready to come after you."

Smiling, Annah turned toward Khawm and Tirtsah. They were silent in the darkness.

Tirtsah spoke, clearly uneasy, but attempting to sound proud, even a little scornful. "I'll stay with you for eight days. After that, if I'm still unhappy, I want you to take me back to my father's house."

Khawm exhaled, holding out a hand for Tirtsah to accept. "I agree. Eight days."

Slowly, Tirtsah accepted Khawm's hand, while Annah leaned against Shem gratefully.

Tightening his arms around Annah, Shem said, "Let's leave this place. I'm sure Yepheth and Ghinnah are wondering where we are."

In agreement, they made their way down to the river and hurried toward the bridge, their way lit by the shimmering moon and stars.

Annah settled a clean fleece coverlet over the bed, then stood back to inspect the room she would share with her husband. The grass mats were comfortable beneath her feet, and the air was scented with the new straw she had used to stuff the bed. She had also stuffed the soft leather pillows with sweet-smelling dried herbs and long, glossy fibers from a hair-seed tree. Earlier, Shem had helped her move their storage chest against the far wall. Inside the chest were their garments, Shem's carving supplies, their work tools, Annah's gold, her veil, and the woven-grass bag. Now, Annah finished her last task: She wiped out the oil lamps, discarded the grass wicks, and packed the lamps into the storage chest. This was Noakh's command; they could not risk an oil fire.

"Ma–adanna–a–a–h," Ghinnah's singsong voice echoed toward her through the pen. "I'm finished with my chores. Will you go outside with me again?"

"I'm coming, Ghinnah." Annah smiled to herself as she walked into the window-lit main living area. Ghinnah wanted companionship whenever she entered or left the pen, like a child needing reassurance. Tirtsah also seemed unsure of herself. Annah had found her wandering through the pen this morning, staring at everything, obviously forlorn—and disdainful—until Annah had coaxed her outside into the sunlight.

Now Annah went out into the daylight with Ghinnah, staring at the confusion below. The area behind the lodge was crowded with tools, cured hides, rolled grass mats, storage chests, and multitudes of baskets filled with the provisions from Naomi's storage room. Tirtsah had apparently gone into the lodge to help Naomi, but Noakh was standing in the middle of all the provisions, arguing with his wild-haired cousin Akar.

"You're welcome to go or stay, as you please," Noakh was telling Akar. "But obviously you don't care to listen to me, so it no longer matters what you do."

"It no longer matters?" Indignant, Akar said, "I've served you all these years—and you say it no longer matters? No, you won't be rid of me so easily!"

"Stay, then." As he spoke, Noakh picked up some of his tools and eyed the broad grinding stone and its mortar. "Stay in our lodge if you like. Whatever you choose, Akar. Soon we won't need the lodge anyway."

Akar snorted, rolling his eyes. "Save me from another story of the Most High."

"I won't bore you again." Noakh beckoned to Khawm and Yepheth, who were coming out of the lodge, laden with the last baskets of grain from the storage room. "Don't forget, my sons, we have to carry your mother's grinding stone and mortar into the pen as soon as possible."

"Then that's all you have to say to me?" Akar demanded, tapping Noakh's back with hard, impatient fingers.

"Why should I talk if you won't listen to me?" Noakh answered, clearly exasperated. "I'll tell you again; if you don't want to leave us, then stay in the lodge tonight. Now, my cousin, take care of yourself, and let me finish my work."

As Noakh rebuked his cousin, Annah saw a pair of brilliantly colored birds, all lustrous green and gold with curving black beaks, alight on Noakh's arm and shoulder.

Noakh blinked at the pair, then chuckled. "You're early," he said to them, shaking his head. "And you've caught me with my arms full." Looking around, he saw Annah and Ghinnah. He smiled at them and tipped his head, indicating the pair of birds. "My daughters, please, come take these two up into the pen. I pray that the Most High doesn't plan to have all the creatures land on me when they find me—it could become quite uncomfortable."

Pleased and amused, Annah went to her father-in-law and offered her shoulder to the pair of green and gold birds. They moved over to her, thoroughly trusting. The smaller one, the female, scrabbled toward Annah's bound hair, apparently enticed by her glittering gold hair bindings. "You can't have them," Annah whispered as it picked at the gold. "You don't need them anyway; you're lovely just as the Most High created you, pretty bird. Come-come."

"Your son deserves such a wife," Akar sneered, fixing his sharp black eyes on Annah. "She's as ridiculous as you are. If she were my wife, I'd beat her for talking such foolishness to a bird."

"But she's not your wife," Noakh answered forbiddingly. "Now, cousin, go or stay as you please, and don't harass us."

Fearful, Annah looked down at her feet, keeping her face expressionless as she went toward the ramp of the pen. Ghinnah followed her silently, carrying a basket of dishes and cooking pots. When they were inside the pen, away from Akar, Ghinnah said, "Just now, I think I saw the nothing-creature-Annah."

"An old habit," Annah acknowledged. "I wanted to get away from that Akar. I was also thinking that except for the care of the Most High, I might have been given to such a man—one who would enjoy beating his wife."

"All men beat their wives," Ghinnah said, as if this were an unchangeable fact.

"Not the men of the lodge of Noakh."

Unable to argue, Ghinnah shrugged and followed Annah through the central level to the ramp leading up to the higher level. The birds were becoming restless, roving along Annah's arm and shoulder. The female finally clawed her way up Annah's hair to the top of her head, making Annah nervous as she carried the birds toward the vast netted enclosure. Ghinnah set down the basket of dishes and opened the curtains so Annah could place the birds on one of the branches hanging inside. Inside the netting, the birds fluttered wildly, shedding delicate tufts of green down as they beat their wings about Annah's head. Annah stood still, shielding her eyes with her hands. If she moved suddenly, she might frighten them even more. Outside the netted enclosure, Ghinnah was agitated, wringing her hands.

"Annah, what's wrong with them? What should I do?"

Steadying herself, Annah said, "Go find the father of our husbands."

Annah waited inside the netted enclosure, trying to remain calm. The birds were flying about now, as if trying to escape. Annah was amazed at their speed and their ability to veer and turn among the countless branches. Then, quite suddenly, they settled near each other in the branches, docile again, as if nothing had happened. An instant later, Annah felt Noakh's presence as he came up the ramp. He was chuckling, followed by the anxious Ghinnah.

"Now, daughter, I hope you haven't changed your hair for feathers. Come out here, little bird!"

"They were frightened," Annah explained. "But the instant you returned to the pen, they became quiet. They sensed your presence before I did."

As Annah slipped out of the enclosure, Ghinnah picked a feather from Annah's hair and laughed, her agitation fading. "Really, Annah, the feathers are quite pretty in your hair. We should show this new adornment to I'ma-Naomi and Tirtsah."

Noakh cleared his throat gently, as if he hated to interrupt. "Daughters, go tell your husbands that I cannot leave the pen. If these two creatures have already appeared, then others will follow. We have little time."

As they left the pen, Ghinnah sniffed doubtfully. "Two birds appear and he says 'we have little time.' It'll take more than two birds to convince me." Tossing her head, she moved ahead of Annah, out of the pen.

"The herds have been restless all week," Naham growled, his voice lifting to the grass roof of his lodge. Seated on a mat beside him, Yerakh grunted and stared into the evening fire. Frowning, Naham continued. "My wives say that they've watched countless creatures on the other side of the river, all moving northward. Although, women being such fools, I should ignore them."

Yerakh grunted again.

Irritated, Naham gave Yerakh a shove. "What use are you, my friend, if you won't talk to me? Where's your laughter? If you give up your will to live, Yerakh, why not just kill yourself now? I haven't said so before, but ever since that Annah-who-is-not-Annah spoke that curse upon you . . . well, you're no longer a man. I should find myself a new friend who enjoys feasting and games and women—and vengeance."

Yerakh looked up. "What vengeance? Who has offended you?"

"Who's offended me?" Naham snorted and spat toward the fire. "I was talking about you. Listen, my friend, it's been months now. You're still alive. Do you need any more proof that your miserable sister was wrong to curse you? You should be angry! She's used her words to escape you and to rob you of your joys." Huffing, Naham said, "I swear, Yerakh, if I hear your pretty wife crying to my wives again that you don't desire her anymore, I'll take her for myself—since you've forgotten how to be a husband."

Yerakh glared at him. "It's easy for you to talk. You didn't feel that presence moving against you. You didn't see the fear of the Nachash—who has feared nothing, until now."

"All the more reason for us to kill that Annah-who-is-not-Annah."

When Yerakh lowered his head and frowned, Naham said, "If you don't kill her, then I will. Your fear has made you weak. And she—that Annah—has even changed Tseb-iy. He swears she's turned all women against him, forcing him to marry."

Yerakh sneered at the mention of Tseb-iy, who had finally chosen to marry Yediydah, K'nan's lovely, pouting-lipped younger sister. "Tseb-iy is getting married because the women of this settlement are tired of him and won't yield to him anymore. His wife, however, must accept him whether she's tired of him or not."

"Then," Naham argued, "if you don't believe Tseb-iy when *he* says he was cursed by your sister, why should you believe that you are cursed? I'm telling you, we should kill that Annah-creature. I'll do it; I'm not afraid of her. In fact"—Naham paused, licking his lips—"it'll be a pleasure."

"Tomorrow then," Yerakh agreed, finally seeming to be persuaded, even pleased by the thought. "I'll go with you; we can sneak away during Tseb-iy's marriage feast. And you can do as you please with her; I'll keep my distance until she's dead."

"Coward!"

For the first time in weeks, Yerakh laughed.

Annah worked with Ghinnah in the middle level of the pen, fastening enclosures and cages. As she worked, she marveled at the orderliness and calm of the creatures as they entered their respective places. They all seemed drawn by Noakh's presence. And they were utterly docile. Even the carrion-eaters, with their endless varieties of claws, horns, and teeth, seemed as easily led as sheep.

"Look at them," Ghinnah said as she fastened another enclosure containing two ponderous, leather-skinned, one-horned beasts. "I don't believe it."

Annah didn't respond; Shem had distracted her. He brushed past her teasingly, going toward the lower ramp, carrying a pair of night-rats and a pair of large-eyed tree-dwellers—creatures that loved the darkness. Other creatures slipped past Annah as well, seeming drawn to various corners, spaces, and levels of the pen. Glancing about now, Annah saw Tirtsah descending the upper ramp, her beautiful eyes huge and a little desperate.

Tirtsah whispered to Annah, "This is not real. There are birds coming down through the windows—some I've never seen before!"

"Are you helping them into the netted enclosures?" Annah whispered back, as she fastened the rows of smaller cages along the walls.

"I'ma-Naomi and Yepheth are up there now," Tirtsah said, distracted. She scanned the central level. "Where's my husband?"

Annah suppressed a smile. Tirtsah had been shunning Khawm for most of the week. Now, she was looking for him. "He's working in the lower level."

"In the dark?" Tirtsah sounded unnerved by the thought.

"Some of the light goes down there," Annah said soothingly. "But, anyway, my husband is with him. And Khawm has a torch."

Tirtsah's eyes widened in alarm, and she darted over to the central ramp leading into the lower level. Shrugging, Annah continued to fasten enclosures and cages, goading an animal here, lifting another there. Now and then, she paused to stare at some of the creatures. Each animal was young, healthy, and seemingly the most perfect of its kind. Annah was amazed and delighted by their beauty and astonishing variations, as well as by their similarities. She thought to the Most High, *What joy You must have had in creating all these animals!*

"Look at these!" Ghinnah shrieked to Annah, laughing. Cautiously she lifted a stocky, spiny, dark-furred little creature that was equipped with a long, slender beaklike snout and oddly turned, bare-clawed feet. "Its beloved looks the same; absurd things!"

"With those feet, they must like to burrow," Annah thought aloud. "Put them in a dark corner cage with lots of leaves and straw."

"You have no sense of fun," Ghinnah sniffed, heading for a corner.

When more than half the day had passed, the sheer numbers of new and different animals dwindled. Then no more came. A muted breathlessness settled over the pen, an almost fearful sense of waiting. Full of wonder, Annah looked around. Naomi and Yepheth came down from the upper level, seeming perplexed. Shem, Khawm, and Tirtsah emerged from the lower level, dousing their torch in a pail of water, then squinting as they walked toward the great side door where Noakh stood.

Puzzled, Annah followed Shem toward the door. Noakh's cousin, Akar, was scoffing at Noakh from the base of the ramp. "Now what'll you do, after calling all those creatures to yourself? What trick did you use, eh? You'll have to get rid of them soon enough, fool. And remember, you've given me your lodge!"

"May we close the door on him?" Khawm demanded from the left of the door. Without waiting for his father's reply, he grabbed a great rope that was looped through iron rings in the base of the ramp and in the doorframe. Noakh motioned to Shem and Yepheth; they grabbed the ropes on the right of the doorframe, while Noakh helped Khawm.

"Pull!" Noakh commanded.

Annah held her breath, watching as they pulled. The ropes went taut, but the ramp door didn't move. Akar cackled from his place outside. "Fools, you can't even close your door!"

"Child, let's help them," Naomi said to Annah.

But as they were reaching for the ropes, the door lifted. Annah gasped, staring, confounded. *The ropes are going slack, but the door is lifting. How can this be?*

"Living Word," Noakh breathed, releasing the rope.

The men were backing away now. Akar screamed from outside, "Wait, wait!"

Annah felt her mouth go dry. She couldn't move. She could only stand there, staring as the great door shut slowly, gently, as if controlled by an unseen hand. *I'm not imagining this,* she told herself, still staring. She could no longer hear Akar's screaming, pleading voice; the door had cut it off. A sudden burst of warmth emanated from the door, and the scents of resins and woods mingled, permeating the air.

"He's sealing the door with His own hand!" Noakh exulted, gazing at the door, delighted as a young child. "Ah, Most High!" Then the warmth dissipated. Instantly, Noakh turned upon them all. "Hurry! Is everything fastened down? If so, then get to the upper level. Go! Go! Go!" He waved his hands, chasing Annah and the others away.

Shem seized Annah's hand, pulling her away from the great door. She ran with the others. *Like sheep,* Annah thought, as they all scrambled up the central ramp. And, almost like sheep, they hurried to the same place, the area surrounding the faintly smoldering hearth.

For an instant, they all sat in pairs—husbands and wives together—looking at each other, still unable to believe what they had just seen. Then the pen began to quiver and vibrate. The tremors intensified, until they could do nothing but kneel, clutching the resin-coated floor and each other. Ghinnah began to scream and cry. Sweating, Annah reached out blindly for Shem, thinking, *This is worse than any of the others.* Then Annah heard a vast, booming, echoing, cracking sound from beyond the windows above them, as if the earth and the sky were splitting and breaking into tiny, irretrievable pieces. Terrified, scarcely aware of her husband's arms around her, Annah began to pray.

Twenty-Two

YERAKH LED Naham along the riverbank to the bridge, talking eagerly. "One thing is true of Annah: She won't stay inside that Noakh's lodge for very long. She likes to wander outside. All we have to do is watch for her."

"You should have given her to me all those months ago when I asked for her," Naham said, his voice deep and rumbling, a sneer on his broad, bearded face. "She'd be no trouble to you now."

"Who would ever have thought she would be trouble," Yerakh muttered darkly. "When you see her you won't recognize her." He paused at the bridge, stepping aside to allow Naham to go first. Naham eyed the bridge warily, then shook his head.

"You go first; that bridge is meant for an ordinary little man."

"Really?" Yerakh asked, hoping to taunt Naham into crossing. "Are you thinking you'll break this thing and fall in? Who's the coward now?"

"Go first!" Naham commanded threateningly, flexing his huge fingers into massive fists.

Reluctantly Yerakh started over the bridge. Now his fears took on a voice in his mind, hissing Annah's warnings to him with renewed vehemence. *You are a fool! You sheltered the Nachash. You killed your father. You willed the deaths of your mother, your wife, and your brothers, and now you seek the life of another. You are cursed!*

The voice seemed to end, but a new thought occurred to Yerakh: *Your feet carry you to your death.* Shuddering, he paused on the resilient reed-and-rope bridge. The bridge shook, upsetting his balance. Without turning, he screamed at Naham, "Quit shaking the bridge!"

"I'm not shaking the bridge!" Naham bellowed from the riverbank. "It's the earth shaking the bridge!"

As Naham was bellowing, the tremors of the earth increased, with groanlike sounds reverberating ominously from deep beneath the ground. All at once, Yerakh lost his footing and went sprawling on his belly, facing north, clutching the ropes of the bridge. Panicked, he looked at Naham, but the giant man was on his knees. Even his great strength was not enough to keep him upright. Yerakh heard an immense burst of noise resounding from the depths of the earth up to the very heavens. In that same instant, he saw impossibly vast geysers of water and plumes of deep gray smoke blasting up from the ground in the distance, tearing through the roseate sky, splitting open the heavens.

Yerakh stared upward, unable to scream, his horror was so great. An immense pattern of waves rippled east to west through the skies above him, as if the heavens were made of water. The physical shocks of these rippling waves, paired with the shaking of the earth, caused the two eastern trees supporting the bridge to lurch threateningly above the now raging current—above Yerakh himself.

Terror-stricken, he clung to the bridge as it sagged into the current. The water dashed over his face, making him raise his head, desperately gasping for air. As he struggled to maintain his hold, Yerakh glimpsed Naham toppling into the white-crested waves. The giant man was swept downriver, howling, raging, all his strength useless.

Suddenly an all-encompassing roar filled Yerakh's ears; the force of the water increased with the noise. Looking up, he saw his death coming: a vast, surging wall of frothing, muddied water, filled with shredded trees, fragments of reed lodges, and battered corpses—animal and human—all sweeping toward him from the north. He could only wait, screaming as the wall finally struck, ripping him away from the sagging bridge. The mighty trees leaning above him fell into the river, rolling and tumbling in the muddy surge, following him downriver. His arms and legs crushed and useless, Yerakh found himself snared among tree limbs in the rapids. He longed, in vain, for a swift and painless death.

Virtually every member of the settlement was gathered in the lodge of Sa-khar, to celebrate Tseb-iy's marriage to Sa-khar's only daughter, Yediydah. Standing near the doorway of the lodge, Ayalah watched the lean, black-bearded, narrow-eyed Sa-khar pronounce his formal approval of the married couple. Though the bride was her sister-in-law, K'nan's sister, Ayalah felt no love or loyalty toward Yediydah or any of her family. By now, K'nan held no attraction for Ayalah. He was a sulking, willful husband, a complete disappointment. Ayalah glanced at him. *Why did I ever want you? You're nothing but trouble to me.* Contemptuous, she looked away from her husband, toward Yediydah and Tseb-iy.

Yediydah, lovely, pouting, and glistening with bride-gold purchased from Yerakh, shifted her gaze from her father to her new husband, the supposedly unattainable Tseb-iy. Ayalah almost laughed at Tseb-iy's grim smile as he waited for the self-important Sa-khar to finish the marriage blessing.

Gloating, Ayalah leaned over to Haburah and the other wives of Naham and said, "Look at that fool, Tseb-iy. By his expression, I think he could spit embers."

"I think he's changed his mind already," said Naham's first wife, Shuwa, her dark eyes sparkling with malice. "Tseb-iy will keep that Yediydah guessing and looking to see where his affections will fall next, I assure you. She's a fool to marry him."

Naham's second wife, Qetsiyah, laughed beneath her breath, nudging Shuwa with one slender, graceful hand. "You're just angry that he has never looked at you. If it weren't for Naham's jealousy, you would have thrown yourself at Tseb-iy long ago."

"May they be barren," Haburah muttered darkly. "I should have killed Tseb-iy for scorning my mother."

Ayalah smiled, deciding that she must encourage Haburah to take vengeance on Tseb-iy—it would be amusing. Suddenly, the earth wavered beneath Ayalah's feet, startling her from all thoughts of Tseb-iy.

Haburah grabbed at Ayalah. "Outside, quickly, before the others trample us!"

Ayalah managed to scramble outside with her sister before the tremors jolted them to the ground. On her hands and knees now, Ayalah looked around, terrified. This shaking of the earth was the worst yet. The lodges were being jostled like loose bundles of reeds. Other members of the settlement were crawling out of the lodge of Sa-khar, unable and unwilling to help those still trapped inside. Shuwa had also managed to escape the teetering lodge. Like the others, she was unable to walk, the tremors were so fierce. Obviously scared, she crawled to Haburah and cried, "Where is our husband?"

Ayalah could not hear Haburah's answer. A deep groaning noise rose from the earth, lifting into the heavens as an immense, distant fissure burst and spewed an endless protrusion of water and smoke upward, rumbling and crackling as it surged past the limits of the sky. *Annah,* Ayalah thought, *you knew this would happen! I hate you—and your Most High! I hope you die!*

Ayalah gaped as boundless shock waves rippled through the sky from the east toward the settlement. The sheer power of these waves caused the lodges to tumble to the ground. Those trapped inside the lodge of Sa-khar screamed and wailed beneath the collapsing roof of the lodge.

"They're dying!" Ayalah screamed.

"We're dead!" Haburah cried, her gaze fixed on the darkening, churning skies. The usual rosy glow of the sky was gone, blotted out by smokelike billows of vapors. Sudden, terrifying streaks of white-blue light flashed downward from these billows, creating a terrible booming noise that shook the air as the tremors jarred the earth.

Stunned, Ayalah could only wait on her hands and knees, watching as muddied walls of water poured down from the dark, seething heavens. The falling waters pounded Ayalah, Haburah, the settlement, and its inhabitants, eventually washing them toward the surging river. Ayalah finally lost consciousness beneath the force of the waters, her life ebbing away. All traces of the settlement were scoured from the surface of the earth.

Its magnificent limbs whipped by the shock waves, its roots loosened by the tremors and the onrush of the waters from the river and the skies, the Tree of Havah creaked and swayed in the earth. At last, weakened and overcome by the power of the waters, the ancient tree groaned and fell into the rising current.

To the east of the settlement, the Nachash and her whisperers tottered outside when the first tremors hit. Hearing the rupturing of the earth and the crackling of the sky, the Nachash screamed, "Most High, will You destroy us? You!"

Shaken to her hands and knees now, the Nachash spat vigorously, her emaciated face defiant. But her whisperers wailed aloud as the shock waves struck, felling the trees to the east of their lodge. And the waters of the darkening heavens descended upon the Nachash and her whisperers, sweeping them away like dry, brittle twigs.

Far to the west, in the most distant grasslands, a small herd of tawny-haired, finely hoofed grazers trotted up to the edge of their watering place. They whinnied to each other, then stepped into the water and lowered their heads to drink. Another herd approached, also grazers, but larger and one-horned, with bare leathery hides. These larger grazers were ungainly on land, but graceful as soon as they entered the water.

Birds, long-necked and elegant, also entered the water, moving lightly between the herds until the earth quivered. Alarmed, the birds took to the air. The sky reverberated and darkened ominously. The two herds milled about, their panic growing with the tremors and the approach of an immeasurably vast, roiling ash-cloud. As the choking, gray, gritty particles of heated ash and gases descended upon them, the herds mingled, struggling to breathe.

The young tried to comfort themselves by suckling, but their mothers were already dying. The birds fell to the earth again and were trampled into the waters. In their blinded terror, the great one-horned grazers charged over the bodies of the delicate tawny-hoofed grazers. One by one, the animals succumbed to the chaos and to the suffocating dust and gases.

Then the waters covered their graves.

To the farthest reaches of the northeast, a large beak-headed female carrion-eater huddled over her carefully arranged nest of eggs. Fearful of the rippling violence of the earth and the sky, the female locked its long, clawed forelimbs together around its carefully arranged nest of eggs.

Then a stifling, life-choking storm-blast of fine red sand buried both the female and her nest of eggs, preserving their remains from the floodwaters that followed.

They sat as a family around the barely flickering hearth of the pen, listening to the storm. This vast downpour of water, punctuated by deafening, inexplicable sounds of destruction, was beyond all of Annah's imaginings. Throughout the evening, everyone prayed and watched in tense uncertainty. No one ate. And although their few conversations were disjointed, they were unwilling to leave each other for very long.

Now, in the nighttime darkness, Annah felt trapped. All the creatures throughout the pen were hushed and stilled, as if they also were listening to the fury of the storm outside. Another jolt of fierce, breathtaking, white-blue light flashed beyond the shuttered windows. Then came a terrible, heart-stopping crackling explosion of noise that shook the very air, making Annah tremble. *O Most High,* she prayed, fingering the cord of the precious shell-carving around her neck, *I realize that this is all happening as You warned, and that You are protecting us, but I am afraid.*

As Annah was thinking this, Shem clasped her hands comfortingly, his eyes encouraging her: *Don't be frightened.*

To answer her husband, Annah nodded, leaning against him. Seated beside Annah and Shem, Ghinnah spoke loudly, nervously as she huddled in Yepheth's arms. "At least the shaking of the earth has stopped for a while."

Yepheth tightened his arm around her and said clearly, "Has it? I didn't notice because you're still shaking."

"Child." Naomi beckoned Ghinnah. "At least have

something warm to drink; perhaps it will soothe you."

Shivering visibly, Ghinnah refused. "Thank you, I'ma-Naomi, but I'm sure I can't drink anything. I don't believe this is happening. . . ." Her words stopped awkwardly and she ducked her head, obviously afraid she had offended Naomi and Noakh.

But Naomi nodded in silent understanding, and Noakh's mouth twitched as if he were reluctantly amused.

Seated near Shem, Khawm grimaced. He was holding the silent Tirtsah's hands, rubbing her fingers as he called to Ghinnah. "Now, sister, if you don't believe what's happening, we'll gladly push you up a ladder to the windows so you can look outside."

Ghinnah stared at him, her eyes huge. "I . . . no—no . . . forgive me. I do believe you."

Hugging her, Yepheth said, "Don't be so frightened. We won't make you go look outside—unless you really want to go."

"No, I don't want to go!" Ghinnah cried, glaring at her husband, almost in tears. "Please, don't make fun of me."

A spectacular flash of light and a rumbling boom from beyond the high windows startled them all, making them look up. As the noise faded, Noakh raised his voice. "O Most High, Living Word, thank You for protecting us according to Your loving will. Save us from our fears this night."

As Noakh prayed, Annah saw Tirtsah wiping her face, and Khawm comforting her. *Tomorrow would have been the eighth day for you, Tirtsah,* Annah thought. *Then you would have been glad to laugh in our faces and call us fools. You would have run in your eagerness to get away from your husband and his family. What are you thinking now? At least you're no longer angry with your husband.*

Tirtsah's scornful, haughty demeanor was gone, replaced by the wide-eyed fearful attitude of a young child. Annah held her breath, praying that Tirtsah would finally accept the Most High, and the Lodge of Noakh. But Tirtsah straightened suddenly and wiped her face. *Like one who will not yield,* Annah thought in despair.

When Noakh finished praying, Annah looked at him expectantly. It was, most likely, their usual time for sleep. Another flash of light illuminated their faces and the darkness behind them, ending with a frightening burst of sound.

The noise finally ended, and Ghinnah pleaded with Noakh. "Father of my husband, can't we wait here tonight? We won't be able to sleep."

"We should try to rest, daughter," Noakh answered kindly. "Even if we cannot sleep with all this noise."

Pressing Annah's hand, Shem spoke to Yepheth and Ghinnah. "If you wish, Annah and I will stay here to keep watch with you."

"We'll stay too," Khawm added, reacting to a nudge from Tirtsah.

"We should try to rest," Noakh repeated. "But perhaps we can make ourselves comfortable here. We have some—" Another startling flash and rumbling interrupted Noakh. He finished his words by pointing to numerous rolls of hides and fleeces stored along the far wall.

Somberly, they arranged their sleeping areas not far from the carefully banked hearth, using the cured hides and fleeces. Annah lay beside Shem, staring up into the darkness. Sleep would be impossible, she decided. Even using the fleeces, the wooden, resin-coated floor was still too hard for comfort. And the noise outside could not be ignored. Even if she covered her eyes or plugged her ears,

Annah could still see the eerie white-blue flashes of light, and she could still hear the terrible outbursts of noise that shook the skies. Then there was the incessant downpour of waters from the heavens; it was too powerful to be soothing. But Annah was glad to be lying down. She was exhausted.

This is like the most terrible dream, she thought, listening to the storm. *But no, truly, the most terrible dream would be to be caught outside.*

Annah stared up into the endless third night of the storm, dazed by fatigue but unable to sleep. Surely it would be morning soon, though the dark days were no different from the nights. She turned uncomfortably and glanced at Shem, who appeared to be asleep. *How?* she wondered, staring at him. *How can you even keep your eyes closed?* Another flash of light made Annah flinch. Shutting her eyes, she curled her fingers around the polished contours of her treasured shell carving. She stilled herself, remembering its glowing colors of luminous pinks and blues, its iridescent sheen, and the endless fascination of the delicately carved waves adorning its edges.

You were considering this destruction when you carved the waves into this piece of shell, Annah thought to her husband. *Have you thought of this storm often? I kept telling myself that this destruction would be later, someday. It never seemed real, but now it's here, like an endless nightmare.*

There was a sudden shifting beneath Annah, an unnervingly buoyant sensation. *We're floating,* she realized, frightened and amazed. The entire pen moved dizzyingly. She lifted her head to look at Shem and the others. They were all sitting up now, looking around anxiously, seeming to question their own senses.

Noakh said clearly, "If we are already floating, then the lodge is covered."

If the lodge is covered, Annah thought, *then the settlement, too, is covered, and they are all dead. Yerakh. Taphaph. Naham. And Haburah and Ayalah.*

Another blinding flash of light and noise resounded outside. Remembering her sisters' faces, Annah pressed a hand to her mouth, startled by her own grief. *Why do I mourn you?* she wondered to her dead sisters. *You hated me, both of you. And I could not bear to be near you. But I never wanted you to die.*

The pen shifted. Annah put both hands on the floor to steady herself. Then, overwhelmed by an unexpected sense of loss, she began to cry.

Shem moved over in the darkness, holding her, kissing her, murmuring, "We're safe, beloved. Don't be afraid."

"They're dead." Annah took a quick, pained breath. "My sisters are dead, and I wanted them to live!" She clung to him and wept.

Twenty-Three

LIGHTING THEIR way with a resin-soaked torch, Annah crept through the second level of the pen, followed by Ghinnah. As Annah held the torch, Ghinnah listlessly checked the animals, making sure they had enough water and food. Not that it mattered; all of the creatures seemed to be in a stupor, moving little, eating less.

Like all of us, Annah thought. *All we want to do is sleep. Just listening to this storm is exhausting. And we've been wandering about like mourners. I didn't expect to feel such grief for so many days . . . weeks now. It's like a continuous bad dream.*

"Poor creatures," Ghinnah sighed. "They're all still moping. But they're alive."

Unlike your uncle, Qeb-al, and his Etsah and their sons, Annah thought, almost able to hear Ghinnah's unspoken words. *Unlike my sisters.* Annah quickly shied away from those thoughts. Both women turned, sensing another person approaching from the central ramp.

"It's Tirtsah," Ghinnah guessed. "Our husbands and the father of our husbands are all checking the animals below. And I'ma-Naomi is above, preparing the midday meal—not that I could eat anything."

Tirtsah came down into the quiet orderliness of the cages, stalls, and enclosures, pausing to look at some of the animals and to touch them, as if she doubted they were still alive. At last she met Annah and Ghinnah, her full mouth set in a grimace, her fine, dark eyebrows lifted in a token greeting. "Ma'adannah. Ghinnah. The mother of our husbands wants to talk to us together before the men come up from the lower level."

The pen heaved swiftly, causing Annah to grab the upright post of a nearby stall. The swinging, sliding sensation nauseated her. With an effort, she remembered to hold the flaring torch out at arm's length to avoid burning anyone or anything. Staggering, Ghinnah and Tirtsah clung to the post with Annah. Ghinnah pressed her hand to her mouth, and Tirtsah held her stomach as if she might retch. As everything seemed to sway about them, Annah shut her eyes. Slowly the pen righted itself in the waters, and the motions eased. Annah leaned against the stall, limp with relief. Sweat prickled over her skin, making her shiver.

Sagging against the post, Ghinnah uttered a despairing groan. "I'm so tired of being ill and creeping around like a would-be-dead person." Then, recognizing her unfortunate figure of speech, she said, "Oh, forgive me. I should have used different words."

"We understood what you meant," Annah assured her. Glancing at the drooping Tirtsah, Annah became concerned. "Tirtsah? Do you need a bucket?"

"No." Tirtsah ran a hand over her ashen face, then looked at Annah, mutinous, as if she expected to be humiliated. "I've been waiting for you to laugh at me, to tell me how wrong I was. And how right you were—that you knew this storm would come."

Clearly aggravated, Ghinnah burst out, "Oh, Tirtsah, I'm sure you've been waiting, but Annah's not ever going to behave so rudely. And she hasn't laughed since this storm began. In fact, I've never heard Annah laugh. Think about it, Tirtsah; your husband and his family haven't exactly been rejoicing in this destruction."

Tirtsah remained stonily silent.

Disheartened, Annah focused on the flames of the torch. *Please, Tirtsah,* she thought, *I don't want to quarrel with you.* Gently she said, "Tirtsah, even now, you don't understand, do you? We didn't care to be 'right' about this storm. It wasn't something we wanted. I certainly didn't want to believe the father of my husband when he first spoke of it."

Pained, thinking of her dead sisters, Annah continued. "But the father of my husband was right. I couldn't deny the truth; outside the lodge of Noakh, I've never met another person who was truly kind and loving, who also loved the Most High. Even my own father—the only person in the settlement who ever loved me—did as he pleased. Everything was according to his own will. He refused to believe in a Creator who desired harmony with him."

"I believe in the Most High now," Ghinnah confessed timidly. Her small round chin quivered as she added, "But I didn't until the storm. And I simply happened to be inside this pen instead of outside."

To Annah's surprise, Tirtsah gave a choked little laugh, and her huge, dark eyes glimmered with moisture. Taking a quick breath, she nodded. "I didn't want to believe either. But now I do. Though if it weren't for the storm, I never would have believed. The Most High was nothing to me but a child's story." Tirtsah bit her lip, and tears slid down her cheeks. "Annah!" she cried. "I've been so afraid! If He destroyed all the others for believing as I believed, then why has He allowed *me* to live?"

"Perhaps because He realized that you would learn to trust Him and to love Him," said Annah, hardly daring to hope Tirtsah would agree.

Gulping down an audible sob, Tirtsah shook her head. "I don't deserve to live."

"None of us deserves to live," Annah said, her own eyes welling, burning as she recalled her previous hatred for Yerakh and everyone in the settlement. "It was the violence of our thoughts and deeds—as much as our shunning of the Most High—that helped to destroy the others. In my heart, Tirtsah, I am just as guilty as you."

Tirtsah cried quietly, her tears gleaming in the light of the resin-soaked torch. At last, sniffling, she said, "I believe you. And Him. I'll never understand why He should—as you say—desire harmony with me, but I'm grateful He does. I pray I never give Him cause to despise me further."

"Turn to Him," Annah urged, wiping her eyes. "That's all He asks."

Ghinnah was also wiping her eyes. She straightened suddenly. "Ugh! I'm tired of crying! I want to do something—anything else. Listen, if the waters have quit tossing us about for a while, then let's go to I'ma-Naomi before our husbands finish their work. We can come back

329

to check the animals later."

"These poor creatures aren't doing anything anyway," Tirtsah agreed. She sighed, as if to clear her thoughts. Then she actually took Annah by the wrist, pulling her along as one sister would naturally behave toward another. "Hurry; I'ma-Naomi is waiting."

Pleased by this new turn in their relationship, Annah allowed Tirtsah to lead her up the ramp to their living area. Naomi was at the hearth, keeping a close eye on the flames beneath a small iron rack, which supported a plump bronze cooking pot. Annah eyed the hearth appreciatively. The crackling glow of the fire was a welcome relief against the continual downpour of rain and chaos outside the pen.

Ghinnah reached Naomi first. "Here we are, I'ma. That last turn made us sick again, so we had to wait before coming up to see you."

"And you've all been crying again," Naomi observed, her dark eyebrows lifting in her calm, commanding face. "Sit down. We need to talk."

Curious, Annah fastened the torch in a sturdy wall bracket and sat with Ghinnah and Tirtsah, facing Naomi expectantly.

Naomi pursed her lips, then spoke severely. "We have been mourning long enough. It's been almost thirty days now. We are alive, and we forget that we should be thanking the Most High for His mercy in sparing our lives. I think even our husbands have forgotten how to laugh, they've been so busy watching the storm and the animals."

Annah heard Tirtsah suck in a quick breath. Ghinnah actually laughed. "I'ma, we were just thinking the very same thing. We've all been crying for so long that we've worn ourselves out."

"Then we agree." Naomi relaxed as if she had been worried that they would be angry with her. "We need to remind ourselves that we are alive, and we ought to praise the Most High for His goodness." Leaning forward, she said, "Also, we need to celebrate my husband's six-hundredth year of life. We passed it while we were harvesting the herds."

"His six-hundredth year," Annah repeated in dismay. "Six kentums. We didn't know. . . ."

Each one hundred years of life for any person, man or woman, was traditionally celebrated by feasting, dancing, visiting, and gift giving. Failure to celebrate was an insult to the person in question, as if that person was despised, and the years of their lives were counted as nothing.

"Does he think we hate him?" Ghinnah asked, sounding horrified.

Naomi smiled and shook her head, the gold talismans of her hair bindings sparkling in the light. "No, child. My dear one doesn't think that at all. It was his choice not to celebrate. At the time of his six-hundredth year, he was mourning for our Methuwshelakh. And we were too busy harvesting the herds to take time for any celebration. After that, again, we were too busy preparing for this storm." Naomi's dark eyes were shining, almost mischievous. "But tonight, we should remind him of how very, very old he is! And we should feast. I've made him a new tunic, and we can prepare all his favorite foods, but I'll need your help."

"We should keep this a secret," Tirtsah added, her lovely face glowing. "It would be fun to surprise our husbands."

As they all agreed, Annah's thoughts raced ahead,

trying to plan some sort of gift for her father-in-law. *Six hundred years*, she thought. *How can we not celebrate?*

"Spiced cakes," Noakh said, his somber face brightening as Annah placed a basket on the mat in front of him. "And beans." His eyes widened as Ghinnah presented him with a large dish of his favorite red beans; thick, sweet, darkened with spices, and simmered until they were almost a paste. Smiling, Naomi and Tirtsah offered Noakh an immense assortment of vegetables, all perfectly cooked and gleaming with olive oil and flecked with fragrant herbs. Now, Noakh became suspicious. "What's all this?"

They waited to answer him, for the storm released a sudden burst of light and a massive, reverberating boom of noise. Glancing upward, Annah sighed, relieved as the noise faded. These vast, overwhelming sounds were less frequent now, thinning out in duration and intensity as the waters deepened over the earth. Hearing the usual rushing downpour, they all relaxed.

"What is all this?" Noakh asked again, bemused, looking at the feast set before him. "How can we eat all this food tonight?"

"You are the oldest, my dear one, with your six-hundredth year," Naomi teased. "In your lifetime, you've eaten more than any of us; you could manage to eat a little more than usual."

"My father's six-hundredth year!" Khawm cried, slapping both hands to his forehead, almost wailing. "How could we have forgotten? We should be beaten!"

Seated near their father, Yepheth and Shem both

groaned and looked equally stricken. But Noakh chuck-led dismissively.

"I didn't forget, but I didn't care to celebrate at the time. We were still in mourning for the father of my fathers, and we were harvesting the herds." He sighed, as if overcome by the memory of those long, miserable days of sorrow and endless work.

Shem hugged his father. "We can still be angry with ourselves for forgetting! Forgive us, Father, and we'll celebrate your sixth kentum now. Look what our wives have done."

Annah watched her husband, thinking, *It's good to see you smile again. I'ma was right; we've been mourning long enough. Even Khawm and Yepheth look happier already.*

"Say you'll play the harp for us tonight," Ghinnah was coaxing Yepheth. "And Shem and Khawm should play the pipes and reeds."

"If they survive this," Tirtsah said. She presented a broad, flat basket of plain, crisp grain cakes and a clay bowl of bright red paste that she had prepared earlier in the day. She had refused all offers of help, and even Annah and Ghinnah did not know the ingredients Tirtsah had used. The paste was a brilliant, glistening, tempting red. Challenging everyone, Tirtsah said, "Some of the smallest, weakest people in my home-city ate this paste constantly. But many of the giants themselves were unable to eat it without crying."

Khawm nudged Yepheth. "I dare you to try some."

Curious, Annah dipped a grain cake into the paste and ate it. Her first impression was of salt and savory herbs, but then her mouth burned, and her eyes teared up as she broke into a sweat. The paste was fiery beyond belief, an intense concentration of all the most searing spices she had ever eaten. Gasping, Annah quickly ate a plain grain cake, then drank some water. By now, everyone had tried some of the fiery red paste, and they laughed at each other's reactions. But only Tirtsah, Khawm, and Ghinnah took more. Noakh chuckled in protest as he refused a second serving, telling Tirtsah, "Thank you, daughter, but I would prefer to live."

"Never make that red paste for me," Shem whispered to Annah. "I think my face is numb. But I'm glad to see Khawm's wife finally behaving as part of this family."

Annah agreed, grateful that Tirtsah had finally accepted them—and the Most High. They ate their evening meal with only one interruption; the pen changed direction again, veering about so quickly that Annah had to put down her dish of food while her stomach settled. Shem continued to eat.

Apparently noticing her aversion and hoping to distract her, Shem nudged Annah, whispering, "We should give my father some sort of gift tonight."

"I made a gift for you to present to him," Annah replied, placing a small fold of leather on her husband's knee. "Perhaps you can promise to carve him a small storage case later."

In honor of this day, Annah had made a pendant of a gold leaf that she had originally created for Tirtsah. To Annah's disgust, the gold leaf had been too long and heavy to use in Tirtsah's hair bindings—but it was perfect for Noakh's pendant. Shem grinned as he felt the weight of the gold in his palm. "I can guess what you've made, beloved," he whispered, his voice making her shiver. "I'm eager to see it." Immediately, Shem gave it to his father.

Seeing the pendant, Noakh protested, "Daughter, you should have saved your gold! I'm an old man, and you will have sons and daughters to provide for later."

"If it were not for you and your family, I wouldn't be alive today," Annah told him. "And I would have had no chance to bear sons and daughters."

Though there is no child yet, she thought, aggrieved. Her longing for children intensified with each passing month. Shem had tried to console her by pointing out all the disadvantages of having a child now, while they were so overwhelmed by the storm, but Annah begged him to stop trying to reason with her. His calm logic only upset her, making her feel irrational.

Sighing, Annah shook off thoughts of children and watched Noakh. He seemed genuinely pleased with the pendant. He had no gold of his own—all of it had been sacrificed to build this pen. He was equally delighted with the others' gifts, a new long leather tunic from Naomi and a corded leather belt and carrying pouch from Khawm and Tirtsah. Then Yepheth and Ghinnah gave him the small, carved, painted storage box Ghinnah had taken from Qeb-al's cart the day of her marriage to Yepheth.

"Open it," Yepheth urged his father, smiling.

They all leaned forward to peer inside the box at what looked like a heap of smooth, waxlike, translucent stones. Noakh seemed perplexed until Ghinnah said, "Father of my husband, please, take the stones into a dark place."

Noakh carried the stones away from the light of the hearth, and even as he was walking, he called out excitedly, "Come look at these!"

Everyone crowded around Noakh to see; the stones exuded a peculiar yellowish light of their own—faint but still impressive. Ghinnah explained anxiously, "They're at their best after a day of full sunlight. I've had the box open all day, but there's no light outside because of the storm. In a little while, you won't be able to see any light from them at all. I've forgotten them for too long."

"Were these fashioned by a man?" Noakh asked, fascinated.

Ghinnah lifted her hands, at a loss to explain. "I believe they were heated somehow, but I don't know the materials or the method used to create them. They belonged to my father, and he forbade me to touch them or to speak of them. I've wondered if he stole them from someone."

Noakh grunted. "When these stones have been in the sunlight for a full day, do they give off any heat?"

Ghinnah shook her head. "No. I told Annah once that these stones are like cold fire—a great mystery."

By now, they were all touching the sunstones, marveling at them.

"I think a man created them," Yepheth said, turning one over in his long fingers. "They don't feel like natural stones."

Noakh sighed heavily. "I agree. They are a secret we may never understand. So many wonders have been lost through man's selfishness and violence."

"We are finished mourning for them," Naomi reminded everyone firmly. "Those violent ones and their knowledge."

"Beloved," Noakh said, smiling at Naomi, "you are right. And perhaps our children will show these stones to their children and teach those children not to forget the true Source of all knowledge." To Ghinnah, he said, "Daughter, thank you for this gift! Now we have another reason to anticipate the sun in ten days."

Khawm agreed happily. "We can use the stones to light our way in the lowest level when we check the animals, without risking a fire."

"Yes, but until then, we will go back to our real fire, and our food," said Noakh. "And my sons—who forgot my six-hundredth year—will play some music to cover the sounds of this storm."

Eagerly they returned to their food and to music as Shem and his brothers played their pipes, flutes, and harp. To Annah's delight, Noakh and Naomi pulled her to her feet, urging Ghinnah and Tirtsah to join them in a dance of pure joy. A celebration of life—although their steps were thrown off more than once by the churning of the storm outside.

Later, when everyone was exhausted, they carried a glowing resin-soaked torch to the far wall, where Noakh routinely carved notations of each day. Annah could not read her father-in-law's series of curling lines, slashes, and dots, but that was unimportant; now she could only think that they were one day closer to the end of the storm.

"Look!" Tirtsah cried, gazing at a stream of light pouring through the high windows some distance away.

Exultant, Annah left her grinding stone and raced with Tirtsah toward the sunlight. The resins of the sunlit floor were warm beneath her feet. *Thank You,* Annah thought to the Most High, deeply moved by the mere sight and feel of this one ray of light. Her feelings seemed to be echoed by the birds sheltered in the branches behind the huge curtain of mesh; a number of them began to flutter, twittering and singing, their notes high and vibrant in the calm.

"This is the morning of the forty-first day," Tirtsah declared, sounding newly amazed. "The storm ended, just as the father of our husbands has said."

They heard Naomi and Ghinnah calling to the others, then running up the ramp, all of them eager to see the sunlight.

"Move over!" Ghinnah commanded Annah and Tirtsah, happily pushing them aside and planting her bare feet in the patch of sunlight. Contented, Annah moved aside. Shem came to stand with Annah, wrapping his arms around her as he looked up at the sunlight. When Noakh came up from the lowest level of the pen, Ghinnah stepped out of the light, demanding, "Father of my husband, how many days before we can go outside again?"

To Annah's dismay, Noakh shook his head. "Who can say but the Most High? Until then, we wait." And he put out a hand, as if he could hold the sunlight in his long, work-roughened fingers.

Shem sighed and stirred in his sleep, unsettled, feeling the light, ticklish sensation of fingers combing delicately through his hair. "Annah," he mumbled into the darkness, "what are you doing?"

Nestled beside him in their bed, Annah sighed drowsily. "I'm sleeping."

Feeling the combing sensation again, Shem said, "You're playing with my hair."

"No," she said, mildly indignant, "I'm not playing with your hair."

Perturbed, Shem put a hand up to grab her fingertips. But the fingertips were not Annah's. A squeak of protest

338

and a light scratching across the back of Shem's hand made him sit up straight. Wide-awake now, he demanded, "What's this?" He swept his hands across his pillow in the darkness and caught hold of a small, warm-furred body—equipped with a long, soft tail that curled over his arm. "It's one of the little tree-dwellers."

"In our bed?" Annah sat up, incredulous. Shem could just see her in the darkness. To convince Annah that he was telling the truth, Shem put the tree-dweller in her arms. Annah laughed. "You thought I was some little-old-woman-of-the-trees?"

"Yes, I thought this creature was you." Baffled, Shem ran his fingers over the top of the storage chest, found his tunic, and pulled it over his head. "Why didn't I sense it there?" he asked Annah. "Did you sense its presence?"

"No." Annah hesitated. "I didn't. That's strange. What are you doing?"

"I'm putting our little visitor back where she belongs." As he bent to take the little creature from Annah's arms, Shem felt the warmth and nearness of Annah's face. He kissed her cheek, delighted as always by the scent and the unutterable softness of her skin. She was still an exquisite wonder to him—an incredible luxury and joy.

"You're sure you are kissing the right creature?" she asked, teasing.

"Beloved," he said instantly, "I forgot to tell you that you need to shave."

"Go away," she said, sounding amused. "And take your little beloved with you. I should be jealous."

"I'm coming right back," Shem told her. "Wait for me."

"Where else would I go?"

Smiling, he ducked past the thick leather door-curtain and headed toward the ramp. It was not until he reached the second level that Shem realized what had just happened. "She laughed. She finally, *truly* laughed!" Studying the tiny, big-eyed creature in his arms, Shem said, "You're one of those night-loving things. You would make me walk all the way down there."

Yepheth was in the second level, making his nightly rounds, using the sunstones for light. Shem almost succeeded in startling him, but Yepheth looked up in time. "You didn't sense my presence quickly enough," Shem told him. "And I didn't sense this creature either. It escaped."

"How?" Yepheth asked, astonished.

"Come with me while I go down to the next level," Shem urged. "You can light my way while I return this creature to its beloved."

"Does the air feel colder to you?" Yepheth asked.

"Isn't the night air always cooler?"

"Not like this. It's strange. Things feel different tonight. And worse, you *did* almost startle me. It's as if I cannot sense things clearly anymore."

Frowning, Shem returned the little creature to its cage—which was half-opened. He closed the cage, warning the creature's beloved, "Keep an eye on her. She wanders."

"I'll give them some more food," Yepheth said. "You go back to sleep."

"Thank you." As Shem started up the ramp, he felt a current of cold air touching his face. "You're right," he said to Yepheth. "The air has changed."

"I don't like it," Yepheth said quietly. "I'm going to make sure all the animals are secured, then I'm going to sit by the hearth until dawn."

"Do you want me to keep watch with you?" Shem offered.

Yepheth hesitated, then shook his dark-curled head somberly. "No. Tomorrow night will be your night. I'll wake Father if anything happens. He'd want to know. Go back to sleep."

"Good night then." Shem climbed the ramp, still feeling the current of air descending on him, chilling as water. *What is this?* he wondered. *It's been one hundred twelve days, and the air is still changing.* Disquieted, he went back to bed.

Annah seemed half-asleep when he returned. She put an arm out to hug him, but immediately pulled away, shivering.

"You're cold!"

"Never mind that," Shem said, kissing her lips, her face, and her throat. "You laughed! Finally—my little tree-dweller." To his immense pleasure, she laughed again and wrapped her arms around his neck.

Twenty-Four

USING A long-handled blade, Annah scraped the boards that slanted downward behind the multitudes of cages in the second level of the pen. *Messy little creatures,* she thought, allowing the mixture of trampled straw, manure, and various scattered foods to fall into the recessed waste pit near her feet. *It's bad enough that I have to scrape their manure down, but look how they mix it with their food. Ugh!*

"You're careless with your food," she told the plump little creatures as she finished scraping. "I should be disgusted with you, but I'm not." Sighing, she reached into a cage and stroked the luxuriant warm, gray-brown fur and long ears of one of the hares, resisting the impulse to pick it up. Instead, she checked the nearby cages containing long, sleek, black tree-foxes and a pair of smaller creatures—odd-hoofed, red-gold puffs of fur with sharp, inquisitive little faces and pointed snouts. "Greedy little ones," Annah muttered, pouring an assortment of grains, nuts, and dried berries into their shared feeding trough. "Don't scatter it this time."

Hurrying through the cool air, Annah reached into a nearby bin for handful after handful of coarse strips of dried meat, which she cast into a waiting bucket of water. Later, when the meat strips were softened, she would return and distribute them to the sleek black tree-foxes, the odd-hoofed creatures, and the other little carrion-eaters in this section of cages.

A sharp whistle echoed at her from the opposite end of the second level. *Shem*, Annah thought, startled. She covered the bin of dried meat strips, put away her scraping tool, and hastily retrieved a long-sleeved leather outer tunic from the floor. More than thirty days past, Naomi had insisted that they should make the long-sleeved tunics and fleece-lined foot coverings to wear against the chilling air. Annah hated the weight of the extra garments and dropped them whenever she could. But Shem was approaching, so she pulled the heavy tunic on again and tried not to look too guilty.

"Where are your foot-coverings?" Shem scolded her fondly.

"I'll put them on," Annah promised, looking for the puffy leather coverings and corded leather bindings. "My feet got warm while I was working."

"You still hate them, I know," Shem said good-naturedly. "But if you don't wear them today, your feet will be cold tonight."

"My feet have been cold every night for weeks, with or without foot coverings, so they can't be very important," Annah protested. She tied the knots of the bindings in place at her ankles, then sighed heavily. Now that she was sitting down, she felt beaten. Looking up at her husband, she almost wailed, "It's well past a month since this cold air has come upon us; will we ever be rid of it?"

"It's that wind more than anything. It'll change again, beloved. We just have to live with it for now." He half-knelt beside her, his long, roughened fingers warm against her cheek.

Comforted, Annah leaned against him briefly. "I want to see the trees again," she told him. "And I want to see the sky—not just clouds and sunlit mist—but the sky. And I want to feel grass beneath my feet. Instead, all I feel are these." She kicked out one fleece-covered foot, knowing she sounded sulky and ungrateful. In another instant, she would be crying. "One hundred and forty-eight days—I'm just so tired!"

"We're all tired." Sighing, Shem rubbed her back. "One day this journey will end, and we can all go out and look at the sky together. Until then, I'ma and the others are waiting for us to join them at the midday meal."

"I'm too tired to move."

"Take my hand; I'll help you up."

Shem offered Annah his hand, smiling—his beautiful, tender, persuasive smile.

There has never been anyone like you, Annah thought. She smiled in return and allowed him to help her to her feet. "I sound like a spoiled child," she said.

Wrapping an arm around her, Shem guided Annah toward the central ramp. "I think you're just tired and hungry and wishing you had a tree to climb."

"You shouldn't tease me about climbing trees. After all, you were the one having your hair combed by that little-old-woman-of-the-trees creature."

"Are you jealous?" Shem asked, his dark eyes shining

merrily.

"No! She can have you." Then, quickly, Annah took hold of his arm. "That isn't true; she can't have you. No one else can have you either, although there is no one else."

"Even so, I would never desire anyone else." Shem paused on the ramp.

Annah waited with him, suddenly tense. The current was changing, and the turning, shifting sensation of the waters seemed to come up through the very planks. Annah hated being caught on the ramps or ladders when the currents changed. It would be too easy to lose her balance and fall.

Shem's lips pressed together in grim patience as he steadied himself. Meeting her gaze, he said, "We're much better with all these turns than when they first began."

"You mean I am," Annah corrected him. "You never had much of a problem."

"None that you knew of," said Shem, smiling secretively. "There now, the turning has stopped. Let's go eat."

As they reached the top of the ramp, Annah felt a breath of light, cool air sweep over her face. The winds had been blustering outside the pen for many days now, and the air of the upper level was chilly and unsettled. As always, she welcomed the glow and warmth of the hearth. She also welcomed the scent of the food: the grain cakes, beans, and vegetables roasted in oil—until her stomach constricted in unexpected revolt.

That last changing of the water currents made me sick again, she thought, surprised. *But why should I get sick after being well for so many days?* She walked unsteadily toward the hearth and knelt on one of the grass mats, her stomach still churning. *The scent of the roasted vegetables is making me sick,* she realized. Swallowing hard, she looked away from the food.

By the time they had finished giving thanks to the Most High, Annah was thoroughly nauseated. And when Naomi passed the vegetables to her, she shuddered, quickly passing them to Shem.

Naomi lifted her dark eyebrows, surprised. "Child, don't you want any vegetables? I thought you liked them."

"I do like them, I'ma," Annah assured her. "But . . ." She pressed a hand to her mouth, too nauseated to explain.

Seated across from Annah, Khawm cackled. "She spends the entire morning scraping manure, but she can't look at the vegetables—I don't believe it."

Naomi's dark eyes sparkled with a dawning joy. "I have been wondering, daughter. It's been many weeks since your last time of seclusion. Now you are ill at the mere sight of those vegetables. Ma'adannah, you are carrying a child!"

They were all exultant, Shem embracing her, Noakh exclaiming happily, Ghinnah clapping her hands together, and Tirtsah calling out, "There, Ma'adannah! And all this time you've been worried."

"Let me know when you've finished the vegetables," Annah told them, scrambling to her feet, unable to endure the smell any longer. "I'll eat later." She hurried to her sleeping area and collapsed on the bed, sighing in relief. She could no longer smell the food. And it was good to lie down and rest. *I'm exhausted. Am I indeed with child?* She was almost too tired and too nauseated to care.

Annah was just dozing off when she heard Shem enter the sleeping area. He set something down on the storage chest, then crept into the bed, sliding his arms around her gently, nuzzling her. "I brought you some plain food. I'ma says you should rest."

"Only for a while," Annah murmured. "I have to finish feeding those little carrion-eaters." Lifting one hand, she reached back to caress her husband's bearded face. "I want our child to look like you."

"Without the beard," Shem suggested. "Particularly if we have a daughter."

She swatted him, then laughed.

Carrying baskets full of seeds, dried fruits, and solid white cakes of rendered fats, Annah and Tirtsah entered the huge netted bird enclosure. To Annah's amusement, Tirtsah scolded the birds, her voice husky and indulgent. "Back away, you silly things, and don't you dare let loose any droppings while we're here, or you won't be fed."

The birds responded by fluttering about on the branches, their eyes bright and watchful, some of them whistling sharply, others twittering as they darted from branch to branch. The larger earth-loving birds approached Annah and Tirtsah proudly, their iridescent plumes sweeping, glowing with every color imaginable. Annah was dizzied just looking at them. But it was better than looking at the disgustingly congealed, oily white cakes of rendered fat she carried in her basket.

Bracing herself against the nausea, Annah placed the cakes of fat and the grains, seeds, and fruits in various trays and troughs scattered throughout the huge enclosure. She would not allow her queasiness to disrupt her chores; it would not be fair to Tirtsah or the others.

As they were leaving the netted enclosure to refill their baskets, Tirtsah put a hand on Annah's arm. Tirtsah's face was claylike and she looked uneasy. Licking her lips, she asked, "When you feel ill because of the child, is it the sight of the food, or the scent of food, or both?"

"Both," Annah said, staring at her sister-in-law. "It's almost like being sick because of the motions of the water. Do you think you might be carrying a child?"

Tirtsah shut her eyes. "I think so. I hope so. Just now, while we were feeding the birds, I looked down at those cakes and felt sick. Don't tell anyone yet. When I'm certain, I want to tell Khawm first. It would be amazing if—just once—I could say something that would leave him too shocked for words."

"He will be so happy," Annah said. She dared to hug Tirtsah. "*I'm* certainly happy, because if you are carrying a child, then I'll have someone else who understands what I'm feeling. And I've been wondering . . . could you show me how to make some of that red spice-paste?"

Tirtsah's lovely eyes widened, and she chuckled—a low, throaty sound. "You didn't like my spice-paste before, but you want it now? Actually, it does sound good. Let's finish caring for these birds, and we'll make some."

They hurriedly fed the birds, checked the water pipes and troughs, and poured out small, coarse rocks here and there throughout the enclosure to aid the birds' digestion. As she was scattering fresh heaps of straw and grass over the floor of the enclosure, Annah felt a firm, jarring jolt. She looked at Tirtsah, who stared back at her, open-mouthed. Trembling, Annah said, "I didn't imagine that."

"If you did, then I imagined it too. And the birds imagined it also."

The birds were flapping their wings or darting through the branches; a few screeched in alarm. Then they settled again, some of them preening, some of them playing in the water and feeding, while others began to sing. Annah released a shaking breath. Her legs felt wobbly. She was used to the motions of the waters now, not this solid stillness. "We've come to rest on the land," she whispered, almost to herself. "We've stopped moving. The waters are going down!"

"Perhaps we can leave this place before too many days," Tirtsah added, some of her natural glow returning.

Tentatively, Annah made her way out of the enclosure, followed by Tirtsah. A long, piercing whistle sounded from the central ramp. *Khawm*, Annah thought. Peering through the filtered rays of sunlight streaming down from the windows, Annah saw him emerge from the ramp.

Immediately he yelled, "Tirtsah? Where are you?"

"I miss it that we can't sense each other from a great distance anymore," Tirtsah muttered to Annah. "The men yell so much more now."

"I hadn't noticed that, but you're right." Annah agreed, amused. She followed Tirtsah, faltering a little, unnerved by the pen's lack of motion.

Khawm met them eagerly and kissed Tirtsah. "I'm going to check the windows."

His gait remarkably steady, Khawm hurried toward the far wall, near the bird enclosure. There he climbed the ladder built into the wall. By the time he reached the top, Noakh and the others had emerged from the lower levels of the pen. They all stood near the base of the ladder, impatient. Hardly daring to breathe, Annah reached for Shem.

"Do you see anything?" Noakh called to Khawm.

Squinting a little, Khawm came down the ladder, his exuberance fading to dejection. "Nothing but too-bright sunlight, mists, and water."

"No land anywhere?" Ghinnah asked, pleadingly.

"Only mists and water."

Annah drooped, biting her lip, unable to hide her disappointment. *One hundred and fifty days,* she thought miserably. *And still nothing but water.*

"This is our two hundredth day," Ghinnah groaned to Annah and Tirtsah as they led the goats, sheep, and oxen out to the central enclosures to exercise them. "The water is still out there, and we're in here. Forever."

"No, not forever." Annah fastened the enclosure, then stretched carefully. The muscles around her abdomen were easily strained now that her pregnancy had begun to show. The sight of Tirtsah, lovely and graceful in her first months of pregnancy, was particularly discouraging to Annah, who felt plump and clumsy by comparison. She tried to reason with Ghinnah. "We're all impatient, but I suppose if all the mountains were covered enough to float this pen—as large as it is—then it will take a long time for the lands to drain and dry."

"You sound like the father of my husband," Ghinnah muttered irritably. "I'm sick of this place! I think I'll be sick of you soon. Wait, I didn't mean that." Flushing deeply, Ghinnah burst into tears.

Annah hugged her, unable to speak, but full of sympathy.

Tirtsah sighed. "When we finally leave this pen, I'm going to run out and roll in the grass. And if there's any water around, I'm going to dance in it!"

Snorting, Ghinnah wiped her eyes. "By that time,

your belly will probably be so big and round, you won't be able to move unless you roll."

"You are such a joy today," Tirtsah said, glaring at her.

Before they could say another word, shouts and screams arose from the other end of the second level.

"I'ma!" Annah gasped, turning away from Ghinnah. They ran toward the screams, toward the cages where the carrion-eaters were held. "I'ma? What's happened?"

As Annah ran around the large wood food bins to help Naomi, she heard Noakh protesting in a pain-edged voice, "It's nothing. Beloved, the creature was not attacking me; it just wanted the food."

Seeing Noakh, Annah cringed. His leg, just above the knee, was torn and bloodied.

Naomi was crying, raging as she inspected his injury. "I could kill that creature! Attacking my dear one . . . Oh, this is going to be such a long time healing!"

Lifting one hand, Noakh interrupted, "But it will heal. Don't blame the creature for my carelessness. Now, help me to stop this bleeding. I think my belt will do to bind the wound."

Annah gave Ghinnah a firm nudge. "Please, go get our husbands. Tirtsah, go find I'ma-Naomi's ointments. I will stay here to help her."

"And boil some water for the herbs!" Naomi cried. To Annah, she said, "Child, come help me. That accursed creature—biting my dear one! I want to skin that lion!" While she talked, Naomi took her own soft leather belt and wrapped Noakh's wound, then stripped some leather cordage from Noakh's belt to tie the makeshift bandage securely. Annah helped her tie the knots.

"Too loose; it'll fall off," Noakh grunted. Fearful of hurting him, Annah held her breath as she tightened the knots. A mist of sweat broke out over Noakh's face, and Naomi's eyes filled with fresh tears.

"I'ma?" Yepheth called to Naomi as he climbed up a side ladder from the lower level. As Yepheth hurried to help his father, Shem and Khawm came running up from the lower level ramp, followed by Ghinnah.

"Don't carry me," Noakh told his sons through his firmly clenched teeth. "I can walk, with some help."

Positioning themselves on either side of their father, Yepheth and Khawm helped him to stand. Shem pulled Annah and Naomi to their feet, then nodded at Ghinnah, saying, "Let's go ahead of them and be sure things are prepared. How did this happen?"

"That accursed lion," Naomi said, flinging a fierce look over her shoulder at the offending creature. "It was hungry and couldn't wait for its food; it chewed on your father instead."

While they were settling Noakh on a pallet near the hearth, he winced. "I think we have not fed that lion enough. Listen to me; we will no longer go into the cages with the carrion-eaters until after they have been well fed. We cannot be so careless, as I was. Beloved," he sighed to Naomi, "you are right; this will be a long time healing." To his sons, Noakh said, "I'm sorry; I'll be useless for weeks."

"The work is nothing," Shem told him. "And you will never be useless."

As she listened to them talk, Annah prepared the bowl of brewed astringent cleansing herbs, then helped Naomi untie their makeshift bandage. Gazing at her father-in-law's wound, Annah longed to cry. *His leg will never be the same; he will never walk straight again.*

"Ick! How can you eat that?" Ghinnah demanded, watching Annah take a second helping of the red spice-paste during their midday meal.

"I crave it," Annah told her, sucking in a quick breath as the fiery paste seared her mouth. Glancing at Ghinnah's fading color, Annah said, "You liked this stuff until you began carrying a child of your own."

"Well, now I know better," Ghinnah said. "That paste will curl your child's hair."

"Is something wrong with curly hair?" Khawm asked Ghinnah, lifting his dark eyebrows in amusement.

Annah laughed as Ghinnah looked from Khawm to Yepheth, who was watching her quizzically, the light shining on his own dark curls. "You know what I meant," Ghinnah replied, lifting her chin at them. "If Annah's child had straight hair before, it's curled now, with all the spice-paste she's been eating."

"Daughter," Noakh interposed gently, chuckling at Ghinnah from the comfort of his pallet near the hearth. "It would be best if you stopped explaining; you are outnumbered by those of us who have curls. And"—he paused significantly—"I wanted to say that we should test the waters today by sending out a kind of spy."

He had their attention now. Annah and the others leaned forward eagerly as Noakh said, "It's been more than a month since the mountaintops were revealed. We should send out a bird to check the waters. Perhaps it will bring some sign to cheer us."

"Which bird?" Khawm asked, his eyes bright with anticipation.

"A clever one," Noakh mused. "One such as the raven."

After their meal, Noakh insisted upon hobbling up a ladder himself to release the clever black bird from a high window. Fearfully anxious, Annah waited with the others in the upper level. Three times Noakh made his way painfully up the ladder, but the raven ignored him, flying back and forth across the waters near the pen.

At last Noakh descended, his patience gone. "I won't go up there again today! That little carrion-eater is out there feasting on floating corpses and refusing to return to us. We'll wait a few days and send out a more discriminating bird. A clean bird, not a carrion-eater. Now I'm going to write this down."

While confined to his bed with his mending leg, Noakh had written his daily notations on a scroll of leather instead of carving them into the far wall. This scroll would be added to the written records already accrued by the fathers of his fathers. Births, deaths, murders, cursings, notations of the giants such as Naham the *Nephyil*, and their rebellious spiritual origins—as well as the creation of the earth and the assurance of mankind's deliverance from the Adversary by the Promised One; all were noted within these scrolls. The scrolls carried the very breath of the Most High, the Word.

In the evenings, Annah begged Noakh to recite the stories of old contained within these scrolls. *They are no longer mere stories*, Annah thought. *They are life.* Hugging the full roundness of her belly, she promised her unborn child, *You will hear all these things from the father of your father. And no one will laugh at you or despise you or threaten you for believing them. You will be free to call to the Most High and worship Him as He deserves. And we will tell you of the Promised One. Then you will always remember Him and tell your children.*

A week later, they all watched as Noakh descended from the ladder again, a dove resting on his hand. "Nothing," he announced resignedly. "She found nothing but barren crests of earth, and the water, as usual."

Annah watched as her father-in-law returned the dove to its special cage. Seven pairs of doves and seven pairs of pigeons were held separately from the other birds, for they alone, along with certain oxen, sheep, and goats were considered worthy of offering to the Most High. By now, Annah knew the purpose of the sacrificial offerings: to cover the sins of mankind before the Most High. She had not yet witnessed such an offering. But each time she passed those seven pairs of creatures, she was filled with a sense of fearful mourning, and of wonder. *It's too much for me to understand,* she thought to the Most High. *It grieves me that blood must atone for our wickedness, so that we can approach You and call upon Your name. Perhaps the Promised One will save us from these sacrifices, though we don't deserve Your love. Why should You desire to welcome us? I think that is the most wonderful question of all.*

Seated on a mat just outside Yepheth and Ghinnah's sleeping area, Annah concentrated on the soft puff of wool between her fingers. Pinching out just the right amount, she rolled it between her left thumb and forefinger to form a continuous twist of cordage while Ghinnah watched. Yepheth had recently constructed a weaving frame for her, and Annah wanted to help Ghinnah prepare the fibers. Discouraged, Annah grimaced. "At least your cordage will be useful. Mine will be odd."

"Yours will do very well," Ghinnah said placidly. "It will add texture to our work."

Annah continued to twist the soft fibers between her fingers, only looking up when Noakh limped by them, heading toward the ladder near the bird enclosure.

Ghinnah said, "I won't follow him this time. Nothing has changed." Sympathetically, she added, "I'm afraid the father of our husbands will never walk properly again."

"At least he can walk," Annah said. Noakh was climbing the ladder, checking again for the dove that he had released that morning. Annah set down her fibers and the cordage. "I'm following him. I still have hope." Pulling herself to her feet, Annah slowly trudged to the other end of the pen. Naomi, Shem, and Tirtsah were already waiting by the time she arrived.

Shem took Annah's hands, whispering, "You're beautiful."

I love you, she thought, recognizing his sincerity. With their fingers intertwined, they watched as Noakh descended the ladder, carrying the dove on his hand.

"Our little spy must think she will build a nest here," Noakh said. "Look what she brought us." Opening his free hand, Noakh revealed a young, fresh, blade-shaped leaf.

"An olive leaf!" Naomi exclaimed, delighted. "O Most High, thank You!"

They gathered around, staring at the leaf, elated. Annah touched it, misty-eyed, longing to see the young olive tree itself.

"This tree must have started growing beneath the waters," Tirtsah said. Looking at Annah, she smiled. "Perhaps our children will be born on dry land after all."

"In three months." Noah pursed his lips, thinking. "Perhaps."

Three months. Annah almost groaned at the thought. But she consoled herself by looking at the leaf again. *Thank you, O Most High.*

"Tonight, we celebrate," Naomi announced. No one argued.

Seven days later, the dove did not return. "She has found food and a place to rest," Noakh said, deeply satisfied.

"I envy her," Annah said, feeling the kicking of tiny feet within. "She's free to fly up into the sky again. How I miss the sky!"

"Soon we will see the sky again, daughter," Noakh assured her. "The Most High will call us out at the proper time."

Do I have such patience? Annah wondered. Her child stirred, restless, agitated.

Moving slowly, Annah scattered grain and straw within the long, communal feeding trough in front of the grazing animals. One of the females—tawny and black-hoofed—whickered softly, seeming to coax Annah to stroke her. Annah stared into the creature's big, gentle eyes, empathizing; the young mare was also pregnant, as were many of the animals.

"I know just how you feel," Annah told her. "Those children and their kicks! But listen to me: Eat and rest, then later I'll take you out of your stall and walk you around. You'll feel better then."

"Ma'adannah?" Tirtsah called from the other end of the stalls. "We're waiting. Are you finished?"

"I'm coming." Annah hurried to join Tirtsah and Ghinnah. It was time to help Naomi prepare food for their evening meal. A clattering, pounding racket greeted them at the top of the ramp. They all looked toward the far end, near the bird enclosure. Noakh was up on the ladder again, while his sons waited below, laughing and passing tools and pieces of wood up and down the ladder. Curious, the women went to see what the men were doing.

Shem greeted Annah with a jubilant kiss. "The clouds are thinning, so we're opening this section above the windows. We should be able to see the sky and perhaps freshen the stagnant air in here."

Noakh wrenched another portion of the covering away. Now, Annah stared up at the sky, confounded. The puffy white clouds were parting, revealing a sky as blue as the color in her precious shell carving. Clear, pale, brilliant *blue*.

"We're going to have these children here," Tirtsah told Annah, obviously disgusted as she struggled to turn the great round grinding stone within the mortar.

Feeling the now familiar contractions of her womb, Annah nodded in wordless agreement, holding her breath, waiting for the contraction to ease. When she caught her breath again, she reached for the wooden handle that protruded from the mortar. Neither she nor Tirtsah could turn the grinding stone alone now; they were too big and uncomfortable to stretch their arms across it for very long.

It's been three hundred and seventy-one days for this flood, Annah thought, watching her entire stomach shift as the child wriggled within her. *But it's any day now for this child.*

They worked until Shem approached Annah and kissed her. "It's time to open the door, beloved, and release all these poor animals. Forget the grain; we need your help."

Twenty-Five

"DON'T RELEASE the animals until the door is opened," Shem warned Annah as they walked down the central ramp.

"Do you think we would do such a thing?" Naomi huffed, pretending indignation.

Grinning, abashed as a young boy, Shem said, "Forgive me, I'ma. Of course you wouldn't do such a thing."

"But you believe *I* would?" Annah asked softly.

Shem's dark eyes were dancing, shining. "I'm going to help my father and my brothers, while I still live."

"That accursed lion is the last to leave!" Naomi called out to everyone. They all laughed in agreement. To her daughters-in-law, Naomi muttered, "If I had my way, that wretched creature would never leave this place."

Unable to believe that this day had come, Annah watched as her husband picked up a hammer and a chisel and headed for the great door. Noakh, Yepheth, and Khawm were already pounding chisels into the sealed edges of the door, the iron splitting into the wood with loud, ringing tones. At last, when the men agreed that they had broken the entire seal, Noakh said, "Why should we strain ourselves further? Let some of the largest creatures help us open this door."

Annah retreated to the central ramp, wide-eyed as Khawm and Yepheth brought out the young elephant and its beloved, urging both creatures forward. At first, the two creatures seemed reluctant, tentatively exploring the door with their long, sensitive trunks. Then, as if suddenly concluding that their freedom lay on the other side of the wooden wall, both elephants pressed against it. The door creaked, then fell open with a crash. The young elephant and its beloved charged forward, clearly eager to leave. Noakh followed them, glanced around outside, studied the ramp, then came limping back inside, his lips pursed.

"Work from the largest animals down to the smallest," he called out, not looking at anyone in his family.

Annah realized that her father-in-law was troubled. Perceiving her look, he said, "Daughter, go with your sister Tirtsah and release the birds from their enclosures. Cut the curtains loose if need be, but keep the doves and pigeons."

"I wanted to look outside!" Tirtsah complained as Annah propelled her up the central ramp once more.

"So did I. But I'm sure the father of our husbands is right; we should release the animals first. I wonder if we'll need to chase the birds out, or if they'll go on their own."

"I think I will miss the birds most of all," Tirtsah confessed.

"We will see them outside." Annah found two of Naomi's cutting blades, and the two women set to work, slicing the mesh curtains apart at their natural seams.

"It's a pity to destroy these curtains," Annah said. Just looking at the long mesh hangings, Annah knew that they represented countless evenings worth of work.

"They are dirty anyway," Tirtsah pointed out. "I'm going to cut that corner away at the top." Despite Annah's protests for her safety, Tirtsah climbed the ladder and cut all the cords and seams in the uppermost corner near the windows.

As Tirtsah descended, the birds began to flutter through the gaping hole to escape through the high windows. The ground-loving birds picked and minced their way through the openings in the bottom of the curtains, then darted away, many of them finally taking flight up to the windows, following the others.

Satisfied, Annah and Tirtsah went to the second bird enclosure at the opposite end of the upper level, where they repeated the process. Annah stood quietly, watching the birds escape, until Tirtsah called to her, "What about these?" Tirtsah was reaching for the doves and pigeons, held in their separate cages.

Annah quickly shook her head. "No. The father of our husbands commanded us to leave them alone. They are for the Most High."

Lowering her hands, Tirtsah turned away from the doves and pigeons. "We're almost done then. Let's drive these last ground-loving ones down the ramp . . ."

And outside, Annah thought, silently finishing Tirtsah's sentence. Gathering baskets of grains, dried fruits, and the last of the white cakes of rendered fat, Annah and Tirtsah slowly coaxed the few remaining ground-loving birds down the ramp. As Annah stepped off the ramp, the birds screeched and squawked around her, then charged toward the brightness of the wide-opened door.

Meeting them now, Shem said, "Let's release these other animals and go outside."

Impatient as a child, Annah helped her husband unbar the numerous rows of stalls. Insects thrummed past their heads as they worked. The animals needed little urging. Even the night creatures seemed eager to go outside into the dazzling sunlight and fresh air. All of them—from the largest of the grazing reptiles and carrion-eaters down to the tiniest of the field-dwellers—scurried toward the great door as soon as they were freed from their stalls and cages.

"It's been easier to chase them out than to close them in!" Khawm called to Shem and Annah while they were releasing the last of the smallest creatures. Then there was a hush within the pen. Except for the multiple pairs of oxen, sheep, goats, pigeons, and doves, all of the stalls, cages, and enclosures were open and abandoned.

Noakh limped toward the door now, his face somber. He put out a hand, silently beckoning Naomi, who was just behind him. She took a deep breath, and they went outside together. Shem took Annah's hand, and they followed Khawm and Tirtsah, Yepheth and Ghinnah, out into the bright, clear air.

A cool breeze played over Annah's face, making the gold talismans in her hair bindings dance against her neck. For an instant she blinked against the fierceness of the sunlight, then she halted on the ramp, too stunned to move.

Nothing is the same, she thought, aghast. *This is not the same earth.*

She had been prepared to see the remote, chilling,

cloud-swept blue of the sky, but not this earth. Not these unbelievably high, awe-inspiring mountain peaks, the abruptly carved chasms, the sloping, water-scoured fields. All traces of the softness of the previous heavens and earth were gone. The low, tender, curving mountains, gently sweeping fields, magnificent trees, and lush vegetation and flowers that Annah had loved were replaced by coarse green grasses, tiny flowers, brutally battered stumps, fragile sprigs of trees, and countless scattered, water-smoothed stones.

There was nothing familiar to cling to. Nothing except her family and the multitudes of still-docile animals, which seemed lost and bewildered as they milled about in the steep, sloping, stone-riddled fields surrounding the pen. Watching them, Annah trembled, and hot tears trailed down her cheeks. Ghinnah and Tirtsah stood in front of Annah on the door ramp, weeping softly as their husbands stared at the harsh landscape in dazed silence.

Standing at the base of the door ramp, the breeze fluttering through his thick, silvering curls, Noakh lifted his hands to the remote blue heavens. Loudly, he cried, "We praise You, Most High, for Your mercy! Who are we that You have spared us from such destruction?"

He turned to face them, and Annah saw his tears and his sorrow.

"Come!" he cried to his sons. "We will build an altar to the Most High."

Exhausted and apprehensive, Annah stood before the stone altar with Naomi, Ghinnah, and Tirtsah, watching the men place the bodies of an ox, a sheep, a goat, a pair of pigeons, and two doves on the wood. Then, deliberately, Noakh took a cluster of dried cleansing herbs, dipped it in blood from the offerings, and whipped it high in the air, sprinkling them all with the blood. Annah cringed faintly as the droplets descended upon her, but she was comforted when Naomi took her hand, patting it kindly. They stood together with Ghinnah and Tirtsah, silent as Noakh took a glowing resin-soaked taper and lit the sacrificial fire.

Nothing is as I dreamed it would be, Annah thought, numbed and bewildered. *This desolate landscape, the cold sky, all these stones instead of sweet plants . . . how will I ever grow accustomed to these distant blue heavens and this terrible new earth?*

Then a sensing swept over Annah. *O Most High,* she thought, feeling His presence descend upon them, covering them all, loving, yet filled with undeniable, majestic, all-encompassing power. She dropped to her knees with the others, lowering her head, quivering. A quiet voice touched her, as if the Most High were standing directly behind her, His words full of blessings and warnings.

Be fruitful and bear many children and replenish the earth. The fear and dread of you will fall upon all the beasts of the earth and all the birds of the air, upon every creature that moves along the ground, and upon all the fish of the sea; they are given into your hands. Everything that lives and moves will be food for you. Just as I gave you the green plants, I now give you everything.

Annah turned her head, gaping as all the creatures scurried away in every direction, terrified, as if scattered by an unseen hand. Annah felt their terror wash over her as well; now she was an enemy to all the creatures she had cared for throughout this past year. Grieving, Annah thought, *They will be prey for my children, and my children will be theirs.* But the Most High seemed to permeate her thoughts, His words quietly admonishing.

. . . for your lifeblood I will surely demand an accounting. I will demand an accounting from every animal. And from each man too . . .

Humbled and shaken by these stern promises of justice and judgment, Annah lowered her head, crying silently. But even in her sorrow, she felt reassured. For beneath these new heavens and on this new earth, only the presence of the Most High had not changed. She could actually sense Him; He was as she remembered Him from the earth before, when she had cried out to Him for protection in her fear. His voice beckoned her now, tender, consoling.

I now establish my covenant with you and with your descendants after you and with every living creature that was with you . . . never again will there be a flood to destroy the earth . . . I have set my rainbow in the clouds, and it will be the sign of the covenant between me and the earth.

As one compelled, Annah looked up at the eastern sky and saw a many-colored arc of light glowing among the clouds—the first truly beautiful thing she had seen in this new earth. She stared at it, amazed, some of the ache in her heart ebbing away.

Never again will the waters become a flood to destroy all life, His voice promised them all, the voice of a Father soothing His precious children.

Annah wiped her eyes and listened, at peace now, feeling the stirrings of the new life within her. *O Most High, You have not changed,* she thought, gazing at the rainbow. *The heavens and the earth have all been swept away and replaced, but You have not changed. Even now, You care for us, and You will fulfill all Your promises to us; this is the comfort I will need more than anything else in this new life.*

"But to eat animals' flesh? I don't think I *could*," Tirtsah moaned as they were sorting out the remainders of various foods from the pen. "If we have enough grains and fruits and seeds—surely we won't need to eat flesh."

"You will have no choice, daughter," Naomi answered quietly. "Look around you at this rugged earth and that cold sky; there is no mercy here. Food may not be as easy to obtain, and what we do find may be less nourishing than what we had before."

Listening to their conversation, Annah dumped the remainder of a basket of dried berries into a larger basket of dried sweet afals. The dried berries would give the pale, thin-skinned afals a pretty, rosy color when they were cooked together.

"We may as well add these," Ghinnah told Annah, passing her a basket of tiny, deep brown, dried vine-fruits.

In time, they would have vine-fruits again. Noakh had stored cuttings of some of his favorite plants in the darkest reaches of the pen, and now he was planning to establish a vineyard in the lower hillsides.

"If we are careful, there should be enough fruit to last us until we find other fruit-bearing plants," Annah said to Naomi.

"But what if there isn't enough?" Ghinnah asked, her pretty eyes wide, apprehensive.

Naomi actually laughed. "Daughter, if the Most High has chosen to save us from the terrors of the flood, I think we may depend upon Him to meet our needs with a few bits of fruit."

And with the grain, Annah thought, eyeing the remaining baskets. Shem, Khawm, and Yepheth already had decided to begin clearing fields and planting various grains. She watched as her husband and his brothers descended from the slopes above, bringing the final cartloads of tools and hides down from the pen, which loomed on the hillside like a dark husk emptied of its seeds. Annah thought it looked permanent, indestructible.

"What shall we do with this?" Ghinnah's tone demanded the other women's attention. She held a broad, deep basket filled with the last bits of dried meat from the pen. "Shall we put it out for the carrion-eaters?"

Naomi frowned and shook her head. "It seems that the carrion-eaters have enough food for now. We need this meat more than they do." Then, as if to console them, she added, "If you find any remaining blood cakes, you may throw them away."

"Gladly," Tirtsah muttered, and the others laughed.

Annah woke, feeling as if she had been struggling in her sleep. Taking a quiet breath, she looked up at the sturdy reed-and-hide roof of the small room she shared with her husband. They had removed some of the partitions and stalls from the pen to build their lodge, and this room. With its hewn-wood sides, low-sloping hide roof, and windows here and there, the lodge was not beautiful, but it was reasonably warm and comfortable. It would serve their purposes until after the fields were planted and this first crop of children was born. Moving her hands over her stomach now, Annah felt another contraction. *A false one*, she thought. But she caught her breath, suddenly struggling against genuine pain.

Gradually, the pain faded. Unable to lie still, Annah

pushed off the warmth of the fleece covers and reached for her long-sleeved overtunic. Softly she made her way outside into the first gray hints of a clouded dawn. She went to the wall-enclosed waste pit just beyond the lodge, then washed her hands in the rushing water of a nearby spring. Another pain struck, making her gasp in deep breaths of the cold morning air. When she could move again, Annah returned the lodge and sat near the banked hearth, silently bracing herself against pain after pain while she waited for Shem and the others to awaken. *Soon,* she thought. *They'll be awake soon. They were so tired last night; I should let them sleep as long as possible.*

Shem found her first. Bending to kiss her, he said, "I turned over in my sleep and you weren't there." He hesitated and stared at her intently, his eyes widening in the dim light. "You're having pains."

"Yes," Annah agreed through clenched teeth, unwilling to communicate further. Another pain closed around her, squeezing her tight. Elated, Shem hugged her; Annah pushed him away hard.

Undismayed, Shem went to wake the others. They gathered around Annah delightedly, discussing her appearance and arguing about when she would actually deliver the child. Annah shut her eyes, struggling through another contraction. When the pain subsided, Naomi, Ghinnah, and Tirtsah helped Annah to her feet. Against her will, they led her back to her room.

The morning passed in a swift, pain-filled blur. Trying to cope with her misery, Annah moved restlessly around the room. All the while, she was vaguely aware of Naomi watching her, while Tirtsah and Ghinnah hovered close by, all of them apprehensive.

"Is the pain too much, Annah?" Ghinnah begged at

one point.

"No," Annah muttered, turning her face away. Another pain gripped her and she clung to the storage chest for support, feeling the urge to bear down, producing a warm, drenching rush of birth water.

Naomi took hold of her and spoke sternly. "Ma'adannah, it's time. You have to let us help you; stop pushing us away."

It's time, Annah thought, repeating Naomi's words in her mind. She obeyed Naomi, finally settling down on the hastily arranged birthing area of mats and hides. Ghinnah and Tirtsah were supporting her back and shoulders, encouraging her through each new contraction. At last Naomi cried out, jubilant, "There! One more breath, daughter, then push again."

Gasping, gritting her teeth, Annah obeyed, thinking of nothing but ridding herself of the pain. It vanished suddenly, as the amazingly angry howl of a newborn filled the room. Tirtsah laughed and hugged Annah, as Ghinnah shrieked into Annah's ear, "A son! You have a son!"

Immediately, Ghinnah and Tirtsah abandoned Annah to watch as Naomi bound and cut the birth cord, then hastily wrapped the squalling infant in a fresh blanket. Annah was leaning forward to catch a glimpse of her new son when another pain struck. Frightened, she called to Naomi, "I'ma, another pain!"

Busy with her grandson, and the admiring Tirtsah and Ghinnah, Naomi answered happily, "It's only the afterbirth, daughter, don't worry."

"I'ma!" Annah cried, enraged, aware of more than just the pain now, "does afterbirth *kick?*"

Gaping in astonishment, Naomi thrust her new

grandson at Tirtsah and returned to Annah. "Another child?" she asked in disbelief. "A hidden one?"

Engrossed with the renewed onslaught of pain and the urge to bear down, Annah ignored the question. After four birth pains, Annah delivered another son. But this second son was different from his howling, shut-eyed brother. This second son cried plaintively at first, then opened his dark eyes and hushed, looking about, alert and curious. Seeing his odd expression of newborn wonder, Annah laughed, overcome with joy. Visibly startled, both of her sons began to cry.

Nestled in her bed, Annah watched the gentle flickering of the oil lamp set on the nearby storage chest. She smiled, listening to the others laughing and celebrating over their evening meal in the main room of the lodge. *They are passing my sons around like little gifts,* Annah thought, pleased by the sounds of their happiness. There were loud discussions earlier, however: Shem had asked Noakh to name the twins, and everyone gave suggestions, each of them groaning when their suggestions were discussed and rejected.

At last, against Naomi's will, Noakh had named the firstborn infant Elam—the hidden one—because Elam would not open his eyes. And Elam's younger brother was called Asshur—the guiding one—because Asshur was alert and watching everything.

"This Asshur will lead his brother," Noakh said, making everyone laugh, including Annah, who strained to hear every word spoken about her sons.

My sons, she thought. *I have two sons. And they are as*

beautiful as their father. Dreaming, Annah closed her eyes. A sound startled her then; a small stone, gently tossed, landed beside her in the bed. *Shem.* She turned to see him watching her from the doorway, his face lit by the flickering of the evening fire.

Shem lifted his dark eyebrows, concerned, questioning: *Are you well?*

Smiling, Annah nodded faintly, motioning with one hand: *Yes. Thank you.*

His answering smile was relieved and radiant. Widening his eyes emphatically, and raising two fingers, Shem silently indicated his joyous astonishment: *Two sons!*

"Move away and let her rest," Naomi commanded him sternly from beyond the doorway. Shem smiled and kissed his fingertips to Annah in reluctant farewell.

Annah repeated the gesture to him, smiling as he retreated to the main room. Then she shut her eyes, clasping the small stone in her hand. Dreaming again, she remembered the first time Shem had beckoned to her from beyond the river near the settlement, silently encouraging her to live. Truly he had acted by the prompting of the Most High.

Annah clenched the small stone tightly, thinking, *O Most High, You sent my beloved to find me that day. You caused him to see me and to save me. You arranged everything according to Your plan. I see that now, and I am amazed. Again I wonder why should You love me—a nothing-creature—when I can give You nothing in return? Only my love, and my thanks. And my joy in Your presence.*

Sensing His unchanging presence now—the presence of a watchful, loving Father, Annah smiled. Wholly at peace, she drifted into sleep. *Thank You always.*

Epilogue

SEATED ON a grass mat just outside the lodge, Annah steadily twisted puffs of wool into long strands, then twirled them onto wooden spindles. Naomi, Ghinnah, and Tirtsah were seated close by, also preoccupied with the wool, which they were planning to use to make tents for the men to take into the fields when they had to watch the herds. As they worked, they talked softly, fearful of waking Ghinnah's daughter, Bekiyrah.

"I wish she would sleep like this at night," Ghinnah sighed, pausing to stroke Bekiyrah's dark tousled curls. "She's going to be impossible when the new baby comes."

Annah studied Ghinnah's fatigue-shadowed face. "Perhaps we should try to keep her awake during the day. Then she'd have to sleep at night," Annah suggested.

"She would be so irritable," Ghinnah groaned. "She doesn't play as long or as hard as your sons do. Look at them."

They all looked at the little boys playing nearby, and Annah had to smile. Her sons were nearly two years old, sturdy, vigorous, and handsome, with thick dark curls and big brown eyes. They were laughing and running in circles with Tirtsah's son, Kuwsh. As the boys ran, they called to each other, "Got-you, got-you, got-you!" Their words became a monotonous chant in Annah's ear.

"Little wild men," Tirtsah laughed, her lovely face glowing with pleasure and with the effects of her pregnancy. Her second child was due within the next two months. Studying the boys, she said, "Kuwsh lost one of his foot coverings. Annah, you're thinner than I am; please go make him cover his feet."

"Thinner by a few months," Annah murmured wryly. Her third child was due after Tirtsah's, near the time of Shem's first hundred-year celebration. Shem was delighted by the coincidence, insisting that this child would be enough of a gift for any kentum.

And you are one child this time, not two, Annah thought, standing, rubbing her full stomach comfortably. This new child already was more peaceable than his brothers—Annah was certain the baby was a boy. Now, picking her way around the crackling, stone-lined outdoor hearth, Annah found Kuwsh's abandoned foot covering and scooped him up, though he was in midstride.

Kuwsh howled indignantly, arching his small, strong, leather-clad back and kicking Annah with quick, hard little feet. Swiftly, Annah turned Kuwsh in her arms until his back was against her, but he continued to kick and scream. *Give up,* Annah thought wearily. *You won't win against me.* Aloud she said, "Kuwsh, stop. You are kicking my baby. Don't kick the baby."

Distracted now, his attention caught by the word "baby," Kuwsh gave Annah a dark little frown and pointed toward the sleeping Bekiyrah. "Baby," he insisted, as if to explain to Annah that he couldn't possibly be kicking the baby; she was too far away.

Annah laughed and kissed her nephew's brown cheek, soothing him as she sat down on the grass to replace his foot covering. She made a game of it, tickling Kuwsh's toes lightly, then hugging him and kissing him again; it was the best way to get the little boy to cooperate. As she tied his foot covering, Asshur and Elam crouched beside Annah, bright-eyed, watching critically.

Asshur stretched a determined little hand toward Kuwsh's foot covering and said, "Me do it."

Kuwsh slapped his hand away hard, bellowing, "No!"

As Asshur prepared to retaliate by slapping Kuwsh, Annah grabbed both their hands, her voice severe. "No. No hitting. This is bad. *Bad.* No hitting each other."

Both little boys were chastened. Briefly. Then Kuwsh lifted his chin at Asshur and said in a husky, self-satisfied voice, "Bad."

"Bad!" Asshur said, accusing Kuwsh in return. They repeated the word back and forth until it was a chant, a game, punctuated by their laughter. Fondly exasperated, Annah turned Kuwsh out of her lap and chased the boys off with a wave of her hand.

Elam stayed behind. Burying his gleaming, black-curled head in Annah's long overtunic, he begged Annah to pick him up, saying, "Ma–ma–ma, up!"

"You're getting too heavy," Annah told him gently. But he was obviously tired, and Annah gave in. Hoisting him up awkwardly to her hip, she returned to the hearth.

Naomi brought out the dough to prepare soft cakes

for their evening meal. By now, they had learned that by making dough and storing it ahead of time, the dough—and the resultant wheat cakes—became puffy and soft inside when they were baked.

While this new type of wheat cake had been an agreeable surprise to everyone, their joy in this new discovery was offset by the realization that cooked food spoiled quickly in the new environment. Annah believed it was because of the change in the air. The air also caused metals to change colors or corrode. Now, blades of stone were easier to make and maintain, because Annah's knowledge of collecting, heating, and working metals was frustratingly inadequate for their needs. It would take years of experimentation before they could create new metal tools to replace their old ones.

So much knowledge has been lost, Annah thought. She settled Elam beside her on a grass mat, then picked up a blade of stone to help Naomi cut the puffy, resilient dough into small cakes. As she worked, she watched Elam drift into sleep. *Perhaps you will help us relearn metalwork later,* Annah told her son silently. *In a few years, I'll show you how to work the gold—though we are too busy now. How I miss working the gold!*

"One day," Ghinnah mused pleasantly, "I will describe the home of my father to our children, and they'll build ones like it: houses of carved stone, with many rooms and two or more levels, and walls encircling them, with beautiful gardens inside. And the gardens will have all kinds of flowers. . . ."

"Tell those two wild men." Tirtsah nodded toward Asshur and Kuwsh. "I think they will accomplish whatever they decide to do."

Annah listened, suddenly uneasy. Would it be right to

create such visions and ambitions in the minds of their sons? Perhaps it would be better to teach them to live close to the earth, remaining dependent upon the land. *Their hearts would be more satisfied by simplicity, and they would remain close to the Most High,* Annah thought, trying to quell her anxiety.

"Ma'adannah." Naomi nudged Annah. "Here comes your husband."

It worried Annah that Shem was returning to the lodge this early—until she recognized her husband's joy. Asshur and Kuwsh were charging at Shem happily. Grinning, Shem paused long enough to allow them to catch hold of his hands. Then he dragged the two little boys toward the lodge, protesting in mock dismay that they were both so strong they would soon pull him off his feet. Their shrieks and laughter awoke Bekiyrah. She sat up, her pretty, rosy little face bewildered, her soft brown eyes enormous with fear until she saw her uncle and her cousins playing. Bekiyrah looked up at Ghinnah pleadingly, pointing to the others. "Me, too."

"Run to them," Annah urged her niece. When Ghinnah nodded agreement, Bekiyrah trotted to Shem, her dark hair shining, fluttering in the light breeze.

"Ugh," Ghinnah groaned, disgusted. "Bekiyrah's wet."

"My husband won't care," Annah said comfortingly. Shem loved Bekiyrah's sweetness—he often expressed hope that their next child would be a daughter. Annah laughed, watching as Shem picked up Bekiyrah and kissed her, then held her out at arm's length, teasing as he brought her back to Ghinnah.

"We're going to douse you in the spring, O daughter of my brother! We're going to rinse you until you squeak, little-wet-one. Then I'll hold you and tell you stories."

As he freed himself from the three little ones, Shem bent to greet his mother with a kiss. Then he gave Annah an enticing smile. "Come, walk with me," he urged. "My brothers and I found something that will please you."

"Go with your husband," Naomi agreed, patting Annah on the arm. "I'll finish making the wheat cakes, and we'll watch Elam while he sleeps. Asshur can stay too."

But Asshur would not stay. He clung to his father insistently. Annah touched Shem's arm, saying, "Perhaps he needs your company today."

Exhaling reluctantly, Shem nodded. "Come then!" He scooped Asshur up in his arms. "Are you wet too? No? I don't trust you."

They made a quick stop at the enclosed waste pit, then rinsed Asshur's hands and face in the spring. Finished, Shem lifted the little boy to his shoulders. "It's a long walk," Shem told Annah apologetically. "If you get tired, let me know and we'll rest."

But Annah did not get tired. The day was clear, bright, and cool. She scanned the grasses and low-growing bushes and small trees for signs of animal life. The animals had been avoiding them completely since their first day of freedom on this new earth, but now and then, Annah would spot the tiny field creatures or one of the great cats. She even saw a small herd of hoofed, tawny, dark-maned grazers, which instantly fled in the opposite direction.

At least we know they are surviving and bearing young, Annah consoled herself. It still pained her to see every sort of animal fleeing from her as if she were a monster. They had not yet killed wild animals for food. It was easier to net fish from nearby ponds. And once they had reluctantly culled animals from their own flocks. The children craved meat, requesting it often. *They will gladly hunt the wild creatures,* Annah thought.

"Your surprise is over there," Shem told Annah, indicating a field that sloped downward to a small, rushing creek.

Wondering, Annah followed him. As they walked, she heard a sharp whistle of greeting from some distance to the east. *Khawm,* Annah thought, smiling at him. Khawm waved briefly, then returned to his work; he was clearing large stones from a field, dumping them into a cart to haul them away. Later, he would harness an ox to a one-bladed plow and drag the plow through the fields in preparation for a crop of grain.

"Here," Shem said, sliding the drowsy Asshur off his shoulders, down into the crook of his arm. "Tell me what you see." He indicated a bare-limbed young tree, no taller than his chest.

Annah stared at the slender, bare, gracefully drooping tree branches, recognizing its form. "The Tree of Havah," she whispered, tears welling in her eyes. "Not the actual tree," she amended, glancing up at her husband.

"But one of its kind," Shem agreed, his voice pleased. "It'll show leaves soon."

Annah smoothed the drooping, bare limbs with their tiny hints of leaf buds. She was smiling and crying at the same time. "I thought I'd never see such a tree again."

"Would the Most High deprive you of such a joy?" Shem asked. Shifting the sleeping Asshur in his right arm, he embraced Annah with his left arm. "Look now, I want to build our lodge here, a lodge of stone and wood. What do you think?"

With an effort, Annah looked away from the graceful form of the young tree. And she saw the beauty of the land, the promising sweep of it, and the rugged charm of the stream cutting downward through the lower hills. *This is right,* Annah thought. *This is where we should stay.* "Yes," she agreed. "Our sons will love it here."

"And our daughters," Shem added, touching Annah's rounded stomach.

"He is not a daughter," Annah said. "But I think he will be your quiet one. He's not like his brothers."

They sat down to rest and to discuss the land. They both agreed that one place in particular, a reasonably level rise not far from the stream, would be the ideal place to build their lodge. As they talked, an eagle circled above them, repeating its shrill cry over and over until Asshur woke up from his resting place in Shem's lap.

Staring up into the sky, Asshur pointed, clearly awed. "Pretty," he said, his small finger following the flight path of the bird. As the great bird flew off and vanished beyond the nearby crags, Asshur continued to gaze at the sky, obviously daydreaming.

Watching him, Annah thought, *I'm glad you love this sky. But you have known no other. What will you say one day, when your father and I try to describe the heavens as they were before? Will you be able to imagine them as they were? Soft and low and pink as the color in my shell carving.*

I pray you'll believe us. And I pray you will remind yourself and your children that this new sky—so beautiful to your eyes—could one day suffer the same fate of total destruction because of the violence of men. How I hope you will listen and remember our words, you and your brothers.

Silent, Shem caressed Annah and kissed her cheek. As she leaned against him, Annah felt their child stirring within her, calm and unhurried. Somehow, the calm of this child reassured her. *You won't forget the words of your parents,* she thought to the unborn one. *And you will tell your children the stories of old, so they will never turn away from the Most High, but be glad and look forward to the day when He sends His Promised One to call to them in love.*

She convinced herself that this would be true; the Promised One would come soon and this formidable new world would not be corrupted in the same way as the world before—by evil from her own children and their kin.

"Pretty," Asshur said again, staring up at the clear, brilliant blue sky.

"Pretty," Annah agreed quietly, feeling her husband's arm tighten around her. "But not as pretty as before."

Glossary

In order of appearance:

Havah (Khav-<u>vaw</u>) Life giver.

Hebel (<u>Heh</u>-bel) "Emptiness" or "Vanity."

Annah (<u>Awn</u>-naw) A plea: "I beseech thee" or "Oh now!"

Yerakh (<u>Yeh</u>-rakh) A lunation of the moon. One Month.

Naham (Naw-<u>ham</u>) Roaring.

Iltani (unknown) Ancient Semitic/Babylonian name

Parah (Paw-<u>raw</u>) Fruitful.

I'ma (<u>Ame</u>-maw) Derived from "Im" or "Em" and the syllable "Ma." Mother. Bond of the family.

Kentum (Ken-<u>toom</u>) Century. From the root words "kmtom" and "centum."

Afal (uncertain) Indo-European root word describing a number of fruits, including the apple.

Tseb-iy (Tseb-<u>ee</u>) Splendor. Conspicuous.

Chathath (Khaw-<u>thath</u>) To break or prostrate by violence.

Tan-neem (Taw-<u>neem</u>) Monster.

Nachash (Naw-<u>khawsh</u>) To hiss. To whisper a spell. Serpent.

Haburah (Khab-oo-<u>rah</u>) Bound. Bruised.

Gammad (Gam-<u>mawd</u>) Warrior, i.e. grasping a weapon.

Ayalah (Ah-yaw-<u>law</u>) Doe.

K'nan (Ken-<u>aw</u>-an) Abbreviated from Kena'an. Merchant.

Noakh (<u>No</u>-akh) Rest.

Naomi (No-om-<u>ee</u>) Pleasant.

Shem (Shame) Denotes honor. Literally means "Name." Also, "Appointed One", and "To desolate."

Khawm (Khawm) Heat, i.e. a tropical climate.

Yepheth (<u>Yeh</u>-feth) Expansion.

Methuwshelakh (Meth-oo-<u>sheh</u>-lakh) "Man of the Darts." In a lesser sense, "He who departs before the waters."

Khawvilah (Khav-ee-<u>law</u>) Circular.
Zahar (Zaw-<u>har</u>) Gleam. Also, "To teach."
Tsaraph (Tsaw-<u>raf</u>) Goldsmith.
Nephiyl (Nef-<u>eel</u>) Bully. Tyrant. Giant.
Taphaph (Taw-<u>faf</u>) Mince. To trip coquettishly.
Tsillah (Tsil-<u>law</u>) Shade.
Shuwa (Shoo-<u>aw</u>) Wealth.
Qetsiyah (Ket-see-<u>aw</u>) Peeled cassia bark.
Bachown (Baw-<u>khone</u>) An assayer of metals.
Dahar (Daw-<u>har</u>) To move irregularly.
Ma'adannah (Mah-ad-an-<u>aw</u>) Pleasure. Dainty. Delight. Also, "A bond"
   or "Influence."
Qeb-al (Keb-<u>al</u>) To acquire.
Kinah (Kin-<u>aw</u>) Wares.
Pa-sak (Paw-<u>sak</u>) To divide.
Saiyr (Saw-<u>eer</u>) Shaggy. He-goat.
Etsah (Ay-<u>tsaw</u>) Trees. Wisdom.
Ghinnah (Ghin-<u>naw</u>) Garden.
Ce'appah (Seh-ap-<u>aw</u>) Twig. Branch.
Tirtsah (Teer-<u>tsaw</u>) Delightsomeness.
Hadarah (Had-aw-<u>raw</u>) Decoration.
Pathal (Paw-<u>thal</u>) To wrestle.
Akar (Aw-<u>kawr</u>) Troublesome.
Othniy (Oth-<u>nee</u>) Forcible.
Sa-khar (Saw-<u>khar</u>) Peddler.
Yediydah (Yed-ee-<u>daw</u>) Beloved.
Elam (Ay-<u>lawm</u>) Hidden.
Asshur (Ash-<u>shoor</u>) To guide. To be level.
Kuwsh (Koosh) Possible meanings: "To scatter." "Confusion." "Chaos."
Bekiyrah (Bek-ee-<u>raw</u>) Eldest daughter. Firstborn.

SINCE 1894, Moody Publishers has been dedicated to equip and motivate people to advance the cause of Christ by publishing evangelical Christian literature and other media for all ages around the world. Because we are a ministry of the Moody Bible Institute of Chicago, a portion of the proceeds from the sale of this book go to train the next generation of Christian leaders.

If we may serve you in any way in your spiritual journey toward understanding Christ and the Christian life, please contact us at www.moodypublishers.com.

"All Scripture is God-breathed and is useful for teaching, rebuking, correcting and training in righteousness, so that the man of God may be thoroughly equipped for every good work."

—*2 TIMOTHY 3:16, 17*

MOODY
PUBLISHERS

THE NAME YOU CAN TRUST®